Praise for the Inside series by
New York Times bestselling author

Maria V. Snyder

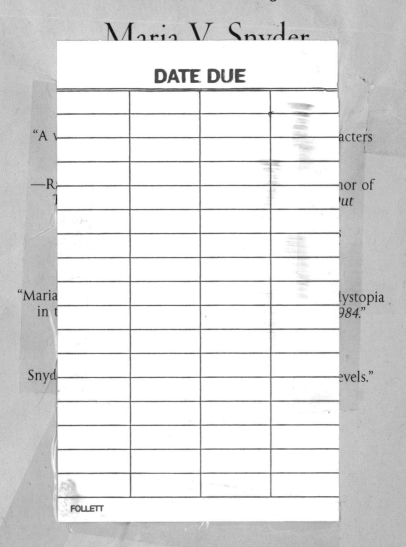

"A v   acters

—R   nor of
     T   *ut*

"Maria   lystopia
   in t   *984.*"

Snyd   evels."

Also by
New York Times bestselling author
Maria V. Snyder

from Harlequin TEEN

Inside series
INSIDE OUT
OUTSIDE IN

from MIRA BOOKS

Study series
POISON STUDY
MAGIC STUDY
FIRE STUDY

Glass series
STORM GLASS
SEA GLASS
SPY GLASS

Healer series
TOUCH OF POWER

inside

Maria V. Snyder

HARLEQUIN®TEEN

(H)HARLEQUIN®TEEN

ISBN-13: 978-0-373-21068-8

INSIDE

Copyright © 2012 by Harlequin Books S.A.

The publisher acknowledges the copyright holder of the individual works as follows:

INSIDE OUT
Copyright © 2010 by Maria V. Snyder

OUTSIDE IN
Copyright © 2011 by Maria V. Snyder

Recycling programs
for this product may
not exist in your area.

This edition published by arrangement with Harlequin Books S.A.

For questions and comments about the quality of this book please contact us at Customer_eCare@Harlequin.ca.

® and TM are trademarks of the publisher. Trademarks indicated with ® are registered in the United States Patent and Trademark Office, the Canadian Trade Marks Office and in other countries.

www.HarlequinTEEN.com

Printed in U.S.A.

CONTENTS

INSIDE OUT

To my niece, Amy Snyder,
for your willingness to read my first manuscript.
Your enthusiasm for my stories sparked the idea
that I could write for a younger generation.

In loving memory of my grandmother, Mary Salvatori,
and my best friend Hazel.

one

A vibration rippled through my body. I awoke in semi-darkness, unsure of my location. Reaching out with my hands, I felt smooth sides arching up and in. My fingers touched overhead. Pipe.

A distant roar caused unease, but with sleep fogging my mind, I couldn't quite grasp its significance. The pipe's vibrations increased as the thunder grew louder. Water. Coming toward me. Fast.

I scrambled in the narrow space. My bare feet slipped on the sleek surface of the pipe as I advanced toward a faint square of bluelight emanating from the open hatch. It seemed an impossible distance to reach.

Cogon's voice in full lecture mode echoed in my mind as the water rushed closer. "Someday, Trella. You'll screw up and there will be bits of you raining out of the showers."

I reached the hatch and dove headfirst through the opening, convinced the water rushed at my heels. Landing on the hard floor, I shot to my feet and slammed the door shut. When I finished sealing the hatch, the whole pipe shuddered, then the vibrations calmed as the water returned to its normal flow. The metal cooled under my fingers, and I leaned my sweaty forehead against it, catching my breath.

That was close. Soft bluelight glowed all around the water-filtering machinery. Hour eighteen: I knew by the rush of water. The upper workers adhered to a strict schedule.

I checked my tool belt to make sure nothing was broken and my flashlight still worked. Then I climbed from the ductwork and made my way to level two by taking a shortcut through an air conduit. Traveling through the pipes and air shafts, I avoided seeing my fellow scrubs. But my peace and quiet ended too soon as I opened the vent, swung down and landed in the middle of a crowded corridor, scattering scrubs.

Someone knocked into me. "Watch it!"

"Come to mingle with the lowly scrubs, your highness?" A mocking bow.

Used to curses and hostile glares, I shrugged. The mass of people in the tight corridor jostled and pushed me along. Life in the lower two levels teamed with scrubs at all hours of the week. They moved from work to their barracks and back to work. We were called scrubs because rust and dust were the twin evils of Inside and must be kept at bay; however, scrubs also maintained the network of mechanical systems which kept both uppers and lowers alive.

The scrubs shoved. They frowned. They complained. I hated every one of them. Except Cog. No one hated Cog. He listened. Empathized with tales of misery. Made people smile. A rare occurrence—as rare as a person like Cogon.

I headed toward the cafeteria in Sector G2. It stayed open around the clock. As far as I could tell, Inside's length and width equaled a square with four levels. All constructed with sheet metal. Overall measurements, by my calculations—for reasons unknown Inside's exact dimensions and specifications were classified—were two thousand meters wide by two thousand meters long by twenty-five meters high. Each level was divided into nine areas.

If I drew a square with two lines across and two lines down inside it, I would end up with nine smaller squares. The first row's three squares would be labeled A, B and C, the next row D, E and F, and the last row G, H and I. With this configuration, there were four Quadrants A, C, G and I, which were Inside's corners, and five Sectors B, D, E, F and H. That was the basic map of each level. Boring, unoriginal, and predictable to say the least.

The cafeteria and dining room for the lower two levels encompassed all of Sector G2. The number two meant it was on the second level. Even a four-hundred-week-old scrub couldn't get lost. Hydroponics resided directly below in Sector G1— the lowest level—making it easy for the food growers to send vegetables to the kitchen scrubs.

The hot, musty smell of people packed together greeted me at the cafeteria's door as the noise of them slammed into me. I paused, deciding if eating was worth being in the same room with so many scrubs. My stomach growled, overruling my reluctance.

The line to get food remained perpetually long. I took a tray and waited, ignoring the stares. Most scrubs changed from their work clothes to wear the drab-green off-duty jumpers before eating, but I was scheduled to scour an air duct at hour twenty. So I remained in my formfitting uniform. The slippery dark blue fabric covered every inch of skin except for my hands, feet and head. The material helped me slide through the tight heating ducts when I cleaned them. And I didn't care if I was the only person not wearing moccasins. My mocs were back at my bunk in Sector F1. With so many scrubs around to clean, the floor didn't even have a chance to become dirty.

Pushing my tray along the metal shelf, I pointed to what I

wanted from three different choices. The big containers held either green-, yellow- or brown-colored slop, and they all smelled like moldy vegetables. The food was easy to prepare, easy to cook and best of all easy to reuse. I didn't even bother reading the names of the dishes. If the kitchen staff called it a casserole, a quiche, a stew or a soup, it all tasted the same. A pulpy, leafy spinach flavor dominated the other ingredients lurking in the recipe.

To be fair to the cooks, hydroponics didn't offer much in the way of variety. Mass production of the hardier vegetables had replaced diversity, and there was only so much a person can do with mutton. I didn't want to be fair, though. I just wanted something different to eat.

After being served, I found an empty seat, and let the discord of multiple conversations roll over me.

"Where've you been?" a voice asked over the din. I looked up at Cog's broad face as he pressed into a seat next to mine.

"Working," I said.

"You were supposed to be done at hour ten."

I shrugged. "Got to make sure the pipes are squeaky clean for the uppers."

"Yeah. Like it would take you that long," Cog said. "You were sleeping in the pipes again."

"Don't start."

"You're going to get hurt—"

"Who'd care? One less scrub to feed."

"Grumpy, aren't we? What's the matter, Trella? Get wet?" Cog smirked, but couldn't hold the expression for more than a second. He was soon smiling, unaffected by my mood.

"Shouldn't you be changing a fan belt or something?" I asked, trying to be nasty, but Cog ignored me, knowing it was all an act—although with any other scrub, I wouldn't be acting.

He nodded to scrubs passing our table, calling out hellos and sharing his smile.

"How's the showerhead in washroom E2?" Cog asked one man.

"Much better," the man replied.

I had no interest in mundane details so I tuned out their conversation. Instead, I contemplated my only friend. Too big to fit into the pipes, Cog worked with the maintenance crew and did odd jobs. Most of it busywork, just like scrubbing. Too many idle hands had been deemed dangerous by the upper workers.

Scrubs also labored in the recycling plant, the infirmary, the care facility, hydroponics, the kitchen, the livestock yard, solid-waste facility or in the waste-water treatment plant. Most scrubs were assigned their jobs. A Care Mother noted the skills and aptitudes of each of her charges and recommended positions. My smaller size automatically matched me as a cleaning scrub. It suited me just fine.

"When's your next shift?" Cog asked.

"One hour."

"Good. Someone wants to meet you." Cog's eyes held an avid glow.

"Not another prophet. Come on, Cog, you know better."

"But this time—"

"Probably just like the last time, and the time before and the five times before that. All talk. No action, pushing false hope. You know they have to be employed by the upper officials to keep the scrubs from rioting."

"Trell, you're jaded. Besides, he asked for you by *name*. Said you were the only one who could help him." Cog seemed to think this divine calling should impress me.

"I have better things to do with my time." I picked up my tray, intent on leaving.

"Like sleeping in the pipes? Pretending you're all alone, instead of crammed in here with everyone else?"

I scowled at him. My fiercest frown, which usually resulted in some breathing room.

Cog stepped closer. "Come on. Hear the guy out."

Again, his face glowed with the conviction of a true believer. *Poor Cog,* I thought. How can he set himself up for another crushing disappointment? How can I turn him down? Especially when he was the only one who remained my friend despite my abuse. And who'd watched out for me, growing up in the care facility together.

"Okay. I'll listen, but no promises," I said. Perhaps I could expose this prophet as a fraud to keep Cog from becoming too involved.

Dumping our trays in the wash bins, we left the cafeteria. Cog led the way through the main corridors of the second level toward the stairs in Quad A2.

The narrow hallways of Inside had been constructed with studded metal walls painted white. Only Pop Cops' posters, spewing the latest propaganda, scrub schedules and the list of proper conduct could decorate common area walls on levels one and two. At least the massive bundles of greenery in every section of Inside helped break up the monotony. Although, if the plants weren't needed to clean the air, I was sure the Pop Cops would remove those, too.

I would never have had the patience to fight my way along the main paths, but Cog's thick body left a wake behind him. I followed along in this space, walking without effort and without touching anyone. A moment of peace.

We descended the wide metal steps. Cold stabbed the soles of my feet and I wished I had worn my mocs. Bare feet were useful in the air ducts, but not in the main throughways.

Cog led me to Sector B1. This prophet showed some intelligence. Sector B1 was filled with laundry machines. Rows upon rows of washers and dryers lined up like soldiers waiting for orders. The laundry was the most populated area, it had the largest number of workers, and every scrub in the lower levels came here for fresh uniforms.

Surrounded by a throng, the prophet had set himself up on an elevated dais near the break room so everyone could see him.

"…conditions are deplorable. The uppers have rooms to themselves and yet you sleep in barracks. But your suffering will not go unrewarded. You'll find peace and all the room you want Outside." The prophet's voice was strong. His words could be heard over the hiss and rattle of the machines.

I leaned over to Cog. "The wheelchair's a different touch. He'll gain the sympathy vote. What's his name?"

"Broken Man," Cog said with reverence.

I barked out a laugh. The prophet stopped speaking and focused his gray eyes on me. I stared back.

"You find something amusing?" Broken Man asked.

"Yes."

Cog stepped in front of me. "This is Trella."

The man in the wheelchair snapped his mouth shut in surprise. Obviously, I wasn't what he had expected.

"Children, I must speak with this one in private," he said.

I had to stifle another snort of disbelief. As if there was such a thing as privacy in the lower levels.

The crowd dispersed, and I was face-to-face with the latest prophet. Long blond hair, thin narrow face and no calluses on his hands. There were no blonds in the lower levels. Hair dye was a luxury reserved for the uppers only.

"Trella," he said in a deep, resonant voice.

"Look," I said. "You're more than welcome to seduce these sheep," I waved my hand at the working scrubs. "But don't sing your song of a better place to Cog. When you go back upstairs to reapply your hair dye, I don't want him left hurting."

"Trell," Cog said, shooting me a warning look.

"You don't believe me?" Broken Man asked.

"No. You're just an agent for the Pop Cops. Spewing the same bull about how our hard work will be rewarded after we're recycled. Oh, you might stick around for a hundred weeks or so, but then you'll be gone with the next shift and another 'prophet' will take your place." I cocked my head to the side, considering. "Maybe the next guy will have a missing limb. Especially if your wheelchair angle works."

Broken Man laughed, causing the nearby scrubs to glance over at us. "Cog said you would be difficult, but I think he spoke too kindly." He studied my face.

Impatient, I asked, "What do you want?"

"I need your expertise," Broken Man said.

"What expertise?"

"You know every duct, corridor, pipe, shortcut, hole and ladder of Inside. Only you will be able to retrieve something I need."

"How did you know?"

"I've heard rumors about the Queen of the Pipes. Cogon confirmed them."

I glared at my friend. The scrubs in my Care group had given me the title and not because they admired my tendency to explore the ductwork. Just the opposite. They had teased me for my desire to spend time alone.

"Will you help me?" Broken Man asked.

"What is it?" I asked.

"You were right," he said. He leaned forward and lowered his voice. "I used to live in the upper levels."

I stepped back in alarm.

"No," he rushed to assure me, "I'm not part of the Population Control Police. What do you call them? Pop Cops? I worked as an air controller, keeping track of the air systems, making sure the filters were clean and the oxygen levels breathable." Broken Man opened his mouth wide and pointed to a large gap in his bottom back teeth. "See the space for my port?"

"Anyone can have missing teeth," I said. "I know a lady in Sector D1 who'll get rid of anything you want. Including body parts."

Broken Man rubbed a hand over his face. His long thin fingers traced a graceful line down his throat. "Look. I *have* to spout the propaganda. If I tell the scrubs Gateway exists and the Pop Cops are lying to them, the Pop Cops will recycle me."

I felt as though he'd shot a stunner at my chest. He mentioned Gateway in a matter-of-fact tone. Gateway was a myth in the lower levels. The Pop Cops insisted no physical doorway existed to Outside. But stories and rumors circulated despite their claims, and everyone liked to speculate on its location.

The Pop Cops' prophets preached that Outside could only be attained after a person's life ends. And only if the person worked hard and obeyed Inside's laws. If a scrub was worthy, his inner soul would travel to Outside while his physical body would be fed to Chomper.

Most of the scrubs believed this Pop Cop dribble. I didn't. Souls were a myth and our bodies stayed trapped Inside.

"Come again?" I asked Broken Man.

"Gateway exists and I can prove it. Before coming down here, I hid some disks in a duct above my sleeping quarters, number three-four-two-one in Sector F3. I need them and only you can retrieve them without being seen. The disks might have information on the location of Gateway."

"Might have?" He was backpedaling already.

"I didn't get a chance to look at them."

"How convenient. I'm not authorized to go above level two. There are locked air filters to keep undesirables out, and if the Pop Cops catch me, I could have an unpleasant encounter with Chomper and end up as fertilizer for hydroponics." I shivered.

Inside didn't have room for many holding cells. Undesirables were simply recycled at the whim of the Pop Cops.

"Hasn't stopped you before," Cog said.

I punched him in the arm. "Shut up."

He smiled.

"Perhaps she's scared," Broken Man said.

"Not scared. Just not stupid enough to walk into a trap," I said.

"I meant that you might be scared because I'm telling the truth, and then you'd have to believe me."

"I don't have to believe anything. Especially not your lies." I turned to Cog. "Watch this one."

When I began to walk away, Broken Man called, "Going to clean air duct number seventeen?"

I stopped.

"I was in charge of the cleaning schedules before my 'accident.'"

I turned back. "Nice try, but cleaning assignments are posted all over the lower levels. See, Cog, he's grasping at air. A true prophet wouldn't have to trick someone into believing him."

"I'm sure no prophet has had to deal with Trella Garrard Sanchia before," Broken Man said.

My blood froze in my veins. Scrubs didn't worry about bloodlines; most knew nothing about their biological parents. Most didn't care. Scrubs birthed more scrubs. We mixed blood like paint. Too many colors combined, and we ended up with brown-eyed, brown-haired babies who were raised in Care groups until they were old enough to work. Me included. With my brown hair and eyes, I blended right in with the scrubs.

Only the uppers worried about bloodlines and maintaining family groups. And Population Control. They kept track of every person in Inside.

Garrard and Sanchia were two of the family names used in the upper levels.

Broken Man watched me. "That's right, Trella," he said. "Your father was from the Garrard line and your mother is a Sanchia. You were born with your father's blue eyes until they changed them." He paused a moment to let the information sink in. "You don't quite fit. Not a purebred by upper standards, but quite the thoroughbred down here."

two

"How do you know?" I asked.

"I told you I used to live in the upper levels. But if you want more information about your parents, you'll have to get my disks first." Broken Man leaned back in his chair with a pleased smirk.

I stepped toward him, planning to agree. A cold jab of logic halted my steps. I couldn't believe I'd almost fallen for it. Why would I care about parents who left me to be raised by scrubs?

"You spout some bull about bloodlines and think I'll get all teary eyed and desperate to find information about my parents. No deal." I grabbed Cog's arm and turned him to face me. "Stay away from this man. He's dangerous." Then I hurried to my cleaning assignment, before Cog could argue with me.

I tried not to think about Broken Man as I scrubbed the air duct, but following the circular cleaning brush with its humming vacuum was mindless work. The cleaning device looked like a hairy troll spinning and singing to himself. All I had to do was turn him on, make sure he didn't break down and then turn him off at the end of the conduit.

Being slender and a little over one and a half meters tall made me the perfect candidate for this duty, but I also knew how to repair the troll if it broke. Thanks to Cog. He had taught me, and I was one of the few scrubs who carried a special tool belt. The black band was constructed of the same slippery material as my uniform. Each of its eight pockets contained a tool. The band held them and my flashlight snug against my waist. Regular tool belts wouldn't work in the tight air shafts. The hanging tools would bang on the metal and impede my motion.

Nothing out of the ordinary happened during my shift. I had plenty of time for the information Broken Man had told me to eat its way through the layers of my mind like acid sizzling through metal.

Devious, the way he had phrased his words. Your father was from the Garrard line. Past tense, meaning he was dead. Your mother is a Sanchia, implying she was still alive. Devious, except he had forgotten I had been raised as a scrub. Family lines meant nothing to me. Biological parents were the concern of the Pop Cops. I might have a fondness for my Care Mother (CM), but that was as far as it went. Broken Man was just trying to con me into his schemes. Give the Pop Cops a reason to recycle me.

The cleaning troll grunted as his motor strained. He had come to a bend. I gave him a little push, and the troll continued on his way. The angle of the air duct started to sharpen. I braced myself in the pipe, using my bare feet to climb behind the troll. The air shaft was one of the main trunk lines, servicing multiple levels of Inside. It cut between the levels and I could follow the troll up to level four if I could unlock the air filter between levels two and three.

Broken Man's voice tapped into my mind. Information

about Gateway might be on some disks hidden on level three. Might be. Most likely not. At least I would have proof the prophet was a fake to show Cog.

During my ten-hour shift of babysitting the troll, I kept changing my mind about whether or not to check Broken Man's story. When the troll finished the last air duct on my schedule, I pulled him out and stored him in a cleaning closet.

Officially, I was off duty until hour forty. All scrubs had the same schedule. Ten hours off, ten hours on, with a break every five hours. There were no such things as vacations or holidays. Since one week equaled one hundred hours, we worked five shifts per week. Everything in Inside could be divided by the number ten. It made life simple so even the scrubs could understand. Work groups comprised ten scrubs. One CM for every ten children. Ten weeks equaled a deciweek, and a hundred weeks was called a centiweek. And so on. Although, a few old-timers called a centiweek a long year, but I had no idea what that meant.

The work shifts were also staggered so only half the scrubs worked at one time. It saved room in the barracks. I shared my bunk with another scrub I never saw. Not that I ever slept there anyway.

My shift ended on level two in Sector D, and I needed to make a decision. Below me were the rows and rows of bunks that filled Sectors D, E and F on both lower levels. From this location, it was just a matter of heading due east for two sectors, then up one level to search for Broken Man's disks.

The uppers filled their two levels of housing sectors with roomy apartments and vast suites for the important officials.

Only certain loyal scrubs had authorization to clean and maintain the upper levels, and to deliver food and laundry. Not me. I had no desire to ingratiate myself to earn the Pop Cops' trust. They rarely policed the ductwork with their sensors, believing in their filters and the passivity of the scrubs. I grinned. Except for a few of us, they were right.

Although I remembered the stories about when the Pop Cops had tried to place video cameras in the lower levels. Each and every one had disappeared. No witnesses came forward, and no evidence had been found. Eventually the cameras became another lost part of our world. Something we once had. Our computers have a whole list of things which met this criterion, but I didn't care. No sense bemoaning what was gone. A waste of time. Better to worry about what weapons the Pop Cops could use now.

It would be a challenge to search for the disks while avoiding the scrubs and Pop Cops. Like Cog had said, the threat of getting into trouble hadn't stopped me before, and I have explored all the upper level ducts more for the challenge than just to break the rules. In the end my curiosity was too great to walk away. I found an appropriate air conduit and slipped inside the tight space.

The rush of air blew past me in the active duct. Closing my eyes, I concentrated on the warm current as it caressed my face. I pulled my hair from its single long braid, and let it flow behind me, imagining for a moment that I flew.

The air shaft ended in a scrubber—a tight wire mesh impossible to bypass without unlocking and removing the cleaning filters nestled inside. This was the barrier to keep the scrubs down in their levels. I could have dismantled it and reattached the lock and filters when I returned, but the effort would eat up a lot of time.

Instead, I backtracked until I found a near-invisible hatch and opened it. Climbing from the duct, I stood on top of level two above Sector F. Pipes and wires hung down, crisscrossed and bisected the open space. I called it the Gap.

Between the levels of Inside, spaces ranged from one meter to one and a half meters high. A two-meter gap existed between the walls of the levels and the true Walls of Inside. The levels were bolted to these Walls with steel I-beams, and foam insulation had been sprayed onto them.

As far as I could tell, no one knew about the Gap. Only four near-invisible hatches offered access to it—one on each level. I had spent hundreds of hours in the shafts before I discovered them. I didn't care what the reason was for such a space around the levels, it suited me just fine.

Bluelight shone and I negotiated the obstacle course of ducts to reach the east Wall. One of the six metal dividers framing our world, it was the barrier between Inside and whatever existed beyond.

A ladder was bolted to the Wall. It stretched from the very bottom of Inside to just above level four. Using it would make climbing to the air ducts above the third level easier. Except for two problems. A two-meter space gaped between where I stood on the edge of level two and the ladder. To use the ladder, I would need to traverse the thin I-beam connecting level two to the Wall. If I slipped, I would plummet about ten meters. The drop might not kill me right away, but if I broke my legs no one would know where to find me.

Breaks in the ladder were the second problem with the route. Someone long ago had cut off portions of the ladder as if they hoped to limit access to the upper levels. I had strung chains between the breaks, but climbing them required a great deal of upper-body strength.

No sense wasting time. A tingle of apprehension brushed my skin. I moved onto the I-beam. The beam was a little wider than my foot. Balancing on it, I placed one foot in front of the other with care. Once I mounted the ladder, I climbed until I reached the chain. Taking a deep breath, I wrapped my legs around the slender metal links and pulled myself up hand over hand to the next complete section of the ladder.

By the time I reached the next rung, sweat soaked my uniform and coated my palms. As I stretched for the bar, my fingers slipped.

I started to fall. Three wild heartbeats later, I managed to stop my descent by gripping the chain. When my body stopped swinging in midair, I grinned at the near miss. My pulse tapped a fast rhythm, matching my huffs for breath. I waited a moment before returning to the top of the chain. My second attempt to transfer to the ladder worked.

Navigating through the ductwork, I found the near-invisible hatch for level three and climbed inside the air shaft, searching for the sleeping quarters in Sector F.

Broken Man had said a duct above his rooms. Logic suggested he wouldn't use a water pipe, too messy, or an electrical conduit, no space. He had been an air controller so it stood to reason I would find the disks, if they existed, in the air shaft. *If.*

I crawled through the shaft above the rooms, counting. Small rectangles of daylight warned me when a room was occupied, and I took extra care to be quiet. Stealing glances into the quarters as I slipped by, I spotted uppers working on their computers.

I usually avoided the populated sections. One sneeze and I would be permanently assigned to the solid-waste-handling crew. The crap cleaners. Nothing like the threat of unclogging *those* pipes to keep scrubs in line.

When I reached number three-four-two-one, I peered into the darkness below. The lack of light noteworthy. Inside had two light levels. Daylight for when people were awake and working and bluelight for sleeping. Bluelight was also used for temporarily unoccupied areas where, as soon as a person entered, the daylights would turn on. In the barracks, the bluelights stayed on all the time.

Darkness in Broken Man's room meant it had been unoccupied for a long time. I shined my flashlight through the vent. The living area appeared normal. Sweeping my light on the walls of the shaft, I searched for the disks. At first, nothing caught my eye, but a strange bulge cast a slight shadow. I rubbed my fingertips over the bump and felt a slender edge.

Booby-trapped, I thought at first. Then I considered what I would do if I wanted to hide something from the Pop Cops. Either find a niche they didn't scan, tuck it behind a lead-lined piece of machinery or camouflage it.

Using my fingernails, I peeled back a thin metal sheet. Underneath was a cloth bag.

I'd been so sure Broken Man had lied, I was almost disappointed. Almost. Let's face it; if Gateway existed, I wouldn't be upset.

I shook my head. These were dangerous thoughts. They led to hope and hope led to pain. I squelched them and focused on the contents of the bag. Four disks with rainbow rays streaked around their silver surfaces. Enthralled, I dropped the bag. It slipped through the vent and floated to the floor.

I shrugged. No big deal. Until a red light pulsed in the dark room below. Then daylight flooded the chamber as gas hissed.

Booby-trapped was right. But not the camouflage—Broken Man's rooms. Smoke filled the air shaft. I held my breath as my eyes stung and watered, blurring my vision. Pushing back, I blindly scooted away. The door banged open and a man ordered, "Halt."

Instinctively, I halted.

"Clear the gas," a female voice ordered.

A pump hummed and the gray fog around me disappeared. Voices echoed in the chamber. Boots drummed on the floor.

"Guard the door."

"Fan out and search."

"Watch for ambush."

I wiped the tears from my eyes, eased back to the vent and peeked in. A woman stepped into my view. An intricate knot pulled her blond hair back from her face. She wore the uniform of the Population Control Police, purple with silver stripes down the outsides of the sleeves and pants. Her black weapon belt bulged to such an extreme that she looked like she wore a tire. A lieutenant commander's insignia glinted on her collar.

A lieutenant snapped to attention beside her. "No one here, sir."

"Impossible. Look again," she ordered.

He rushed off.

She scanned the room, then spotted the bag on the floor. She tipped her head back and looked directly into the vent. Every cell in my body turned to ice.

"All sectors clear, sir," another Pop Cop said.

"Get me some RATSS," she yelled. "Post guards on all air vents in Sector F3. Now!"

Her order shocked me into action. I hustled along the duct with as much speed as I could muster one-handed. The Pop Cops' Remote Access Temperature Sensitive Scanner (RATSS) would search me out through the ducts using heat-seeking technology. I had to leave Sector F3. Now. I had to find a hot spot to hide in.

As I slid through the air shaft, snatches of conversations reached me from the corridors where an alarming number of Pop Cops rushed to take up positions under the vents. I just stayed ahead of them.

"Someone sprung the trap."

"Escaping through the vents."

"Use the gas."

"Stunners only. No kill-zappers."

"Alert all sectors on level three."

My heart hammered, driving me forward on the edge of panic. With the Pop Cops in every room, I couldn't get to the near-invisible hatch. Instead, I raced toward Sector B3 where

I knew of a well-placed laundry chute I could use. Impossible to climb up, laundry chutes only worked one way.

Just before I reached the chute, something bit my foot. Yelping, I twisted around. A RATSS had clamped on my toe. Damn!

Its little antennae vibrated, probably reporting my position. Imagining the information racing through the complex network of wires crisscrossing every level, I yanked my wrench from my tool belt and smashed the RATSS. After reducing it to scrap, I jerked it off my foot.

When I reached the laundry chute, I slid down two levels without having any dirty garments tossed on my head. A small bonus. I landed in a half-full bin.

The dryers hummed productively, creating one of the warmest sections of Inside. If a RATSS had followed me here, it would lose me in the heat from them and from the mass of scrubs who labored here.

I found a small crawl space behind a row of dryers and collapsed into it to catch my breath.

Questions swirled in my mind. Where to go now? I couldn't give the disks to Broken Man. He might have orchestrated this whole thing. Obviously the Pop Cops had set a trap for whoever came to collect the disks. But why not rig the vent? Maybe they hadn't known where the disks were located. That would mean Broken Man wasn't involved. So why hadn't they interrogated him before sending him down here? I hadn't wanted any trouble. Now I swam in it.

I could hide the disks on level three for the Pop Cops to find. If Broken Man wasn't a plant, then they'd known someone had come for them, but not who. Then I could walk away. Stay uninvolved. It was the safest course of action. The smartest move. The Pop Cops would have what they wanted.

Broken Man had said the disks might reveal the location of Gateway. Why risk my neck for a possibility? For something even I didn't believe in.

I just couldn't give the Pop Cops what they wanted. It rankled too much. Shoving the disks into a pocket of my belt, I hurried to find Broken Man.

Pop Cops had infested the lower level. Groups of three and four scanned the scrubs, occasionally stopping and questioning one. My skin burned where it touched the pocket concealing the disks. Trying to remain calm and invisible, I searched for Broken Man.

The dais he had used as a pulpit was empty. Cogon sat on the edge of the platform with his head in his hands.

"What happened?" I asked.

"Broken Man's gone," he said to the floor.

"Disappeared?" Figures, I thought. He was a plant and I had fallen for it like a gullible three-hundred-week-old.

"No. Taken." Cog looked up. Blood ran down his face from a gash on his forehead.

"Cog!" I ran and grabbed a towel from one of the laundry bins lining the hall. A few scrubs folded sheets nearby, appearing to ignore us, but I knew better.

"Here." I wiped Cog's eye and cheek, pressing the cloth to the cut. "Who did this to you?" Cog was a big man. No scrubs would dare fight him.

"Pop Cops," he said.

The significance of Cog's word *taken* finally sank in. My world shrank, tightening around my body until I felt like I was being crushed. Interrogation of Broken Man would lead the Pop Cops to me.

"When?" I demanded.

"Just now." Cog gestured down the hallway. "I tried to talk to them. Stop them. But…" He touched his forehead.

Figures. The Pop Cops knew a good beating was an effective way to warn a scrub. Give them trouble another time and a scrub is arrested and never seen again in the lower levels.

"How many?"

"Three to subdue me," he said with a smile, "but only one took him away. He can't do much from a wheelchair."

"You could have been fed to Chomper," I admonished him, but I was distracted.

"Could have, Trell. Doesn't mean I would have. Besides, I would have felt terrible if I didn't try to help." He sighed. "I'm talking to a wall. You don't care about anyone in this place."

An old argument. My response would be how I cared about him, and he would claim I had a funny way of showing it. But not this time. "You're right. So why do you bother with me? Why do you drag me to listen to every prophet?"

"It's called hope. It's called seeing the best in people despite the miserable conditions." He grabbed the towel from me. His shoulders sagged as he covered his face with the bloody cloth. "Maybe you're right and it's all a lie." He gestured to Broken Man's dais.

The prophet hadn't lied about the disks, but soon the Pop Cops would know about them, too. A plan raced along the circuits of my mind. "Which way did the Pop Cop take Broken Man?"

"Why?" Confusion pushed his thick eyebrows together.

"Just answer."

"Toward Quad A1. Probably going to take him up the lift to level four."

I had to hurry. "Cog, you better get to the infirmary. I need to go."

"Go where?" He glanced at the clock. "Your shift doesn't start for another two hours."

"Not your concern," I said, looking up at the ductwork. I quickened my pace, planning the best route to Quadrant A's lift.

But Cogon trailed after me. "Why do you care which way he went?"

I ignored him.

"He must be right," Cog called. His voice bright and strong again. Back to normal. "Broken Man's right about Gateway. Why else would the Pop Cops take him?"

I just shook my head.

The corridor to Quad A1 teemed with scrubs and Pop Cops, hopefully delaying progress of the Pop Cop pushing the wheelchair. When I spotted an air vent, I climbed up the metal wall. Metal rivets on the walls were the perfect size for my toes and fingers. Once inside the air duct, I scurried through the horizontal tube, using my hands and feet while sliding on my belly.

The hum of the lift set every nerve in my body afire. If they were in the elevator, I was too late. Occasionally, I slowed to peer through the air vents, trying to spot Broken Man.

I grunted with frustration. A Pop Cop wheeled Broken Man into the open lift.

three

I had mere seconds to rescue Broken Man. Good thing level one's near-invisible hatch was next to the lift. I scrambled out of the air pipe and hunched my way over to the shaft. The elevator's shaft was solid except for half-meter openings at each level's Gap. If the lift passed level one's, I would be too late.

Reaching the opening, I glanced inside. The lift remained on level one, but the doors hissed closed. I squeezed through and landed on the lift's roof. I held still, listening as something scraped against the doors before they shut.

"Stop," a voice ordered.

The lift began its ascent. I clutched a cable to keep from falling. Huddled on top, I regained my balance. Risking notice, I pried up the roof hatch just enough to see inside.

A meter below me, Broken Man slumped in his wheelchair, while a Pop Cop stood with his stunner pointed at Cog. The big oaf must have squeezed into the elevator to rescue his prophet, and now he was caught.

I altered my plan. Tracing wires, I found the electric feed

into the elevator and fitted the white electrical wire between my rubber-handled pliers. I opened the emergency control panel on the roof, yelled, "Fire drill" and punched the stop button while cutting the wire. The lift jerked to a halt.

The occupants of the elevator were now in total darkness. I hoped Cog knew what to do. My call had warned him. As I lifted the hatch, a soft thud, a loud grunt and the unmistakable sizzle slap of the stun gun reached me.

"What's going on?" Broken Man asked with a nervous tremor in his voice.

I sucked in my breath, biting my lip.

"We need to get out of here," Cog replied.

Relief washed over me as my clenched muscles relaxed. I pulled the hatch wide open. It squeaked.

"Trella?" Cog asked.

"Hold on. I'll get a light." I fumbled for the flashlight on my belt as Broken Man repeated my name in shock.

I leaned through the open hatch, dangling upside down from my waist and held out my light. The Pop Cop lay on his side. His wide-eyed, lifeless gaze stared at nothing.

Cogon gaped at the Pop Cop's weapon in his own hand in horror. "This is a stun gun," he cried. "Why would it kill him?"

"What's the setting?" I asked.

Cog just looked at me. His eyebrows pinched together, and confusion shone in his eyes.

"The intensity." I tried again. "It's on the side."

Cog turned the weapon over. "Ten."

"That's why. It's on the maximum setting. A ten blast could easily kill an average-sized man." I still didn't see understanding in Cog's creased face. "You're twice the Pop Cop's size. I would have set the damn thing to ten, too, if I had to incapacitate you. Look, we don't have time for this. We need to get Broken Man to a hiding place."

"Impossible," Broken Man said. "Inside has no hiding place." His face looked pale in the light.

I smiled at Broken Man's regurgitation of Pop Cop propaganda, then pulled myself back onto the roof. Using my rubber-handled pliers again, I fixed the broken wire, restored the lights and accessed the lift's controls.

"Push the button for level two," I called.

When we reached level two, I opened the back doors. A maintenance room was located adjacent to the elevator shaft.

"Cog, wheel him out and take the Pop Cop, too."

Cogon finally realized how dangerous it was to delay. Galvanized into action, he cleared everyone from the elevator.

"Leave them here, and get back on the lift," I said through the roof's hatch.

"He can't stay here. It'll be the first place they'll look," Cog said.

"I know, but he can't travel through the corridors. We'll have to camouflage him."

"How?"

"Laundry bin."

Understanding smoothed Cog's face. He delivered the laundry to the upper levels, so it wouldn't look out of place if he was seen pushing a bin.

With Cog as the sole occupant, I sent the lift back to level one, and again opened the back doors. This time the doors led to the laundry. Bins full of clean laundry filled the area by the lift. Cog grabbed one, waved to the working scrubs and pushed it into the elevator. I brought him back to level two.

"Stand in the doorway," I said. Returning the controls to the panel inside the lift, I swung down. "Help me put the hatch back on." I sat on Cog's broad shoulders and replaced the cover.

We joined Broken Man in the maintenance room as the lift resumed its regular service. The bin was full of towels. We removed them and Cog lifted Broken Man into the bin.

Before we covered him, he asked, "My wheelchair?"

"It's too big. We'll have to leave it behind," I said.

"Now what?" Cog asked as he finished arranging the towels.

"Take him down to Quad C1, but don't use this lift."

"To the Power plant?" Cog asked.

"Yes. I'll meet you there."

"What about the Pop Cop?"

"Leave him. Someone will find him."

"And the stun gun?" he asked.

"Put it back in his belt. It's too dangerous to keep." The Pop Cops would be mad enough once they discover a fallen colleague, but it would be worse if they believed one of the scrubs was armed.

Kneeling beside the prone form, Cog shoved the weapon into the Pop Cop's holder, but he paused. He closed the man's eyes and smoothed his limbs to a more comfortable position— not that the Pop Cop would care. Cog rested a large hand on the man's shoulder, bowed his head and whispered. Only the words *sorry* and *journey* were audible to me.

I suppressed the urge to hurry him, knowing Cog needed this time. When he finished, he stood and wheeled the bin from the room. I waited for a few minutes before climbing into the air shaft. I traveled to level one to assess the situation.

Walking through the corridors, I scanned faces. Level one appeared normal. So far, the Pop Cops hadn't raised an alarm. I headed to Quad C1.

I pressed past some scrubs until I found a heating vent near the floor. After sliding inside, I replaced the vent cover and rested in the warm metal tube, catching my breath. The enormity of what I had just done slammed into me. My body shook as doubt and fear fought for control. With effort, I pushed the ugly thoughts away; I had no time for recriminations. Right now I navigated by instinct alone.

Propelled by the need to keep moving, I followed the heated

air to its source. The Power plant in Quad C1 was Inside's beating heart. It pumped out electricity and heat to keep us all alive. Encompassing all of Quadrant C on the first, second, third and fourth levels, the plant's main controls were located on level four. Noise, excessive heat, dirt and fuel tanks filled level one, and hardly anyone worked in this area.

The air burned my lungs as I drew closer to the plant, forcing me to leave the vent. Sweat soaked my uniform, but a sudden chill gripped my spine when I couldn't find Cogon and Broken Man anywhere near the plant.

My name sounded in the thick air and I spun in time to see Cogon waving me over. He had hidden behind one of the fuel tanks. Broken Man was propped up in the laundry bin.

"Now what?" Cog shouted over the chugging engines.

"There's an abandoned controller's room by the fuel-intake valve." I pointed. "The door's locked, but I can open it from the inside."

Finding the air return duct crossing over the controller's quarters, I had Cogon lift me up to it. I crawled through the duct until I found a vent into the controller's room. I had discovered this small living space on one of my excursions. Thinking it was a perfect hideaway, I had proceeded to make it my own. It hadn't taken me long to figure out why it had been empty. The intolerable noise from the plant, the oppressive heat and the fine coating of black grit covering everything had eventually driven me away despite the rarity of such a space.

As Cog wheeled Broken Man in, I cleaned the room as best as I could with the towels. Cog lifted the prophet into a chair. Dust puffed out from the cushions.

We stared at each other for a moment as the engines roared.

"We're in trouble," Cog yelled. "This isn't going to work. They'll find us."

"They'll think I killed the Pop Cop. I'll be recycled," Broken Man said.

"You were going to be recycled anyway," I said.

Broken Man jerked his head in shock.

"What did you think they would do after they interrogated you?" I asked.

"But what happened to you?" the prophet asked.

"Yeah, why are you here, Trella?"

Broken Man's nose crinkled in confusion. He was either a good actor or genuinely flustered. Drowning in trouble and still unable to trust the blond-haired man, I hesitated. Cogon stepped toward me, a mixture of fear and anger twisting his face. An expression I had never seen on Cog. There was only one scrub I cared for in this whole metal world, and he wallowed in this predicament with me.

Damn. I pulled out the disks, spreading them in my hands like a fan. Cog's mouth dropped open as though someone had slapped him.

Broken Man raked his fingers through his hair as understanding dawned. "But the Pop Cops didn't know about the disks," he said.

"Why not?" I asked.

"I used an untraceable port and covered my tracks for the file transfer. However, I wasn't as clever with my other forays into the computer system and was caught. When they questioned me before my accident and exile, they hadn't a clue about the hidden files."

He glanced around the room. "Unless they suspected."

"So the Pop Cops rigged your former quarters just in case," I said.

"Why not just pick me up and ask?" Broken Man shuddered. The Pop Cops had a gruesome reputation.

"They knew where to find you. They knew you didn't have the disks on you. Plus if they waited, they could see who you recruited to break the rules in order to help you."

"That's why you rescued him," Cog said. "You started this whole mess by getting the disks."

I bit down on my retort. In my mind, Cogon had started it when he introduced me to his prophet, but in fairness I had made the decision to retrieve the disks. "All right," I said to Broken Man. "Cog and I'll have to lay low for a while. Let's hope no one spotted Cog entering the lift. You'll have to hide here."

"The scanners?" he asked.

"The power and heat coming off those engines plays havoc with their scanners. This room hasn't been used for hundreds of weeks. Keep the door locked at all times."

Cog rubbed a hand over his face. "I could put a blind in front of the door."

"A blind?" I asked.

"It's a thin sheet of metal. The maintenance crew uses them to cover holes and dents in the walls. If you match the rivets up right, no one can tell what's behind the blind. I'll do it during my next shift," he said.

"Good. Make sure no one sees you. And when you're done, keep far away from this room. I'll take care of Broken Man."

Cog nodded, pulled out a set of earplugs from his belt and handed them to Broken Man. "I'll also bring some insulating foam to cut down the noise."

The quarters had a bathroom, but I had to make sure the water was turned on. Our shifts started in a few minutes. "Can you take care of yourself for the next shift?" I asked the prophet.

"I'll be fine for now," he replied though his eyes looked a little wild. He held his hand out. "I'll keep the disks."

"No. If they find you, they find the disks. I'll hide them," I said. I stuffed the disks back into my belt. Broken Man pulled his hand away. His expression guarded.

Cog left through the door, and I locked it behind him. "I'll be back after my shift with a few supplies."

The prophet blinked at me, but said nothing as he pushed the green foam plugs into his ears.

I climbed into the vents and found the valves to turn on the water. Then I hurried to level two to report for work.

Ten hours seemed like an eternity as my thoughts dwelled on the need to hide the disks.

After my shift, I climbed to level four. This time I didn't slip and I didn't encounter any RATSS. Ultrasonic scanners and RATSS they might have, but I knew plenty of hiding places all over Inside where the electromagnetic currents scrambled ultrasonic waves. Spots that reflected a solid wall on their scanner displays. I stayed in those hidden areas as I traveled.

In the Gap on top of level four, I had hidden a small box where I kept my valuables. It was difficult to find and dangerous to reach. Perfect for hiding Broken Man's disks.

My niche appeared untouched. Until now, I had stored only two items in this cabinet. I placed the disks next to the thread-picture of my Care Mother. Colored threads had been sewn onto a white handkerchief, and, from a distance, her face and kind eyes could be seen.

She understood my need to disappear in the pipes. Her support when Cog grew out of our group had made living bearable. I wondered what my CM would think about the trouble we were in now. Considering the problems my care mates and I had managed to cause during our stay, I imagined she would sigh with exasperation.

Imagining her frown, I smiled because, no matter how hard she had scowled, she couldn't stifle the gleam in her eyes. The gleam that said she was proud of our inventiveness. The gleam that encouraged us during lessons to think for ourselves even while she taught us the standard Pop Cop propaganda.

It must have been difficult for her, getting a new child when one of the older kids reached the age of maturity and left. Our ages had ranged from newborn to fourteen centiweeks old.

I folded the handkerchief and smoothed a few wrinkles before returning it to the cabinet. The other item in my niche was a comb decorated with pink pearls along its spine. The smooth spears pushed into my fingers as I pulled the comb through my long brown hair. With all the excitement, I had forgotten to rebraid it and it had knotted.

Thoughts of the comb wove through my mind as the comb's teeth worked at the knots in my hair. According to my CM, it had been a gift from my birth mother. My CM had kept it safe for me until I reached 1400 weeks, the age of maturity. The age when you were no longer considered a child. It was when you became a scrub and the reality of what the rest of your life would be like became suddenly and brutally apparent. The old-timers called it sweet sixteen, but there wasn't anything sweet about it.

I finished combing my hair and examined the gift, wondering which adult scrub cared enough to part with such a precious item, yet didn't care enough to contact me. Even though it was forbidden, a few mothers kept in touch with their offspring.

Damn. Every moment counted. I shoved my comb back into the cabinet. These stolen glances were a nasty habit that I needed to break. I slammed the door shut and bolted.

Never taking the same route to and from the cabinet, I snaked my way west before entering an air conduit on level four, which would lead to a laundry chute I could use. The air conduit passed above an abandoned storeroom. I always shone my light down through the vent to marvel at the wasted space. A perfectly good chamber big enough to house four scrubs comfortably was being used for broken furniture.

Ghost furniture. Each time I checked, the pieces lost more

of their color and texture under a coating of dust—one of the evils of Inside.

This time, when I paused a bluelight glowed, and the room appeared to be different. The couch cushions had been cleaned, revealing a brown and green geometric pattern. The mess of broken chairs had been piled in a corner. The junk on the desk in the opposite corner had been removed and an upper sat before it, working under a small lamp.

Startled, I pulled away and hit my head on the top of the shaft. The noise vibrated and the upper turned to look. With careful and slow movements, I started to cross the vent.

"Who's there?" he called.

I paused, resting my knees and most of my weight on the vent. Big mistake. The vent cover groaned and popped free. Scrabbling with my hands for purchase, I felt my legs drop, pulling my body down. The last thing I saw before hitting the floor was a black-haired man with a shocked expression.

four

As I crashed to the floor, I pulled my body into a protective
ball. I kept a fetal position as waves of pain pulsed up and down
my legs. I braced for the cry of outrage from the occupant of
the room and the call for the Pop Cops.

Instead, a concerned face came into my view.

"Are you all right?" he asked. His blue eyes held a touch of
awe as he stared at me with parted lips. No immediate threat.

I grunted and stretched, feeling for injuries. It wasn't the first
time I had fallen, and it wouldn't be the last. My leg muscles
would be sore for twenty hours or more, but otherwise no
broken bones. Rising with care, I leaned on the couch as a
dizzy spell washed through me.

The young man stepped back as if afraid. I suppressed a
laugh; I had probably given him a real scare. Smoothing my
hair, I glanced around the room. Food bowls, glasses, markers
and a wipe board littered the area, suggesting the room was in
use.

The tenant wore a black-and-silver jumper, indicating a

level-four resident who was in training for whatever job the Controllers had assigned him. Having never met an upper besides the Pop Cops, I had learned about them and their families from the computer's learning software in the care facility.

"Are you a…scrub?" he asked.

Oh, yes, a young one probably around fifteen hundred weeks old. Well, close to my age, but the uppers coddled their children, babying them until they were seventeen hundred weeks old.

I pointed to my work suit. "Guess."

"Oh. Yes. Well. Sorry," he said. His pale skin flushed pink.

My head cleared. He seemed in no hurry to call for help, probably didn't even know he should be reporting me. I wasn't taking any more chances; I climbed onto the couch, trying to reach the air duct. It was another meter beyond my grasp. The vent was in the middle of the ceiling, and I couldn't use the rivets to scale the side wall.

My first attempt to jump was unsuccessful. I thumped to the floor with an alarming bang.

"Stop it," he said.

His firm tone gave me pause. "Why?" I asked.

"With all the noise you're making, someone will hear you and come to investigate."

"Why do you care?" I shot back at him. "I'm the one who isn't supposed to be here. It's not like *you'll* get in trouble."

He frowned. "I don't want anyone to know about this room," he said. "It's where I come for privacy."

I couldn't help it—I laughed. "What? You have to share a room with a brother?" I guessed. "Poor boy," I mocked. "Try sharing a barrack with three thousand others."

Fury flashed in his eyes. But I had to give him credit for controlling his temper.

"When I'm here," he said evenly, "no one can find me.

No one can give me assignments. No one can harp at me about shirking my duty. No one makes me pledge loyalty to the Controllers." He stepped toward me. "And I'm not about to give it up because some scrub doesn't have the sense to be quiet."

"Well, then, it's to our mutual benefit that I disappear and we both forget about this little incident. Agreed?"

"Yes. No. Yes, but I want to know what you're doing up here."

I thought fast. "Cleaning the shaft like a good little scrub." Climbing back onto the couch, I said, "I'm finished, so I'll be returning to the lower levels where I belong. Can you give me a leg up?"

He laced his fingers together, but before I could step into his cupped hand, he pulled back.

"What? If I'm caught here, I'm in trouble."

"What's it like in the lower levels?"

"Why?"

"I'm curious."

"Go log on to the computer, look under scrubs," I said.

"I already tried. All I found was one paragraph of information. I want to know more."

"You shouldn't. Curiosity is a fatal trait in here."

He set his legs slightly apart and tucked his hands under his crossed arms.

I sighed at his stubbornness. "Imagine every space in this room filled with people. Moving from one end to the other is like swimming in a thick human tank. Constantly being jostled and pushed. Smells of scrubs invading your senses, overwhelming you to the point of nausea. Always waiting in line for food, water and for the washroom. Mind-numbing routine with change a rare event. Being battered by the noises of people eating, moving, snoring, mating and talking over the constant roar of the machinery. In the lower levels, there is no quiet place. No peace."

I drew a deep breath. My speech had come in one burst. The young man had unknowingly unleashed a deluge, which had propelled him onto the couch. Looking around the chamber, I said, "To a scrub, this room is paradise."

We stared at each other for a few heartbeats.

"No one should live like that," the man said in a quiet voice.

"Over eighteen thousand and counting do." I tried to be flippant, but my words felt heavy. A woman caught in the illegal act of terminating her pregnancy was bred until her fertility ceased. Our population bulged. Children were our future, said the Pop Cops. But why? Especially since the future looked like life crammed into every available space. None of the scrubs had a clue.

I pointed toward the duct. "I should go before I'm missed." A lie. I doubt I would ever be missed. Noted absent, charged delinquent, reprimanded but never missed.

He stood on the couch and created a step with his hands. After I had wiggled inside the air shaft, I called down my thanks.

Before I could move he said, "My name's Riley Narelle..." He paused as if embarrassed by his family names. Clearing his throat, he continued, "Ashon. Anytime you need a moment of peace, you're welcome to use my hideaway."

If he noticed the shock on my face, he didn't show it. I gave him a curt nod and hurried away, shaken by his offer. An offer that would be too dangerous for me to accept. Scrubs and uppers don't mix. Ever. The Pop Cops had specific guidelines for keeping everybody where the Pop Cops decided they belonged. Besides, we hated each other. The uppers lived in spacious quarters with their families. Their work schedules were shorter and they had more freedoms. They made the decisions and we followed.

The time I had spent at my niche and with Riley had used up most of my off hours and I needed rest. Moving through the pipes as fast as I dared, I made it to the lower level, found a comfortable shaft and fell asleep.

Empty corridors should have been my first warning. I had woken after a couple of hours to a strange hush and dropped down to level one to investigate. Pop Cops herded scrubs into the dining room. Surprised, I tried to retreat but was spotted and pulled into the flow.

Shoulders pressed against shoulders. I gagged on the overripe smell of tightly packed humans. When no more scrubs could be wedged into the room, the doors were shut and guarded by the Pop Cops. There were three "meeting" locations in the lower levels, and I guessed the Pop Cops also had our two common areas in Quads A1 and A2 filled with scrubs and sealed off just like the dining room.

I started to sweat, and not just from the excessive body heat. Standing on top of a table in the middle of the dining room was the female lieutenant commander who had ambushed Broken Man's quarters. I glanced at the clock. Hour sixty. My troubles started only twenty-five hours ago. It felt more like a week.

"Citizens of Inside, I realize this is unusual," said the LC. Her voice boomed from the speakers. "Our hundredth hour assembly isn't due for another forty hours, but we are missing a citizen."

Murmurs rippled across the scrubs. Everybody reported in at the end of each week. We all had assigned locations so we could hear the news and get updated on the rules and regulations. The Pop Cops called it an end-of-week celebration, but I knew it was just a device to keep track of the scrubs, checking for pregnancies and making sure we behaved.

"All citizens will remain in their secure locations until we find our missing person," the LC continued.

It made sense; their RATSS got confused when so many people milled about.

"We are looking for a man who calls himself the Broken Man. He uses a wheelchair, so we're most concerned he might have been injured. If any citizen has information regarding his current location or information that would lead us to him, you may be promoted to any posting of your choice."

My guts turned to metal. I couldn't move, couldn't breathe, couldn't feel. Lovers would snitch on each other with an offer like that. Cog and I were sunk. I shouldn't have gone for those damn disks. We might as well turn ourselves in. Who knows, maybe they wouldn't recycle us. Yeah, and maybe I'd be invited upstairs and given a family, a room and an interesting job. If I was going to delude myself, might as well dream big.

Oh, well. No sense wasting energy on what I shouldn't have done. I had made my choice. I'd see it through and resign myself to whatever fate had in store for me.

Numbly, I watched as different scrubs pushed their way to talk to the LC. After two hours of waiting and sweating, the air in the room felt like a sauna and smelled like week-old dirty laundry.

The LC listened to the scrubs and inputted notes in her hand-puter until her communicator beeped. She pressed the device to her ear. Little tongues of red streaked up her cheeks as she listened. She gripped the knot of hair behind her head in a tight fist. Gesturing with curt motions, she issued orders to the other Pop Cops. They snapped to attention and marched from the room.

Turning on her microphone, she said, "Citizens, we have yet to locate the Broken Man, but we cannot keep you here any longer. Report back to your work areas or barracks. Anyone else with information is to see me at once."

The Pop Cops opened only one door to let the scrubs out. I sighed. It would be another hour for me to reach fresh air.

When I finally arrived at the door, I was directed to one of the many Pop Cops in the hallway. They registered each of us in their black census recorders that kept track of the population. The LC stood nearby. She seemed tense as she talked rapidly into her communicator.

"Name, barrack and birth week?" the male ensign asked me.

"Trella. One-one-seven. 145,487," I replied automatically. Identification was required every hundred hours. I calculated my exact age. I was 1,514 weeks old or fifteen point one four centiweeks or if I used the old-time measurement, I was seventeen point three years old.

He entered my data and waved me off. I was just about to slip past him when the LC grabbed my arm.

"Trella?"

Darts of fear raced through my shoulder and stabbed my heart. My thoughts scrambled as I stared at her violet eyes and angular features. I used all my energy to nod, keeping my face calm.

"Come with me," she ordered.

She still had a firm grip on my arm; I had no choice but to accompany her along the corridor. Once we were far enough away from the noise of the Pop Cops, she stopped and released me. I glanced around, considering escape. The array of weapons hanging from her belt kept my feet planted.

"My sources tell me you spoke with the Broken Man around hour nineteen this week. Is this correct?" she asked.

Not trusting my voice, I nodded again. Those little laundry weasels. Scrubs complained about the Pop Cops and how they hated them and weren't to be trusted, yet the first chance a scrub had to ingratiate themselves, they jumped. Granted, the offer was stellar, but I knew I'd never squeal on my fellow scrubs.

"Then why didn't you come tell me?" she demanded.

"It didn't seem important."

A condescending smile twisted her lips. "*I'll* decide what's important. Tell me what you and—" she consulted her data screen "—Cogon talked about with Broken Man."

Damn. She knew about Cog. Did they have him? I worried. It was common knowledge Cog had a weakness for the prophet-of-the-week so I went from there. "Cogon wanted me to meet this Broken Man. He said this new prophet had proof Gateway existed."

I shrugged. "Cog's my friend. I met the prophet in the laundry. He started spouting some crazy crap about using meditation to transport yourself through Gateway to Outside. Yet he didn't have a shred of proof."

"Yes. You scrubs seem to have a fascination with Gateway despite the facts." The LC shook her head. "Go on."

"I told Cog to stay away from him, that he could get in trouble. Then I reported to my work shift." I shrugged again, hoping to appear nonchalant.

She studied my face. I feigned innocence.

"Have you talked to Broken Man or seen him since hour nineteen?"

"No."

"If you hear anything or see anything, you're to report it to me immediately. Understand?"

"Yes, Lieutenant Commander…?"

"Karla Trava. Report to your workstation."

"Yes, sir." I walked away. I felt her gaze drilling holes into my back. The desire to run, to jump into one of the ducts and hide pushed at my muscles. Instead, I kept a steady rhythm and only looked back as I turned the corner. Lieutenant Commander Karla met my glance with a thoughtful and lethal squint.

five

Once I was out of Lieutenant Commander Karla's toxic sight, I sighed with relief. It was short-lived. I had gotten off easy. Too easy. I had the feeling I was now in LC Karla's crosshairs. A dangerous position to say the least.

The Pop Cops tended to be cocky in their dealings with the scrubs. Yes, they arrested and recycled without any backlash, but they seldom jumped to conclusions. They watched. They waited. They knew they could find a scrub without much effort, and they enjoyed seeing who else the bad scrub could draw into trouble.

That's why I had always thought the prophets were Pop Cop spies. The prophets preached about Outside and the final reward for enduring the horrible living conditions just to see who believed and who remained a skeptic. The skeptics seem to vanish as if the Pop Cops sanded them out of the masses like rust spots, removing the defective genes from the general population.

I had been wrong about Broken Man being a spy. The Pop

Cops wouldn't be searching so hard for him if he were one of theirs. And now the Pop Cops had learned a person could disappear in the lower levels, which meant their flippant attitudes would change.

Instinctively, I knew LC Karla wouldn't give up her search for Broken Man. So I was screwed and destined to become fertilizer for hydroponics. What could I even hope to gain from this situation? I doubted finding Gateway would make everything rosy.

Longing for Outside to be a real place welled up from the tight corner of my heart where I had squashed it. The type of longing that could overwhelm me and reduce me to a mental case, chanting "a million weeks, a million weeks," as I dashed through the plain hallways of Inside. Hallways so empty of character that if the sector and floor level hadn't been painted on every wall, people would be lost for weeks and no one would miss them. Scrubs as empty of character as the walls. Because we all knew that hope and longing and desire were deadly to our peace of mind.

My involvement with this search for Gateway was to prove it didn't exist. To show my heart it was wrong to long for change, forcing it to accept my life and focus my energies on finding the small joys Inside might have to offer. Joys that Cogon had already found. And yet, he had always been drawn to the prophets, seeking their stories about the rewards given for good deeds.

Unwanted thoughts swirled in my mind. The time spent at the assembly in the dining room followed by the interrogation by LC Karla had run well into my hour sixty to seventy shift. Five hours remained.

Forget it. I looped back to the dining room, hoping Karla and her goons were gone. A few Pop Cops lingered nearby—normal for this area.

As I stood in line for food, I could feel the tension pouring off the other scrubs. Taking a bowl of the leafy green slop, I found an empty chair. The meal failed to improve the mood of the room. When I stood, a scrub pushed me aside and sat in my seat. Typical.

Only the vision of Broken Man starving made me return to the food line. After a half-hour wait, I filled another bowl with the spinach casserole. By the time I reached the tables, most of the scrubs I had sat with were gone. I threaded my way through the dining room, pretending to search for a seat. Once I reached the back, I checked to see if any Pop Cops had noticed me, then slipped out the door. Taking food from the dining room was not uncommon, but since the Pop Cops searched for Broken Man, I knew carrying a bowl of food would draw immediate suspicion.

Sliding into the nearest heating vent, I pushed the casserole ahead of me as I crawled through the duct. The warm air flowing across my skin turned hotter as I drew closer to his room, but I stayed in the vent. The risk of being spotted outside his door was too great.

"Trella! Where the hell have you been?" Broken Man demanded as soon as I poked my head through the heating vent.

I didn't answer him. Dripping with sweat, I rolled from the shaft and onto the ground.

Broken Man lay sprawled on the floor. Black streaks of grit striped his clothes.

"What happened?" I asked.

"You were gone so long, I had to use the bathroom."

A man-sized, clean track on the floor from the chair to the bathroom. His present position made it clear getting into a chair was harder than sliding out.

I stood and helped him back into his seat. My assurance to Cogon that I would take care of Broken Man's needs seemed foolhardy once I fully realized his physical limitations.

I handed him the food. As Broken Man shoveled the casserole, I realized the ear-aching noise of the Power plant was muted. Foam had been sprayed onto the walls, and, when I opened the door, a sheet of metal covered the entrance.

When he finished his meal, I took his bowl. The rank aroma of stale sweat filled my nose, and I coughed to cover my expression. From the way he wrinkled his face, I could tell I didn't smell any better. Funny how people can stand their own stink, but not others. I explained to him what had happened since Cog had been here.

"The Lieutenant Commander was quite upset about your disappearance," I said. "Do you know her?"

"Lieutenant Commander?" Broken Man tapped his spoon against his lower lip. "Which one?"

I blanched for a moment, envisioning an army of LCs patrolling the lower levels like clones. "Said her name was Trava."

He huffed. "Trava is a family name. Almost all the Pop Cops are Travas."

"Oh. Karla Trava. Why doesn't she have another family name?"

"Travas don't take on any other names. Not even the children who are born to a Trava and another family member. In fact, if you mate with a Trava you are then registered as a Trava." He considered. "Unfortunately, I know Karla. You never did ask for more information about your biological parents."

"I've been a little busy," I said, my words laced with sarcasm. "Besides, you fed me a line of bull just to get me to help you."

"Believe what you will, but watch out for this LC. She's intelligent, cunning and intuitive. Her family is not only in charge of the Pop Cops, but work closely with the Controllers, as well. She's well connected to all the powerful people."

"Why worry about the Controllers? Aren't they just in charge of the uppers?"

"They tell the Travas what to do. And the Travas make all

the decisions for Inside. Every admiral is a Trava, and every time an upper links with the computer, a Trava knows. Every mechanical system running Inside has a Trava at the switch."

"That's the way it's always been. Why do you make it sound as if it's wrong?"

"It hasn't always been this way. You scrubs know nothing of what goes on in the upper levels. Exactly what the Trava family wants."

I really didn't care what the uppers did or didn't do. My throat burned from the heat and dust, and my short nap hadn't been enough to fully revive me. "I need more sleep before my next shift."

"I need more food," Broken Man said. "I did some exploring. There's a kitchen here, but no electricity."

"I'll turn on the juice, but it may take me a while to get you other supplies. I'll see what I can do."

Broken Man nodded even as he frowned at me. "I should get a few hours of sleep, too."

I helped him into bed and felt a twinge of guilt as the black dust puffed from the mattress, causing him to choke. It would probably be another twenty hours before I could bring him food and help him shower.

The bedroom and bathroom were two small squares adjacent to each other. Both led out to the living area, another square which bordered the equally tiny kitchen. Inside was divided into rectangles and squares. The designers had to have been obsessive-compulsives, and I cursed them for their lack of imagination. Again.

Grabbing a couple of drinking glasses from the kitchen, I filled one with water. I set the glasses on the night table beside the bed. When Broken Man peered in confusion at the empty glass, I told him it was for urinating into so he wouldn't have to drag himself to the bathroom. His face muscles drooped in sad understanding as I waved goodbye.

Reconnecting the electricity to the small apartment proved arduous. If I hadn't been tired, it would have taken me half the time to find the connectors.

Finally, I found a quiet place to sleep in one of the heating shafts. As I drifted off, an odd thought touched my mind. Why was Inside always heated?

I awoke at hour seventy-nine. Clocks had been installed in every room and corridor of Inside so scrubs couldn't use the excuse of not knowing the time. I had an hour until my next shift so I headed toward one of Sector F1's washrooms. Peeling off my sweat-stiffened uniform, I stood under the shower's warm water. Once I dried off and put on a clean uniform, I checked my tool belt, making sure all my tools were in the right spots and that my flashlight still worked. I never felt properly dressed until the familiar weight of my belt settled on my hips.

I fought my way through the corridors to my scheduled air shaft. On the way, I encountered Cog. He scraped paint chips from one of the corridor walls. Patches of rust sprinkled the metal. Another of Inside's evils, rust was not tolerated and repainting remained a constant chore.

Glad to see him, I touched his arm. His honey-brown eyes slid in my direction. Tight lines of worry streaked across his sweaty face. Cog pulled the scraper from the wall.

"What's going on?" he whispered. "Is everything okay with—you know?"

I nodded. "He's fine."

Cog pointed with his nose toward the two Pop Cops who hovered at the end of the hall. "They're watching me."

"What happened?" I asked.

Cogon winced. "The Pop Cops escorted me to their office for questioning about my little skirmish before they arrested Broken Man."

I studied his face in concern but didn't see any bruises. Understanding my look, Cog touched his ribs and winced again. This time in pain.

"They said I was their best suspect. They threatened to recycle me just for defending my prophet. Told me I might as well confess to killing their colleague, and tell them where Broken Man was hiding." Cog clamped his teeth together as defiance flashed in his eyes. "I'd confess to murder, but I won't give him up."

"Why? You could negotiate and tell them where he is in exchange for not being fed to Chomper."

He stared at me as if I had spoken gibberish. "He's important, Trell. He can find Gateway."

"He *might* have a location. Big difference, and one not worth being recycled for."

"He knows. I can feel it."

I huffed in annoyance. "Come on, Cog. You're an intelligent man. How can you believe in Gateway without proof?"

"The disks—"

"Could be part of the ruse."

He smiled. "Then why did you risk punishment to get them?"

"To prove Broken Man wrong."

"Then go ahead, prove us wrong." His confidence turned smug and he watched my expression with a knowing grin. "You can't resist a challenge. It got you into all kinds of trouble in the care facility."

"We're not in the care facility anymore." I tapped his bruised ribs, emphasizing my point. "The stakes are higher."

"So is the reward."

I shook my head. We had lapsed into the same old argument with no ending and we had talked too long. The Pop Cops headed our way. Their continued interest in Cogon meant he remained their primary suspect.

"Why did they let you go?" I asked.

"Two scrubs came forward while I was being questioned and claimed they saw Broken Man wrestle the Pop Cop for his weapon before the elevator doors closed."

My breath locked in surprise. After a moment I asked, "Did you get their names?"

"Not yet. But I will."

"Keep playing innocent," I whispered to him as the Pop Cops came within earshot. Then in a louder voice I said, "And my cleaning device has been making weird noises."

"I'll let maintenance know," Cog replied.

"Thanks." I walked away.

Another twist. I sighed. Why would two people lie? Especially when the right information could make their lives a lot easier.

The questions would have to wait while I dealt with my supervisor. She paced the hallway in front of my cleaning troll's storage area. A red cuff clenched in her long-fingered hands. She frowned at it.

"Trella," she said with a snarl. "Going to show up for work this shift?"

I braced myself. What rotten luck. The supervisors checked to make sure each scrub assigned to them was at the proper work location about once a week. My bad luck to have her looking for me during my last shift. At least I hoped it was bad luck and not the directive of a certain lieutenant commander.

"Where were you?" she asked.

"Special assembly." I glanced at the cuff. If she snapped it around my wrist, I would have to report to the Pop Cops for discipline. They would probably assign me to work in waste handling during my off hours. When I completed the punishment, the cuff would be removed. Until then, everyone would know I was in trouble.

She hissed in exasperation. "The assembly lasted two hours. You were missing for eight." She pulled the cuff open.

"It took me almost two hours to get out of the dining room, and then I had to wait to speak with Lieutenant Commander Karla."

The LC's name elicited the desired effect. Her hand paused in midair and she shot me a white-faced look. Usually only ensigns and lieutenants policed the lower levels. LCs were as rare as a change in routine, and all the scrubs knew to keep their distance.

"Oh, well, in that case." She lowered her arm, probably assuming time spent with a Pop Cop lieutenant commander was worse than working in waste handling.

I never thought I would use fear of the Pop Cops to my advantage, but I knew my supervisor wouldn't check my story with the LC. Watching me pull out my cleaning troll and heft it into the air shaft, she stayed until I had climbed into the shaft to begin my shift.

While I followed my troll through the air ducts for the next ten hours, I planned the best way to gather supplies for Broken Man. My choices were limited. The only time I could take enough food from the kitchen to stock Broken Man's refrigerator was when everyone was at the hundred-hour assembly. Problem was, my presence was required, too.

When the buzzer sounded for the assembly, I dutifully reported to the dining room and stood in line.

"Name, barrack and birth week?" the Pop Cop asked without even looking up.

I repeated my stats.

"Health changes?"

"No."

"Blood test." He pointed toward another Pop Cop.

Waiting in this line, I held my arms close to my stomach

as a Pop Cop drew blood from a scrub's wrist using a device we had nicknamed the vampire box after reading one of those mythical stories in the computer. The stories we had been allowed to access chronicled myths and legends of strange creatures like vampires and ghosts. They also mentioned things and animals we have never seen. When questioned, my Care Mother explained those items were no longer available.

I shuffled forward in line, dreading my turn. After you insert your arm in the vamp box, two prongs jabbed into the skin and sucked a couple drops of blood out through a tube and into a chamber where it was analyzed in an instant.

The Pop Cops checked for illegal substances, pregnancy and other health markers the scrubs didn't really care about. Blood tests were done at random hundred-hour assemblies, but they were never more than six weeks apart. The Pop Cops had them scheduled in advance and, for a price, you could find out when the next test would be. A scrub named Jacy had a whole network of informers, and he always knew when the Pop Cops planned tests and inspections.

The next scrub to be checked was a woman. The ensign running the analyzer grabbed her arm. Before the woman could react, he clamped a bright yellow bracelet on her wrist. She was pregnant. Shock, fear and surprise warred on her face as she tried to cope with this new information.

"Eight week checkups required," the ensign droned. "Schedule with the infirmary."

The woman was waved on. She staggered toward the dining room with her other hand gripping the irremovable bracelet. Now the entire population of scrubs would know she was with child. She'd work her shifts until she gave birth, spend a week in the infirmary, hand her baby over to the care facility and then return to work. It felt more like a breeding program than a miracle of life. One of the many reasons I would never have a child.

I took my turn with the vamp box and wove my way through the dining room toward the kitchen, finding a seat as close to the kitchen doors as possible. LC Karla stood on one of the tables. A fire burned in her eyes as she barked orders to the Pop Cops around her. I wondered why she chose this location instead of the other two meeting areas. Perhaps she enjoyed standing on the table. Yeah, right, just like I enjoyed these assemblies.

Another buzz sounded, signaling all scrubs were in their designated locations.

Karla addressed the crowd. "Citizens, welcome to the end of the week celebration. Now begins week number 147,002."

An old scrub sitting next to me chanted. "A million weeks! A million weeks! A million weeks!"

Another scrub leaned over to him and said, "Hush, old man, you'll be lucky to see another two weeks. No one cares about the millionth week. We won't be here."

His companion laughed. "Just think," said the second man, "in another seven thousand weeks or so, everyone in this room will be gone and there will be a whole new generation forced to listen to the same crap."

They chuckled together as the old scrub squinted at them. In the minds of the scrubs, the millionth week had been blown to mythical proportions. Some prophesied that on week one million, our fuel and air would run out, ending all our lives. Others claimed we all go Outside. But when you considered the average life span of a citizen was sixty to seventy centi-weeks, and there would be roughly a hundred and twenty-two generations of scrubs before the millionth week, it was hard to get too concerned.

With a gnarled finger, the old scrub tapped the man who had hushed him. "Laugh all you want, but the millionth week isn't the end. It's the beginning."

"...Broken Man." Karla Trava's voice cut through the buzz of voices around me. My attention snapped back to her.

"Information is still needed. You will be rewarded for any tips that lead us to him." She stopped for a heartbeat. "But don't lie to me." Her tone turned deadly. She gestured. Two Pop Cops pulled a scrub forward. Karla yanked the poor guy up to the tabletop by his collar. He swayed on weak legs and his face was a mask of fear. His hands trembled. Silence blanketed the dining room.

Karla patted her weapon belt, looking as if she debated. With a blur of motion, her kill-zapper jumped into her hand. She pressed the nozzle to the scrub's chest.

"This," she said, "is what I do to liars." A crackle built to a crescendo as the man jerked and twitched.

When the lieutenant commander pulled the weapon away, the man dropped to the floor with an echoing thud.

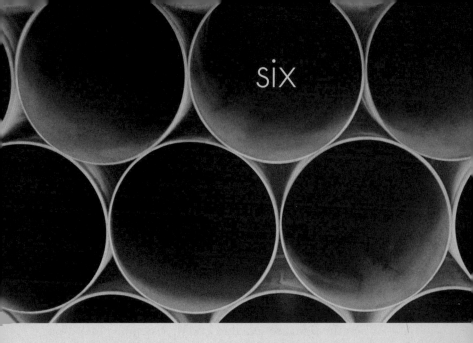

six

The sound of the scrub hitting the floor burned into my mind like the kill-zapper had burned into the man's chest. I shook in my chair, feeling hot and short of breath. It didn't take much imagination to envision myself an arm's length away from LC Karla with a kill-zapper at my breast.

She stepped off the table and let the usual ensign read the weekly announcements. The ensign stumbled over his words, probably thrown by the unnatural silence in the room.

Little by little, whispered conversation spread, and the ensign's voice evened out. My plans to collect food during the assembly took on a higher level of danger. Karla Trava had raised the stakes.

Even so, I couldn't let Broken Man starve. Time was running out. I faked a coughing fit. My seatmates glanced at me in annoyance. I sputtered and choked for a while then stood and headed for the kitchen doors, hoping anyone who was interested would assume I sought a drink.

As soon as the doors closed, I bolted to the refrigerators.

Grabbing cheese, sheep's milk and containers of vegetable casseroles, I piled them on one of the stainless-steel counters. I shut the refrigerator and sprinted to the freezer, tossing a few hunks of frozen mutton onto my pile. With panic fueling my actions, I leapt up on the counter next to the food. Right above my head was a vent to an air duct. I opened it and loaded the shaft with the provisions. Careful not to block the airflow, I shoved and stuffed until my breath came in puffs.

When finished, I replaced the vent cover, hopped down and filled a glass with water. I slipped back into the dining room, covering my gasps for air with the drink as I reclaimed my seat. None of the scrubs gave me a glance, and I hoped no one suspected.

When the signal sounded to end the assembly, I filed out with the rest of the scrubs. The line of people bulged sideways. Even though the scrub's body had been removed, everyone avoided the spot where he had fallen.

As I passed Karla, she pressed her lips together and cocked her head to one side. I dropped my gaze and tried to look as inconspicuous as possible, which only resulted in her calling out to me.

"Trella, come here," she ordered.

I stepped out of line. My heart jumped in my chest. "Yes, Lieutenant Commander?"

"Feeling better?"

"Excuse me?"

"Your cough. I hope you're not getting a virus."

Her concern was frightening. "No, sir," I said, my mind roiling. "I just must have swallowed something wrong."

"Oh, yes, I understand," she said with an even flat tone. "I find myself having to swallow wrong things all the time. They leave a bitter taste. Makes me choke. Churns my stomach."

I had no answer. My mind buzzed with warning signals.

She studied me for an eternal minute, then said, "Hour zero.

Time to report to your station for your next shift. Air duct twenty-two, I believe."

"Yes, sir," I managed to squeak out. I joined the flow of scrubs to the hallway, not daring to look back at the LC. She had been reading my file. She knew all about me, and she wanted me to know. Damn.

An interesting fact about air duct number twenty-two was it crossed right above the kitchen, and eventually, if you followed it far enough, it passed right on top of Broken Man's hideout.

Once I reached my cleaning station, I hefted the troll into the air shaft. Then I raided a maintenance closet for extra supplies. Crawling behind the troll, I built a crude skid. I kept glancing behind me, checking to see if LC Karla had sent a couple of RATSS to spy on me.

When the troll reached my stash of food, I shut it down while I rigged the skid up to it. I peered through the vent. The kitchen bustled with activity. Scrubs filled containers and chopped vegetables. Two ensigns strolled through the chaos. They were probably keeping track of the knives, counting in their heads to make sure a scrub didn't steal one and attack the Pop Cops.

No sign of Karla. My relief surprised me. Subconsciously I must have been expecting her to ambush me; to reach through the vent and cry "Gotcha!" before she kill-zapped me.

With that awful image in mind, I loaded the food onto the pallet as fast as I could, then restarted the cleaning troll. The troll's engine strained with the extra weight. I had to smile when I flipped open one of the control panels on the side of the troll and turned a tiny thumbscrew. Cogon had shown me how to increase the machine's throttle, so it could move faster. An increase of speed meant I would finish my work sooner, and would have more time off—provided no one caught me.

The troll lurched forward as the engine roared. Its speed stayed the same, but it had no trouble pulling the skid.

Paranoia made me keep checking for RATSS, but the troll and I reached Broken Man's rooms without incident. I popped the vent off and swung down, dropping to the floor.

"Hello, Trella," he said.

I spun. He sat in a corner of the living room. I smelled him from here. He was ripe.

"I don't have a lot of time," I said. Pulling a chair under the open vent, I used it to reach the food.

"Here, let me help." Broken Man sprawled on the floor and used his arms to drag himself across the room. He wriggled into a sitting position and held his hand to me.

I handed the supplies to him, and he made a pile next to his legs. When the skid was empty, I hopped off the chair and carted the food into the kitchen.

"Hungry?" I asked from the kitchen.

"Very."

I brought him a spoon, and he dug into one of the yellow vegetable casseroles. When everything was put away, I stepped onto the chair again.

"I'll be back after my shift with fresh clothes," I called. He waved his spoon in goodbye. I climbed into the duct, turned the troll on and completed the air shaft.

When I finished my assigned ducts, I headed to the washroom. Fresh laundered uniforms and clothes were always stacked in large canvas bins on wheels. Empty bins were then used for dirty garments.

I collected a bunch of clothes, linens and soap and bundled everything together with a towel. At my next stop I added some cleaning supplies, hoping to reduce the black dust coating every surface of Broken Man's rooms.

He had returned to the corner when I plopped down with my bundle. I showed him what I had brought. He smiled in relief, but I cringed over the black grit between his teeth.

"Shower?" I asked.

"Please."

I hesitated for an awkward moment. How to go about this? Fortunately, he had thought ahead. Poor man, he had hours alone with nothing to do, and I didn't think to bring him anything to occupy him.

"Get a chair from the kitchen and put it in the shower," he said. He set a businesslike tone as he gave me instructions.

As I placed the seat under the nozzle, he pulled himself into the bathroom and began to undress. His short commands only faltered when I tugged off his pants and underwear and hoisted him into the chair. I turned on the water and gave him the soap and the washcloth, leaving him to wash himself in private.

As I cleaned the dust, I wondered how he had gotten the long jagged scar stretched across his lower back. Shorter scars marked his arms and torso. His withered legs had flopped when I had moved him. I stopped wiping for a second to try to envision his life before the accident. One insight I did have while helping him into the shower. He was a natural blond, and I should probably apologize for the harsh comment I had made when I first met him about going back to the upper levels to have his hair dyed.

When I checked on Broken Man, he had turned the water off and sat dripping. I handed him a towel and assisted in drying and dressing. I debated how to move him. Despite my smaller size, all the time I'd spent climbing through the ducts and pipes had strengthened my muscles. Not wanting him to drag his clean clothes over the floor, I wrapped his arms around my neck, pulled his weight onto my back and in a hunched-over shuffle managed to get him into the chair in the living room.

"Thanks," he said as he combed his fingers through wet hair.

"Food?" I asked.

He nodded. I brought him a bowl.

As he ate, he pointed to one of the walls where a rippled pattern was the only notable feature.

"See that? I bet it's a computer terminal. I couldn't reach it from the floor. Can you lift it?"

I studied the pattern. It consisted of horizontal sheets of metal about two-centimeters wide connected like a curtain. A dent at the bottom allowed my fingers to slide under.

"That's it," he said.

I pulled it up, then stepped back in alarm as the metal curtain disappeared under the wall with a rolling sound. Behind the sheet were a flat computer screen and a console of buttons and plugs.

"Yes!" Broken Man said. For the first time since we had rescued him, his face glowed with excitement. "Help me get closer."

I pushed his chair next to the wall. He reached out to touch a button.

"Wait," I said in alarm. "If you turn it on won't the Controllers know about it?"

"No. It's only when you hook up to the internal system. The basic public system for the scrubs doesn't require a port. Besides, I just want to see if it works."

He pressed a series of switches. His hands moved with a practiced grace. The computer screen brightened, and the symbol for Inside appeared. Typically unimaginative, the symbol looked like a cube with a capital *I* on the front panel. As the children in the care facility would say, "Boring." Little did they know the activities and schooling in the CF would be the most interesting part of their lives. I shook my head of the gloomy thoughts as Broken Man changed the image on the screen.

After a while he said, "It's still connected to the main system. We could access my disks from here."

"Which would lead the Controllers right to us?" I asked,

again afraid this seemed too easy. Too convenient. It made sense the upper worker who used to live here had a computer hookup, but that it still worked was suspect.

"Yes, it would. Except I have a program to reroute the tracking software, so the Controllers would be led to another computer station on level four."

"You know it works?"

"Well…" Broken Man rubbed his back, considering. "Obviously my original program had a few flaws, but I had found another more effective program hidden in the system. I copied it onto my disks. Unfortunately I was caught before I could use it." The memory of pain spread across his face. His gray eyes squinted into the past.

"Who created the other program?" I asked.

"The security on it was too good to crack. But I believe it was probably a member of the Garrard family."

"Garrard?"

"They are unhappy with the status quo. All the major families were upset with the Trava takeover, but in time they grew complacent and believed there was nothing they could do to restore the original balance of power."

"Hold on. The Trava takeover?" I asked. "The Travas have always been in charge."

"No, they haven't. The Travas want the scrubs to believe that, and they're hoping eventually, with enough generations born, the uppers will forget they ever had a say in the running of Inside. But I've uncovered the truth. All nine families at one point had an equal vote. Each family elected one of their members to be a part of Committee. This Committee made decisions and supervised the various mechanical systems of Inside." Broken Man frowned. "Each family had a specialty—air systems, waste water, electrical—which turned into a major disadvantage."

"Why?"

"The Travas' specialty was security and only they had access to the stunners and kill-zappers."

"Oh."

Broken Man met my gaze. The wrinkles on his face deepened as if he alone shouldered all the responsibly in letting the Travas dominate. I guessed he was around forty-five centi-weeks old.

"There was a group of uppers who tried to regain control of a few systems, but they failed," he said.

"Would the group be willing to help us if you actually find Gateway?" I asked.

"No." Broken Man fiddled with the computer. "The consequences of getting caught are too great for the uppers."

It had been a hypothetical question. I planned to prove there was no Gateway. Prove to Cog that the people of Inside had been sealed off from Outside.

Besides the Pop Cops' insistence of a purely spiritual final resting place for the good people, the rumors surrounding Outside ranged from wild guesses to tales of horror. I knew *something* had to be beyond our walls. And whether this place was Outside or something else, speculation ran rampant.

A few scrubs claimed it was a vast wasteland, others a magical kingdom where fairies flew through the air, a number declared water surrounded us and a couple maintenance scrubs thought our own garbage was piled around us. We reused and recycled everything, but a small portion of pure waste disappeared through a flushing system the Controllers maintained. Cog had tried to use that fact in his argument about Gateway.

All the rumors didn't sway me. I didn't care. Why worry or speculate about an inaccessible place? We were trapped in Inside until we ceased to exist and Chomper turned our bodies into fertilizer. End of story.

I concentrated on Broken Man's statement about getting no help from the upper families. It fit—uppers wouldn't risk themselves and their cushy life for a bunch of scrubs. Although, I couldn't help thinking about Riley in his hideout on level four.

His family names seemed important to him—a source of pride. How did he feel about the Travas controlling our world? Maybe Riley and a few uppers would like to see life altered? I grimaced. Sappy bull. I was getting soft, letting hope grow a centimeter. Snip. Snip. I mentally cut it back.

"If the computer works, all I need to do is retrieve your disks and you can access them? Right?" I asked.

Broken Man bit his lip and said nothing.

"What's wrong? I thought you have a gap in your mouth for the port."

"I have the gap." He paused. "Problem is…I don't have my teeth."

"What?"

"They're not real teeth. We just call them that. They're needed to access the internal computer network. They're designed so the Pop Cops can keep track of who is in the network and restrict access to the computer system by pulling an upper's port."

I sank to the floor. Rubbing my face in my hands, I said, "Now you tell me."

seven

Nothing more I could do. The end. The Pop Cops had Broken Man's port. Without his port, he couldn't access his disks and the information. No information meant no proof or disproof of Gateway's existence.

"Lieutenant Commander Karla has my port," Broken Man said.

I stared at him. Was he serious? "You want me to ask her for it back?"

"Think, Trella. She doesn't know about the disks. Pulling my teeth is standard procedure. She would have sent it to computer ops to check what I've been accessing in the system, and they would have returned it with their report." Sudden understanding lit his gray eyes. "The report! I should have known. A few of the files I'd viewed probably made Karla suspicious and she set a trap in my room. If only I heard about you before she rigged my quarters."

His comment reminded me of how I had gotten involved.

Cog knew I couldn't resist a challenge. "If Cog hadn't told you about me, we wouldn't be here now."

He shook his head. "Your reputation as Queen of the Pipes intrigued me first."

"Yeah, but Cog was the only person who knows what I'm really capable of. And he's too quick to trust, he falls for any line and is too eager to get involved."

"The opposite of you?"

"Of course. I'm not the one getting my hopes dashed every time a new prophet arrives."

"Yet here you are."

In trouble with no solution in sight. "A moment of weakness and an excellent lesson on what *not* to do in the future. Provided I even *have* a future."

"From what I've seen in the lower levels, do you really want to live the rest of your life in these conditions?" he asked.

The standard scrub reply was to shrug and say there was nothing I could do about it or to regurgitate the Pop Cop line about a better afterlife. But I had the opportunity to actually prove or disprove the theory about Gateway and Outside. If I wanted to risk my life. Was being alive enough for me? Could I really walk away without trying?

Broken Man could see the answer in my eyes. "Karla's office is on level four, Sector—"

"A. I know. It's the only area I avoid." Last thing I needed was for the Pop Cops to catch me in an air duct above their offices and holding cells. I enjoyed a challenge, but I wasn't crazy. And I limited my time spent in the Gap above four to trips to my box.

Contemplating the theft of his port from the lieutenant commander, I crossed over from rational to insane. "Do you know what type of security measures are installed in her office?"

"The door's always locked, but I'm guessing you're not going to use it." He smiled. "Probably the usual motion sensors."

LC Karla knew someone had used the pipes to get the disks. Would she rig the air ducts above her office with sensors? Broken Man had said she was smart, so I assumed she had. But did she know about the Gap above the ductwork? I needed to do a reconnaissance mission to her office. It would require a great deal of planning.

"How do I know which port is yours?" I asked.

"There's an identification number etched into the bottom." Broken Man recited his number and I committed it to memory.

"I need to eat before my next shift. Hopefully I'll think of a way to bypass the LC's security measures."

Various scenarios ran through my mind as I returned to the main corridor of level two. No brilliant ideas had formed by the time I shuffled through the cafeteria line and sought a free seat. And consuming the casserole of the day failed to ignite any exceptional plans.

The only way I could enter Karla's office would be to find the wires for the motion detectors and disable them without setting them off. It would be time-consuming and dangerous. The probability of missing a sensor would be high.

The noise in the room rose to an uncomfortable level. I grabbed my tray, intent on leaving, but two scrubs stood right behind me. A young man and woman. They both had the same nose—a distinctly petite feature with a perfect shape. Combined with their matching oval faces and light greenish-brown eyes, I knew they were related. They wore the drab-gray and shapeless overalls of the recycling-plant workers.

Pitching his voice so the sound cut through the din, the man said, "We want in."

I stepped aside so he could claim my seat.

He shook his head. "We want to help you."

"With what?" Confused, I glanced at each one.

She gestured to the table. Two more seats were empty. The scrubs sat and she pulled me back down.

I yanked my arm away. "Who do you—"

"I'm Anne-Jade and he's my brother, Logan. We want to help you find Gateway."

Stunned, I gaped at them a moment. "But, I'm not—"

"Save it for the Pop Cops," Logan said. "We know what you've been up to. We saw you with Cogon before he entered the lift. Saw the lift stop and Cogon leave the elevator's maintenance room with the laundry bin. It wasn't hard to figure out."

They hadn't told Karla, which meant a bribe. "What do you really want?"

"To help," Anne-Jade said. Her lips pressed into a thin line, drawing her oval face into a serious expression.

"Why? You could get recycled."

She swept her hand out, indicating the mass of people. "This is intolerable. I'd rather be recycled than to continue to live as livestock."

Instinct kicked in. Too many people increased the chances of getting caught. Besides, I couldn't trust them and I preferred to work alone. "Sorry, no. I can't get anyone else involved."

"We're already involved," Logan said. "Who do you think covered for Cogon?"

I scrambled for a reply. "Look, I'm thankful you saved Cog, but I really don't know how you can help right now, and—"

"Listen." Logan held up a metal wind-up toy near his ear then handed it to me.

"What—"

Logan gestured for me to listen to the toy. Not happy, I brought it close and almost dropped it when Broken Man's voice whispered in my ear. He talked about Gateway and the disks, and I heard my own harsh reply. I stared at the little mouse murmuring in my hand. Its metal key turning. "How?"

Logan grinned. "Voice transmitting device sewn onto Broken Man's shirt. This—" he picked up the mouse "—records and replays the conversation." He held the device in the palm of his right hand, acting indifferent to the incredible danger he had placed us all in.

Realization finally clicked, and my bad situation turned downright rotten. I groaned. "You're Tech Nos."

Working in the recycling quadrant, Tech Nos "rescued" certain discarded items from the upper levels. They played around with the illegal technology—illegal for scrubs to have—and made it better. The Pop Cops hunted and killed these Tech Nos as fast as they would disease-carrying vermin. It was amazing Logan and Anne-Jade were still alive.

"How do you… Where do you…" I couldn't finish. The recycling-plant workers were monitored, their bunks searched on a regular basis.

"We're allowed to make toys and different supplies from the metal waste." Logan twisted the key. "Most of our toys are delivered to the uppers for their children, but we keep a few *special* ones."

With space at a premium, scrubs owned few possessions. "Where?"

"Here and there. A few stay with us. This little guy is my favorite right now, and if a Pop Cop asks about it, I just say I'm doing safety testing on it before sending it to the uppers."

Impressive and scary. "How much did you hear?"

"The conversation you had with Broken Man and Cog," Anne-Jade said, "and the rescue. But wherever you have hidden him, we can't get a signal."

At least they didn't know about the port. "I still don't think you can help me."

"We're assuming you're going to need to enter a few secure

locations in search of Gateway. We have *other* gadgets," Anne-Jade said.

When I didn't respond, she huffed in frustration. "How did you plan to get past the motion detectors?"

"With creative wiring."

"No need. We've built an invisibility device," Logan said with pride.

I couldn't mask my disbelief. "You can make me invisible?"

"To the sensors. When you turn on our Not-There Machine, the sensors won't detect your presence."

Passion shone from Logan's eyes, but I wasn't a sucker. "You two are either working for the Pop Cops or delusional." I stood to go.

"This isn't proof enough?" Logan held the toy mouse up.

"Yes. Proof you're working with the Pop Cops."

Logan opened his mouth to speak, but Anne-Jade shot him a look. "Fine," she said. "Think what you want, but you owe us one for covering for Cog."

"I don't—"

She ignored me. "In the supply closet in Sector H1 is a small cleaning device."

"Anne-Jade, if she doesn't trust us, we shouldn't trust her," Logan said.

She frowned at him. "Someone has to take the first step." Returning her attention to me, she said, "Do you know the one?"

"Zippy?" He was a quarter of the size of the regular trolls, and made to fit into tight pipes.

"*You* have names for the cleaning devices, and you call *us* delusional?" She tapped her chest to emphasize her point. "If you hold down its…Zippy's on button for ten seconds, it not only cleans dirt, but will suck up all evidence of your presence in a place where you shouldn't be."

I'd heard more believable fairy tales. "How can Zippy suck up the evidence?"

Logan perked up. "Motion detectors emit pulses—"

"She doesn't need to hear a bunch of technical mumbo jumbo," Anne-Jade snapped at him. "It comes down to trust, Trella. You take Zippy out for a spin, and then let us know what else we can do to help you."

They wove through the crowded cafeteria, taking their "toy" with them. The harsh clamor of multiple voices seemed louder than before. I suffered the noise as long as I could before leaving the room and reporting for my next work shift.

My thoughts replayed the encounter with the Tech Nos. If I was found associating with them or using illegal technology, I would be kill-zapped in an instant. I didn't doubt I would be caught. I just wanted to… What? Find Gateway first?

I chided myself for such mushy thoughts. The end result would probably be exposing the whole endeavor as a hoax. Instead of wasting time, I concentrated on the next task, letting no emotions cloud my judgment. If Zippy worked, then it would make retrieving Broken Man's port a whole lot easier. And if it didn't? Then I hoped I could outrun the Pop Cops again.

During my shift, I planned how best to approach LC Karla's office. I overrode the speed control on the cleaning troll and increased the pace. If I finished all my scheduled ducts early, I could sleep for a few hours before sneaking to level four.

"What do you want to know?" Jacy asked in a low voice. The scrub leaned against a column of bunks, appearing relaxed, but tension rolled off him. Two of his buddies hovered nearby. They kept watch, ensuring our conversation wouldn't be overheard by the Pop Cops. Bluelight lit the scrubs' barrack in Sector D1, and the snores and heavy breathing of sleeping scrubs filled the room. The musty smell of dirty socks mixed with sleep-breath, creating a rank odor. No wonder I slept in the pipes.

"I need to know Lieutenant Commander Karla's schedule," I said.

We were in a poorly lit corner. Rows and rows of bunks, reaching from top to bottom filled the room. Three beds per column. One meter of headroom per bed. The wooden dividers between them contained two drawers. One for the possessions of the first shift scrub who slept there and the other for the second's.

Right now the row we occupied was half-empty. Most scrubs had finished their shift at hour thirty and were in the cafeteria.

"Why do you need her schedule?" Jacy's dark brown bangs hung over his eyes. He studied me through the gaps.

"Doesn't matter."

"Yes, it does." He straightened.

He had grown since our time together in the care facility. I tilted my head to meet his gaze. If he tried one of his old tricks, I already knew the location of the closest ceiling vent. The design of the bunks made it easy for me to scale them if I needed to escape.

"Lieutenant Commander Karla's been causing a lot of trouble for us. I don't want to upset her any further. In fact, she asked me about you."

A stream of cold fear shot down my back. Jacy dealt with information. His group of five always knew where the Pop Cops were. They warned their clients of surprise inspections and raids. Even though the scrubs worked hard, they found time to engage in a number of illegal activities.

"What did you tell her?"

"I had a kill-zapper at my chest so my memories are a little fuzzy. Perhaps if you tell me why the LC's interested in you, it'll help me remember."

His expression remained guarded and I guessed the bastard already knew but wanted to confirm his suspicions.

"You'll live longer if you don't know." Ha. I managed to surprise him. "Are you going to tell me Karla's schedule or not?"

"And what do I receive in exchange?"

Typical scrub. Nothing without a price. "I'll act as a lookout for you. One time only."

He laughed. "I have a ton of people willing to watch for us."

"From air duct seventy-two?"

His smirk died. "You can get in there without an upper's help?"

I nodded. Number seventy-two crossed over a few highly sensitive areas, including the Control Room and Pop Cop headquarters. The uppers didn't want a disgruntled scrub near them. The two scrubs allowed in the shaft always had a Pop Cop escort.

Energized, he paced. "Can you install a microphone in seventy-two for me instead?"

"A mic is illegal. How did you—?" Tech Nos. I didn't need to know more. "You want me to put it where the cleaning trolls won't suck it up?"

"Yes!"

I considered. "It's more dangerous than acting as lookout. It's worth two requests—Karla's schedule and what you told her about me."

"Deal."

His response was too quick. I should have negotiated for more.

"I'll have her agenda in an hour." His posture relaxed, but concern lingered in his eyes. "I told the LC the truth."

My stomach felt as if I had fallen off a pipe. "And?"

He huffed. "Same old Trella, giving nothing away. Not even for your fellow care mate."

"The mate who bullied and tormented me? I guess you would find it odd I don't hold any fond feelings from our time together."

He waved my comment away. "You were cold from the start. We had to bully and torment you just to get a reaction from you." Jacy bent close and lowered his voice. "I told her all about it. How you escape into the ducts to be alone. No friends. No interest in associating with your fellow scrubs. But I neglected to inform her about your Queen of the Pipes title."

"Why? It's just a taunt." Even Broken Man had heard about it.

"Really? You spend hours in the pipes. You must know every nook and cranny of Inside. If I searched for a missing prophet and had exhausted every known area, I would turn to the Queen of the Pipes for guidance." He paused, giving me time to understand. "She already suspects you're involved, telling her about your title would give her a reason to arrest you."

"But you could have earned a better post."

He shrugged. "I did it for old time's sake. Besides, if you're hiding Broken Man, that means you actually *care* for another person and there's hope for you yet. Meet me here in one hour." He strode away with his friends at his heels.

I spent the time sifting through all Jacy's comments. He had been wrong about me. I'd had friends in the care facility after Cog left. Before I was picked on and teased—the victim of multiple pranks and nasty rumors. At least one or two girls. I just couldn't remember their names.

When I matched LC Karla's work schedule to mine, I found I would have a single two-hour window between hours thirty-eight and forty to search her office.

The heating ducts would be my best bet to enter Karla's office. Low to the ground, the vents opened into every room in Inside. Although they were small, Zippy and I just fit. They also snaked between the rooms. One of the drawbacks to using the heating system was that there were no connections between levels. Since the Power plant spanned all four levels, each level had its very own network of ducts. The other limitation was the heating system couldn't be accessed from the Gap.

I needed to ascend to the fourth level, then enter the heating system. Aiming for the abandoned storeroom, I hoped Riley wouldn't be there. As I moved through the air shafts with Zippy tied to my tool belt, my thoughts turned to the young upper I had surprised.

Riley's comments replayed in my mind. He used the store-room to escape assignments and avoid having to pledge loyalty to the Travas. Perhaps his life wasn't as easy as I had thought.

I slowed when I reached my destination. Peering through the air vent, I scanned the room below with care. The furniture had been rearranged again, but no one was there. The green-and-brown couch was now located right below the hole, and a metal stepladder leaned against the side wall. Riley must have moved it for me. I smiled, but then dismissed the notion. An upper caring about a scrub? No way. And I wouldn't let myself believe it. Stick with the plan, I chanted under my breath.

Hanging from the air duct, I dropped onto the couch. I waited a moment. When no one rushed into the room, I slipped into the tight heating vent. Pressing Zippy's on button, I counted to ten. He hummed and chugged along the duct as I pulled myself by my elbows and pushed with my feet.

I hoped any noise I made would be dismissed as the regular cleaning. Even if he didn't work, having Zippy along would help my cover if I was caught.

By the time we drew near LC Karla's office, sweat soaked

my uniform and my arms ached. Switching Zippy to Neutral, I examined the room through the vent's cover.

From my limited vantage point, a large desk dominated the space. I counted three computer monitors. On the wall opposite the vent hung a variety of weapons and handcuffs. My heart stuttered for a few beats, before settling into a fast pace.

Again, I waited and listened for sound. LC Karla was supposed to be off duty, but Jacy had warned me the schedule wasn't completely reliable.

I wiped slick hands on my uniform, unscrewed the cover and pulled it slowly into the vent. According to Broken Man, the Pop Cops motion sensors would be in the four corners of the room for maximum coverage.

Nothing else left to do, I pushed Zippy through the opening and held my breath, preparing to flee. He rolled a couple feet and stopped. His hum transformed into a low chug. When the alarm failed to sound and no Pop Cops burst through the door, I eased from the vent.

I searched the desk and opened all the drawers as fast as possible. Karla's office also contained a long worktable, a couch and a bench with chains and cuffs. A sudden vision of me secured to the bench while the LC questioned me jumped into my mind.

Shelves filled with RATSS decorated another wall. I ignored their mechanical stare, yet prepared to dive back into the heating vent if one moved.

My desperation increased. No sign of Broken Man's port anywhere. Closing my eyes for a moment, I drew in a few deep breaths. Think. Where would you put his port? I scanned the room once more. A gray closet in the corner drew my attention.

My joy when the closet's door swung wide disappeared in a heartbeat. A metal mesh gate covered shelves filled with various items—evidence, probably—and was locked. A small keypad had been installed on the lock's outer plate. None of the tools in my belt would be able to bypass the bolt. I would need a code to open the gate.

The third shelf down held a row of ports. Broken Man's must be among them, sitting mere inches from me. So close.

"Don't move," a voice ordered from behind.

eight

I closed my eyes as a hot flush of terror liquefied my muscles for an instant.

"Put your hands where I can see them. Slowly," he ordered, but his voice squeaked a bit. Either from nerves or youth.

Perhaps I could talk my way out of this. I moved my hands to the side.

"Turn around. Slow."

I faced him. My surprise transformed into suspicion. "Did you follow me?"

Riley lowered the stun gun. "No, I— What are *you* doing here?"

"I could ask *you* the same thing. Unless you're Lieutenant Commander Karla's assistant? Why didn't you tell me you're a Pop Cop?" My bold response seemed to have the desired effect as Riley struggled to answer questions I had no authority to ask.

"I'm not.... I monitor the electrical system." He gestured to his headset. "There was an electrical drain coming from here. I came to investigate."

"All right then. Investigate." I swept my hand, indicating the room. "I'm finished cleaning the ducts." Picking up Zippy, I headed toward the open vent. The little troll was hot.

"Wait." Riley stepped into the room, closing the door behind him. He still held the gun, but he aimed it at the floor. "You're not cleared to be on this level." He glanced at the open evidence closet. "Why are you here?"

I dodged the question. "How do you know I'm not cleared?"

"I checked."

"But you don't know my name." And unlikely to find it.

"I pulled up the approved list. Assuming your birth week is close to mine, I only found one scrub under sixteen hundred weeks old, but I forget *his* name."

"I'm on special assignment this week. The records haven't been updated yet." The heat from Zippy grew intolerable. I dropped him by the vent and crouched to enter the duct.

"Stop or I'll stun you."

I looked over my shoulder. He pointed his gun at me. By the intensity radiating from his blue eyes, I knew he was serious. And he seemed taller than before. Why hadn't I noticed his muscular build?

"You're not going to tell me why you're here, right?"

"Right," I said.

He sidestepped to the closet, keeping his weapon trained on me. A quick glance at the shelves, then his focus returned. I met his gaze. He squinted as if his thoughts raced.

"There are weapons and devices free for the taking, but you stood here. You want a port. Except you wouldn't be able to use it. No scrub can."

Riley was smarter than I had thought. Too smart.

Hoping to throw him off, I said, "I was just curious, seeing what would be important enough to be locked away. I stopped in here to fix my cleaning device." Zippy's hum increased and small tendrils of smoke reached for the ceiling. Good boy.

"No. I've been learning about the lower levels. Being caught in the upper levels is bad enough, but to be found in Karla's office…to risk your life… Wait. Something big is going on in the lower levels. Someone can't be found." His eyes unfocused as he followed the logic.

No time left. I spun Zippy. The metal burned my hand.

He snapped his fingers. "You want Domotor's port!"

I switched Zippy off and raised my arm, triggering the motion sensors. A shrill clang pierced the air. Distracted by the noise, Riley sought the source. Without hesitation, I shoved Zippy into the vent and followed the troll, pushing him as fast as possible through the narrow space despite the heat searing my fingertips.

"Listen!" Riley shouted after me.

An odd request. I craned my neck to look back. His hand grabbed the vent's cover and slammed it closed. After a few moments, the alarm cut off in midclang. Damn. I wanted the noise to mask my retreat. As I debated how much sound I was willing to risk, the rumble of many feet and the crash of a door reached me.

Reinforcements. Crap.

I had managed to crawl three meters from the vent. All the Pop Cops had to do was send one of Karla's RATSS after me and I would be caught in no time.

"What's going on here?" Karla demanded.

Her voice stopped my heart and I wondered, if she kill-zapped me, would it resume beating?

"Sensor malfunction, Lieutenant Commander," Riley said.

"But the alarm—"

"My fault. I accidentally triggered it while repairing the device. I apologize for any inconvenience to you, sir."

"Inconvenience! *Your* accident disrupted our meeting and

woke every off-duty officer on level four. You'll have to be reported. Name?"

"Riley Narelle Ashon." His voice remained calm. Impressive, considering how terrifying Karla's scrutiny could be.

"Narelle? What are you doing monitoring security systems?"

Good question. Only the Trava family had access to the security network.

"I'm with electrical, sir. When the device malfunctioned it sent a spike through my workstation and I came to investigate. I thought I could fix the sensor, sir."

"You thought wrong. What's your birth week?"

"It's 145,414, sir."

Ha. He was only seventy-three weeks older than me.

"You're just out of training. How did you get assigned electrical?"

"It was my choice, sir."

"Your choice? Oh. Top of your class. Well, you obviously need more training. Report to Commander Vinco Trava for extra duty."

Extra duty meant the dreaded red cuff and hard physical labor in the lower levels. The uppers were probably assigned a boring or mindless task nobody else wanted to do.

"Yes, sir," Riley snapped.

After a few seconds of quiet, it dawned on me. Riley hadn't reported me again. Even faced with a punishment, he still kept quiet. A strange sensation rolled through me—relief mixed with… I couldn't name it. Odd.

"You're dismissed, Mr. Ashon. Lieutenant Arno, your unit can return to their stations, but I want you to stay," she ordered.

The shuffle of feet faded and the door clicked shut. I decided to wait. No sense alerting Karla to my presence. I wondered how long I would be stuck here.

"Where were we, Arno?" Karla asked.

"Discussing the situation below," Arno said.

"Anything?"

"No. No one is talking. The scrubs are terrified. They're ratting out their friends. We've uncovered more illegal activities this week than in the past thirty weeks. Caught a woman who was raising her own children. A whole family unit."

"That's new. What did Vinco do?"

"The kids were too old for the care facility. They would remember a mother and might band together. He sent them to Chomper, and the woman was assigned to the *sheep* breeders."

He reported the demise of three children in a bored voice. Enraged, I wanted to strangle him.

"Harsh." A hitch cracked her voice, but then she continued speaking without emotion. "But appropriate. It would be dangerous if the scrubs formed loyalties." She paused. "You've increased the pressure to find Domotor and still no results?"

"Yes, sir."

Domotor? Riley had mentioned his name, too.

"Cogon's our best suspect, but he's had dozens of scrubs vouch for him." She paused.

Dozens? Wow. I knew he was well liked, but didn't think so many would risk their lives for him.

"He knows something, I can feel it," Karla said. "What about our informers? Have they heard any rumors?"

"No. Everyone's keeping quiet. No speculation. No gossip. It's as if Domotor never existed. Usually when a prophet disappears, there are rumblings of unease and talk of martyrs. This time nothing."

Domotor must be Broken Man's real name.

"What about the young girl…Trella?"

All of a sudden it felt as if the air shaft tightened around my body. I struggled to draw a breath.

"I had a few of my men ask about her," Arno said. "Keeps

to herself. No absences. No reprimands on her record. No friends except Cogon."

"There's an interesting connection. Arrest them both. Perhaps Cogon will be more informative if we threaten Trella's life and vice versa. Put them each into an interrogation room. Inform Commander Vinco when they're there."

"Yes, sir."

I had to warn Cog. He needed to disappear. But where could I hide the big man? With Broken Man? No. Cog had sealed his door.

Arno left the office, but Karla remained. No more time. Risking capture, I slid through the vent, pushing Zippy ahead. Cooler to the touch, the little troll had worked. I wondered if Logan and Anne-Jade had invented a device to open locks. I bit down on a laugh. I would be lucky to survive the next ten hours let alone make another attempt to steal Broken Man's port.

I reached Riley's storeroom. No sounds, but I paused for a few precious minutes before opening the vent's cover. The place was empty. However, the ladder had been set up underneath the air shaft, and a wipe board rested on the couch. A note for me written on the surface.

It read "I've covered for you, now it's your turn. Meet me here at hour fifty-eight."

I erased the message with a corner of my sleeve. By hour fifty-eight, I would either be in custody or on the lam. It was doubtful I could meet him. A tweak of disappointment surprised me. I repeated my mantra. Never trust the uppers, the Pop Cops or the scrubs. It all boiled down to survival.

As I climbed the ladder I wondered, was survival enough?

"Shouldn't you be in an air shaft working?" Cog asked. He was elbow deep in a piece of machinery in the Waste Handling

Plant. Black goo smeared his coveralls and dripped onto the floor. A fetid stench fogged the air.

"The Pop Cops are coming to arrest you and me."

He ceased tugging. "How do you know?"

"Overheard Lieutenant Commander Karla. They're going to threaten to recycle me if you don't tell them about Broken Man. You need to hide. Now."

Instead of pulling his arms out, he resumed his work.

"Cog!"

"Hush a minute. I need to think."

"I thought it out. We both hide and then…"

"What? We live like fugitives for the rest of our days? Or do we find Gateway and leave? Do you believe in Gateway, Trella?"

"I believe something is going on in the upper levels. I believe the Pop Cops are lying to us."

"No kidding. You need to answer my question. Do you believe in Gateway?"

"It doesn't matter. We need to get you somewhere safe first and then we'll worry about the next step."

Cogon grunted and pulled a wad of black cloth. "Contraband." He unrolled the mass and a bottle fell. "Flushed through the waste system during a Pop Cop raid."

"Cog!" My panic increased. He acted so casual.

"It does matter if you believe or not."

"Why?"

"Because there is nowhere for me to hide. They'll find me pretty quick and keep searching for you. I'm going to let them arrest me, and I'm going to confess to killing the Pop Cop on my own and clear your name. And I'm going to eventually tell them I hid Broken Man, sending them to various hiding spots. And when they don't find him, I'll confess to killing him, too, and dumping his body in a number of tanks and feeding bits of him to machines. Hopefully they'll investigate each and every claim."

I stared at Cog as my body numbed with horror.

"See, Trell? It does matter. Because for me to endure, I need to know you believe in Gateway and know you're searching for it. To know I am helping by keeping the Pop Cops occupied while you find it."

"But you'll be fed to Chomper!"

"I don't have a problem with that."

"But I do."

"It's not your decision."

"You think finding Gateway is more important than your life?" I asked him.

"Yes."

"Why? Aren't you happy with the status quo? You smile at everyone. You have a ton of friends."

He held up his filthy foul-smelling hands. "This *is* the rest of my life. Nothing is going to change unless *we* do something. I've been waiting for the right circumstances. This is it."

One of the maintenance scrubs hustled over. "Cog, a group of Pop Cops are looking for you. Want us to distract them?"

"No thanks. Go back to work." Cogon met my gaze. An unanswered question still hovered between us.

"I don't know if I believe in Gateway or not. But I won't stop searching for it until I prove beyond a doubt it does or doesn't exist. Will that help you?"

Shouts and loud voices reached us.

He smiled. "Yes. Now, shoo." He waved me toward the heating vent. "Won't help my story if you're found in here with me."

"What about the maintenance scrub?"

"He'll cover for me."

I raced for the vent and scrambled through. The Pop Cops must have been prepared for a fight. Surprise laced their voices when Cog agreed to go with them. Sure enough, the other scrub never mentioned me. He could have used the information in exchange for a better position. Proof of Cog's uniqueness.

Lying in the warm duct, I felt truly alone for the first time in a long while.

If Cog was going to sacrifice himself, the least I could do was report to my work shift and pretend nothing had happened. Catching up on the three hours I'd missed, I toggled the troll to move faster, reminding me of Cog.

We had been care mates. My earliest memories involved a confusing array of new faces, being upset and longing. Even though Cog was two hundred and sixty-eight weeks older than me, he befriended me. Life in the noisy and chaotic facility was bearable with him. Then Cog had his fourteenth centiweek celebration and "graduated" from the care unit, leaving me.

I had known he would go, but I hadn't been prepared for the devastation inside me. He visited and he was reachable, but his new life and friends kept him busy. The change from having him as my almost constant companion to seeing him for an hour every two weeks left me distraught and an easy target.

My other mates didn't understand. Life in the pipes was preferable to being taunted by everyone. Once I had my celebration, I left the facility and Cog found me. I vowed not to get too close to him or anybody, fearing the return of pain. But Cog just wouldn't give up. And now he was gone again.

I let the waves of anguish pound in my chest. Abandoned and alone. I rode my emotions as I would surf in a water pipe, allowing the force of the liquid to take control.

Eventually, I fought for control and won. I shoved the sadness deep within me, locked it down and focused on the present. My shift was over.

The cleaning troll slowed as it neared a turn. Access to a

maintenance area was a few meters ahead. When we reached the area's door, I stopped the troll and slid the panel wide. Wrestling with the awkward device, I stored the troll in a cleaning cabinet for the next scrub.

As I debated whether or not to travel through the pipes or main corridors, the door opened. Three Pop Cops entered the small room.

My heart desired immediate action, screaming for my legs to run. Logic forced my body to ignore the panicked commands. I gave the newcomers space and stepped closer to the access panel, planning to escape through the air shaft if needed.

A lieutenant eyed my work suit and bare feet. "Finishing your shift?" I recognized his voice from Karla's office. Lieutenant Arno.

"Yes, sir." I kept the quaver from my voice.

"You're under arrest."

The quaver dropped into my stomach. "Why, sir?"

"For lying to Lieutenant Commander Karla," he snapped.

"Lying, sir?" Cog wouldn't have given in so fast. Unless… My thoughts shied away from how horrible it would have to be for Cog to tell her about me.

"We know you're involved with Broken Man's disappearance despite what you said. You *will* tell us where he is." His tone left little doubt.

The Pop Cop on his left pulled a pair of handcuffs from his belt. I gauged the distance to the panel, but hesitated. Running was the action of a guilty person and I—well, I was guilty, but I trusted Cog. It seemed too soon.

One of Arno's gadgets beeped. He grabbed the black communicator. "Yes?"

The Pop Cops waited as he listened.

"Are you sure?" He shot me a nasty look. "All right. I'll be there." Replacing the device, he reported to his companions, "Looks like the little scrub is clean." Then to me he said,

"Your friend Cogon just confessed to killing my officer by himself. You're free to go…for now."

He strode from the room with the Pop Cops a step behind. When the door clicked shut, I sagged against the wall, letting the metal cool my hot skin. I didn't linger long. My next shift started in ten hours and I had a promise to keep.

After a meal and a few hours of sleep, I aimed for Broken Man's hideout. I hadn't visited in over thirty hours, but at least he had enough food. When I slipped into the room, he sat at the computer terminal, looking well groomed for a man in hiding.

He smiled with relief. "Thank air you haven't been caught."

"Not yet."

He sobered. "Will Cogon tell them where I am?"

"How do you know about Cog?" I glanced around. Was someone else coming here? The place appeared to be clean.

"The computer. I can access general information. When I saw Cogon's shifts had been reassigned, I assumed he was arrested."

"He was. But don't worry about Cog ratting you out. He can be stubborn when he wants." I explained Cog's sacrifice to Broken Man.

He closed his eyes and pressed his hand over them. "A martyr. He will be remembered."

My throat felt as if Zippy had lodged there. I swallowed, and focused on the ground. Broken Man's chair legs had wheels. "Where did you get the chair?" I demanded.

He wiped his eyes and squinted at me. "Chair?"

"The wheels?"

"Oh. I made it. I found an old toolbox and a broken cart. With nothing else to do, I had plenty of time to rig this up." He straightened in his chair, grinning slightly. "In fact, I've gotten pretty good at helping myself. I can take a shower and pull myself into a chair. I guess my muscles are getting stronger." His posture wilted a bit. "Trella, will you do me a favor?"

I stiffened. What more could he want? "Depends."

"If you are caught, tell the Pop Cops where I am."

"Why?"

"I'd rather be kill-zapped than starve until I expire."

Good point. "I'll make sure someone knows where to find you, *Domotor*," I promised.

His defeated attitude changed into surprise. "How do you know my name?"

I related my adventures in LC Karla's office. "Riley knows I wanted your port. We'll have to find a way to access the computer without it."

"Impossible." He stared into the distance for a few moments. "What are the boy's family names?"

"Narelle Ashon. Why?"

"He's Jacob's boy." He peered at me. "You never asked me about your family."

"The family *you* invented so I would help you?"

"I didn't—"

"Doesn't matter. Even if you were serious, from what I read of the uppers, no *real* family would abandon their child in the lower levels, so I have no desire to know anything about them."

He put his hands up in defeat. "All right. Have it your way. We still need my port, though. Any ideas?"

"I make another attempt." How remained the problem. Zippy worked but would tip Riley off again, and the lock was impossible to pop. Unless the Tech Nos had another useful device.

"Do it when Riley's on shift."

"Why?"

"He covered for you before and might do it again. Hopefully he's sympathetic to our cause."

Broken Man's words reminded me of Riley's note. He asked me to meet him. And to trust him. I did owe Riley one, and would meet him at hour fifty-eight. But trusting him was out of the question.

nine

The recycling plant occupied the entire I1 quadrant. Piles of discarded and broken items littered the space. Scrubs sorted the heaps of trash into smaller loads. Other scrubs moved around the plant's machinery, feeding metal into the blast furnace, glass pieces into the kiln and thread into the looms. And, beyond the equipment, another set of workers crafted goods from the melted glass, from the sheets of metal and the bolts of cloth.

I wore the shapeless coveralls of the workers, blending in with ease. A few Pop Cops wandered around, and I practiced my cover story in my mind just in case.

Heat from the machines thickened the air, and a film of fine grit formed on my clothes and skin. A hot metallic smell dominated. I pushed through the noise and activity, looking for Logan and Anne-Jade.

The reason thick-soled boots were required for this area crunched under my feet, and I skirted piles of kitchen utensils and torn clothing. Nothing was wasted. Everything was recycled and reused. Human waste and food traveled to the

waste-handling system to be turned into fertilizer for hydroponics. Water looped through the water-treatment plant and
air blasted through a series of tanks and scrubbers.

Even people contributed when their life ended. Their lifeless
bodies were sent to Chomper's Lair—a room next to the solid-
waste facility—to be transformed into…I wasn't sure. Wild
rumors and creative speculation circulated about the place. Not
many scrubs were allowed in there—well, not alive anyway.
A few called the room the Final Gateway.

My thoughts drifted to Cog. When a well-loved person
died, scrubs would line the corridors to Chomper's Lair to
pay their respects. I yanked my morose thoughts away. They
distracted from my mission.

Anne-Jade and Logan sorted a number of small circuit
boards. I joined them. Anne-Jade shot me an annoyed look,
but Logan smiled in welcome. In order to appear to be working, I moved items around.

"What are you doing here?" Anne-Jade asked. The words
hissed.

"I need your help."

She scanned the Pop Cops nearby. "Couldn't you wait until
our shift is over at sixty?"

"No, I work the even shifts."

Logan leaned close. "Did Zippy help you?"

"Sort of."

They waited, and I explained about the power drain being
noticeable to the electrical systems manager.

"That *is* a problem. We will have to install a—"

"Not now." Anne-Jade's long golden hair swung as she
shook her head in exasperation. "What do you need?" she
asked me.

"I could use a new-and-improved Zippy and something to
open locks."

"Zippy's it for now. If I had some time…" Logan stared into the distance, probably reassembling Zippy in his head.

"How much time?"

He shrugged. "A week."

"Too long." I considered. Since I knew where to find Broken Man's port, I could reduce my time spent in Karla's office and be gone by the time the spike registered. "What about the lock?"

Logan flashed me a bright smile. He pulled a narrow timer from his pocket and handed it to me. "I thought you would need this. Place it below the keypad and press the button. Instead of the time, the display will show the code for the lock in about three to four seconds."

I marveled at the device. "How?"

"Do you really want to know?" Anne-Jade asked.

"No. This is wonderful."

"Anything else?"

I hesitated. Broken Man had said it was impossible, but, with these two, impossible could be possible. "Do you have a device to access the uppers' computer network?"

Anne-Jade and Logan exchanged a glance. Once again, she scanned the room before asking, "Like a port?"

I nodded.

Another significant look flashed between them. "That's the *ultimate* goal of a Tech No," Logan said. "I managed to hack into the uppers' computer system about as far as I can go without one. All I need is a port to open the door, then I would *own* the system. Own it!"

"Has anyone achieved that goal?" I asked, wondering just how many Tech Nos there were.

"No, but…" He sought Anne-Jade's permission. She waved him on, despite the strain lined on her face.

Logan stepped close to me. "But, we're almost there."

"How soon?"

"Twenty weeks, maybe more."

Too late to help me. "Any chance you could speed it up?"

Anne-Jade turned on me. "No. Crafting these devices takes an immense effort. And it's just us. You're looking at the entire Tech Nos. The Pop Cops have decimated our group, and the only reason we're still alive is because we move slow and proceed with the utmost care. So far, we have outsmarted the uppers." Twin circles of red spread on her cheeks.

"We know we'll be found out eventually," Logan added. His tone remained flat as if he discussed a routine event. "We just want to impart the maximum damage before we're fed to Chomper."

With Zippy leading the way, I crawled through the air shaft on level four. The trip here felt routine. Bad sign. Before Broken Man, I had limited my trips into the upper levels to once every five or ten weeks. Now I popped up here every off-shift.

I turned Zippy off as we neared Riley's room. No sense alerting him to our presence even if hour fifty-eight was only minutes away. Peering through the vent, I searched for Pop Cops.

Riley sat on the edge of the couch. After a moment he stood, glanced at the clock, smoothed his shirt and adjusted his headset. Nervous or bored, I couldn't tell for sure. The Pop Cops could be waiting in the corridor for Riley's signal. And why would he be wearing his headset?

Now or never. I reached the vent above the couch and removed the cover. Riley jumped at the sound. I suppressed a grimace. He was nervous. Because of a trap or because of me? At least he wasn't armed.

I dropped Zippy onto the couch and climbed down the ladder. Keeping my feet on the lowest rung, I prepared to bolt at any sign of trouble.

"I thought you wouldn't come," Riley said.

He appeared older. No longer in training, he wore a plain gray shirt and black pants. Fresh scratches marred his cheek and neck, and his left sleeve was torn and bloody.

"What happened?" I asked, gesturing to his arm.

A wry smile twisted his lips. "Extra duty with Commander Vinco. The commander delights in knife fighting and uses his unarmed *helpers* for target practice."

I couldn't resist. "Unarmed?"

Impishness lit his face. "So far, I've managed to survive the duty, much to his annoyance." He rubbed his shoulder as the humor faded from his expression. "But he's getting creative, which is not the reason you're here." He stared at me for a moment.

Warmth flushed through me. I imagined I was quite the sight. Wisps of brown hair had sprung from my braid long ago and clung to my sweaty face. Stains and tears marked my one-piece cleaning uniform, which felt rather tight all of a sudden. Bare feet roughened with calluses completed the picture. I don't know why I cared about my appearance. I hadn't before.

"Aren't you going to come down?" Riley pointed to the couch.

"I'll stay here."

"You still don't trust me even after I covered for you?"

No sense sugarcoating it. "Yep."

"Then *why* are you here?"

"I owe you one."

"Wonderful," he muttered. He crossed his arms and frowned. "You might as well go then. I can't help you if you don't trust me." Riley turned to leave.

Not the reaction I expected. "Help me with what?"

He paused. "Getting Domotor's port."

"Why?"

Riley faced me with a challenge in his blue eyes. So used to the various shades of brown in the lower levels, the color still amazed me.

"If you want to know why, then have a seat." He swept his arm wide.

Curiosity was a lethal trait. Scrubs learned in the care facility not to ask too many questions or challenge what you were taught. To accept and agree meant more privileges, fewer punishments and a decent work assignment. A few had learned this lesson quicker than others. A few still hadn't accepted it.

My Care Mother followed the Pop Cops' rules, but she lacked the inner conviction. She punished because she had to, not because she agreed with the rules. If one of us found a loophole, she honored it and applauded our inventiveness.

Unfortunately, my talents in creative explanations had been limited. And the faded scars crisscrossing my body reminded me I should squelch all curiosity. But should didn't mean I would. I settled on the couch next to Zippy.

Riley pointed to the little cleaning troll. "Is that what you used to keep the motion detectors silent?"

"I'm not answering anything until you tell me why you want to help me."

He swallowed his first comment, drew a deep breath and said, "After meeting you the first time, I searched for more information about life in the lower levels. My interest triggered a warning. Good thing I was still in training, the warning was sent to my trainer who's also my father instead of the Controllers." He touched his left arm. Blood still welled from a number of cuts.

"What happens when the Controllers are alerted?"

A wince flashed across his face. "You don't want to know."

"Yes, I do. You're an upper. How bad can it be?"

He paused. "Interesting. The ignorance goes both ways." Balanced on the couch's armrest, his gaze slid past my shoulder.

"Makes sense, though. The Trava family wouldn't want uppers and lowers to unite." Riley's focus returned to me.

"Nor would we. You uppers think we're filthy livestock bred for one purpose. To work."

"I see the propaganda has worked. You believe the Pop Cops."

I jumped to my feet. "I'm not like those sheep. I don't listen to all that bull."

"Really?" He raised one eyebrow in a mocking sneer. "Where did you acquire your vast knowledge of life in the upper levels?"

"In the care facility."

"Which is run by the Pop Cops." Smugness replaced his scorn.

I preferred the sneer. "So your purpose in inviting me here was to prove I'm an ignorant scrub?"

"No." The word ground out as if it originated deep within him. He held up both hands in a stopping motion. "I'm trying to understand why you automatically assumed I'm a spoiled brat. And I wanted you to think about where you've gotten your information. It's either from the Pop Cops or from the computer system, which is run by the Controllers. Both can't be trusted."

"Gee, thanks for that little nugget of advice. I wonder how I survived all these weeks without it." I headed to the ladder. What a waste of time.

"Wait." He grabbed my arm.

I yanked a screwdriver from my tool belt. He let go.

"Please listen," he said to my back. "This isn't going the way I thought it would. When my father asked why I was so interested in the scrubs, I told him—"

I rounded on him. "I knew this was a trap! Is your father waiting outside with a troop of Pop Cops?"

"No." This time the word growled. Riley's hands shook

as if he fought to keep from grabbing me again. "I told him I wanted to help the scrubs, to do something…anything to ease their horrid living conditions."

"Really?" Disbelief tainted my voice.

"Yes." He practically shouted the word.

"Why?"

"Because of what you told me when you…er…visited last week. Before you dropped in, I thought scrubs were…" His arms moved in a vague all-encompassing gesture. "Were like your little device there, but bigger. We're taught nothing more about scrubs than they clean and work. We're threatened to be exiled to the lower levels if we do anything really bad. It's implied that if we survived, the rest of our weeks would be filled with hard physical labor." He held a hand up, stopping me from contradicting him. "Look. There are no pictures in our training computers. Truthfully, I hadn't really thought about who lives in the lower levels at all. But there you stood, a real human being. My age, with…" He dropped his arms, slapping his hands against his legs. "Never mind, you wouldn't believe me. My father said there was nothing I could do to help. He was right until Domotor went missing and I caught you in LC Karla's office."

"Caught?" I feigned innocence—all I could manage. His speech rolled around in my mind, and I couldn't quite grasp the significance. "Don't you mean found?"

"No. Caught. You didn't see the petrified look on your face when you turned around. It was gone in an instant, but I'll never forget it." He smiled at the memory.

He *could* smile. *He* wouldn't be fed to Chomper if caught. "Is there a point to all this? My work shift starts in an hour."

"My father had told me about a few uppers who'd tried and failed to circumvent various security systems in the computer network long ago. Domotor was rumored to be trying again before his accident and banishment to the lower levels. When you showed up looking for Domotor's port, I guessed you know where he is and you're helping him."

"Why would I care if Broken Man is trying to bypass computer systems?"

Riley stepped closer. "If the other upper families regain control of Inside, then we can make life in the lower levels better."

I studied his expression for signs of deceit. Broken Man had said the upper families wouldn't want to help. Or did he tell me that so I would focus all my energy on finding Gateway? Riley seemed sincere and he already knew most of it. How much worse could it be for him to know?

"You're right. I'm here to fetch Broken…Domotor's port."

"You'll let me help?"

He managed to downplay his triumph. Impressive. I nodded.

"I'm monitoring the electrical usage for level four during the next shift. I can't disable the motion sensors because it would be recorded, but I can hide the spike from your device." He glanced at the little cleaning troll. "Smoke was coming out of it before. Will it work?"

"Yes." Logan had repaired Zippy before I left.

"Good. I wasn't able to find the code for the lock. How do you plan to get into the evidence closet?"

"I have another…ah…device."

He raised his eyebrows, inviting me to elaborate.

"It's better you don't know."

"As long as it works fast," he said. He slid his hand into a pocket.

I tensed, but relaxed when he withdrew a port. He handed it to me.

"What's this for?" I examined the white interface. The size and shape mimicked three molars in a row, but underneath a square-shaped metal piece stuck out. Small numbers had been etched into the metal box. It was hollow except for a line of copper pins. I guessed the bottom piece was inserted into a person's jawbone to anchor the port.

"To exchange for Domotor's. An empty spot will alert LC Karla. Do you know his ID number?"

"Yes, but what about the LC? She's also scheduled to work the next shift."

"All the high-ranking officers have a meeting in the Control Room at hour sixty. It lasts about an hour. She's usually there."

"Usually?"

"Wait to enter her office until a few minutes past sixty. The computer lists the whereabouts of important people so if there's ever an emergency they can be contacted. If she's not listed in the meeting room, I'll flash the lights in her office to let you know."

"Do you always know where she is?"

"No. I only have second degree security clearance. The hour sixty meeting and its attendees are general knowledge."

General knowledge to the uppers. The scrubs hadn't a clue, and what we did know was doubtful. So much for reporting to my shift on time.

"Get in position now," Riley said. "I don't want to open the door until you're hidden from sight. Just in case someone is out in the hall."

"How come you're the only one who uses this room?"

"It's hard to find and has been forgotten. I doubt anyone is outside, but it never hurts to be too careful."

I agreed with him, being extra careful should be our motto. Turning away so Riley couldn't see my smirk—our motto, like we were a gang—I opened the heating vent and slipped inside, taking Zippy with me.

Riley crouched down to help replace the cover. But before setting it in place, he touched my arm. This time I didn't flinch as the heat from his hand sizzled in my blood. I met his gaze.

"Be careful," he said.

Cog constantly told me to be careful, but Riley's voice sounded different. I wondered if it was fear or genuine concern.

"You, too," I said.

He nodded then replaced the vent's cover. Rolling Zippy ahead of me, I slid through the tight space toward Karla's office, but my mind reviewed the strange conversation with Riley as I traveled. Could the Controllers be as bad as the Pop Cops? It was hard to imagine and yet I couldn't shake the image of blood dripping from his arm, nor could I forget the warmth that still lingered on my skin from his touch.

I reached Karla's office and slowed. Creeping toward her vent, I listened for any noise. The soft bluelight shone through the vent cover, signaling an empty room. My body was so used to the ten-hour system, I felt rather than knew when it was hour sixty. I hoped my supervisor wasn't looking for me.

The glow remained steady. After a few minutes, I removed the vent's cover. Another couple passed before I turned Zippy on and pushed him out. When the alarm failed to sound, I hurried over to the gray evidence closet. Opening the doors, I pulled out Logan's device and placed it under the keypad, pressing the button.

It hummed and a series of numbers filled the small screen. Typing in the code, I braced for an alarm, but the bolt slid back. I exchanged the fake port for Broken Man's, checked the ID numbers twice, then relocked the closet.

The room's daylights flashed a few times. I grabbed Zippy and dove into the vent. Voices sounded beyond the office door. The vent cover stuck in the hole. I tugged on it as the pings of someone entering a code rang. It jerked free. I placed it over the vent as the door opened.

"Alarm off," Lieutenant Commander Karla said.

Daylights swept over the blue glow, trapping me and illuminating a frowning Karla. I couldn't ever recall seeing the woman smile.

"This had *better* be important," she said to the lieutenant following her into the room.

"Our detainee just gave us a clue to Domotor's location. I need your permission to assign a search team," the lieutenant said.

"Has he implicated anyone else?"

"No, sir."

"Hard to believe he managed to hide a physically disabled man without help." Frustration tainted her voice.

"He's strong and has a high pain tolerance, sir."

My heart stumbled. Only one way to discover how much pain a person could tolerate.

Karla grunted. "But he's too big to fit in the air shafts. Another scrub had to be involved."

"But we have no real evidence, sir. That cloth bag could have been blown down to the floor. It's light enough to have been sucked up by the return air."

"No. I know a scrub was there, and I'll find out who was in the air shaft," she vowed. "No *scrub* gets away from me."

"What about the search team, sir?"

"Take team four and report back to me immediately. Understand?"

"Yes, sir." The lieutenant strode from the room.

The LC scowled at his retreating form. She stood gazing at the door as if lost in thought then left her office, pausing only to reactivate the alarms.

I waited a few minutes to ensure she was gone. The need to act pulsed in my body. Cogon suffered while I wasted time. I headed toward Riley's room with reckless speed. Even knowing Riley wouldn't be there, disappointment still jabbed me when I reached the place. I hid Zippy under the couch and hurried to Domotor's room. My shift be damned. Cogon would not suffer in vain.

ten

I held Domotor's port between my finger and thumb, flourishing the unit.

The prophet pumped a fist in the air and grinned. "Good work!"

"How long to get the information?"

"It'll take about forty to fifty hours," Domotor said.

I groaned aloud.

"If I'm not careful, I'll alert the system to my presence and we'll be discovered." He studied my face. "Trella, get a few hours' sleep. You look terrible."

I ignored his remark, but thought about Riley's comment about circumventing computer systems. "Are you going to tell me your real agenda?"

He fidgeted in his chair. The ecstatic expression faded and wariness touched his eyes. I hadn't given him the device.

"Are you really seeking Gateway's location? Or was that my incentive for retrieving the disks and your port?"

"It's complicated," he said.

"Meaning a dumb scrub wouldn't be able to understand?" My hand fisted around his port.

"No." He pushed the hair from his eyes. The long blond strands hung loose. "Meaning you don't know enough about the upper levels to realize that even if we find Gateway, we might not be able to unlock it without gaining control of key computer systems."

"Do you even believe Gateway exists?"

"Yes, I do." His gaze remained steady.

Damn. Either he was a good liar or he told the truth. "How do you gain control of the systems?"

"Through the computer network, but I need to find out who the real Controllers are."

"You mean which Travas?"

"No. All the upper families think the admiral, vice admiral and captain, who are all Travas, are the Controllers. But I found a command flow chart in a forgotten file that put the Controllers above the admiral."

"Then who are the Controllers?"

"No one knows. Not even the Travas. But I've overheard them speculating, and they believe the Controllers live Outside and send instructions through the computer. Sort of a divine influence."

Shock rolled through me. The thought of people or even a divine being dictating what we did Inside from Outside was hard to grasp.

"Just because the Travas believe it doesn't mean it is true."

"Do they know what is Outside?"

"No. No one does. It's all speculation. A few Travas think the divine presence lives in the computer network. Others think the computer itself has become intelligent." He shrugged. "Knowledge of before was erased from the computer system thousands of weeks ago. Something has to be beyond our walls. The Controllers must know."

I mulled over the information. "Gateway could just be a computer link to the Controllers, and not a physical exit."

"It's possible. And you're holding our only chance to find out."

I unfurled my fingers. His port rested in my palm. Cog's life in exchange for this. No turning back now. I would stay the course until the end.

He snatched his port as a hungry man would grab food. Relief washed the worry from Domotor's expression. He inspected the device and then inserted it into the gap on the right side of his lower jaw. I wheeled him over to the computer.

"Get some rest," he said half-distracted. "You're welcome to use my bed."

A few hours remained in my shift, and I needed to put in an appearance. But I entered the kitchen first to inventory his food. Not much left. A few lonely bowls of casserole occupied the small refrigerator. More than thirty hours remained to the next assembly, and I doubted I could cough my way into the kitchen again. The prospect of standing in line multiple times for extra food seemed daunting.

I straightened the dishes and checked his bedroom. The clicks and taps from the keyboard followed me. His sheets hung to the floor and his blanket was a balled-up wad. Must be hard to make a bed when you couldn't use your legs.

Pulling everything off, I remade the bed with clean linens. A mistake. The fresh sheets called to me. My body ached. My thoughts pushed through a numb fog. A sense of loss pressed between my shoulder blades. I settled on the edge of the bed and rested my head in my hands.

What had I expected? Give Domotor his port and voilà! Directions to Gateway would appear in a matter of minutes. Huffing in tired amusement, I admitted that, yes, I had been expecting instantaneous results despite all my efforts to believe Gateway didn't exist and to not get my hopes up. I guess a part of me really desired a true exit to Outside. Now the possibility of a computer Gateway instead of a physical Gateway sucked all hope away.

I should be happy. Domotor's discoveries would prove me right. Yet the possibility of the Controllers not living with us or even being a person caused a finger of fear to brush my spine.

Morbid thoughts circled and conversations replayed in my mind. To escape them, I lay down. I would rest a few minutes.

"Lousy son-of-a-Trava!" Domotor's curses woke me from a dreamless sleep. Hours and not minutes had passed. So much for my shift. I hoped my supervisor hadn't checked on me. I stretched and padded to the living area.

Domotor scowled at the computer monitor. He punched a few keys then slammed his fist on the table.

"What's the matter?" I asked.

"New security systems have been installed."

"And?"

"I might not be able to get around them." He typed a few words. "The program is…odd. The Controllers aren't usually this…creative. They stick to what they know and what has worked."

"Perhaps your earlier forays into the system alarmed them?"

"Possible. But this other program should work. It's just complicated." His attention returned to the screen.

I left him to his work and showered. My stomach growled with urgent need and I resigned myself to spending the next five hours gathering food for me and Domotor.

He grunted when I said goodbye. I traveled through the heating vents until I reached one of the main hallways. The scrubs traveling through the corridor ignored me. No curses. No taunts. I joined the flow and aimed for the cafeteria in Quad G2.

Standing in line, I noticed the stiffness of the people around me. It was well known I didn't like them and they didn't like me. They called me Queen of the Pipes, believing I thought I was better than them. Used to glares and sneers, I now had scrubs avoiding eye contact. Different. And the ones who met my gaze, nodded. A few smiled in encouragement. Stranger still was the muted hum in the room. Pop Cops patrolled the aisles between tables, and a mist of fear hung in the humid sweat-scented air. Yet a sense of purpose emanated as if no matter how afraid they were, the scrubs were determined to endure the Pop Cops' scrutiny.

I pushed my tray along the metal track and pointed to a vegetable casserole. The scrub spooned a ladleful into a bowl then added in a second scoop. I glanced at the man in surprise.

"There's a clog in the kitchen's air shaft," he said. "Can you clean it out for us?"

It took me a moment to realize he was talking to me. "Report it to the kitchen manager."

He stared at me. "I did. She said to have *someone* check the shaft at hour eighty." He returned to filling bowls and the press of the scrubs waiting behind me propelled me toward the tables.

Odd. The whole exchange worried me. The scrubs couldn't know about me. Could they? No. They'd rat me out in an instant. I shoveled the food into my mouth, but didn't taste a thing.

There had been plenty of chances for scrubs to gain favor by implicating me. Yet here I sat with a double portion. Enough for Domotor and me. Instead of standing in line again, I stored the leftover food and checked the cleaning schedule.

My next shift started at hour eighty. Air shaft twenty-two was the first job listed on my sheet. Twenty-two crossed over the scrubs' kitchen. I licked my dry lips. The man had said there was a clog. Could it be an ambush? No. Why go to all that trouble? A simple anonymous note to the lieutenant commander would do the trick.

Something was going on. I searched for Jacy. He held court in his corner of the barracks. A tone signaled the end of a shift. I hung back, waiting for the crowd to thin. He spotted me and soon the scrubs hurried away.

After scanning the barracks, he pulled two round disks from his pocket and handed them to me. "The listening devices," he said.

I remembered my deal to plant them in air shaft seventy-two. The metal felt cold in my hands. About a quarter inch thick, the silver circles fit within my palm. An inner circle of gold-colored mesh coated the one side, and a black magnet clung to the other.

"Stick them close to the vents. They won't come loose even when the cleaning trolls go through," Jacy explained. "Put one in the Pop Cops HQ and the other over the Control Room."

I hid them in my tool belt. "I have another question."

"Goody. I have more listening devices."

"Not that type of question. At least I think the answer wouldn't be worth anything."

He brushed away his hair, revealing his dark eyes. "Now, I'm intrigued."

"I just want to know the latest gossip, what rumors are circulating."

Jacy studied my face. "You never cared before. Why now?"

"The lower levels feel…odd."

"With twice as many Pop Cops patrolling, people are scared and nervous."

"I get that, but…" How to word my questions without giving too much away? "But they have the chance to…make their life better, and I don't know why they don't take it."

"You should know why. Do you really need me to spell it out for you?"

I nodded.

He shook his head. "It'll cost you two more devices."

Figures. "Only if it isn't some bull."

"It's not. This is serious." He stepped toward me and lowered his voice. "Despite what you think, scrubs aren't stupid. We put it together. One missing prophet, Cogon arrested for hiding him and LC Karla asking questions about you." He held up three fingers. "If we rat you out to the Pop Cops, then the prophet is found and you and Cog are recycled." His fingers curled in and formed a zero with his thumb. "We're left with nothing. No hope, Trella, is worse than fear. Right now, we hope you're up to something that will benefit us all."

All feeling drained from my body. Logic leaked from my brain and panic filled the empty space. "And if I'm not?"

"No one will believe you. See we know something big is going on. Big enough to cause the Queen of the Pipes to come down from above and mingle with her fellow scrubs."

"But…but…" My vision turned to static. I drew in a few breaths. The air smelled musty and damp with a hint of body odor. "But what if I fail?"

"Doesn't matter."

"What?"

He gave me a sad smile. "It's the *effort,* not the results that matter."

Coming from the man who was all about getting something in exchange for his information and services, I didn't believe him. The scrubs were either holding out for a better offer from the Pop Cops or waiting for me to perform a miracle for them. Sheep don't risk their necks for other sheep.

Yet my conviction faltered when I discovered what clogged the air shaft above the kitchen a few minutes past hour eighty. Food containers filled the duct. Enough food to feed me and Domotor for weeks.

I peered through the vent and watched the bustle of the

kitchen scrubs. Pop Cops also kept an eye on them, but they had still managed to hide food despite the danger.

They counted on me. Again panic threatened to overwhelm me. If nothing changed in the lower levels, the scrubs would be disappointed and upset for risking the little comforts they had.

Shoving the confused terror into a deep corner of my mind, I concentrated on the task at hand—getting the food to Domotor's hideout. With my makeshift skid and the troll's help, I transported all the containers to the air shaft over his quarters then continued to work my shift.

The hours crept by. Each time I changed air ducts, I kept expecting to be arrested. When I encountered the first RATSS, I almost screamed. The thing focused its antennae on me.

"Name and birth week," a mechanical voice ordered.

I answered.

"Noted. Continue working," it said.

It drove away and my heart resumed beating. I was questioned by two more RATSS in two other shafts.

By the time hour ninety arrived, my muscles were so tight I could have climbed a vertical shaft without breaking a sweat. Grateful to be done, I returned the cleaning troll to his closet.

"There you are," my supervisor said. Her eyebrows pinched together with annoyance and a red cuff hung from her fingers.

I bit down on a sarcastic reply. No sense upsetting her further.

"I waited for you at the end of your last shift, but you never showed. Where were you?"

My thoughts raced. "My cleaning device broke in the shaft and I had to repair it. Took me an extra hour to finish." I hoped she hadn't waited an hour.

She tapped the red cuff on her thigh. I kept my face neutral.

"Next time, leave it behind and check to see if I'm waiting.

I've got Pop Cops breathing down my neck. They want to know if anyone misses a shift."

"Yes, sir." Calling her sir always mollified her.

As expected, her expression smoothed. "I wanted to let you know there will be a lot of RATSS in the pipes. The Pop Cops believe there's evidence hidden in one of the air ducts." She huffed in disbelief. "We're *supposed* to work around them. Just try not to break any of the RATSS during your next shift."

"Yes, sir."

She checked my name off her list and left to find the next scrub. I waited for my pulse to calm before sliding into the heating ducts and heading toward Domotor's room. The air shafts wouldn't be safe for me to travel in for a while. And I hoped the RATSS hadn't discovered the cache of food above Domotor's hideout.

I entered his quarters through the vent. Domotor was slumped over his keyboard sleeping. Wasting no time, I transported the food containers from the air shaft to the refrigerator and freezer.

When I finished, Domotor straightened a bit in his chair, but he rested his forehead in the palm of his hand. His hair covered his expression.

Not able to wait anymore, I asked, "Any progress?"

His reply was muffled so I stepped closer and touched his shoulder. He dropped his arm and met my gaze. Hollowness lurked in his eyes.

"What happened?" I asked.

"We're done."

eleven

I understood the look of defeat in his face, but not the reason for it.

"What happened?" I asked.

"I hit a wall. The security system has been enhanced and I couldn't bypass it."

I ignored the tightness gripping my throat. "Is there another way?" The question squeaked out.

"No."

"There has to be." A whisper, all I could manage. My body felt as if it were trapped in a metal compactor.

"There isn't." He rubbed a hand over his cheek as he stared into the distance. A combination of emotions crossed his face, but they moved too fast for me to decipher. "Unless...I follow Cog's example and reveal myself to the Travas. They'll know I have my port and where I am, but I could find the information we need before they get to me."

I searched his expression. He was committed to sacrificing

himself. Good to know. "You said 'could find,' does that mean the information is there to retrieve or you think it might be?"

"The information is there, but I can't guarantee I'll access it before the Controllers sever my link."

Too big a risk right now. I thought about the problem. Even though I knew nothing about the computer and its security, I remembered a comment Logan had made about the uppers' computer system.

"Wait until I return before you attempt to retrieve the information. I need to check a few things and report for the hundred-hour assembly."

He agreed to wait and I hurried off. I had much to do in the hours remaining before assembly.

"Sure can," Logan said. A delighted smile spread across his face.

"No," Anne-Jade said at almost the same time.

Once again I had donned the shapeless overalls of the recycling-plant workers and joined the Tech Nos in sorting through a pile of clothing. We pulled buttons and cut zippers from the ruined garments before feeding them into Shredder. The device had a more technical name for how it recycled the threads, but the scrubs nicknamed everything.

"No as in he can't do it?" I asked Anne-Jade.

"No as in I won't let him. It's too dangerous. He'll be caught."

"We're going to be discovered anyway. Might as well go out with style," Logan said.

She scowled as Logan pouted, but by the tight set to Anne-Jade's shoulders I knew she wouldn't change her mind. A Pop Cop sauntered by and we concentrated on our work.

Her reaction didn't make sense. They had covered for Cog and told me about Zippy. Why was this different? I ran a tattered shirt through my fingers. The steady plink of buttons dropping into a bucket and clack of zippers kept time with my thoughts.

The answer was right in front of me in the movement of their hands. They worked as one, progressing through the pile of clothes without any signs of communication. Anne-Jade wasn't afraid he would be recycled, but that he would be recycled without her. They were a matched set.

I used logic. "If he doesn't help, Broken Man will go after the information anyway. He'll be arrested and interrogated, which will lead the Pop Cops to me and I'll lead them to you." I suppressed a shudder. The pain would have to be horrible for me to rat on them.

"Are you threatening me?" Anne-Jade thrust her scissors in my direction.

"No. I'm just stating the facts. We've come too far to back off now. If Broken Man's efforts fail, then you and Logan will be recycled without causing any damage."

Her arm dropped and she returned to cutting zippers. "When do you need him?"

"Right after assembly is over. Logan, meet me in the hall-way outside the care facility."

He flashed me a grin, but Anne-Jade kept her eyes on her work, ripping threads and seams with more force than needed. The sound of tearing cloth followed me as I left the plant.

I had a few more bits of unfinished business. Jacy's listening devices needed to be installed. Air duct number seventy-two was located above the fourth level. It didn't cross over Riley's room. In fact, it supplied air to two areas only. The main control room in Quad G4 and the Pop Cops headquarters and holding cells in Quad A4. Extra filters had been installed and a few special scrubbers.

Remembering the gas hissing from the canisters in Domotor's room, I guessed the extra precautions kept an enemy from sending airborne poisons through the vents.

The known ways into seventy-two were either through the vents in the actual rooms or at the air source. Since I doubted LC Karla would let me use her office to climb into the duct, I headed to the air plant in Quad I4. I could cut a hole into the shaft from the Gap, but the ducts weren't labeled and the effort to figure it out would consume more time than I had available.

I wore the air workers' plain white jumper, tucking my hair under the bump cap. The air filters and scrubbers were cleaned on a regular schedule. Between shifts only a few scrubs lingered to keep an eye on the equipment. I strode to a two-meter-high rectangular box as if I had an urgent purpose. A large air shaft entered the side of the container and another exited the other end. No one questioned me as I climbed the ladder to the top of the container and the access ports that allowed the scrubs to remove the filters, clean them and return them.

Lowering myself, I squeezed through the rows of filters. Soft and made of a cloth mesh, the bags trapped the dust particles in the air. A strong current pushed through the chamber. I tried hard not to damage the filters as I swam through them. On the intake side of the container, I climbed into the oversize trunk air shaft and followed it up to one of its branches—air shaft seventy-two.

Working my way through air filters and wire security screens, I reached the Pop Cops headquarters and placed a microphone near a vent.

I couldn't resist making a side trip to the holding cells. Risky, yes, but there could be a way to rescue Cog, I rationalized. When the covers on the vents turned into solid bars, I knew I had reached my destination. Slowing, I moved with care. Only a slight whisper of fabric sounded.

Harsh daylight streamed from below. Armed Pop Cops occupied the room. Desks and chairs with handcuffs littered the space, appearing to be a processing area for the inmates. Double doors festooned with locks filled the back wall.

Farther along the shaft the light changed into a muted yellow. The smells of sweat, blood and fear created an acidic stew. Taking shallow breaths, I peered into the dank cells. Black bars caged tiny areas only big enough for a bed and toilet. Although, calling the metal slab a bed was being generous. Three cells lined each side of the room with a short corridor between them. Cog was the sole occupant.

His bulk filled the slab and his feet dangled off the end. In the sickly half-light the raw and bleeding bruises on his face resembled rotten meat. His eyes were swollen shut and his breath rattled. I rested my forehead on the duct for a moment, trying to see past the fog of horror and guilt clouding my vision. Pressure built inside my skull and chest as if I would explode. I fought to muffle my sobs.

My fault. Retrieving those disks had been a lark. I didn't believe in Gateway, didn't care about the prophet. One mistake, letting the cover slip through my fingers, and Cog… I wanted to shy away from the vision, but I forced myself to face the image of Chomper crushing and pulping Cogon's lifeless body, and to hear the sound of splintering bones and the wet smack of bodily fluids. I let the consequence of my actions burn into my mind.

No way to change the past, I could only hope to affect the future before I met the same fate. For Cogon, and in Logan's words, I would inflict the maximum damage.

"Cog?" I whispered. When he didn't stir, I cupped my hands around my mouth and called louder. After the fourth try, he moved his head.

"Trella?" His voice rasped like a rusty hinge. "You caught?" He struggled to sit up with frantic haste.

"No. I'm in the air shaft above you."

He relaxed, resuming his prone position. "Good, 'cause I

can't break those bars to the duct to help you escape. So don't get caught."

"How are you—"

He waved his hands in a pushing motion. "No worries. Did you find Gateway yet?"

Despite being beaten, his confident tone astounded me. I squashed the honest reply between my molars and hedged. "Not yet."

"How soon?"

"Don't know."

"I hope I'm alive when it's opened. Just to see the look on the lieutenant commander's face."

My jaw ached as the Chomper vision flashed. "Cog, can I bring you anything?"

"No, but you can do something for me."

"Name it."

A harsh bark erupted from him, and, at first, I worried he was choking but then realized he was laughing. Between gasps he said, "And I...had...to *beg* you...to see Broken... Man. Wish...you were this...cooperative before."

"Cogon," I warned.

"Whew. Back to your old...self. I need you to plant Broken Man's clothes to help my alibi. Obviously, the Pop Cops haven't found him and they think he's moved to another hiding place. But after the next—" he drew in a deep breath "—next round of torture, I'm going to confess to killing him and I need evidence. I'm going to tell them I shoved his clothes into the space behind storage closet two-two-one in the care facility. Do you know where it is?"

I smiled at the memory of Cogon showing me his hidey-hole. "The one where you hid your...what did you call them?"

"Spirits."

"Now I remember. So called because they burned on the

way down and floated right to your head, making you feel as light as a ghost."

"And you believed me, too."

"Did not."

"Did, too. You used to follow me around the common room, making sure I didn't turn into a ghost."

"You have it all wrong. *You* followed *me*. And I'm the one who kept *you* from getting into trouble."

"Me? Who covered for *you* when you went exploring? Me. That's who! And I'm still protecting you."

The dagger of truth popped the warm bubble of memories. Cold reality rushed in, shocking me into the present.

A bang echoed through the cells, and a wedge of daylight sliced the yellow glow.

"Who're you talking to, scrub?" a man asked.

"The rats," Cog said.

The man's harsh laughter grated on my nerves. "Did they respond?"

"No."

"I'm not surprised. Rats wouldn't demean themselves by interacting with a low-life scrub."

"*You're* talking to me, Vinco. Does that make you worse than a rat?"

Vinco growled. "That's *Commander* Vinco, scrub. Since you're in such a chatty mood… Porter bring me my knife!"

There was a muttered reply. I strained to see Commander Vinco. I wanted to put a face to the man who hurt both Riley and Cog.

"Damn assembly. My *knife* will be talking to you on my next shift," Vinco said.

The white light shrank then disappeared with the slamming of the doors.

"Trella?" Cog pitched his voice low.

"Still here."

"You shouldn't be. Get going before you're marked tardy for assembly."

"But I need to hide Broken Man's stuff for you."

"You have time. The Pop Cops won't be looking for it until hour twelve."

His matter-of-fact tone about the exact time had an ominous ring. A cold unease crept up my spine. "How can you be so sure?"

"Vinco's next shift starts at hour ten. I can take a beating and I can endure most pain. But two hours of Vinco's knife is all I can bear."

The bell rang for the hundred-hour assembly as I climbed from the bag-filter's chamber. Damn. No time to change the stained and sweat-soaked uniform. I raced to my assembly station—the cafeteria—and ended up last in the short line. Only three scrubs between me and LC Karla. She leaned against a table, watching the check-in process. I wondered why she was here again.

My voice didn't waver when I repeated my stats, but my heart beat a faster rhythm when Karla eyed my work suit with a contemplative purse on her lips. I tried to sidle past her.

"Running late?" she asked.

"Sorry, sir." I stepped toward the dining room.

She blocked my way. "You weren't scheduled to work. What have you been doing during your off time?"

Her stare could have frozen the warmest heart. I blinked. Caught by surprise, my mind blanked.

"Hey, Trella," another scrub called. An older man with short gray hair and a stooped posture, he had gone through check-in just before me. "Thanks for helping with that clogged drain. Without your little hands, I don't know what we would have done."

"Anytime," I said, waving.

Karla snatched my hand and inspected my short fingernails. "No dirt under your nails?" She waited.

"I washed my hands, sir. They were in raw sewage."

She dropped my hand as if I were contagious and gestured for me to join the scrubs assembled in the cafeteria. I stood next to the man who had covered for me. As Karla pushed her way to the front, I leaned close and whispered my thanks.

"Anytime," he said, winking.

LC Karla climbed onto a table to address the crowd. "Citizens, welcome to the end-of-the-week celebration. Now begins week number 147,003." She scanned the scrubs. "I have good news. We have caught the man responsible for my officer's untimely recycling, and we will find Broken Man soon. However, if you know of anyone who may have helped hide Broken Man, you are to tell me immediately. Rewards for accurate information may result in promotion to the upper levels."

Absolute silence filled the room. All moisture evaporated from my mouth and gushed from my pores. I couldn't help glancing at the man beside me. Why didn't he raise his hand and tell the LC about lying for me? He didn't move. No one did.

LC Karla's body stiffened and she shook as if waves of pure anger pulsed off her. She glared at the crowd. "Fine, then you *all* will be interrogated. One at a time."

She relinquished her tabletop position to the ensign on duty. As he read the weekly announcements, murmurs circled the room. But the whispers held a timbre of outrage.

The man leaned over. "She's made a mistake." He met my gaze. "Whatever you're up to, do it quick. I think you'll be first on her interrogation list."

I listened to the rest of the ensign's message without hearing a word he said. My thoughts tumbled in circles, ending at the same point. I stifled the desire to jump on a tabletop and shout to the scrubs, "Don't get your hopes up!"

When the assembly was over, I bolted into the kitchen. Karla stood at the exit and I didn't want to remind her about me. If she caught me later, I could say I had needed to start my cleaning shift. True to a point.

No Pop Cops had arrived yet, and the kitchen scrubs took my presence in stride, preparing food for the next meal. I could reach the air vent above the countertop, but would have difficulty getting inside. Scanning the kitchen, I searched for a stool to stand on.

A thud sounded behind me and I turned. On the counter rested a stepladder. The type with only a few rungs and used to reach into high cabinets. Without delay, I climbed on the counter and up the ladder.

"Thanks!" I called as I pulled myself into the air shaft. The ladder was gone by the time I closed the vent's cover. I traveled through the shaft to the hallway outside the care facility in Sector H2. Once there, I glanced down. A stream of scrubs heading toward their work assignments flowed below me. I waited a few minutes then dropped down on the stragglers.

No curses. No taunts. I could get used to it. Although if I failed to help the scrubs, the verbal abuse would resume. I laughed. If I failed, the scrubs would be the least of my worries.

Logan paced the hallway, biting a nail. I scanned the hallway to make sure no Pop Cops lingered nearby. He stopped when he saw me. I pulled his hand down.

"Try not to look so nervous," I said. "How do you manage to work on Zippy and the other technology without giving yourself away?"

"Anne-Jade. She has nerves of glass. It has to be pretty hot for her to melt."

"We'll be out of sight soon." I guided him to a small door near the care facility. Taking his decoder from my tool belt, I whispered, "Keep an eye out." Then I placed the device near the door's lock, pressing the button.

"Anne-Jade? What are you doing here?" Logan asked.

I looked over my shoulder. Barefooted, Anne-Jade wore a skintight dark blue work uniform. Her thick hair had been wrestled into a single braid.

"I need Trella's birth week and barrack number," she said.

"Why?" Logan asked.

"Good idea," I said, rattling off my stats. "I'm supposed to be in—"

"Shaft one-eleven. Got it." She hurried off.

I reviewed my cleaning schedule in my mind—two water pipes and a bunch of air ducts on level one. Nothing too challenging for her.

The decoder had finished. I unlocked the door and pulled Logan into a small storage room filled with stacks of linen diapers. Closing the door, I switched on my light. Situated under the shelves was a heating vent. My fellow scrubs didn't bat an eye when I wormed into the heating system, but Logan's presence would draw unwanted attention. I had thought ahead, remembering this closet. However I had failed to find a solution for missing my shift, hoping we would be done in time for me finish it. But Anne-Jade figured it out.

"Oh," Logan said. His puzzled expression smoothed. "She's pretending to be you so the Pop Cops won't be suspicious. Smart!"

"So are you," I said.

"Not that kind of smart."

"There's another kind?"

"Oh, yeah. I know the tech stuff, but she's the one who disguises it. The Pop Cops walk by our stuff all the time and don't know it's there. She's the one who figures out what we can take from the recycling plant and when. She's the one who insisted we not tell the other Tech Nos about us."

"That is smart," I agreed. Pulling the vent cover down, I pointed. "Follow me, it's not far. Close the vent when you're through, and keep quiet. Voices carry in there."

He nodded and then gnawed on a fingernail. I squirmed into the vent and moved ahead to give Logan room. My sore forearms protested. From all the time spent in the ducts, I would develop calluses on my elbows and wrists. How would I explain them to LC Karla?

The trip to Domotor's room took twice as long as usual. Logan's slight build fit into the shaft, but his arm muscles weren't used to pulling his weight. When we finally entered the hideout, Domotor woke with a jerk. He had been sleeping on the couch. He pushed himself into a sitting position and studied Logan in alarm.

"I hope he is one of the 'few things' you needed to check on. And not a Pop Cop in disguise?" he asked me.

"Yes. Logan's here to see if he can help with the computer system."

"Unless he's a technological wizard, he—"

Logan spotted the computer and wasted no time. He settled before the monitor. I helped Domotor into his chair and wheeled him closer to Logan.

The Tech No squealed in delight. His fingers flew over the keyboard. "You have a port!" He grinned.

"Yes, but you can't—"

"I know stealth mode. I'll be like a ghost. What are you trying to do?"

Domotor launched into technical double-talk. Logan's eyes lit with the challenge. The prophet nodded and made impressed noises as they worked. I settled on the couch. My desire to interrupt to inquire about clothes for Cog's ruse warred with my desire for sleep. I tried to remember the last time I slept. The effort needed to calculate proved too much for my exhausted brain, so I rested my head on the couch's arm.

★ ★ ★

"…need an upper computer to access the data," Logan said.

I sat up and rubbed my eyes. The vision of Logan and Domotor peering at me with twin concerned expressions failed to dissipate.

"What happened?" I asked.

"We figured out where the information is," Domotor said. His demeanor didn't match his words. "But…"

"It can only be accessed from a computer on the upper levels." He gave me a few seconds to let the news sink in. "Can you get Logan to level four?"

"Doesn't he need a port?" I asked.

"Not anymore." Logan smiled with smug satisfaction. "I set up my own account; all I need is a password and the right connection."

"Why won't it work here?"

Logan tried to describe the inhibitor function on a lower-level computer. I lost him after the second word.

Domotor thankfully interrupted. "Five minutes is all he would need. Can you do it, Trell?"

Could I? Crawling through heating vents was easier than climbing to another level. I doubted Logan had the upper-body strength needed to pull himself up the chains. Unless… We could ride on top of the lift. But where would we find an unoccupied computer and, if we did find one, then how long would it remain unoccupied?

"I need a few hours to think about it."

"Perhaps Riley could help," Domotor said. "I'm sure he would know where to find a computer."

"I don't think we should involve him," I said.

"Who's Riley?" Logan asked.

"It's better you don't know." Too many knew about us already. Our chances of getting caught increased with each new person. Maximum damage, I chanted in my mind.

"He's proven himself trustworthy. This is too important to leave to chance," Domotor said.

I grumbled even though he was right.

"We'd better go. I don't want to be late for my shift," Logan said.

His words reminded me to ask Domotor about his clothes.

"Sure, take what you need."

When I returned from his room with the pants and shirt he had worn the day we had rescued him, Logan grabbed the shirt. He jerked off the top button. I remembered the microphone.

"Don't want to lose this," he said, then handed me the disks. "We don't need these, though."

I looked at Domotor. He avoided my gaze and shifted in his chair as if searching for a more comfortable position. Waiting, I tapped the disks—the irresistible bait that lured me on this fool's errand—against my legs.

Eventually, he gave me a sheepish grin. "The programs on them are worthless *now*. If I could have used them *before* I was caught, they would have worked."

"But they can help Cog," Logan said.

They would delay the inevitable. I pushed those morbid thoughts away. "It's better than nothing."

Hour ten and Logan had reported to his shift on time, the clothes and disks had been hidden in the storage closet and I had to figure a way to get Logan to level four. I stopped by the laundry room. All the clothes for Inside were washed here. Scrubs rolled big white canvas bins to transport piles of clean and dirty garments. Bins also stood under the chutes to collect the uniforms and clothes from the upper levels.

Along the left side wall rested stacks of clean uniforms for the scrubs. Each pile was specific to a different work area and was sorted by size. The blue color of the pipe scrubs seemed bright compared to the rest. Laundry and kitchen scrubs wore the same white uniform.

Stealing scrubs' clothes was easy. A steady stream of people headed to and away from the stacks and no one cared if you picked up one or a hundred. The uppers' clothes, though, were placed in marked bins—one per family. Pop Cops kept a close watch over them.

After a circuit around the room, I left knowing I would be unable to borrow a few uppers' garments from the bins. However, if I wasn't picky, I could intercept a few items as they traveled down the chutes.

I rigged a net in one of the shafts. Clogs in the chutes were rare, but not unheard of. Hopefully, I'd catch a Logan-sized disguise.

My next problem would be harder to solve. Climbing to Riley's room on level four, I reviewed my options for finding a computer terminal. I could spy on one of the upper's suites. Keeping track of their comings and goings, I could determine when the suite would be empty. But how long would it take? And, working my own shifts, I would only have half the picture.

Bluelight shone through the vent into Riley's room. When I was certain it was empty, I dropped through the vent and onto the couch. The daylights turned on automatically and I jumped to my feet in surprise—it had never happened before.

I found the tiny motion detector. Its sensor was aimed at the couch, and the simple device had been wired to the light switch. Everything else appeared to be the same. The ladder leaned against a side wall, and the furniture remained in place. A moment passed and nothing happened. I checked under the couch. Zippy looked undisturbed in his hiding spot.

I relaxed. Riley had spent time fixing the place up. Wandering around the room, I found a few of his possessions. A broken keyboard with a tangle of wires streaming from under it, a chewed marker, a wipe board with a technical diagram of circuits drawn on it and a stuffed sheep. Not made with the skin of a real sheep, but the wool was genuinely fuzzy and soft, and the rest had been constructed of cloth. A child's toy. And from its worn and threadbare appearance, I knew it was well loved.

I picked the sheep up and stroked its wool. The care facility had few toys for the children to share. Most of our time in the facility had been spent training for our future jobs. Cleaning trolls instead of dolls, and engines to take apart and repair. The Care Mothers evaluated us and decided our careers based on our aptitudes.

The memory of Cog racing Jacy to see who could rebuild an engine first caused me to smile. Cog loved to get his hands dirty and he probably would have gotten the maintenance job even if he hadn't grown so big. My tendency to explore the ducts also made my Care Mother's job easy in placing me. I didn't have the patience to be a Care Mother or a gardener for hydroponics.

Computer time had dominated our learning hours. Teaching stories to read, mathematics to learn, our society's customs and expectations, and a basic knowledge of the physical machinery and how our world worked had all been the main focus of learning. According to Riley, the information we learned had been Pop Cop propaganda. I wondered just how much was accurate.

A click sounded behind me. I spun, reaching for my tool belt. Riley slipped into the room and closed the door without making any more noise. He wore his headset and work uniform.

He raised an eyebrow at my defensive posture. "I see you found Sheepy."

"Sheepy?" I replaced the toy. "That's not a very original name."

He shrugged. "I was three hundred weeks old when I got him and his mother as a present."

"What's her name?"

He grinned. "Mama Sheepy."

I laughed.

"You *do* know how to smile and laugh," he said. "I was beginning to worry."

Sobering, I searched his expression. "Worry about what?"

"That you had no joy in your heart."

What an odd statement. "What do you mean?" I demanded.

"I put myself at considerable risk helping you and it's good to know you can...that you're not...that you have..." He slapped his hands to his face and then dropped them as if in surrender. "I always say the wrong thing around you. Look, can we start over?"

"Over?"

"Yes. Over. Wipe the board clean."

"But I would have to go back to hating you and not trusting you," I said.

"Oh, well, don't do that." He paused and chewed his lip. "Does that mean you like and trust me now?"

"I don't hate you."

"Trust?"

"The debate is ongoing."

"You're giving me squat. You know that, don't you?"

I suppressed a grin, but couldn't keep a straight face. "Yes."

He shook his head. "Okay. We won't wipe the board clean, but how about we ignore all our previous misconceptions and biases about each other and start as two regular people who *don't* hate each other. Agreed?"

"Agreed."

"Great. Hi, I'm Riley Narelle Ashon and this is Sheepy Narelle

Ashon." He picked up his stuff toy and waved the sheep's paw at me. Then he held out his hand to me. "And you are…?"

I grasped his hand, marveling at the feel of his smooth skin. "Trella Garrard Sanchia."

twelve

The name had popped from my mouth without thought. I was sure Riley's shocked expression mirrored my own. He let go of my hand.

"How do you know?" he asked, recovering faster than I did.

I waved a hand as if I could erase my words from the air. No luck. They hung in the thick silence between us. I pulled my uniform away from my chest. The fabric peeled off my sweaty skin. Why was this room so hot?

He squinted at me, his demeanor stiff and cold. "Are you a spy?"

"No. Domotor told me the names, but I don't care."

"I see." His tone implied otherwise.

"Look. I'm just a stupid scrub. Domotor wanted me to help him and he offered to give me information on my birth parents as a bribe. Except I don't care who they are or why they abandoned me in the lower levels. I'm helping him for my friend Cog. End of discussion."

Understanding lit his eyes and another emotion softened his

posture. When I realized he pitied me, I crossed my arms over my chest to keep myself from punching Riley in the face.

"Since we already did a partial board-ectomy, let's just move on. What do you say, Sheepy?" Riley pressed his nose against the sheep's as if communicating with the stuffed toy telepathically. He pursed his lips and nodded. "Sheepy says he's hungry." He quirked a smile at me. "Sorry. Oh…wait." Once again, Riley stared at his toy. "Sheepy also says he doesn't believe you're a stupid scrub. In fact, he thinks you're quite smart and if you say otherwise, he'll bite you on the leg."

Amused, I huffed in mock outrage. "Tell Sheepy that if he bites me on the leg, I'll send Zippy after him."

"Zippy?"

"My little cleaning troll. He has a nasty habit of shredding dust bunnies."

He laughed. "Sheepy's not going to back down. He meant what he said." All humor evaporated from Riley. He pressed fingers into his right temple, wincing in pain. "My break's over. I need to return to my station." He met my gaze. "Did you come here for a reason?"

"Yes. I need help…" How should I phrase the request?

"Name it."

I stared at him. He used the exact same words I had when talking to Cog. Did he overhear us?

"What? Did you expect me to say no?" His confusion seemed genuine.

"I…"

"I have to go."

I told him about needing a computer, but didn't mention Logan's name. "Preferably one located in an isolated area."

"I'll see what I can do, and let you know during my next shift." He strode to the door.

"How?"

He paused with his hand on the knob. "Come to our room,

I'll try and schedule my break time to coincide with your visit again, but you might have to wait a bit."

"You knew I was here?"

"Yes."

"How?"

He gave me a mischievous smile. "Sheepy told me."

On my way back to level two, I checked to see what I had netted in the laundry chute. A couple shirts, three pants, a handful of undergarments and a Pop Cop's uniform. I debated about the uniform as I sent the rest down. It could be a great disguise, but it also could be trouble. Did the Pop Cops keep track of their uniforms? Did they all recognize each other by sight? If a person wore a white kitchen uniform, I wouldn't know if they were scrub or spy. Postponing my decision, I rerigged the net and left the uniform within its black web.

I stopped at the cafeteria, pushing my way through the miasma of so many people gathered together. When I reached the serving scrub who had mentioned the clogged air shaft, I paused.

"Your problem is fixed," I said.

He nodded.

"Thanks."

He made eye contact and resumed filling the bowls with food. But he squared his shoulders, stood a little straighter and the barest hint of a smile settled on his face. The image of his smile hovered in my mind. Even though we had a limited variety of food, the kitchen scrubs worked hard to cook meals for the rest of us.

Cogon had always thanked the servers, calling them by name as he moved through the line. I remembered being annoyed and impatient with him as he held up the rest of us who waited. Considering Cog's present situation, I regretted every harsh word I'd said to him.

I fought my way around filled tables, searching for a seat. Jacy and his buddies occupied an entire table. When I glanced back at them, Jacy patted the vacant seat next to him. Funny. There hadn't been an empty one there a second before.

Understanding the hint didn't mean I would take the hint, I hesitated, but couldn't produce a good reason to avoid him. I sat next to him.

"The microphones are working well. Thanks," Jacy said.

"No problem." I shoved a spoonful of green bean casserole into my mouth.

"We've already gotten a few nuggets of useful intelligence. Do you think you could install a few more?" His casual tone didn't match the intensity in his eyes.

"Where?"

"Over the Control Room and in the lifts."

"Monitoring Pop Cops not enough?"

His gaze slid over the mass of scrubs. I copied him, trying to see the people through his viewpoint. Clusters of miserable expressions dominated, but a few smiles and a couple of laughing faces stood out from the crowd.

"No. Not enough at all," he said. "Can you do it?"

"Sure." I ate a few more scoops of casserole. When I realized I hadn't even tasted the food, I slowed down and made a conscious effort to savor it. Not bad. Did the cooks change the recipe?

"What do you want in return?" he asked.

Interesting question. He dealt in information. "How about you tell me if you hear anything I would consider important through those microphones?"

"Deal. In fact, I'll start now. I heard Cog confessed to killing Broken Man and dismembering him." Jacy watched my expression. "Gruesome, I agree. And despite the evidence the Pop Cops found, I don't believe Cog is capable of harming anyone." He gestured to the scrubs around us. "And neither do they. *If* Cog killed the Pop Cop, we all know it had to be an accident."

He waited, but I wasn't going to confirm nor deny his theory.

"Cog has taken the blame for everything. However, Lieutenant Commander Karla knows Cog is too big to fit into the air shaft above Broken Man's room, and she's determined to find the scrub who started this whole mess." Jacy stared at me. "And do you know what Cogon did then?"

Icy fingers of dread clutched my heart. "No."

"He saved your ass. Again. He told Karla that Roddie was in the air shaft."

Roddie? I spun the name around my mind, but failed to recognize him. "A friend of Cog's?"

"You don't know who he is?" Jacy's face creased as if he smelled a rotten stench.

"Should I?"

"You damn well should! He was the man who Karla kill-zapped at assembly 147,002. He was recycled because of you and you don't even know his name!"

Stunned, I lost the ability to even form a reply. He was right—when he…Roddie had been kill-zapped, all I had worried about was my own skin. Karla had claimed he lied to her, but I didn't know why he had lied.

Jacy answered my question before I could voice it. "Roddie told LC Karla Broken Man hid in the recycling plant to help Cog. When the Pop Cops discovered the ruse…well you know what Karla did. But Cog told Karla she had been too hasty in kill-zapping Roddie and he was in on the plan from the beginning." Jacy leaned closer to me. "Karla didn't want to believe the explanation. Too easy, she said. But her boss ordered her to close the case. So you…" He jabbed me in the shoulder with a stiff finger. "You are clear. Unless you do something stupid, you're no longer a suspect."

He grabbed his tray and stood. "I hope you're worth the effort. I hope you manage to do something with all of this, because as a human being, you're worthless." Walking away with his cronies in tow, Jacy didn't look back.

The seats at the table remained empty as I moved the food around my plate, building heaps and creating designs out of the cold vestiges of my casserole. The bell sounded for the new work shift, jarring me from my morbid thoughts.

I hurried to my assigned ducts and went through the motions. Insert cleaning troll, turn on and follow. Turn off troll, remove and lug to the next shaft. Gratitude to Cog for taking the heat off me warred with Jacy's admonishments. Worthless might be the right word for me. Events had spun beyond my control. I relied on Logan and Riley to reach the next step.

I dragged the troll to the cleaning closet when my shift ended. Every muscle in my body ached and my head felt as if it were stuffed with wet towels. I wanted to find a warm spot and sleep, but Riley worked the odd-hour shift and I needed to climb to our room.

Our room. I stifled a laugh. Riley's name, not mine for where we met. The trip was a hard slog. Bluelight from the room shone through the vents and, after checking for ambushes, I dropped to the couch. White daylights switched on. My tired brain connected the dots and linked the motion sensor with Riley's precognitive knowledge of my arrival. Too bad. I liked his explanation better.

After scanning the room, the only change of note was the presence of Mama Sheepy. A twin of Sheepy except for her larger size. He rested in the space under her belly and between her legs, protected and safe. Mama Sheepy's wool was flat in the middle as if she had been used as a pillow. An image of a young Riley with his black hair mussed, sleeping on Mama while clutching Sheepy formed in my head. I braced for a stab of jealousy, but I couldn't produce the emotion. Instead, I kept the pleasant image in my mind as I carried the sheep family to the couch.

Squirming into a comfortable position, I waited for Riley. I played with the sheep. Not caring that I had lost it and gone soft. Not caring about Gateway. Not caring about what might happen the rest of the week. I enjoyed the moment.

"Trella."

His voice pierced the bubble of my dream. Cold reality replaced the feelings of warmth and safety. I blinked awake. Luckily Riley hovered over me and not a Pop Cop. Falling asleep up here was deadly. I wanted to blame the couch, but knew my erratic snatches of sleep were to blame.

He straightened with a smile on his face. "Sheepy told me to let you alone, but I only have thirty minutes."

His stuffed toys were still clutched in my hands. I sat and placed them on the cushion next to me. Riley settled on the opposite end. I smoothed my hair and wondered how long he had been here before waking me.

"I've been searching for a computer terminal, but every one up here is either in constant use or located in a populated area. The only option left is for you to use the terminal in my room." He held up a hand, stopping my protests. "My father works even shifts. You can come during the next one."

"What about the rest of your family?"

An odd half-flinch creased his face for a second. "He's all I have, so no problem there."

"What happens if the Controllers find out we used your computer?"

"As long as you don't use my port, there is no way to prove I'm involved."

"It's still a big risk."

"So is this." Riley gestured to me and him.

"Good point." I considered his offer. "Where is your suite located?"

"Sector E4."

I waited for the number, but he stared at the wall as if making mental calculations. "What's your—"

"Are you going to tell me why you need access to the computer?"

"No."

"You still don't trust me." He stated it as a matter of fact, but his arm muscles bulged as he pressed his palms into his legs.

I looked at Sheepy and his mother lying between us. The information about the uppers circled in my mind. Coddled, pampered and privileged had been the line. Yet it missed the mark with Riley. "I trust you."

"Then why won't you confide in me?"

"Partly for damage control and for selfish reasons."

"We're not accepting cryptic and vague answers right now. More detail, please."

"We?" I asked.

He pointed to the sheep. I couldn't help smiling. Such a stupid little toy, yet I admitted he filled the missing gaps deep within me. Picking up Sheepy, I held him close to my face. He was easier to talk to than Riley. "Damage control is to minimize the number of people who could expose this whole adventure. The selfish reasons are mine. Eventually, I'll be caught and fed to Chomper. I'm hoping to cause a lot of trouble before then, and I hope I can convince the Pop Cops you were just a dupe. Someone I used and who didn't know what was going on. I'm already responsible for sending one person to Chomper and another..." I swallowed as a shudder of guilt and horror swept through me. "It's only a matter of time before he is sent. Don't you see, Sheepy? I don't want anyone else to be recycled because of me."

Silence stretched, but I kept my gaze on the sheep, avoiding Riley's expression. I couldn't face his censure.

"I didn't know you were a Trava," Riley said.

"What?" I glanced at him. His eyebrows hovered midway between his eyes and hairline in almost thoughtful surprise.

"The Trava family decides who is fed to Chomper. I hadn't realized you were a part of them."

"That's too easy. I can't blame them. The Travas set the rules and carry out the punishments. My actions caused another to break the rules."

"Oh. So you forced this person?"

"No, but—"

"But what? I'm trying to understand how you're responsible. Is the blame all yours? My father told me the Travas aren't supposed to be setting the rules—that it should be a Committee of all the families. The rules themselves are suspect. And there is also a thing called free will. I had a choice back in Karla's office. You never asked me not to tell. I decided to help you instead. Are you responsible for my extra duty? No. I am."

"You can twist the argument any way."

"Exactly. You can shoulder all the blame and become a martyr. Provided anyone knows what or who you're martyring for. Or you can accept that some things are important enough to fight for and realize there will be sacrifices along the way." He peered into my eyes. "I've assumed this is one of those important fights. An effort to regain some of the freedoms we all lost. I'm well aware of the danger, but am still committed to helping you. You trust me and I need to trust you. So let's take it to the next step. Tell me why you need access to an upper computer."

I debated. If I told him about Gateway, he might think I was delusional. Yet he risked his life for me. "We're hoping to find a way to circumvent the Controllers' security measures in the network so we can access a few files and retrieve critical information."

"Which information?"

"About how the various mechanical systems are set up and how to alter them without letting the Controllers know." So I omitted a few facts. At least I wasn't lying.

He relaxed. "See? That wasn't so hard." He stood and pulled a stack of clothes from underneath the couch. "I've borrowed a training uniform for you." Riley gestured for me to stand and held the uniform against me. "Looks like it will fit."

His knuckles touched my shoulders and a ripple of warmth spread through my body.

Riley continued to study me. He tossed the uniform over one arm and reached for my hair. More than a few strands had escaped my braid. He smoothed them next to my face. "Leave your hair down. It makes you look younger." His fingers brushed my jaw.

I suppress the sudden desire to press his hand against my cheek. "Younger?"

"You're supposed to be a student."

"We'll be in your suite. Are you expecting visitors?"

"No. But there's a chance someone might come, and I'd have a harder time explaining why two scrubs were in my room."

"Good point."

As he rummaged through the pile of clothes, I tugged the rest of my hair from the braid. Combing my fingers through it, I separated it into three sections.

"Don't," Riley said.

"Why?"

He didn't answer. He pushed my hands away and drew my hair over my shoulders. Stepping back, he cocked his head as if contemplating. "You look so stern and serious with your hair tied back." He gestured. "That's more like the Trella I first met. But it's not quite…right." He mussed up my hair, pulling a few strands over my face. "Ah-ha! Perfect!"

I shot him a withering look.

His smile widened. "Even better. It's like I've been transported back in time."

"Ha. Ha. Funny," I said in a flat tone. Sweeping the hair from my face, I tucked it behind my ears. "Do you have a disguise for my companion?" I asked, trying to return to the point of my visit.

"I didn't know who you were bringing along, so I found a basic coverall worn by the maintenance workers. It's one-size-fits-all and we're used to seeing the crew with rolled up sleeves and pant legs."

He handed me the clothes. The fabric on the student's garment had the same coarse and durable weave as the jumpers worn by the lower kids in the care facility.

A pained expression crossed his face. "Break's over. I'm in three-six-ninety-five in Sector E4. Will you be able to find it?"

"Yes."

"When?"

I calculated how much time I needed to find Logan and lead him to level four. I hoped Anne-Jade would cover my shift again. "Around hour forty-two."

"See you then." He slipped from the room.

I waited a moment just in case an upper saw him leaving the room and investigated. Diving behind the couch probably wouldn't be the best hiding place, but it was better than being caught halfway inside the air duct. After enough time elapsed, I set the ladder under the vent. But before I climbed, I snuggled Sheepy back in his protective spot under Mama Sheepy.

On my way to find Logan, one of Jacy's guys bumped into me. He slipped me two listening devices without a word and ambled on his way. Laughter echoed through the hallways and people lingered in small groups, talking. The tension in the lower levels had eased.

After a few moments, I realized why. The number of Pop Cops patrolling the area had dropped to normal. As I hurried to Logan's barrack, scrubs tried to catch my gaze. A few smiled at me with hope shining in their eyes and others cocked an eyebrow with a questioning look.

For the first time, I was the center of attention. Everyone watched me as if I were a bomb. Would I explode and cause a disaster or would I pop and cause a miracle? The pressure of their stares squeezed my chest until my lungs wheezed with the effort to draw a breath.

Pop Cop spies still worked among us. It amazed me that they hadn't discovered my involvement. Perhaps Karla waited for me to make a mistake. Right now she had no evidence I was involved in Broken Man's disappearance, but if she stalked me for a few weeks, she would eventually catch me breaking the rules. Hard to believe, but breathing became more difficult, and I wished for simpler weeks. My lonely life in the pipes seemed a distant and pleasant memory.

I met Logan and Anne-Jade as they entered the barrack. Odd-hour shifts had finished and even would begin soon.

Logan's light brown eyes sparkled. "Time to play?"

Anne-Jade shot him a sour look.

"Meet me in corridor A2-5 in one hour," I told him. "Anne-Jade, can you cover my shift?"

"Sure." She met my gaze. "Please don't let anything happen to him."

"I'll try." My throat felt hot and dry.

"Hey," Logan said. "I'm a grown man. I can take care of myself."

"Are you kidding?" Anne-Jade shot back. "If it wasn't for me, you'd be late for everything. Too busy playing with your toys."

I left. The sounds of their mock argument followed me from the barracks. One of Jacy's men waited in the hallway. He fell into step beside me.

"Boss wants to see you," he said.

"When?"

"Now."

"I can't. My shift's starting. Tell him I'll stop by later."

He wrapped his strong fingers around my right elbow. "You'll see him now." He pulled me along.

I squawked in protest, but he stared straight ahead. Twice my size, I knew I couldn't pry his grip off, but I could jab him with a screwdriver. My left hand closed on the tool.

"I wouldn't do it," he said. "It would…annoy me."

Interesting choice of words. I rationalized my cowardice and decided to wait. After all, there was no sense making a scene.

Jacy held court in his corner of Sector D1's barrack. At least six unhappy expressions turned to me as my companion delivered me to his boss. My worry switched from annoying the man clamped on my elbow to Jacy's livid face.

"I knew it would happen eventually," Jacy said. The muscles along his arms quivered and his eyes held a wild shine. "I just wasn't…prepared." He swallowed and his anger eased a bit.

"What happened?" I braced for the answer.

"I want to blame you, but I can't." He looked away.

My guard's fingers dug into my skin and I yelped.

Jacy's attention snapped back to me. This time grief lined his eyes. "Cogon's been scheduled for execution."

thirteen

His words sliced through my heart, cutting it into little pathetic pieces. I understood how he could feel unprepared. The knowledge that the Pop Cops would recycle Cog had been trapped deep within me and ignored. I planned to deal with it later or, better yet, hoped it would disappear altogether.

"When?" I asked.

"Hour ninety-nine. They plan to walk him down to Chomper's Lair and kill-zap him there." Outrage filled Jacy's voice. "They figured it would be easier than lugging his body down there. The timing is so Lieutenant Commander Karla can use his execution to lecture us during the hundred-hour assembly on the consequences of disobeying the Pop Cops."

I did the math. Fifty-eight hours left.

"If what you're doing can help Cog, you'd better do it quick," Jacy said.

"I can't do anything with a broken arm."

He nodded and the big guy released my elbow. I rubbed the joint and turned away.

"Trella," Jacy called.

"What?" I almost growled at him.

"Let me know if you need anything. Anything at all."

It was a generous offer, considering the last time we conversed he had called me worthless. "Got it."

With my emotions spinning, I hurried to meet Logan. I walked right past my turn and had to stop. Distractions would be dangerous, and all our efforts would be for nothing if we were caught before accessing the computer. I squashed my fear and worries into a small metal box and dropped in the shattered remains of my heart for good measure. Locked with an obnoxiously big lock, I pushed the container into a far corner of my thoughts.

Focused and almost robotic, I marched toward corridor A2-5. Logan fidgeted and paced, trying to appear nonchalant, but failing miserably. At least he wasn't chewing his nails.

I led him to the door of the maintenance room next to Quad A's lift. While he watched the hall, I opened the door's lock. Memories of Cog and I hiding Broken Man in a laundry bin in this room threatened to overwhelm me. I clamped down on the feeling. No emotions allowed. We slipped inside and locked the door.

Pushing the air vent open, I pulled out a bundle. "Here, put this on." I handed Logan the coveralls Riley had given me. While he dressed, I donned the student's uniform. The black jumper with silver piping along the pants and sleeves sagged around my waist, but I cinched it tight with the belt.

When he was ready, I climbed into the air shaft and helped Logan inside.

"It's bigger than the heating vent," he said.

"Sounds still carry, and I'm about to show you a place only I know about. You can't tell anyone. Not even Anne-Jade. Promise me?"

"Ooh. Sounds like fun. Of course, I promise."

I slid through the shaft, stopped under the near-invisible hatch and pushed it open. Logan pressed a hand to his mouth to smother his cry of surprise. Turning on my light, I climbed into the meter-and-a-half-high space and moved aside so Logan could join me. He stared at his surroundings while I closed the hatch.

"What is this place?" he asked in a whisper.

I shrugged. "I call it the Gap. There's one between each level."

"Wow. What's it used for?"

I gestured around. "Space for the pipes and wires. I think everyone's forgotten about it. I can only get in here through one near-invisible hatch on each level. Come on, but crawl quietly." I hurried toward the lift. The easiest way to get Logan up to the fourth level was by riding on top of the lift.

A meter-high metal barrier divided the Gap from where the lift cut through the four floors of Inside. From the inside of the lift, it appeared the shaft was solid, but each level had a half-meter opening into the Gap. I pulled my extendable mirror from my tool belt. Shining the light in the shaft, I used the mirror. The lift was on the third level.

"When the lift comes down to our level, we don't have much time but we need to quietly move onto the roof and stay there until we reach the top," I said.

"What happens at the top?" Logan bit his thumbnail.

"We climb into the Gap before the lift descends."

Logan stared, and nibbled on his nails. If he were a computer, he would be making the rumbling crunching noise that meant it was calculating.

"Once we're on, do we have to wait until an upper wants to go to level four?" he asked.

"No. Once it's down, there are override controls on the roof."

Logan shivered as we waited. "It's cold here. I wonder why

there is all this extra room. Does the Gap run the entire length of Inside?"

I explained how each level was connected by steel I-beams to the Wall.

"How about under the lower level, is there a Gap there?" he asked.

"Yes. All the levels are surrounded by Gaps."

"What's beyond the Gaps on the sides?"

"The Walls of Inside."

He considered. "What do the Walls feel like?"

"There're covered with insulating foam."

"I meant temperature. Hot or cold?"

"Oh. The foam's room temperature, but the few places where there isn't foam, it's ice-cold."

He grinned. "Have you pressed your ear to it?"

I admitted I tried to listen for sounds from the other side. "I heard nothing besides the Hum." Produced by the machinery, the Hum was a constant background noise. It seemed like Inside's breath, and most scrubs no longer noticed the Hum.

"Too bad."

Eventually the lift passed with a chilly blast of air. We scrambled over the barrier, but landed with care on the lift's roof. I pressed the override button for the fourth level. I didn't think it would concern the occupants too much. The Pop Cops always complained about the lift's odd quirks.

Voices reached us from below, but they were indistinguishable. I put a finger to my lips as Logan's eyes flew wide when the lift ascended. It moved fast and in a handful of seconds we reached the top. I waved Logan on. In his haste, he fell with a grunt and a bang over the barrier into the fourth-level Gap.

We halted, listening for sounds of discovery. Nothing but the hiss of the lift's door shutting. I grabbed the edge of the barrier and pulled until my hips rested on it. The lift dropped away, leaving my legs dangling. Logan scooted back and I joined him on solid ground.

After taking a moment to recover, I led him through the maze of pipes and ductwork to the hatch. Finding the hatches the first time had been difficult. I'd spent hours exploring each Gap for the near-invisible hatch. Grinning, I remembered how disappointed I had been when I found the last one. The search had provided me with a challenge unlike my prior week-to-week pointless existence.

When we reached it, I whispered in Logan's ear, "No talking, no sounds at all from now on. Got it?"

"Yes."

The fourth-level hatch opened into air duct number fifteen, which crossed over the giant water storage tanks in Sector H4 before cutting through the uppers' rooms in Sector E4. I counted the suites, but then realized I didn't need to as I felt Riley's impatience through his air vent before seeing his worried face staring at the ceiling.

Under the vent, he had a stepladder set up on a table. Removing the cover, I slid my legs out. "Feet first," I said to Logan before lowering myself down.

Riley hurried to put the ladder away after Logan had reached the floor. We stood in the middle of a small living area. Couch, two chairs and one low table decorated the room. The two men eyed each other.

"It's safer if I don't introduce you," I said into the uncomfortable silence.

"He's a scrub," Riley said.

"So?" I shot back.

"He doesn't have a port and can't access the computer network."

Logan smirked. "Don't need a port. Where's your terminal?"

Riley failed to look reassured but opened a metal curtain

just like the one in Broken Man's hideout. He pulled over one of the chairs and gestured for Logan to take a seat.

"What about your port?" I asked. "If you're too close—"

"Took it out and put it in a metal box." Riley rubbed his right jaw as if he were unused to having it missing.

Logan wasted no time. His fingers flew over the keyboard. "This is going to take a while. I have to distract the Controllers and take a circuitous route in. Don't want anyone to know I'm in here." He flashed us a wild grin.

Riley and I stood next to each other, looking over Logan's shoulder. The strange symbols popping up on the screen meant nothing to me. Riley, though, frowned. Time to distract him.

"How about a tour?" I asked. "I've never actually been inside an upper's suite."

He turned his displeasure on me. "Really? But you've spied on them from above?"

For a moment, I wished for the goofy Riley. The one who mussed my hair and communicated telepathically with stuffed sheep. "I don't spy on anyone. I avoid the living areas, they're too dangerous. The places I've been on level four are the store-room and Karla's office." And the holding cells, but I didn't think it would be wise to tell him. I pointed to a half-open door on the opposite wall. "Is that a bedroom?"

Still unhappy, Riley showed me his room. The tiny interior had two beds with a table between them and two desks. A few metal sculptures were propped against the light blue walls, and circuit boards littered the one desk, the other was neat. Same with the beds, one was made, the other was heaped with blankets.

He followed my gaze. "I share the room with my father. He's always harping on me to make the bed and clean up my stuff."

No other items decorated the space. "Where's Dada Sheepy?" I asked.

A half smile flicked on his lips before sadness dragged it down. "With my brother." Turning away, he strode into the living room and opened the door next to Logan. "Standard bathroom." He waved at the remaining door. "Suite entrance."

Except for the small peephole and extra locks, it mirrored the other two.

"There. That's the grand tour," he said.

"That's it?" Surprise tainted my voice.

"Yep."

"But I thought the uppers lived in apartments with lots of rooms."

"The admiral's and vice admiral's families do, but most have suites like mine. If my mom were still alive, we would have two bedrooms and a small kitchenette. But since it's just us, we get this and a refrigerator."

The rumors about the uppers' living quarters had been exaggerated. I wondered what else had been blown out of proportion. "What happens if you…want a family?"

"If I find a mate, my father would be reassigned to share a suite with another single man, and if he finds a mate then I would move."

"Does he want another mate?"

"No."

The whole mate thing was odd to me. Scrubs hooked up with others and stayed together for as long as they desired then moved on. Any children from the pair went to the care facility. A few couples never parted. The Pop Cops tracked the pairings, and would separate them if their bloodlines were too close.

Logan whooped with joy. "I'm in!"

Riley stood behind him and watched the screen.

"Do the uppers mate for life?" I asked Riley, hoping to pull his attention away from the computer.

"Most do, but if a union isn't working then they'll split."

"What do you do for fun?"

Riley glared at me. His stiff posture radiating his ire. "Trella, I know what you're doing. You haven't asked questions about the uppers unless it was directly related to your *mission*. You have a very strong opinion about the uppers, and you haven't shown any interest in us before. But I do know the systems your friend is accessing can only be seen by people with ten-degree security clearance. So unless he's a rear admiral, he's neck-deep in serious trouble—"

"Only if I get caught," Logan said. "Don't worry, I'm ghosting."

"Ghosting? What the hell is that?" Riley demanded.

"Not leaving a traceable trail," I explained. Coming here was a bad idea. I hoped Logan would finish soon.

Riley's anger flared. "You didn't tell me the whole story. Time to talk, Trella. What *exactly* is this man looking for?"

"Well…" To tell him we were looking for Gateway might have ruined whatever credibility I had left with him. He knew Domotor had been trying to find ways around the Controllers to seize control of the computer for the rest of the upper families.

He studied my face and when I opened my mouth he said, "Don't lie." His words growled and I knew I trod on dangerous ground.

"Got it!" Logan whooped.

"Got what?" Riley asked.

Before I could say anything, Logan, who hadn't listened to anything we'd said, proclaimed with pride, "The coordinates to Gateway."

"Yes!" I jumped and slapped Logan on the back. Cogon was going to be ecstatic and very smug. I could already hear his *I told you so*. But my jubilation died when a strangled sound escaped Riley's throat. The anger drained from his face. His

flushed cheeks and red-tipped ears turned white, and I suddenly wished I could ghost back to the lower levels.

"Hold on," Logan said. His attention returned to the screen.
"No…no…you lousy unrecyclable…"

"What's wrong?" I asked.

"It requires a password."

"But you just said you got it."

"I have the file. To open the file we need a password. Any
ideas?"

I wanted to shake the screen until it surrendered and let us
read the file. To come all this way and to put so much at risk…
I shoved my crushing disappointment aside and concentrated.

"How about *Gateway?*"

"Nope."

"Inside? Outside?" I looked at Riley for help. He just shook
his head. A horrified fascination settled on his face.

"No and no. Wait!" Logan sat up straighter. "There's always
a fail-safe."

"A what?" I asked.

"People forget things. It's part of being human. You don't
want to risk someone discovering your password by writing it
down, so the computer has a way to help you remember your
password." He typed for a while.

"How?"

"It will ask you a question and the answer is the password."

"What if we don't know the answer?"

"Then we don't get the coordinates and we have to guess
again. Except…" He leaned forward. "There's a limit on the
number of guesses. After ten, the computer notifies the Controllers someone is trying to access the file."

"Not good." Horrible in fact.

"No." The clicking keys filled the silence. "Okay. I found
the question."

"And?" I prompted.

"I don't know the answer," Logan said.

I reached out but managed to stop my hands from wrapping around his neck. "What *is* the question?"

"Oh. *It's the end and the beginning. What is it?*"

fourteen

"A circle?" Riley suggested. He had recovered from his shock about Gateway, and was now intrigued by the mystery question. "A circle doesn't have an end or a beginning."

Logan moved his hands over the keyboard.

"Wait," I said. "How many other passwords have you tried?"

"Three so we have seven guesses before the computer shuts down."

"A circle is good, but let's think this through logically." I swiped hair from my face and tucked it behind my ear. "The question has to refer to something about Inside. We know it is an object or place and not a person's name."

"We do?" Logan asked.

"Yes, the question contains the word *it* and *what*. *It's* the end and the beginning. *What* is *it?* A person would be *who,* and a place would be *where.*"

Riley sat in the remaining chair, and covered his eyes with a hand as if blocking out all distractions. "Everything in here is squares, rectangles and cubes. No circles."

I settled on the couch. The living room was too small to pace. Searching my memory for circles, I tried to find a connection. "If you think about it, everything in here is a circle. The air circulates throughout Inside, going through the filters and purifiers. Same with the water and sewage. Reused and recycled, nothing wasted."

"Should I try circle?" Logan's fingers hovered over the keyboard.

"Yes." I held my breath.

"Nope. Try again."

Damn. I repeated the question in my mind. It sounded familiar as if I read it or heard it before. Maybe when I was living in the care facility. But there had been so many weeks of lessons in math, biology, science…. "Water?"

"How does it fit?" Riley asked.

"It has a cycle. Evaporation, condensation, freezing and melting as it changes from a gas to a liquid to a solid. Water is a vital resource for Inside, without it we couldn't exist."

"So is air and food." He considered. "Air has a cycle. We breathe in oxygen and breathe out carbon dioxide. The plants in hydroponics absorb the carbon dioxide and release oxygen. Growing food is also a circle with eating and producing. Think of the sheep."

"Sheepy?" I wished he were there. "Would Sheepy know the answer?" I joked.

He removed his hand and shot me a smile. "No. Sheep eat grass and vegetables and produce manure which fertilizes the grass and plants in hydroponics. Another cycle."

Logan tried, *water, air* and *food*. "No. Three guesses left."

Thinking along those lines, I realized a hundred different aspects of our life were cycles, including people. Perhaps the answer wasn't a representation of a circle, but more a concrete object or mathematical symbol. "Zero is circular. Isn't the symbol for infinity a sideways eight?"

"That's assuming the answer is a circle of some kind," Riley said.

"Can you think of another answer?"

"No, but to try and connect it to a mathematical number or concept…" He threw his hands up. "There could be a million different possibilities. I wouldn't—"

"Stop!" One of his words triggered a memory. I replayed the incident in my mind, searching for reasons why it wouldn't work. Certainty bloomed in my chest. I knew the answer.

Logan and Riley stared at me, waiting.

"The millionth week. That's the answer." I remembered the assembly and the old man's words: *the millionth week isn't the end, it's the beginning.*

Riley groaned and the hope dimmed in Logan's eyes.

"That's just a myth to scare people. Week one million will be like all the others. Its importance doesn't exist," Riley said.

"People said the same thing about Gateway." I gestured to Logan. "Yet we're one password away from the location."

Logan met my gaze. "How should I type it? *Week one million* or *the millionth week?*"

"Try both."

Unable to remain seated, Riley and I joined Logan at the computer. I held on to the back of his chair as he typed *the millionth week* and hit Enter. The words disappeared and the password prompt returned. This time he entered *week one million.*

"Are you sure?" Logan's finger was poised over the key.

I let go of the chair and clutched Riley's arm. "Yes." I wanted to turn away, but I watched the screen. It turned black then lines of text raced across, matching my heart's rhythm. I couldn't read the words; they kept jumping up as more white lines streaked on the screen.

"Logan?" I didn't care if I used his name.

"Yes! Got it!"

I wrapped my arms around Logan's neck and kissed him on the cheek, then turned and hugged Riley. Caught up in the excitement, he leaned back and picked me off the floor, spinning me around.

Logan rattled off a bunch of numbers.

"How do I find it?" I asked, still dizzy and thrilled Riley's arms supported me.

"Oh, right." Furious typing and a crude schematic of Inside appeared, showing a cube with a pulsing dot near the bottom of one side. "It's along the west wall in Quad G1. That's hydroponics."

"You'd think the workers would notice it," Riley said.

"Maybe it's one of those near-invisible hatches Trella found," Logan said.

"Near-invisible?" Riley looked down at me.

He held me close. Tall and with his strong arms wrapped around me, I knew I should extricate myself from his embrace, but a part of me wanted to stay. "Some doors are hard to see. Perhaps the vines have grown over it," I said.

"Oh, yeah. Lots of vines," Logan said.

Annoyed, Riley's muscles tightened. "Your friend's a lousy liar. What are you hiding?" When I hesitated, he moved his hands to my shoulders and pushed me back so he could see me better. "Enough. The location…the existence of Gateway is huge. No. It's way bigger than that…it's a whole other phenomenon. The repercussions are going to be unimaginable if it is really there and it works. I need to know everything right now, or I'm going to…"

"To what? Report me? You risk being implicated."

"No. I'm going to follow you. Yes, even through those vents until I know the whole story."

Logan eyed him. "You'll get stuck."

"It's ridiculous. He's not going to do it," I said.

"Then I won't let you leave until you tell me." Riley straightened, trying to look bigger.

"Two against one," I said. "And I'm armed." I rested my hand on my tool belt.

He deflated and dropped his hands, but, by the gleam in his eyes, I knew he hadn't given up.

"How about in exchange for Sheepy?"

"Really? You'd give me Sheepy?" I called his bluff.

"Yes."

He meant it, and my reaction surprised me. I would have loved to have the little sheep. "No. Sheepy stays with his mama." I put my hand up to stop Riley. "Just let me think."

As Riley had said, discovering Gateway's existence was a whole other realm of problems and possibilities. If caught right now, Riley would be recycled just for knowing about it. Too late to save him. Remembering his lecture about choices and sacrifices didn't make me feel any better.

"You'd better sit down," I said. "It's a long story."

"So Gateway wouldn't be on the wall in hydroponics, but on the *real* outer Wall?" Riley asked.

"Yes," I said.

"And no one knows about this except the three of us?"

"As far as I know. I've never seen anyone in the Gap, but it's possible high-ranking uppers could know or find it in the computer."

"Complete and detailed diagrams and blueprints of Inside have been deleted," Logan said. He had been searching through the computer, trying to gather as much information as he could about the Controllers.

"Are you sure? Wouldn't the engineers need them?" Riley asked.

"Each system—water, air, electrical and heating—has its own blueprints. Let's see...if I put them...together." Logan typed. "Still not showing Trella's Gap or Gateway. Lot's of other stuff's missing, too. Historical records and logs have been wiped clean up until…week 132,076."

Almost one hundred and fifty centiweeks ago.

"The first log is written by Admiral Peter Trava. He mentions saboteurs wielding magnets and trying to destroy Inside. He says they were stopped with no loss of life, but with major damage to the computer, causing data loss." Logan scrolled through a few more pages. "Something's wrong. The deletion was too clean for a magnet."

"Do you know when the files were deleted?" I asked.

"The same week Admiral Pete's entry was written, which was only fifteen centiweeks ago. Whoa! It's bogus."

"What happened that week?" I asked.

"Could have been when a few of the uppers tried to get into protected files on the system," Riley said. "My dad told me about it. Maybe they got too close to the truth, and the Travas decided to delete all the data prior to their takeover and write the bogus entry to explain it."

"Not all the data," Logan said. "There are about ten hidden and protected files in the system. I bet the Controllers don't know about them. The location of Gateway was one of them. Maybe the dissenters buried these files. They're all password protected." He clucked and hummed like a child with a brand-new toy.

"Could those be the files Domotor wanted?" Riley asked me.

"I don't know."

"Trella, what's your birth week?" An odd tone shook Logan's voice.

"It's 145,487. Why?"

"And the hour?"

"Why do you need to know?" I asked.

"Humor me."

"Hour four point fifteen."

He whistled.

"Logan, tell me."

"There's a file here named with your birth week and hour."

"What?" I moved closer to the monitor. He pointed.

"Why did you think it referred to me?"

"It says, 'For my daughter born on…' It's one of the ten files Domotor or whoever thought was important, so I just guessed it might have something to do with you."

"Can you open it?"

"Nope. Just like the others. The password question is 'Smile and show me your pearly teeth. How many do you have?'" He glanced at me. "Count your teeth."

"That's too easy, and what if I lost one?"

"Have you?"

"No, but I think it's referring to something else." The words *pearly teeth* had jumped out at me. My sole possession. The comb with the pearls. The answer was the number of teeth on my comb.

"And it would be…"

"Something I don't have with me, so we can't answer the question anyway."

"It's getting late. The next shift starts in an hour," Riley said.

I looked at the clock in surprise. So engrossed in our puzzle, I hadn't kept track.

"I just need a couple minutes." Logan's fingers danced on the keyboard. "I want to put these files where I can get to them from the lower level computers."

Anxious to get moving, I fidgeted behind Logan.

Riley also had a worried look. "Are you sure all this time you spent on the computer hasn't been recorded or traced?"

"Yep. I'm ghosting. No port. No problem."

"What does that mean?" Riley asked.

"Uh…just that I can get into the system without a port."
Logan was a bad liar, but his cry of alarm distracted us both.

"What now?" I really didn't want to know the answer.

"Gateway's going to suck a lot of energy when it opens. Plus it has a command to alert all of Inside's systems. We're going to need people in the network to cover the call," Logan said.

Yet another problem. Nothing was simple.

"I can cover electrical," Riley said, "but we'll need to recruit other uppers to help." He considered. "There are a number of uppers who supported Domotor and have been lying low since his capture. But if I tell them we found Gateway, they'll probably laugh in my face."

"But you believed us," I said.

"I saw Logan using level-ten clearance, and I saw the file. This is a huge risk for the uppers. They don't know me and they won't trust me. But they'll trust Domotor. Can you get him up here?"

He would probably do all right pulling himself through the air shaft, but he couldn't go between levels. "Only if we can use the lift."

"Too exposed. Domotor is too recognizable in the upper levels. His capture and punishment was discussed for weeks. He wouldn't be able to blend in up here, and I doubt we could get him from the lift to a room without being seen." Riley rubbed his face. "Also I'm not one hundred percent sure the people I'm thinking about are really supporters. My dad might know."

More problems. More people involved. To me, trusting uppers felt like the wrong thing to do, but we needed them. "Domotor would know who to trust. I can get the names from him and some kind of code word or something you can say to them to prove he's involved."

"That could work. But I'll need you here, too."

"Why?"

"To prove the scrubs are serious about opening Gateway," Riley said.

"And if I get into these hidden files," Logan said, "the uppers might have a way to bypass the Controllers and regain control."

"Sounds like a plan." Riley smiled.

Uneasiness swirled in my stomach as I steadied the ladder for Logan. I hated having to trust uppers. I trusted Riley, but he was different. Or was he?

"Thanks for your help," I said to Riley as Logan climbed the table.

"How soon can you get me those names?"

I needed to take Logan back, then go to Domotor's hideout. "Four hours give or take an hour."

"I'll meet you in our room during my break." Riley grasped my sore elbow to help me up the table.

I yelped and he let go.

"Sorry." Riley watched me rub the tender spot.

"Must have bumped it."

Logan called for help. His legs dangled from the vent. I pushed him into the air shaft. When his feet disappeared, I reached for the vent.

A click slide sounded.

"Get down," Riley ordered.

I didn't hesitate. He pulled the stepladder from the table, folded it and leaned it against the wall. In two strides he sat at the computer and whispered, "Stand behind me. Follow my lead." He rested his fingers on the keys.

The door opened as I reached Riley's chair. We both glanced at the man entering the room. He stopped short when he spotted us.

"Hi, Dad," Riley said. "You're back early."

fifteen

The surprise on Riley's father's face transformed into a smile. He had the same build as his son, but his thinning hair was brown and cut short. Riley's blue eyes must have been inherited from his mother. His father's brown eyes and beak nose gave him a friendly and inquisitive appearance.

"I see we have a visitor," he said as he stepped into the room and closed the door.

"Dad, this is Ella, the student I've been training," Riley said. "Ella, this is my father, Jacob."

"Hello, Ella, I've heard so much about you."

I shot Riley a look.

His father chuckled. "Don't worry. Nothing bad. Riley says you're a quick learner and coming from him that's high praise."

"Thank you," I said.

"Something happen?" Riley asked his dad.

"No. I had to work through my breaks, so my supervisor let me leave a little early." He glanced at the clock. "Shouldn't you be reporting for duty? Or are you training Ella here?" He smiled broadly with a gleam in his eyes.

Riley stood. "No. We need to go. Just need to get…something." He strode into the bedroom.

Jacob stepped closer to me and whispered, "You're as beautiful as Riley claims. I hope you'll visit us again." He winked.

I smiled and wondered what the real Ella looked like. Riley returned.

His father spotted the ladder along the wall. "What's this?"

"Oh. Maintenance was testing air flow again. They must have forgotten it. I'll return it on my way to work." He grabbed the ladder and turned toward the door.

"Wait," his father said, staring at the ceiling. "They forgot to cover the vent, too. Hand me the ladder."

"I'll do it, Dad." Riley set the stepladder on the table.

"No. You're going to be late." He shooed us out.

Riley shrugged and opened the door. I hoped Logan had the sense to scoot away from the vent and to keep quiet. Jacob reached for the air shaft as Riley escorted me into the hallway. The door clicked shut.

"Let's hope Logan doesn't give himself away." He strode down the corridor. "Does he know where to go?"

I hurried to follow. "No. I'll have to go back and get him. Isn't this dangerous?" I swept my arm out, indicating the hallway.

"Not really. Just act like you belong here. Walk with confidence. No one knows who you are. Since you're wearing a student jumper, they'll assume you're from another sector."

"Don't you know everyone up here?" My vision of the upper levels as one big happy family was being shredded strip by strip.

He laughed. "No. Do you know all the scrubs?"

"There are ten times as many of us."

"Well, up here everyone keeps to themselves. I have a few

aunts and uncles, some cousins, a friend or two and I know my fellow workers of course, but that's about it."

"What about the real Ella? What if she sees me?"

A few uppers walked toward us, and I braced for their cry of alarm. They nodded at us and continued past. Riley was right. I relaxed a bit and looked around. There wasn't much to see. Doors and plain white metal walls, the same as in the lower levels. The only difference was the thin strip of gray carpet on the floor.

When the uppers moved out of hearing range, Riley said, "You *are* Ella."

"I am?"

He gave me a don't-be-stupid look. "How do you think I justify all my time spent in our storeroom? My father likes to know what I'm doing during my off hours, so I tell him I'm training a student. Actually, his unexpected arrival helped me. Now he has met Ella and knows she's a real person. It should keep him happy for a while. Although…"

"What?"

"He might start bugging me to bring you around more."

Confused, I asked why.

Riley's stride slowed as he stared at me. "You really don't know anything about families do you?"

"Scrub, remember? We have care facilities not families." I believed I did a good job of keeping the bitterness from my voice, but he still frowned.

"Well, parents want their children to grow up, earn important positions and find mates. According to them, that's the key to happiness. My father, being no different, wants me to find a mate. It's the reason why he was grinning so much. He's hoping I have found someone."

I considered his explanation. In the lower levels, scrubs waited until after their tenure in the care facility to become couples. Care mates didn't hook up. It was frowned upon.

"Don't you already have someone? Another upper?" I asked.

"No."

"Why not?"

He stopped and searched my expression. I tried to let my genuine interest show. He had been right about my lack of curiosity and my assumptions of upper life. I was determined to learn more.

"I haven't met the right woman yet. Guess I'm waiting for someone to…surprise me." He continued walking.

"Surprise you how?"

"Oh, the usual way, I guess. Suddenly appear out of nowhere and completely change my life. You know, boring stuff."

He increased his stride so I couldn't see his expression, but I thought he might be joking with me.

"How about you?" he asked in a too-casual tone. "Anyone surprising?"

Domotor would qualify for appearing out of nowhere and changing my life, but I didn't think he was referring to him.

"No," I said.

"Why not?"

I huffed in annoyance.

"You have to answer," he said. "I answered you—it's only fair."

I bit back a sarcastic comment about fairness and sighed. "Would you bring a child into the scrubs' world? Add yet another body into an already overcrowded place? To be raised unloved and ignored as one of too many? I won't do it."

He remained silent for a while. "You don't have to have a child."

"But when you're intimate with someone, it's usually just a matter of time."

He slowed, glancing at me as if puzzled. Up ahead was a large intersection with many uppers grouped together, talking.

A bunch of Pop Cops strode into view and turned toward us. Without thought I stepped back.

Riley grabbed my hand, pulling me beside him. "Confidence," he whispered. "You belong here." Riley squeezed my hand in encouragement.

Easy to say, harder to act. Especially when Lieutenant Arno was among them. I gazed at the floor, but realized it was a scrub reaction. Uppers made eye contact and nodded in greeting. With effort, I returned Arno's semidistracted nod and continued down the hall as if my heart wasn't trying to jump out of my body.

Riley kept my hand as he turned left at the intersection and increased his pace. He made another left into a smaller corridor without doors and which ended. He headed straight for the end.

I scanned the ceiling, looking for air vents. "Riley, where are we going?"

"Trust me."

Almost running now, I kept close to him. When we reached the end, he let go of my hand and stepped to the side, disappearing.

"Hey," I called and he poked his head out.

"Optical illusion. Pretty cool, isn't it?"

I felt around. The wall on the left side of the end was solid. The right side appeared to have a solid wall, but the wall was actually a meter past where it should have connected to the end. The corridor jigged to the right for a meter before going straight again, but it looked like another end. After I made the turn, I glanced back. The illusion worked from both sides.

However this hallway was only about two meters long and contained one door. Riley typed in a number sequence on the lock and the door opened into our storeroom. Relief coursed through me when we entered and I plopped on the couch. I couldn't believe I had just strolled through the upper level.

"That's why no one knows this room is here," he said.

It made sense. Unless you put your hands on the walls, you wouldn't discover the illusion. "How did you find it?"

"Lightbulb duty." When I didn't say anything, he continued, "During training, the newbies get assigned lightbulb duty. We go around changing lightbulbs in the corridors and public areas. Then we fix the broken filaments. A painstaking process." He waved his hand as if pushing away the memory. "Anyway, I was assigned this sector and the bulb at the end must have just burned out. It was still hot and I dropped it. The bulb landed on the rug and then rolled through the wall."

He grinned. "It's amazing, but that bulb has never burned out since I found this place." Riley pulled a drawer open. It was filled with lightbulbs.

After stashing the upper's training uniform under the couch with Zippy, I found Logan in the air shaft not far from Riley's room. We returned to the lower levels and he raced to make his shift on time. The poor guy would be awake for thirty hours straight. Not fun, but doable. Having worked my shift, Anne-Jade would also be dragging. Perhaps the news of Gateway's existence would wake her up.

Gateway. I still couldn't wrap my mind around all the implications. But I did know actions and alliances needed to be made and I couldn't do it on my own. So I climbed into the heating vents to visit Domotor.

He sat in front of the computer, but turned an expectant expression toward me. I kept my face neutral, but couldn't maintain it for long.

"You found it!"

I smiled. "We know the location."

"Yes." He shouted and banged his chair's arms with his fists. "When are you going to open it?"

"It's not going to be easy." I explained what Logan had said about the alarms. "We need trustable uppers and we need to know more about Outside. Do you even know what's there?"

He played with the long strands of his hair. "Not really. I was hoping there would be more information in the computer system."

"Logan said there were about ten hidden and protected files. He moved them."

"Protected how?"

"With passwords."

"Passwords are the old security system. Those files are probably what I've been searching for. Did Logan move the files so we can access them down here?"

"Yes."

"Maybe I can find them now." Domotor returned his attention to the computer.

"Wait for Logan. He mentioned how the ports log your ID number every time you open a file."

"I've very familiar with the security system, Trella. I don't need Logan." His voice huffed.

I tried to reason with him. "I'd rather we all be together when you try to open those files. You only have ten guesses. The way we figured out the password for Gateway was by all of us bouncing ideas off each other."

"Fine. I'll wait. With nothing else to do, I've become an expert in waiting."

I ignored his snippy tone. "What about the uppers? Do you know who would be willing to help us?"

"I can give you the names of those who *said* they would support me. For security, I made sure no one knew who the others were. But one of them ratted me out, and once I was arrested and interrogated—" he shuddered with horror "—I couldn't hold out. I gave her a few names, hoping one of them was indeed her spy. Karla was a power-hungry lieutenant then, but she arrested all the people I named and recycled them all."

A hitch caught his voice, and his eyes shone with grief. "At least I saved the others, and they wisely stopped looking for the files, keeping quiet."

"Why didn't they recycle you?"

"Karla suspected I knew more, but her superior officer was satisfied. I spent two centiweeks in the holding cells before the Travas released me. They claimed I was spared recycling for cooperating with them. I went back to my duties, but no one would talk to me or even look at me. The rumors had spread, and everyone feared I was a Trava spy." He huffed. "Ironic."

"When did all this happen?" I asked.

"About sixteen centiweeks ago. After I was released, I played the game, acting timid and obedient. Eventually, the Travas stopped monitoring me. I waited another three centiweeks before searching the network for the location of those hidden files. Guess I didn't wait long enough." He rubbed his back. "Karla hadn't forgotten about me."

I waited for the rest of his story.

"She suspected and had me interrogated again." He closed his eyes and hugged his chest for a moment. "He broke my back, but I didn't say a word about the disks I hid. After I recovered, Karla sent me down here as punishment, but also to wait and see what I would do or who I would contact."

"The spy?"

"I guessed wrong. I doubt Karla would kill her own, so he or she is still spying for her." Domotor pulled out a wipe board and wrote down five names. He handed the board to me.

I scanned the list. Most of them were women. One name jumped out at me.

Domotor watched me. "Call me old-fashioned. When I implicated my cohorts, I named mostly men."

"Who did you implicate?"

"Do you *really* want to know?"

"Yes." The word was a whisper.

Domotor gazed across the room, seeing into the past. "There were ten of us." He huffed in sad amusement. "Ten—the magic Inside number. Before I knew about the Trava takeover, I always wondered why there were nine major families. I learned later that Inside's original power structure had a voting system, which needed an odd number of voters." He paused. "I had supporters from each of the eight remaining families. A few were mates."

He returned his focus to me. "One of the couples was your parents."

I didn't care about my parents. To prove it, I imagined a thin coat of metal along my skin. So they tried to help Domotor. So what?

"After being tortured, I named your father, Nolan Garrard, as an accomplice."

His name clanged on my defenses even though I already knew he had been recycled.

When Domotor didn't see any reaction he continued. "I also named Blas Sanchia and Shawn Lamont. Ramla Ashon was also recycled."

The other names didn't clang. "I thought the uppers all had two family names."

"The children do. Once you find a mate, then you pick one family to be a part of. If you don't find a mate, then you have the support of two families."

With this new knowledge, I read the names on the board again. Jacob Ashon was listed. "Is Ramla Ashon…?"

"Riley's mother."

"And…Kiana Garrard?"

"Your mother."

Her name stabbed through my metal defense. My parents had tried to change things, and my father had been recycled. But those events happened after I was born. No. I didn't care. I forced my metal skin to grow thicker.

"Do you want to know about your—"

"No." I read the list again. Kiana Garrard, Jacob Ashon, Hana Mineko, Takia Qadim and Breana Narelle. "Do you know which one of these uppers is the spy?"

"No. I thought it was Blas Sanchia."

How would I isolate the spy? My limited knowledge of the uppers once again hindered me. I trusted Riley, but could I trust his father? Perhaps Riley would have a few ideas or Logan could track the uppers' computer usage and see if one of them could access restricted Trava files.

"What about Gateway?" I asked.

"Find it underneath the foam. Dissolve the insulation and expose the door for now."

It was hour fifty-two. Eight hours remained before my next shift. I calculated the time needed to sleep, eat and get to the outer wall. Not enough, searching for Gateway would have to wait until my next break. Although, I had time for one errand.

I left Domotor and climbed to level four. Reaching my hidden cabinet, I removed the comb. It was a beautiful gift and should be used and displayed. After counting the teeth, I pocketed it in my tool belt and headed down.

Finding a warm spot to sleep, I dozed in the shaft. If I was Queen of the Pipes, I should request a better throne. Dreams of Outside swirled through my mind. The doorway hovered in front of me, but stayed the same distance away no matter how fast I ran.

My supervisor waited for me at the beginning of my shift. She scowled at me, and I knew it wouldn't be good. It wasn't. She yanked my arm out and slapped a red cuff around my left wrist. It bit into my skin.

"For failure to finish your shift. Explain," she ordered, "and don't try the broken troll excuse. Your troll was found in the air shaft in perfect condition, but no one could find you."

My thoughts raced. "I fell asleep."

"Where?"

"Air shaft seventeen."

"You're lying." She uncapped a marker and wrote the number ten on the cuff. "Report to Emek in solid-waste handling for ten hours extra duty. It can be broken into five-hour increments during your next two off-shifts."

"But that's—"

"Have Emek sign the cuff and return to me after assembly. Failure to comply will result in your permanent reassignment to Emek's team."

Her punishment was extreme for a first offense. "But—"

"*My* supervisor was not happy over your disappearance. Now *I'm* on notice. I'll be watching."

True to her word she stayed until I hefted the troll into the shaft, and she waited at each transition point during the next ten hours. I thought she would follow me down to the solid-waste plant in Sector H1, but she just made sure I headed in the right direction.

Emek smiled broadly when I arrived. Blood seeped from under the bright-colored cuff on my wrist. "Welcome to the crap cleaners. Grab a pair of overalls, a plunger and follow Rat. He'll be your partner."

"Rat?"

He pointed to a young scrub. Despite the name, Rat wore clean overalls and his brown hair was trimmed and tidy. His manner remained pleasant even when we unclogged a bilious wad, reeking with the most horrible stench. My eyes watered and I almost lost the contents of my stomach.

To distract myself, I asked him, "How did you get the name Rat?"

"It's my nickname. My real name is Mark."

"Okay, so how'd you get your nickname?"

"Rats like me. I keep their population down and make sure the rest are healthy."

"Healthy rats?"

He laughed. "Most people don't want to know what goes on in solid-waste handling. All they want is clean water and fertilizer. Rats are important to our world. Bet you didn't know that."

"You're right."

"Bet you don't know about the bugs, either."

I held a hand up. "I don't, and I don't want to. For certain things, ignorance really is bliss."

My comment turned my thoughts to Gateway. What if I couldn't open it? What if I was caught and killed before seeing Outside? I berated myself. One minute I was convinced Gateway didn't exist, the next, I waxed maudlin over the possibility of not opening it. Just because we found a few coordinates in the computer, shouldn't make me an instant believer.

I forced that line of thought away. It wasn't helping, and I could what-if myself until I was reduced to a nervous mess. Instead, I followed Rat and tried not to breathe through my nose.

Shoveling black goo from the bottom of the incinerator was my last task.

"Isn't this maintenance's job?" I asked.

"Nope. This is good stuff." He dumped a shovelful into the bin. "That's it. Take the bin to the recycling plant and then you're done."

"Where are you going?"

"To the sheep's pen. Want to come? I'm good with sheep, too." He winked.

"No, thank you. Ignorance remember? Best I don't become an expert in waste management."

He waved as he left. And I realized he enjoyed his work. His job was used to punish other scrubs, but he didn't see it that way. He knew his job was vital to Inside and was content. Why couldn't the rest of the scrubs be content? Maybe they were, and I hadn't noticed.

"Trella? What are you doing here?" Logan asked as I pushed the bin through the sorting piles. Dark half circles hung under his eyes.

I waved the cuff in front of his bleary eyes. "I pissed my supervisor off. She assigned me extra duty."

"Anne-Jade will be glad. She's worried because she fell asleep in the air shaft, but she didn't see your supervisor, so she hoped it would be okay."

"She did fine. I'm glad you came over. Broken Man wants to open those files. When can you get the password questions?"

"My next off-shift."

"Great. Also can you—" I checked for Pop Cops "—get security information about the uppers?"

"Depends on what you want to know."

I'd already memorized the names Domotor had given me. Reciting the list of uppers to Logan, I asked, "Can you find out which one of these people is working undercover for the Travas?"

"If the information is listed in the computer system, but it's unlikely."

"Why?"

"Because someone could find it."

"Like Broken Man?"

"No. You need level-nine clearance...oh!"

I smiled as Logan realized only a few Travas had the required security clearance.

"It's still unwise to have such sensitive information listed," Logan said.

"I agree, but I'd bet the higher Pop Cop officers feel rather confident about their security network, believing no one, especially no *scrub* could breach it. So try not to bust their illusion."

"Oh, don't worry, I'm like a—"

"Ghost. I know." Two Pop Cops headed in our direction. "I better go. I can't miss any more shifts, but I'll stop by your barrack during one of my breaks."

Logan nodded and returned to work. I left the recycling plant and hurried to find Emek. Only five hours remained in my off time and I was determined to locate Gateway.

Emek issued orders to a couple scrubs. When they left, I pushed a marker into his hands. "Sign, please."

"Hold on, you still owe me five hours," he said.

I met his gaze. "Cogon's execution is in twenty-four hours. I don't have time."

Understanding softened his face; he signed the cuff. "Ever have a cuff before?"

"My first."

"Put a little sheep's oil on your wrist under the cuff before the Pop Cops remove it. Otherwise, the sucker tends to grab a hunk of skin when it's cut off."

"Thanks." I strode from solid-waste handling and headed to the right. My supervisor's voice called from behind me. She wasn't kidding about watching me. Suppressing a groan of annoyance, I turned.

My heart dropped into my stomach and ran laps. Lieutenant Commander Karla and three Pop Cops followed my supervisor. The LC's smug expression and the terrified fury on my supervisor's face told me all I needed to know.

Without hesitating, I ran.

sixteen

My supervisor's shrill voice called for me to stop. One of the Pop Cops threatened to shoot me, but LC Karla's calm order to stun me made my legs run faster. I reached an intersection just as a sizzle slap sounded behind me. Diving into the hallway on my left, I felt the pulse clip my legs.

I rolled along the floor. A burning pain danced along my calves and left my muscles numb. Scrubs yelled and scattered. The corridor filled with noise and confusion. Regaining my feet proved difficult, I used my upper arms to balance on numb legs. The quickest of Karla's Pop Cops reached the intersection.

Pushing scrubs out of his way, he aimed his stun gun at me. Without thinking, I grabbed a screwdriver from my belt and flung it at him. The tool knocked into his arm. His shot flew low, hitting me below the waist.

I fell over, landing on my back, feeling as if a million needles jabbed through my uniform and into my thighs. The Pop Cop stepped closer, raising his gun again.

He was bumped from behind. Cursing, he turned to stun

the closest scrubs. I hurled my wire cutters at him. They grazed his head, so I lobbed my flashlight. A direct hit. His gun clattered to the floor with a satisfying crack. Surprised, he stared at me a moment, then glanced over his shoulder.

His buddies should be arriving any second, but sounds of a commotion reached us from the other hall.

Taking advantage of his hesitation, I rolled onto my stomach and pulled my body away from him—the benefits of having strong arm muscles. A heating vent beckoned from two meters away.

"Oh, no, you don't," he said.

Too much weight on me, I strained to a stop. He had latched onto my ankles.

"Don't you want to help your boss? Sounds like she's in trouble." I transferred my weight to my left elbow, turning my body sideways and freeing my right arm.

He paused. Karla's voice boomed through the sounds of panicked scrubs, ordering them to get out of her way. The sizzle slap of a stun gun increased the noise level.

"She can handle a couple of scrubs. You should worry about yourself." He reached for his handcuffs with his right hand. "You're under arrest for—"

I stabbed my needle-nose pliers into his left forearm. He yelled and let go. I continued, gaining another meter before he lunged for me. I managed to roll away, but he snaked an arm around my waist, pinning me down. He grinned as I searched for another tool.

"You're out, but I'm not." He pulled a knife.

The ruckus in the other hallway spilled into ours. The LC was caught in the middle of stampeding scrubs. It would have been comical if I didn't have an armed Pop Cop wrapped around me.

Taking advantage of the distraction, I grabbed the comb from my belt. I poked the teeth into his eyes as the crowd reached us. He let go of me, and I lost track of him as we were stepped on, kicked and crushed. The comb dropped from my hand, but all the while, I closed the distance to the heating vent. Removing the cover, I wormed inside, and replaced the metal grate.

I pulled my aching body through the semidark shaft until my arms shook with exhaustion. Laying my head down, I listened as the clamor from the hall died and the angry voice of LC Karla echoed.

Only a few of her words were coherent, but two stood out. Injured and blood. Then the grating sound of a metal cutter vibrated. I turned my head. In the faint light, a thin black trail shone. I wasn't in pain, but then again the lower half of my body remained numb. Running my hands along my skin, I stopped when my fingers encountered wetness.

The Pop Cop's knife had sliced a gash near my hip. I couldn't tell how deep, but I needed to stanch the blood. The rumble of the cutter stopped and a bright light glowed behind me.

The slide step rasp of a person in the shaft reached me. I continued, but I still left a blood trail. When I arrived at an intersection, I tore a part of my coveralls and made a make-shift bandage which became soaked in no time, alarming me.

Not much more I could do, so I kept moving. If LC Karla knew about me, she must know about the others. I wondered what had tipped her off. Concentrating on losing my tail, I glanced over my shoulder. I no longer left a smear of blood. Good. Next I needed to figure out where I was.

The light had changed from weak gray to blue. Bunks were visible through the slats. I had reached the scrubs' bar-racks. Trying not to make a sound, I removed a vent cover and slipped out of the shaft. I replaced the cover and peered around. It was hour seventy-six and most of the bunks were occupied with sleeping scrubs.

My legs remained numb, which, by the amount of blood pouring from the gash, was a good thing. I crawled across the barrack to another vent on the opposite side. This one would take me to Domotor's hideout. Once inside the shaft, I rested. My arm muscles burned with fatigue.

The trip to Domotor's room seemed unending. By the time I reached his vent, I didn't have the energy to remove the cover.

"Domotor," I called. No answer. I yelled louder.

"Trella? Where are you?" he asked.

"In the heating duct."

He rolled into view. "What's the matter?" He bent over and yanked the cover off.

I stayed in the duct. "LC Karla tried to arrest me. She knows."

"How much does she know?"

"I didn't hang around to find out."

Concern and fear filled his expression but not surprise. He had come from the right side of the room. "What have you been doing?" I asked.

Guilt flashed before he covered it. "Cleaning."

"You haven't tried to access those files?"

His gaze dropped to the floor. All the answer I needed. "Domotor, I told you to wait!"

"I was careful. There has to be another reason Karla's after you," he shot back.

"I doubt she'd bring along three Pop Cops if she wanted to follow up on my reprimand."

"You were reprimanded?" His voice held an accusatory tone.

"For failure to finish my shift. Which is pretty damn good, considering all the extracurricular activity I've been doing for you." This wasn't productive. I drew a breath. "If she knows where you are, she'll try and cut through the door. At least you'll have a warning. Once you're in custody, hold out for as long as you can before naming anyone. Give her Cog's and Roddie's names and then mine."

"Who is Roddie?"

"The man who was kill-zapped back when you first went missing. Hopefully, she'll be happy with those names."

"What are you going to do?"

"Warn my friends."

It was a good plan. Warn Logan then find Riley. However, the numbness wore off my legs. It was a bonus to have the use of my legs, and I switched from the heating system to the air shafts. But the sizzling pain shooting from my hip created a big problem.

After climbing to level two, I knew I wouldn't be able to find Logan. Light-headed and weak, I lay in the shaft, wishing for one of those pocket communicators the Pop Cops carried. A sudden memory flashed and I checked my tool belt.

Yes! I still carried the two listening devices Jacy had given me. Palming one, I toggled the On switch. I was supposed to plant it in air duct seventy-two, but hadn't gotten the op-portunity. I chuckled wildly, thinking I could only break one rule at a time.

I wasn't sure if Jacy or his buddies would be monitoring the devices or even listening, but it was worth the effort.

Moving the device close to my mouth, I whispered, "Jacy, remember when you said to let you know if I needed anything? Well, I need your help." I paused, collecting my thoughts. To tell Jacy Logan's name could result in more danger for Logan. All Domotor knew about Logan was his physical description. My head spun and I realized I might not be conscious for too long. Better to tell Jacy then pass out.

I asked Jacy to warn Logan. "I also need you to *borrow* all the metal cutters, chisels and crowbars in the lower levels and hide them. The Pop Cops are going to want to cut a hole and the longer it takes them to complete this task, the better. Anything you can do to make the Pop Cops' lives difficult would be appreciated." I flipped off the device and returned it to my tool belt.

After the wave of dizziness passed, I decided to try to climb to the fourth level and warn Riley. Even if he wasn't in our room, I would leave him a note. And then what?

To distract myself from the pain and effort of climbing, I planned my next task. I could hide from the Pop Cops, but eventually they'd know about Gateway from Domotor. I had to get there first and open it. And then? No clue.

My progress slowed and I gasped for breath. Focusing all my energy into moving my body, my awareness shrank to pushing forward one foot at a time, to pulling with one arm then the other. Black and white dots swirled in my vision and I bit my lip to keep conscious.

A single goal propelled me forward, and the last thing I remember was the sensation of falling.

Sharpness jabbed my arm. I tried to jerk away, but my arm was stuck. My whole body ached and a hammer kept striking the back of my head. I retreated to the darkness, leaving all those annoyances behind.

The pricking and pulling around my hip demanded attention. I opened my eyes, but shut them against the harsh daylight. Two people stood over me.

"She's waking. Quick, more thiopental!"

Another painful prick on my arm, and fire raced through my veins. I welcomed the return of darkness.

Foggy thoughts floated sluggishly. Pain radiated from my hip, but only spiked when I moved, which proved difficult to do. My right arm was trapped. Squinting, I braced for the bright daylight, but sighed in relief. Soft bluelight glowed in the room.

The familiar shapes of our storeroom surrounded me. Reclined on the couch, I still couldn't comprehend why my right arm wouldn't move. I wore a soft robe. A liquid-filled bag hung above my head with a tube snaking down. I followed the tube and found the reason for my frozen arm. It was tied to a white board. The tube ended in a metal piece protruding from my skin.

Memories of being chased by Pop Cops sprang to life. They must have caught me and were using a drug to torture me. I struggled to sit up. Every muscle in my body hurt and I felt as if I'd been chewed by Chomper.

"Easy there," a woman's voice said. She knelt next to the couch and laid a cool hand on my shoulder. "You shouldn't move."

Panicked, I swatted at her hand with my free arm, but the effort was weak and she caught my wrist. The cuff was still in place around it.

"If you move, you might pull your stitches out and I'll have to sew you up again." She used the stern tone of a Care Mother.

Stopping, I peered at her clothes. An upper, but not a Pop Cop. Her words finally pushed through the fog of fear and I realized she worked in the infirmary. Yet I was in our storeroom. Could the Pop Cops be waiting outside? "What...? Who...?" My throat burned.

"If you promise to lie still, I'll get you a drink and tell you what happened. Promise?"

I debated. Knowledge versus promising an upper. "Yes." But if she turned out to be a Pop Cop in disguise, then I could break my promise.

She moved away and returned with a cup of water. I grasped

the heavy glass in my left hand, and she supported my head while I drank. The cold water felt wonderful going down, but turned my stomach.

"Sip it slowly," she said. "You just had surgery."

"Surgery? It was just a cut." I strained to sit up.

"Remember your promise."

I wilted. Who was I kidding anyway? I could barely lift a glass of water.

A fleeting smile crossed her lips. Her brown hair had been braided into a single long rope. The end reached her waist and she flicked it aside when she sat on the edge of the couch. In the bluelight, it was hard to see her eye color, but I guessed by the fine lines on her face she was around forty centiweeks old. Her thin fingers checked the metal thing stuck in my arm. She moved with a competent grace as if she did this all the time.

I winced when she touched my hip.

"Sorry, but I want to be sure you didn't pull a stitch." She pressed her fingertips through my robe and along my cut. "Feels fine."

"Okay, Doctor. Care to explain what's going on?" I asked.

"I was accosted by a very persistent young man who insisted I was needed for an emergency. Imagine my surprise when he led me here. You were on the couch, unconscious and bleeding. After an initial check, I determined you had a concussion and had been stabbed."

Which explained all the blood.

She watched my expression for a moment. "The young man would not let me take you to a proper surgical room, so we had to make do." The doctor fiddled with the tube. "I'm giving you an antibiotic, but the risk of infection is still very high."

"How deep?"

"The knife penetrated to your pelvic bone, damaging your large intestines and your ovary. I stitched you up as best I could, but you might have trouble conceiving a child."

Not a concern for me. "When will I be able to move?"

"You can walk around in a few hours, but it's going to take a week for you to regain your full strength."

A week! I'd be recycled in a week. Sooner if the doctor reported me to the Pop Cops.

"Now it's your turn. Care to tell me why you're here?"

"No."

"How about if I threaten to tell the authorities?"

I considered. The doctor could have reported me hours ago. "No."

She grinned. "You called my bluff. Good thing your young man is a friend of mine." Then her smile dissolved as sadness pulled on her features. "I'm not an idiot, though. A rogue scrub wearing a red cuff has been reported to be in the air ducts and, although injured, is potentially dangerous. The uppers have been ordered to listen at vent covers and alert the authorities about any suspicious noise." She gazed at me as if memorizing my features. "Once the game is up, it never ends well."

Jacy's comment about results repeated in my mind. "Better to make an effort, than do nothing."

"When the effort fails, is it worth the cost?"

A tough question to answer. Failure meant Domotor, Logan, Anne-Jade, Riley and I would all be recycled along with Cog. Six people. A high cost. "No."

"Then why try at all?"

"Because there is a chance for success. Maybe not complete success, or even the hoped-for results, but maybe just planting a seed to grow long after I'm gone. It doesn't have to be a total failure." Logan already knew this. I understood his words about causing maximum damage on a deeper level.

"Good answer. It's the reason I'm here." She glanced at the clock. "Now that you're in stable condition, I need to report to the infirmary." Standing, she bustled about and gathered her supplies. "I'll be back later to check on you."

"Doctor?"

She turned.

"Thank you."

Flashing me a smile, she left. The bluelights remained on, and I wondered why her motion hadn't triggered the daylights. Perhaps Riley had turned off the sensor. Her comments about Riley as my young man made me laugh. Pain flared near my hip and I stopped.

I scanned the room for the fifth time. Nothing to do or see, I was alone with my thoughts. Funny how I had craved to be alone and now I wished for company. Wished to see Cog's happy face. I had been avoiding the clock, keeping my gaze away. If I didn't know the time, then Cog was still alive.

Instead, I reviewed my conversation with the doctor. This quest to find Gateway had started because I wanted to prove Broken Man wrong and save Cog the disappointment when his prophet disappeared without keeping his promises.

A simple task which had blown into a complicated mess, involving six—seven if I count the doctor—people. Actually, if I included Jacy and his group, the scrub who covered for me and the kitchen scrubs, I was well past twenty.

Not the actions of sheep at all. In fact, if I was honest with myself, I'd wanted to prove Broken Man wrong to save myself from hoping. To give myself permission to not care about the scrubs. So I could view them and treat them just like the Pop Cops did. As sheep.

Some Queen of the Pipes, I thought. I'd believed I was better than a mindless drone. But I was the mindless one, hiding away. Even now I referred to them as if I didn't belong. I had completely fallen for the Pop Cop propaganda. The computers in the care facility listed all the wonderful things the uppers did and their wonderful lives. Being a scrub was undesirable and hard work, living in crowded conditions with no privacy and just being one of many. Undistinguishable.

The propaganda was crafted to make scrubs distance themselves from other scrubs so they wouldn't be lumped into one universal category. Queen of the Pipes was better than being a scrub. I fell for it, but others hadn't. Cog, for one. He remembered names and treated everyone as if they were special. Rat in waste management. He was proud of his work, despite his job being considered even beneath a scrub.

Shame over my behavior pulsed in my chest. I dug deeper into my motivations for pursuing the location of Gateway and my entire body cringed. I covered my eyes with my free hand, yet the darkness didn't block the realization. *Selfish*. The word flashed in front of my eyes as if burned in the underside of my eyelids.

In my small metal heart, I'd wanted to find Gateway for me. So I could escape from being a scrub. I could try to rationalize it—my desire to help Cog was genuine—but my desire to help myself was stronger.

Disgust, self-loathing and guilt all rolled into a noxious mix, filling me until I acknowledged them and had wallowed in them for a while. Then I purged them. Gateway existed and the game wasn't over yet.

Maximum damage.

Unflinching, I looked at the clock. Hour ninety-six. Cog was still alive. I had three hours to… What? I couldn't even laugh without pain, and couldn't count on Riley's help. His shift lasted until hour hundred, and I assumed he would come straight here.

I scanned the room for ideas. My tool belt and blood-stained clothes lay tangled together in a heap by the desk. The tools were long gone, but I hoped the pouches still held Logan's decoder device and Jacy's microphone.

A small amount of liquid remained in the bag over my head. I wiggled into a sitting position, closing my eyes against a burst of pain and wave of dizziness. When my head stopped spinning, I examined my arm. My wrist had been turned to expose the underside of my arm. The top of the metal needle at the end of the tube had been taped to my skin on the opposite side of my elbow.

I pulled the tape off the tube. Each tug caused a pinching jab. When the tube was free, I tugged the needle out. Blood welled. Another round of dizziness claimed my attention for a few moments. Unwrapping the rest of the tape to remove the white board, I focused on the positive. There was less hair on the underside of my arm. If my wrist had been turned the other way, the sting from removing the tape would have been worse.

Once I was free, I paused to catch my breath before working the stiffness out of my arm. Bending over to retrieve my tool belt from the floor, I toppled. Bad idea. Daggers of pain robbed me of breath. On the upside, I landed near my tool belt. Sheer willpower kept me from passing out.

I found both Logan's and Jacy's devices close to the heating vent. My initial idea had been to bring Logan's decoder to Cog. He could unlock his cell door and escape. Pure fantasy. If the air shaft vent in the cells had been barred, it stood to reason that the heating vents would also be secured. Plus where would he go?

But I could do one thing for him. Determined, I found the student's uniform I had stashed under the couch. I wore nothing but a bandage under the robe. I wondered if Riley had helped the doctor. Heat flushed my face.

My line of thought wasn't conducive to my mission so I concentrated on getting dressed. I taped a small pillow to my wound before donning the uniform. Ignoring the pain, I crawled over to the heating vent and opened it.

Amazingly, the pillow did a decent job of cushioning my injury as I slithered/crawled through the duct. However, my battered muscles protested each movement and dizziness plagued my efforts. I paused often, and set little goals for myself.

Just make it to the bend, I willed, and I celebrated each one with a rest before setting the next. I had no idea how long I spent traveling to the holding cells. All that mattered was reaching Cog before they led him down to Chomper.

There was no mistaking the feeble light or the rancid stench of the holding cells. I peered through the bars, searching for Cog. Nothing but empty cells until I reached the third vent.

Cog sat on the edge of the bunk. Old black and yellow bruises painted his face, and the swelling around his eyes was gone. Bleeding cuts crisscrossed his legs and torso. He hugged his arms tight to his chest as if trying to stanch the blood. He rocked either in agitation or pain.

I called his name.

Cog jumped to his feet and looked around. "No, Trell, you shouldn't have!"

"Shouldn't have what?"

He cocked his head.

"I'm down here. In the heating vent."

He sagged back on the bunk. Keeping his voice low, he said, "Don't scare me like that."

"Sorry." I hated to see him so frazzled. "Cog, what shouldn't I have done?"

"I thought you had turned yourself in."

"Why?"

He gestured toward the door. "They came asking more questions about you. They found out Broken Man is still alive and you're involved."

"I know. Broken Man tipped them off."

"Really?"

"Yes. He used the computer, and then I was reprimanded for failing to finish my shift. Karla's suspected me all along, so the reprimand gave her enough reason to *try* to arrest me."

Cog smiled with glee. "That's my Trella, hiding in the pipes."

"You used to yell at me for it."

"You should have seen her. Bright red, sputtering with rage and I swear I saw fire coming out of her nostrils. That was worth every cut from Vinco's knife." He grew serious. "She said you were injured. Are you all right?"

"Fine." It was a good thing he couldn't see me. I thought about his earlier comment. "Why did you think I turned my-self in?"

"Karla asked me stuff like what you knew, where you might be and who you were working with. I couldn't tell her any-thing. Then she said she would offer you a deal." He stopped.

"What kind of deal?"

"I'll only tell you if you promise *not* to take it."

I connected the clues. He didn't need to tell me Karla would offer to spare his life in exchange for me. "I'm not promising, Cog."

"You have to. Otherwise everything I suffered through will be for nothing."

"No, it wouldn't. You gave us time and freedom. We found Gateway."

He slid off the bunk and onto his knees as pure joy lit his face. "Did you open it?" The question was a reverent whisper.

"Not yet. I've been a little...busy."

"All the more reason to *not* take Karla's deal. *You* need to open it."

"Why can't I do both?"

"Not possible."

"Yes, it is. I can stall for time." But how much time? I needed to heal first if I planned to climb between levels. "Are you still scheduled for..." I couldn't speak the words.

"No. My appointment with Chomper has been delayed until further notice. I guess if they recycle me, the LC wouldn't have any bait for her trap." A tired resignation colored the tone of his voice. "How are you going to stall for time?"

"Don't worry about it. You just need to hold out for a little longer."

He huffed. "You have no idea. Do you?"

My thoughts raced. Communication with the LC would have to be through a third party, which would be time-consuming. "I can make a few unreasonable demands, and by the time we negotiate Gateway will be open. And then…" I couldn't speculate any further.

"Everything changes," Cog said.

seventeen

The trip back to the storeroom progressed at a much slower pace. No longer driven by the need to speak to Cog, I tended to stop often and lay my cheek against the cool metal of the duct. The warm air flowing through the shaft didn't help either. I dozed off a few times.

My sense of accomplishment on reaching the storeroom evaporated in an instant. Riley occupied the couch. I couldn't call it sitting. Every muscle was so taut he appeared as if welded in place. His furious expression matched his posture.

I concentrated on pulling my body from the vent. My adventure ended on the ground in a painful and exhausted heap. Wondering how I would find the energy to endure the inevitable recriminations and questions from Riley, I rested my head on the floor.

Instead, he gathered me in his arms and carried me to the couch. "This is the second time I've had to pick you up. At least, this time you're conscious." He knelt and set me down with care. All signs of his anger had dissipated. "Good thing you don't weigh much, either." He fussed about, propping cushions.

I was half asleep when he said, "Let's see what damage you've done." He pulled back my uniform to expose my injury. "A pillow." He shook his head as he peeled off the tape.

Blood soaked the underside of the pillow. I closed my eyes against the sudden queasiness in my stomach. He probed the cut and I hissed in pain.

"Amazing. You didn't rip any stitches, but you need a new bandage."

I peeked at him. His tone was matter-of-fact and he moved with confident efficiency as if he changed bandages all the time.

"It's going to hurt." He gloated.

"You need to work on your bedside manner," I said.

"And you need to listen to your doctor. Now hold still."

I bit my lip as he removed the old dressing and replaced it with a clean one. He covered me with a blanket. Rummaging around his desk, he returned with a tool resembling bolt cutters but smaller.

"Cuff."

I held my arm out. "Any chance you have some sheep oil?" I asked as he tightened the clamp.

"Nope. And this *will* hurt." He grunted and the metal cuff buckled.

It broke with a crunch snap, gouging a hunk of skin in the process just like Emek had warned. Riley pulled the damaged cuff from my wrist and bandaged the bleeding gouge. He poured me a glass of water. Remembering the doctor's instructions, I sipped it.

Riley sat on the edge of the couch, and I knew the questions would start. He didn't disappoint me. "What was so important?"

I told him about Cog. About his strength, his sacrifice and

his beliefs. "I couldn't let him be recycled without knowing about Gateway."

Riley listened without interruption. "Then we need to open Gateway before he's recycled." He glanced at the floor as if undecided, then met my gaze. "You said you didn't have a mate."

I almost laughed, but remembered the pain it caused. "I don't. Cogon is like…" I cast about for the right upper word. "A brother to me. You should know how that is, you have one."

"I saw him once, and then he was gone." He frowned. "I thought scrubs didn't have families."

"We don't. I was trying to match the feeling. Cog was my care mate. Which means we grew up together, looked after each other." I struggled to keep my eyes open.

"Get some rest, Trella." Riley smoothed a few hairs from my face and stroked my cheek.

"We need to plan."

"We'll make plans when you're stronger. Rest now. Doctor's orders."

This time I listened.

I woke to the ungentle prodding of the doctor.

She perched on the edge of the couch and held up the needle I had yanked from my arm. "I see you decided to stop your medicine. Are you feeling better?"

"Yes." The dizziness and nausea were gone. My stomach rumbled, and I had no energy. The doctor helped to prop me up, bending caused too many spikes of pain.

"Here." She handed me a warm bowl of tan-colored water and a spoon.

I sniffed the strange substance.

"It's broth. It'll help you recover." Amusement filled her voice. "If you keep that down, I'll give you a thicker soup."

Sipping a spoonful of broth, I waited for my stomach's reaction. My hunger strengthened, and I abandoned the spoon to drink right from the bowl.

"Enjoy being able to recover quickly. When you get past thirty-five centiweeks old, it's harder to heal." She handed me the soup. "In a few hours you can return to your normal diet." Rising, she glanced around the room. "Eventually, you're going to want to take a shower and sleep in a real bed." Her gaze returned to me. "You already have the student's uniform, and I have an extra bed in my rooms next to the infirmary you can use. It's supposed to be for an intern, but none of the current class has the skills needed, and I'm waiting for a few of the younger kids to grow older."

A generous and dangerous offer. She would be recycled if I was found in her rooms. "Wouldn't my presence be suspicious?"

"Not really. Students have more freedom and aren't tracked as closely until they choose a profession and are given a port. My supervisor would actually be happy to see I have selected an intern—he's been nagging me about it for weeks." She checked my pulse. "Strong. You should be fine."

Collecting a few medical items, she headed toward the door. Before she left, she looked at me. "Think about my suggestion, Ella. Riley knows where to find me."

Her offer was out of the question. Karla would not stop until she found me and I needed to confirm Gateway's location, talk to Logan about those files, open Gateway and turn myself in to the Pop Cops for Cog. Playing Ella the upper with a very nice lady wasn't included in my to-do list no matter how much I wished it was there.

Instead I reviewed each task. Confirming Gateway's location would require climbing through the shafts. Not possible right now, but could be accomplished in another ten hours or so I hoped. The concern was if Karla had gotten the coordinates from Domotor or Logan and beaten me to Gateway. What then? The Pop Cops would control it. I could tell the scrubs about its existence. I barked out a laugh. I'd be the new prophet, raving about Gateway for everyone's amusement. No. If Karla had Gateway, the game would be over.

If I found Gateway, I would need to learn more about Outside and how to open the door. Logan guessed the needed information hid in the old files. Opening the files required passwords and Logan. Again I needed to be able to climb to contact the Tech No. If Karla held Logan, or if we couldn't deduce the correct passwords, then it was game over.

Opening Gateway depended on the success of task two, plus we would need uppers to cover the computer alerts. I had a list of possible sympathizers, but one of them was a spy. Logan had planned to check the computer records of the uppers. If he couldn't discover who worked for Karla, we'd need to find another group via Riley, and hope we didn't contact another spy. If we did—game over.

The last task, turning myself in to Karla had the least problems. And once the game was over, it would be the only job left for me to do.

I needed to communicate with Karla somehow, and I really needed to find out what she knew and what she planned. Too bad I couldn't crawl through the heating vents again and maybe listen—

Jacy's device! I had planted one above Karla's office. If I could pick up the audio signal, I could listen in. I ignored the fact I had no idea how to do it. My whole future depended on so many ifs and hopes and assumptions and possibilities that I would consider it impossible right now if I thought about it too much.

I decided to think positive and impart maximum damage. My tool belt was close enough to reach with a minimal amount of bending. I removed the microphone. Jacy might regret his offer to help.

I flipped it on and said, "Jacy, I need your help again. Lieutenant Commander Karla is offering me a deal and I need you to be my negotiator. Tell Karla that I will turn myself in if she promises to free Cogon so he can return to work in the lower levels and promises she won't recycle me. She won't accept those terms and she'll make a counteroffer. Tell her you'll communicate with me and let her know in twenty hours. Drag the negotiations out as long as possible. I don't care what the final terms are for me as long as Cogon stays alive and no one else is arrested. I'm trusting you."

"You don't care what the final terms are?" Riley asked. He closed the door and stood there holding a steaming bowl.

"No. As long as I cause problems and do maximum damage." I wondered how much he had heard.

"What about your friends? Don't you think they care?"

"But I would be helping them. And besides, it's my decision."

"Maybe they don't want you to help them. Did you ever think of that? Did you think about how *your* decision impacts others? Those you leave behind to deal with the gaping hole in their existence?"

Riley's agitation seemed excessive. He noticed my confusion. "I guess it must be a family thing. Something a scrub wouldn't understand. Although I wouldn't call me and my still-grieving father a family."

I remembered. Riley wasn't angry at me, but at his mother. Her name was on Domotor's recycled list. "I know you miss your mother—"

"You don't know. You're a *scrub*. You don't have a family."

Now I was livid. "Of course I do. The scrubs are my family. I have a Care Mother. I shared her with nine brothers and sisters, but she loves us all. And I have Cog, who I will give myself to Karla in order to save." My outburst surprised me, but not as much as the realization that I truly believed what I had said.

Riley couldn't keep the smugness from his voice. "Your description of life in the lower levels is completely different from how you described it to me when we first met. Perhaps uppers and lowers have more in common than you first thought." He tried to suppress a smirk and failed. "Come on, admit it."

"Did you come for a reason? I'm *supposed* to be resting."

He held the bowl up. "Admit it and I'll give you this stew." He blew over the top, sending a delicious smell my way.

"You're obnoxious."

"I've been called worse." He swept the food under my nose.

"All right. All right. Maybe I judged the uppers too soon."

"Nope. Not good enough for this wonderful meal. I want three words: *I, was, wrong.*" He held up three fingers and waggled them.

"You're mean. I'm injured and need nourishment to recover."

"The stew's getting cold."

"Fine. I was wrong. Happy?"

"Ecstatic." He gave me the bowl and a smile.

At least he didn't gloat. After scraping my spoon to retrieve the last bit, I decided the stew was worth my admission.

Riley hovered. I moved my legs so he could join me on the couch.

"You look better," he said. "Your face isn't as pale."

"I have you to thank. You risked a lot by fetching the doctor."

He shrugged. "Doctor Lamont is a friend of my father's." He pulled at a thread on the couch. "Considering the extent of your injury and blood loss, the doctor was amazed you made it up here."

"You know how stubborn I can be. I wanted to warn you

about Domotor. Once they break him, he'll tell the Pop Cops about you and Logan." I looked at the clock. Hour twenty-one. Plenty of time for Vinco's knife to have done its job.

"They don't have him yet," Riley said.

I straightened, tugging my stitches. "What happened?"

"LC Karla knows he's been using his port, but her computer experts can't trace it back to an exact location. All she knows is he's on level one. She's been trying to search the entire level."

"Trying?"

He grinned. "The Pop Cops have been besieged with a run of bad luck. Malfunctioning equipment, missing tools, miscommunications and a broken water pipe."

Jacy had heeded my request, which meant he'd warned Logan and probably received my most recent communication. I wondered if Logan was the reason for Karla's computer woes. "How do you know about her troubles?"

"One of the metal cutters overheated and injured an ensign. Doctor Lamont treated him. Nice, chatty fellow." He leaned forward. "Now we have a little time to find Gateway."

"Yes. But we'll need Logan and a bunch of uppers to help."

"We have me, my father and Doctor Lamont. I have a cousin in mechanical that I can trust. Who else did Domotor mention?"

"Kiana Garrard, Hana Mineko, Takia Qadim and Breana Narelle. But one of them works for the Trava family. Logan might be able to tell us which one."

Riley wound the couch's thread around his hand. "I've heard of Takia. She works in the Control Room. One of only two people who are not Travas. I've met Breana and Hana. They were part of my father's training group, but he hasn't visited with them in hundreds of weeks. I never heard of Kiana Garrard. Do you know which system she works in?"

"No. We need Logan."

"You're in no condition to bring him through the air shafts."

I agreed. LC Karla was occupied with locating Domotor. Perhaps Logan could take the lift. It would be a matter of timing, and Logan being able to find the Pop Cop uniform I had hidden. I shared my idea with Riley.

"It could work as long as his nerves don't give him away. How are you going to contact him?"

I showed Riley the listening device.

He whistled. "When you decide to break the law, you certainly don't skimp. Illegal technology *and* a stolen Pop Cop uniform."

"Borrowed. You're not exactly Mr. Law-and-Order. In fact…" I had an idea.

"Oh no. This can't be good."

"Is there any way you can pick up an audio signal?" I asked.

He took the device and examined it. "If I had the frequency, yes. Why?"

"There is one of these hidden in Karla's office. Knowing her plans will help us."

His surprise didn't last long. "Gee, I wonder how it got there," he said with a light sarcasm.

"No idea," I said, playing along. "Kids these weeks." I tsked. "Always getting into trouble. Not like me, I'm the soul of conformity."

He laughed. "We should make that your code name. Soul of Conformity or SOC for short."

After Riley left, I contacted Jacy through the device, telling him about our plans. "Send Logan up at hour twenty-six. He tends to get nervous so it would be a good time for another distraction. I also need the frequency of the bug in Karla's office."

If all went as planned at hour twenty-six, Logan would dress in the Pop Cop uniform and take the lift to level four where Riley would be waiting to escort him to our storeroom.

Realizing I'd used *our* instead of *Riley's,* I grunted with amusement. Storeroom also failed as a descriptor. Recent events had transformed the room into an infirmary, a hideout and a bedroom. Riley had ordered me to rest.

I wormed into a comfortable position, but my thoughts swirled with worries and my hip ached. Giving up, I scanned the room for something to distract me. Besides Riley's electrical sketches, nothing caught my eye. I could understand why Domotor hadn't waited for Logan. Boredom was worse than unclogging pipes for waste handling.

A little gray lump rested under the desk. Careful of my stitches, I eased to my feet and shuffled to pick up Sheepy. His mother was a few feet away. I carried them both to the couch. Small flecks of blood dotted their coats and I used the water in my drinking glass to clean them off.

I wondered about Riley's brother. From his comments, I guessed the boy died right after birth. So where was Dada Sheepy?

Eventually, I dozed, dreaming about sheep. I held a bleating lamb as I waded through a hallway filled with sheep. A wet crunching sound chased me. It grew louder as I stumbled over the animals, convinced Chomper's blades would soon bite me. I tripped. Rolling over, I pushed the lamb behind my back to face the threat, but Cog stood between me and darkness.

He offered his hand. I grasped it and he pulled me to my feet. Then he stepped aside and flung me toward the LC.

"Use her to ensure their cooperation," he said.

His laughter followed me as she dragged me away.

"Game's over, Tre… Trella. Trella. Wake up."

I squinted into the daylight. Riley stood next to a Pop Cop. Wide awake in an instant, I nearly tore my stitches sitting up before I recognized the face. "Anne-Jade? What happened?"

"Logan's being monitored," she said. "A Pop Cop noticed he was spending a lot of time on the computer."

"I thought they were all busy with the search," I said.

"Most are, but a few Pop Cops are convinced the missing scrub is being helped and are determined to be the one to find you and get a promotion. They've made life in the lower levels even more intolerable." Her gaze swept the room. "Although, I must say I'm disappointed by level four. Is level three any better?" Anne-Jade asked Riley.

"No. It's about the same."

"Pity."

"Anne-Jade, do you have any news?" I asked.

She settled on the couch, leaving Riley to sit on the floor. "The first thing I'm supposed to tell you is from Jacy." Her nose creased with distaste. "He says you owe him big and when this whole mess is over, you're his slave for a week."

Nice of him to be optimistic.

Riley's mouth opened in stunned outrage. "He doesn't mean—"

"No." I assured him. "Jacy'll have me planting his bugs all over Inside. Go on, Anne-Jade."

"Logan gave me a list of password questions to memorize. Do you have a wipe board?"

Riley rummaged through the desk, and wrote down the questions. All were vague yet had enough information to make them seem possible to answer. The third question mentioned a platitude about being unable to see. No quick answers jumped to mind.

"What about the uppers? Did Logan have time to check them?" I asked.

"Yes. He said he found one of the names mentioned as an informant in the security files. The rest had clean records."

"Which one?" I asked.

"Kiana Garrard."

Her name banged hard against my metal heart, sending vibrations along my skin. I shouldn't be surprised. If she could abandon her child in the lower levels, she could rat out her husband and others.

"Anything else about the uppers?" Riley asked.

"Yes, Logan said Takia Qadim would be the best person to have on our side as she has access to multiple systems."

"How will she and the others know to trust us?"

I shuffled through all the information Domotor had told me. "This is going to sound hokey, but tell them the Force of Ten is back in action." Which was true. If I counted Logan, Anne-Jade, Riley, Doctor Lamont and myself the number was ten.

"I don't know if I can say that with a straight face," Riley said.

"Just think of the consequences if they don't help us."

"Good point."

Anne-Jade had been fidgeting with the top button on the Pop Cop uniform. Dipping her head down, she spoke to her chest. "Did it work?" Then she pressed a fingertip to her ear-ring, cocking her head.

Riley and I exchanged a significant look. Had the pressure been too much for her?

"Okay. I'll give it to her. Thanks." Anne-Jade noticed our dubious expressions. "I can't keep playing messenger between you and the lower levels." She pulled the small blue earring from her earlobe. "Receiver." She dug into her pocket, and removed a strange metal device that resembled a rivet gun. She placed the earring in the gun and pressed it to my left earlobe. "Hold still."

Before I could protest, she squeezed and a loud pop sounded in my ear followed by a sharp pain. Anne-Jade batted my hand away as she finished, wiping my lobe with a medicinal-smelling cloth. It came away wet with my blood.

"Now you can hear Jacy." She yanked on her top button. It

popped off with ease and revealed an identical button underneath. "Microphone. It's built into a standard issue button and
attaches with ease. Go on, try it."

I clipped the metal microphone to my top button.

"She's on," Anne-Jade said.

"Trella?" Jacy asked.

I started and glanced around. His clear voice sounded as if
he stood next to me.

"Trella, are you there?"

"Yes."

"No need to shout, I can hear you just fine. These devices
of the Tech Nos are wonderful. Once they make more, we can
coordinate our team's efforts."

"What team?"

Anne-Jade averted her gaze.

"The Gateway team of course." Jacy's matter-of-fact reply
contrasted with his upsetting revelation.

"How did you—"

"He threatened to report us to the Pop Cops," Anne-Jade
said in her defense.

Under normal circumstances, Jacy wouldn't interact with
the Pop Cops.

"You fell for his bluff. How much did you tell him?" I asked
her.

But Jacy answered. "Everything and you should have come
to me right away instead of blundering around."

Riley's confusion increased as I talked to Jacy, but he kept
quiet.

"Blundering? You would have done better?" I asked.

"Of course. I would have assigned people to cover your
shift, to help smuggle food and to supply you with information."

"But I couldn't—"

"Trust anyone. I know."

I had planned to say "get you in trouble," but he was right, too. "You're helping now." With Jacy, we were the force of eleven. It didn't have the same cachet.

"Small consolation, considering the havoc down here." Yet a gleeful challenge spiked his tone as if he looked forward to the upcoming difficulties.

"What's the status?" I braced for his answer.

"Pop Cops everywhere, snooping around. It's only a matter of time before they do a full level-wide search, and there are certain…things I'd rather they not find."

"What about the negotiations with Karla?"

A pause. "There are none. Before you yell, hear me out."

I growled my assent.

"Karla offered every enticement possible to get the scrubs to rat you out. Failing that, she has announced Cogon's life could be spared if you turn yourself in. Wait! Since nothing has resulted from her efforts, she believes you're hiding in the ducts, wounded and close to expiring. The air shafts are filled with RATSS. And I don't want to bust her illusions."

"What about Cog?"

"He's been protecting you since we were toddlers, and the worst thing you can do for him is to undermine his efforts and turn yourself in. Besides, once you open Gateway, it'll be a whole new world."

"But what if—"

"Stop! Don't what-if me. Do your part and get Gateway opened, and I'll do mine, making life miserable for the Pop Cops. Time to go. I'm needed elsewhere, but I'll keep a man monitoring this frequency."

His comment reminded me. "Jacy, what's the frequency for Karla's bug?"

"Ninety-eight megahertz."

"Thanks for your help."

He chuckled. "Don't worry, you *will* return the favor. And once the Tech Nos build more of those receivers, I'll contact you."

I turned off the button microphone, and filled Anne-Jade and Riley in on what Jacy had said.

"What's to stop the Travas from picking up the frequency?" I asked.

"Nothing, but with a large number of frequencies, the odds are small they would find it," Riley explained. He stood and brushed off his pants. "I'll escort Anne-Jade back to the lift." He handed me the board with the password questions. "You work on these, and I'll start recruiting uppers."

I couldn't help smiling at his bossy tone. "Who put you in charge?"

"Sheepy."

"Are we the Force of Sheep now?"

"No. We are the Force of Onaaaaae." He bleated the word as if he were a sheep.

eighteen

I threw a pillow at Riley for his awful pun. He ducked easily and escorted Anne-Jade from our storeroom. Before he left, he poked his head back into the room and said, "Byaaaaae."

My aim was off and the next pillow hit the closing door. I debated the merits of standing to retrieve the cushions and decided to stay on the couch and study the list of ten password questions. We had solved the one to gain access to Gateway's coordinates, and the other referred to the number of teeth on my comb with the pearl handle—which I had counted before losing it when the Pop Cop had attacked me.

Eight questions remained. I puzzled over them, but I couldn't solve any of them with one answer. Number six was, *What do you turn to get the outside in?*

The answer could be a doorknob, a handle, a lock or a screw. With no one for me to bounce ideas off of, I wrote down as many possible answers and tried another.

Your eyes can see, but mine don't work, yet I see what you can't. What am I? And tried another. After a few hours, my head ached. I abandoned my task and rested. Hour thirty meant Riley had returned to work and it would be a while before my next meal. My empathy for Domotor increased with every passing hour. Those first seventy hours in his hideout had been rough. At least he had a washroom and kitchen. I calculated how long he could survive on the food stocked in his refrigerator. His continued freedom still amazed me.

I tried to sleep, but my empty stomach complained, and Doctor Lamont's offer of using her shower tempted me. The floor plans of the four levels of Inside matched for the most part. Quad C4 was dedicated to the Power plant, and Sectors D4, E4 and F4 contained living areas. The biggest difference between level four and one was the water tanks.

Sectors B4 and H4 housed large water-storage tanks, while on level one those sectors held the laundry and the waste-water treatment plant. The infirmary for the scrubs was in Sector H2 along with the care facility.

I had limited my excursions to the upper levels to avoid being detected, but I remembered seeing the uppers' infirmary on level three Sector B. To gain access through the air shafts, I would need to climb into the Gap. My tender hip would be a problem.

I still wore the upper's student jumper. Could I stroll through the upper levels as if I belonged there? More importantly, would I? Anne-Jade had worn Jacy's listening device in plain sight. Zippy appeared to be a regular cleaning troll. Even the decoder had an ordinary disguise as a timer.

Was a shower worth getting caught? No. But it was worth testing if I could travel through the upper levels without being recognized. A thin rationalization. And the Pop Cops wouldn't think to look for me up here. Right? Decision made, I searched for a good spot to leave Riley a note, hoping he wouldn't be too upset.

Before leaving the storeroom, I combed my hair with my

fingers and let it hang down past my shoulders to cover the earring. I used the water in my glass to wash my face and rinsed the dried blood from my hands. A tool belt around my waist would appear odd to the uppers. Funny how I felt improperly dressed without its comforting weight, but all I had left was the decoder. It fit into a long pocket in the uniform's pants. Once I tucked the wipe board of password questions inside the top of my jumper, I was, at least physically, ready to go.

I mapped the shortest route from the storeroom to the infirmary in my mind, drew in a steadying breath and left the room. After a quick peek around the optical illusion of the hallway to check for people, I strode with purpose as if I had an important message to deliver.

A few uppers met my gaze and nodded, others ignored me and the three Pop Cops I passed didn't show any signs they recognized me. With my heart somersaulting in my chest, I arrived at the infirmary. The possibility that Doctor Lamont wouldn't be there didn't occur to me until I pushed open the door. The rectangular room duplicated the scrubs' infirmary, containing a row of beds against each long wall, with a narrow path between them. But the privacy curtains hanging from a U-shaped metal track on the ceiling above the beds weren't included in the scrubs' room. Two beds were occupied with sleeping patients. A high counter arched from the back right wall next to a wide entrance.

When I was halfway across the room, Doctor Lamont bustled from the entry, carrying a tray. A slight hitch in her step indicated her surprise, but she smiled.

She gestured toward the back room. "I'll be there in a minute. I need to give Izak his meds."

I aimed for the door. Shelves filled with medical supplies hid behind the high counter on the right. Through the entrance was an examination room. Stainless-steel instruments glinted in the harsh light. I balked at the threshold. The flat table covered with a black pad, straps and stirrups reminded me of my first medical examination.

Scrubs were required to have a complete physical at fourteen centiweeks. No part of my body had been left unexamined. I shivered at the memory of the cold probes. The Pop Cops claimed the exam ensured the scrub's health and ability to perform the job they had been assigned.

I jumped when Doctor Lamont placed her cold hand on my back, guiding me into the room.

"The surgery is over there." She pointed to a wide door on the right. "And my office is back here."

We entered a small alcove in the back left corner, which opened into her workplace. A far friendlier place than the last. My gaze was drawn to the oversize quilt hanging on the wall. Small squares of color had been sewn together in a pattern. I squinted and stepped back, trying to discern it.

She noticed my gaze. "It's a stethoscope."

The shape of the long tubes and round bottom became clear.

"You're wondering why a stethoscope." Her thin eyebrows arched as if inviting me to speculate.

"No. It's one of the tools of your trade."

"But why not a thermometer or a scope or a scalpel?"

"It's your quilt. I think you would know the answer better than me."

She laughed. "Yes, but I want your opinion."

I hid my surprise by focusing on the quilt. All the doctor's instruments were important. Each played a role. A stethoscope listened to a patient's heart and lungs. I imagined working as a doctor as patient after patient came through the doors. After a while, I thought doctors would view their work as just another job. How would a doctor make a connection with so many different people?

"You picked the stethoscope because hearing a person's heart beating is a…" I moved my hands as if I could pull the right word from my throat. "Treasured part of being a doctor. No one else can hear it unless they're really close to the person. By letting you listen to their heart, they're trusting you."

She nodded her head as if impressed by my answer.

"Am I right?" I asked.

"There is no right or wrong answer. You could have said it was my favorite instrument, which is also true. One thing I like to do with my stethoscope is listen to Inside's heartbeat." Doctor Lamont pulled it from her neck and handed it to me. "Go ahead. Press it to the wall."

Curious, I placed the ends in my ears. My left lobe throbbed when the instrument brushed the earring. Touching the wall with the round sensor, I braced for an amplified Hum. Instead, a distinct rumble sounded, alternating from louder to softer. A series of knocks also repeated in a steady beat. I returned the device.

"Interesting, isn't it? Our ears can't discern all those mechanical noises. To us it's just the Hum. Unnoticed until we make an effort to hear it. I enjoy listening to the different components of Inside's heartbeat. It comforts me." She swept her hand out in a dismissing wave. "Silly, I know."

"It's not silly."

"Well, I'm sure you didn't come here to discuss my quilt. I'm guessing my offer sounded more inviting with time."

"Yes."

"Any trouble on the way over?" she asked.

"None at all."

A tired sadness filled her olive-colored eyes. "I'm not surprised. People have been afraid to get to know others who are outside their families. The halls are filled with strangers."

Sounded liked the scrubs. "Why?"

"When noticed by the Travas, the friendship is immediately a cause for suspicion. The Travas view any group of people as potential rebels. Also, people are afraid of being reported. If you don't have a friendship with another, then when they get mad at you, they can't call you a scrub-lover and have you arrested."

I stared at her. If I exchanged Trava for Pop Cop, she could be talking about the lower levels.

She shook her head. "You don't want to hear about this. Wait here, let me check to make sure my clothes aren't all over the floor." The doctor disappeared through another door.

This place reminded me of a maze. I glanced around the rest of the room. Her computer occupied the middle of her neat desk, and two big armchairs faced it. A basket of toys sat on the floor. I knelt next to it and rooted through the meager contents. When disappointment stabbed, I realized I had been searching for Dada Sheepy.

"For my younger patients," she said behind me. "The shower is clean, but I want a peek at your incision before your stitches get wet."

She led me to her suite. Bigger than Riley's, it had two bedrooms, a sitting room, a small kitchen and a washroom. I peeled the uniform down and showed her the cut. In the brutal glare of the daylights, the bruises appeared purple, and black thread held together a swollen and angry red line. I swayed and rested against the wall.

"Healing nicely despite your adventures."

I gave her a dubious look.

"Trust the doctor." She sniffed and eyed my uniform. "Shower. I'll bring you a bowl of hot soup and a change of clothes."

I removed all the devices and decoder and hid them under a towel. The warm water felt wonderful despite the sting of the soap. When I finished, a steaming cup and a clean jumper waited for me as promised. I could get used to this attention.

Perhaps I could let Trella die in the air shafts so Ella could remain here.

"Better?" Doctor Lamont asked.

"Much."

"Your room's on the right. Get some sleep."

My room, I repeated in my mind. My room. With a narrow bed and single table with lamp, it wasn't elaborate or even special. But it was a rich luxury compared to sleeping in the barracks. The mattress springs creaked when I sat on the bed. Fun. I bounced, enjoying the feel. The bunks in the lower levels were cushioned with thin mats. Not that it mattered to me, I could sleep in an air shaft. But this was the first time I felt a real difference between the uppers and lowers.

If my parents hadn't abandoned me, would I be living in a similar room? Would I be happy? I imagined my life before the whole mess with Domotor. Would I trade that life for this? Yes. But trade my life now? No way.

As I stretched out on the bed, I worried I would be spoiled and unable to sleep in the vents after spending time here. For once, I decided to enjoy the moment.

Riley's insistent voice roused me from a dreamless slumber.

"…need to speak with her."

I stepped from the room feeling stronger and followed the voices to the doctor's office. Riley sat on the edge of one of the armchairs, leaning forward as if ready to launch himself across the desk. He sprang to his feet as soon as he spotted me in the doorway.

"You *are* better. When I saw your note…" Riley glanced at the doctor.

"He thought your condition had worsened and you sought medical help." A glint shone in her eyes. "He didn't believe me."

"Do you know how long it took her to trust *me?*" he asked

the doctor. "I couldn't imagine Ella risking so much for a shower."

He had a point. Normally, I would be very suspicious of the doctor's motives. But my regular instincts no longer felt right. All I thought I knew had been wrong.

"Not just a shower," Doctor Lamont said, "but a bowl of my famous soup. And I'm sure she's ready for another serving." She winked at me as she left the room.

An awkward silence descended.

"I'm sorry you worried," I said.

He smiled. "It's not all bad. At least now I know to offer you a shower and soup if I need you to trust me again."

With the tension broken, I settled into the other armchair. "You were talking about others when I first came in. Do you have any news?"

"They're being difficult. The near miss before has convinced most of them it won't work, but they're willing to at least listen to you." He paused in thought. "If the doctor is agreeable, I can have the others come to the infirmary at different times, complaining of a headache or something. You can talk to them here. It wouldn't draw as much suspicion and we can still keep our room a secret."

His plan made sense.

"And it avoids having the group members find out about each other, making it safer," Riley added.

Domotor had done the same thing, yet four people had been recycled. Keeping the others ignorant sounded logical, and my initial reaction was to agree. But the notion clanged. The atmosphere of the upper levels mirrored what the Pop Cops tried to do to the lower levels. Keep to yourself. Trust no one. Report your fellow to gain favor. I fell for it. From my ease in traveling in plain sight, I knew the uppers had fallen for it, too.

And so had the scrubs. Before.

Before what?

My thoughts raced over the past four weeks. They had kept my secret despite enticements and threats from Lieutenant Commander Karla. The kitchen scrubs worked together to stow the food for Domotor in the air shaft. Jacy and his buddies. Logan and Anne-Jade. They never would have risked themselves before.

Before…Broken Man and the promise of Gateway. He gave them a reason to join together and risk themselves for another.

"No," I said. "It will fail."

"What do you mean?" Riley asked.

The doctor came in carrying a bowl of soup, but I had her full attention. I wondered how much she had heard or what she suspected.

I answered his question regardless of the doctor. "Keeping everyone separate won't work. They all need to know who is in the group. They need to talk and make a connection." I looked at the doctor. "Hear each other's heartbeat, and know they're all risking themselves for the same reason. It's too easy to report a name. Or to give up when you don't know who you're letting down." I glanced between Riley and Doctor Lamont, willing them to understand.

"She's right," the doctor said. "If you don't hear a heartbeat, it's easy to send the body to be recycled."

"Full disclosure?" I could see Riley struggling with my complete reversal.

"Yes. And we can start with the doctor." I turned to her. "You saved my life and performed surgery in a storeroom because Riley asked you to. Why?"

Taken aback, she frowned. "He's the son of a friend."

"You know him."

"Right." She relaxed a bit.

"But you don't know me. You suspect I'm the missing scrub, so why not report me?"

"Again, for Riley."

"But you offered me a shower and a bed."

"Don't forget the soup," Riley said.

I shot him a look.

"What? I'm trying to help." He feigned innocence.

"Yes, and soup. Why?" I asked her.

"Curiosity mostly. Your strength is remarkable. The fact that you're up here instead of at the wrong end of a kill-zapper is impressive. I want to know why you're here. And, I wanted to get to know the person Riley would risk his life for."

"You wanted to hear my heartbeat?"

She smiled. "You're going to overuse that analogy, aren't you?"

"It works, though."

"Yes, it does and, yes, you're right."

I drew in a breath. "If I ask you for more help, would you be willing?"

She considered. "It depends on what you need."

"We need a meeting place and we think the infirmary would be ideal."

The doctor stiffened as a guarded expression blanketed her face. "What for?"

Time to slide down the chute. The scrubs needed Broken Man to rally around, and in order to be successful, the uppers would need someone, too.

Locking gazes with her, I said, "So we can coordinate our efforts in opening Gateway."

She gasped as all color flew from her face.

Riley elbowed me. "The whole heartbeat thing—does it work in reverse? 'Cause I think the doctor's heart has stopped."

"You…found it?" The doctor gripped the edge of her desk.

"I know where it is, but opening it is going to be difficult, hence the need for help. Are you willing?"

"Of course," she said without hesitating.

★ ★ ★

A meeting time was set and Riley planned to contact the uppers with the details. Before he left the infirmary, he gave me a narrow metal box as long as my hand. The number ninety-eight was on the digital readout.

"So you can listen to the bug in Karla's office," he explained. Then he paused as if struck by a notion. "It works the same as the receiver Anne-Jade made. With the batteries, that's the smallest space I could cram everything in." He touched the earring. "That's some serious tech. We have nothing like that up here. The Travas don't encourage invention."

"Then we have an advantage." I hoped it would be enough.

I kept Riley's device close by, but no sound emanated. Karla must be off-shift or elsewhere. I also worried because I hadn't heard from Jacy in a while. Feeling stronger, I paced around the infirmary.

Finally, Doctor Lamont said, "If you're going to be in the way, you might as well help me." She showed me the supply cabinet behind the high counter, and asked me to organize the contents. "In an emergency, it saves precious time."

The shelves bulged with various sizes of bandages, packages of sutures, tape, splints and packs of gauze all heaped together. As I worked to put order to chaos, uppers stopped in, seeking medical treatment or advice. Most ignored me. But on occasion, Doctor Lamont would ask me to help with a patient. If they asked, she introduced me as her new intern, Ella.

At one point, Lamont placed a bin full of clean bandages next to me. "Can you roll those when you have time?"

"Sure. With such exciting tasks as these, I'm surprised you don't have a ton of students volunteering to be your intern," I teased.

"Watch it or I'll have you scrubbing bedpans."

"Rolling bandages right now, Doctor." I saluted her, and exaggerated my enthusiasm for the task.

She laughed. I liked the sound of her laughter. Light and carefree and warm. She wasn't quick to laugh; grief clung to her skin like perfume but hadn't doused her empathy for others.

Around hour forty-five, my energy level dropped. A nap was more appealing than the last three shelves. I sat on the floor, resting my back when a shrill voice broke through my drowsiness.

"Doctor?" A woman's panicked voice.

I stood as Lamont rushed past. A very pregnant woman clung to the door. Her face ashen, she swayed on swollen feet. Bright blood stained her pants.

"My water broke," she said.

Lamont held her elbow and half carried her. I rushed to support the patient's other side.

"It's not supposed to be red, is it?" she asked.

"Where's your mate?" the doctor asked.

"Won't come. Too hard." The woman slurred her words. We reached the exam room.

"Surgery?" I asked.

"Not yet. I need to determine what's the matter."

Hoisting her onto the table, I grunted with pain, but soon forgot about my injury as the woman's condition worsened.

Lamont shouted orders to me and the patient. I fetched bandages and sterilized instruments.

The woman groaned and shuddered. "The baby wants to come out."

"Not yet. Hold on a little longer."

Doctor Lamont examined the patient and I held her hand. She squeezed my knuckles so hard, I thought she would crack my bones. The hand-crushing grip came every minute and was accompanied by moans from the woman.

"Contractions," the doctor said. "Flip that switch there." She pointed to a wall and I extracted my hand long enough to comply.

"Surgery now." Lamont pressed a pedal and the table sprouted wheels.

We rolled it into the surgery.

"Don't you need more help?" I asked.

"Called with the switch. He should be here soon." She launched into a flurry of instructions, leaving me no time to think.

The events blurred together. Another upper arrived and I had two people yelling orders at me. The woman's cries mixed with the loud bawl of a newborn. And somehow I ended up out in the exam room, holding a swaddled infant while the doctors attended to the woman in the surgery.

If Cog could see me now, he would be incapacitated with mirth. At least, the baby was asleep. Although I marveled that she could sleep after what had happened to get her out. The doctor had said the placenta blocked the birth canal and the woman needed an emergency C-section.

The baby weighed the same as Zippy, my small cleaning troll. More than I expected. I peered at her tiny face and wondered what name the woman would give her. Naming a person seemed a huge responsibility. In the lower levels, the scrubs handed their babies over and the Care Mothers assigned them names.

The male doctor bustled from surgery, peeling off bloody gloves. "She'll be fine. Thanks for your help." He came over and examined the baby. "The mother doesn't want to see her." He took a small bottle from his breast pocket. Unscrewing the strange rubber-topped lid, he withdrew a thin glass tube. "Hold her still," he instructed as he opened one of the baby's blue eyes. He squeezed the rubber and a drop of liquid splashed into her eye.

She startled and blinked. The doctor quickly doused her other eye, and retuned the bottle to his pocket. He held out his hands. "I'll take her now."

As he settled her in the crook of his arm, she opened both eyes wide and gazed at me with brown eyes. I almost stumbled. He had changed her eye color! Is that what Domotor meant when he had said I had been born with my father's blue eyes?

Doctor Lamont wheeled the woman from surgery, and I helped transfer the patient from the table to a bed. The woman cried in silence. Tears flowed down her temples and her mouth gathered into a tight grimace.

Lamont stroked the woman's head and squeezed her hand. "It'll be all right. The baby's healthy. She'll do fine."

Nothing the doctor said eased the woman's misery. When we returned to Lamont's office, she collapsed in a chair behind her desk and opened a drawer. Taking out a small glass and a bottle filled with an amber-colored liquid, she poured herself a drink. She considered, then reached for another glass and poured another albeit smaller portion.

"Sit down, Ella. Your performance in surgery was exemplary." She pushed the second glass toward me as I settled in the opposite chair. "Most people would faint on seeing so much blood, and to see the inside of a person's body."

I sniffed the contents of the glass. The fumes stung my eyes. "I tried not to think about what it meant. Just followed orders."

The doctor sipped her drink. I copied her, and almost spat the burning liquid out. She chuckled. "Haven't had spirits before?"

"No. My friend did once, but he wouldn't let me try it." Good thing, too, or I would have yelled and brought unwelcome attention.

"It's an acquired taste. The burn down your throat and the numbing warmth in your stomach become a pleasant experience."

Knowing what to expect, I swallowed the second sip without choking. The doctor rested her head on the back of the chair, closing her eyes.

"I do have a question," I ventured.

Without opening her eyes, she raised her glass in a swirl. "Go ahead."

"Why is the woman so upset?"

Her eyes snapped open and she fixed me with an incredulous expression. "You don't know?" Seeing my evident confusion, she straightened. "Aren't the women in the lower levels upset when they give their babies away?"

"Some are, I guess. But this is the upper level. You have families."

Understanding smoothed her sharp features before lines of grief deepened. "Yes, we have families, but, up here the rule is one couple, one child. We don't have enough room for more people, so if a couple has an accident and conceives another child, the child is sent to the lower levels."

The unexpected information slogged through my brain. Had she just said the child was sent to be a scrub?

The doctor continued, "The woman is upset because the baby is her second, and the infant will be sent to a care facility in the lower levels."

nineteen

Once I understood, the doctor's explanation slammed into me, shattering my beliefs. "Uppers are only allowed one child?" The foreign concept refused to find an empty seat in my logic.

"Yes. We have limited space, so the Travas have made it a law." The doctor peered at me in concern.

Perhaps if I broke down her information into manageable bits. "You mentioned the couple having an accident. How can getting pregnant be an accident? If you have sex, you're bound to have a baby in time."

"We have birth control, Ella. Women can choose if they want a baby or not. I'm guessing by your horrified surprise, scrubs don't have that option."

The revelation made perfect sense and yet made no sense at all. My mind grappled with it. It explained why Riley only saw his brother once, why he had said you don't *have* to have a child, and it meant perhaps my mother hadn't abandoned me. I could have been a second or third child—an astounding notion! Finally Domotor's comment about my blue eyes made sense.

"Those drops?" I asked.

"Drops?"

"In the baby's eyes."

"Oh. To change the color so the babies blend in with the scrubs and don't get teased for being different."

It didn't always work. I mulled over what she had said about birth control. Why not let the scrubs use birth control? With the overcrowded conditions getting worse every hour, why not limit the number of children born?

"Ella, are you all right?" Doctor Lamont stood beside me. She placed a cold hand on my forehead. "You lost all color in your cheeks. Take another sip of your drink."

I gulped the spirits, welcoming the harsh sting as it ripped down my throat. I asked Lamont why scrubs weren't offered birth control.

"Truthfully, I'm surprised they don't. The uppers have assumed scrubs don't cherish their offspring. That they keep having babies because they don't have to care for them. Basically, we all thought the crowding in the lower levels was your own fault." She returned to her seat. "Interesting how certain facts have been ignored in the computer. Or deleted."

I mulled over the ignorance on both sides. The results created two groups of people who distrusted each other, which would be ideal if you didn't want them to join forces. Again my contemplations looped back to why they let the scrubs grow in number.

We did the grunge work, but even if we limited births, there still would be plenty of scrubs to work. Another theory popped into mind. "Is the birth control hard to make? Or of limited quantity?"

"Not really. It's grown in hydroponics. You only need to ingest it when you're planning to be intimate." She jerked her head as if struck with a sudden thought. "You didn't seem concerned about your damaged ovary. Was it because you don't want children?"

"Yes. I'm not going to be intimate with anyone so that—" I waved toward the infirmary "—doesn't happen to me or to a child."

We discussed various reasons the Travas would allow the scrubs to increase in number, but we couldn't find a logical explanation.

"I'll ask LC Karla next time I see her," I joked.

But Doctor Lamont's demeanor turned to ice. "If that woman was injured, I would not save her life. In fact, I would happily feed her to Chomper myself." She stood and strode from the room, claiming she needed to check on her patients.

While I agreed with the doctor about Karla, I wondered what the LC had done to cause such a strong reaction from a caring individual.

The meeting with the uppers who'd agreed to help us convened in the doctor's sitting room at hour sixty. Riley and Doctor Lamont stood apart from the group, who talked among themselves in low whispers, getting acquainted and reminiscing about prior events. Riley's father, Jacob, kept peering at his son as if amazed the boy was there.

After learning about the uppers' birth control, I had wanted to discuss so much with Riley, but the group arrived and we had limited time.

Takia Qadim was the most vocal and spoke for the group. "Why will this attempt work when our first one failed?" Her sharp and intelligent gaze focused on me.

I willed my heart to stop its panicked thumping, and reminded myself about the need for full disclosure. "First we already know where Gateway is." A mixture of expressions spread over the four uppers. I waited for the information to sink in.

"Second, we have access to the other hidden files. One led us to the location, and I'm reasonably sure the others will tell us how to open Gateway and what to expect on the other side."

"Why do you need us?" Hana Mineko asked. Her black hair had been piled on top of her head in a pleasing twist of curls. She fiddled with a curl hanging by her ear, pulling it straight and releasing it. The hair sprang back each time.

"When Gateway is open, it will alert all the systems in Inside, and we need you to cover the alert so the Controllers and the Travas don't know. Once we know exactly what to expect on the other side of Gateway, then we can plan how to use it."

"Why don't you know what's in the rest of the files?" Takia asked.

"They're protected by passwords. We haven't figured out the rest of them yet." A rumble of alarm rolled through the uppers. "We have the password clues, and I hoped as a group we could deduce the answers."

"Let me get this straight," Jacob said. "Provided you open the files, we then have to hide your activity from the Trava family while you open Gateway." He looked around. "You're going to need to recruit more uppers."

"We have two scrubs willing to ghost through the network and aid in hiding data. And don't forget Domotor." As long as he listened to Logan's instructions.

Breana Narelle pulled her shirt down over her pregnant belly. "Four people were recycled last time because Domotor was caught. This time we all know who's involved. What if someone here is the person who ratted us out?"

"We know who spied for Karla and she hasn't been invited back. Obviously you don't say anything to anyone, but especially not to Kiana Garrard," I said, proud I didn't stutter over her name. It's possible she hadn't abandoned me, but she still caused much pain and suffering.

Most of the group nodded with understanding, but Jacob flashed the doctor a strange, pain-filled look, which she returned. I wondered if they both knew Kiana.

"Why should we risk our lives for the scrubs?" Breana asked. "They hate us and are jealous of us. They won't do anything to help us. Why should we help them?"

I counted to ten before answering her, reminding myself she has been fed lies about the scrubs all her life. Then I explained to the group just how much the scrubs had done to get me here. The ghosting through the network, Cog's sacrifice and Jacy's risks as well as the amazing fact that not one scrub had yet to provide information to the Pop Cops despite the fantastic rewards offered by the LC.

"The Travas are our mutual enemy. They have lied to you and to the scrubs to keep us from joining together. Think about it. The scrubs outnumber the uppers ten to one. But you have control of the systems keeping us alive, and the Travas have control of us both. Teaming up takes the Travas out of the equation. We can return to the times when each family had an equal say."

My speech worked and the uppers set about planning. They wanted to hear the password clues and I read them aloud. Two questions produced answers right away. Six left. I repeated the first question and everyone brainstormed.

During an unusual lull in the conversation, LC Karla spoke from my pocket. Terrified faces turned to me and I hurried to explain about the listening device and Riley's receiver. I retreated to my room to hear the conversation better.

"…another busted scanner? That's three this shift. Something's going on," the LC said. Her voice strained with frustration.

"It can't be sabotage. No scrub was allowed near them. They

were guarded the entire time by my men," a man said. His voice sounded familiar.

"Eyes on the devices? Or an ensign stationed outside the supply cabinet?"

"Why would it matter?"

"The scrubs are using the air shafts to get around, you idiot!"

"Lieutenant Commander, no one is in the shafts. The RATSS have found no evidence."

"I saw her with my own eyes, *Commander.*" Karla's tone was even, but each word had a little kick to it as if she bit back her anger.

She was talking to Vinco, the knife-wielding bastard.

"I believe you. But she's not there now. She's hiding with this Broken Guy. We need to entice her out," Vinco said.

"I've tried. I promised to not recycle her friend if she turned herself in. It didn't work."

"Perhaps we need to find someone she cares for more," Vinco said.

"She has no other friends. The general opinion is she's a loner and detests being among the scrubs. Not that I blame her."

"She might think you're bluffing about her friend. Schedule him for execution. Parade him down through the lower levels on his way to Chomper's Lair, take him inside and kill-zap him if she doesn't give herself up."

"And if she does?"

"Contact me and I start the interrogations." I shuddered at the delight in his voice.

"Then what should I do about her friend?"

"Keep him alive. He's fun to play with."

"What time should I schedule him?"

"Before the hundred-hour assembly."

"All right. Go spread the word, Commander."

The sound of a shutting door echoed through Riley's metal box. I stared at the clock. Hour sixty-two. Thirty-eight hours to turn myself in. Yet another countdown. I felt as if I had already grieved for Cog, either that or I felt more confident of our success.

I rejoined the others. They had answered another two questions. Four left.

"What's the one about turning something in?" Takia asked me.

"Oh. It's number six. It's *What do you turn to get the outside in?*"

A discussion ensued, producing the same answers I had. Riley sat in the midst of them, adding his own arguments to the debate. But Doctor Lamont kept her place along the wall. Her pale face appeared strained. I walked over to her.

"Do you feel all right?" I asked.

She gave me a wan smile. "Isn't that my line?"

"When you look as white as the lady sleeping in the infirmary, it's a valid question."

"Just tired." She pushed away from the wall. "I better check on her and make sure there's no internal bleeding." Doctor Lamont hurried from the room.

That's all the poor woman needed, I thought. She had lost so much blood; I hoped she wasn't bleeding on the inside.

Daylights flooded my mind. Of course, how stupid! I punched the wall. Everyone quieted and stared at me.

"I know the answer to number six!" I cried.

"Don't keep us in suspense," Riley said.

"Inside out! You turn the inside out to get the outside in."

The group worked another hour, then each left at different times. We had answers, or what we thought were the correct answers to six out of eight questions. Not bad. I turned on my button microphone and hoped someone was listening like Jacy had promised. I sent a message, asking Jacy to bring Logan to Domotor's hideout at hour eighty-one. His hidden room would be the best to access the network without interruption and without Pop Cops looking over his shoulder. I toggled off the microphone.

Riley returned to his workstation and Doctor Lamont rested in her room. Exhaustion pulled at me, but the doctor had asked me to watch over her patients while she slept.

They all appeared to be asleep, and I wasn't sure I would even know if they were in trouble. Watching them sure beat scrubbing air ducts. At one point the woman moaned and I rushed over. Lamont had left a few pain pills by the patient's bedside in case she needed more.

"Are you in pain?" I asked.

"Yes," she said. Her voice was thin and weak.

"The doctor has pills." I moved to get her a glass of water, but the woman grabbed my arm.

"A pill can't ease this kind of pain. Can you sit and talk to me?"

"Sure." I pulled a chair beside her bed. We sat in uncomfortable silence for a while.

"What's your name?" she asked.

"Ella."

A half smile played on her white lips. "That's it? No family names?"

"Oh. Ella Garrard Sanchia."

"Still no mate, then?"

"No. I'm Doctor Lamont's intern." I pulled on my sleeves, reminding myself to tread carefully and watch what I said.

"Did you… Did you see her?"

Only one possible "her." The baby. "Yes. She is beautiful."

"Really?" The woman bit her lip.

Instinct took over my voice box. "She has long dark eye-lashes and already a full head of hair. Her face was a perfect oval, her chin came to a little point with a dimple. Skin so smooth and as soft as the underside of a sheep's ear." My surprise matched the woman's. I'd held the baby for minutes, yet I could form a lifelike picture of her in my mind's eye.

Unfortunately, my description caused the woman more pain. Tears flowed and her chest heaved in quiet sobs. Feeling terrible, I tried to ease her anguish. "Don't worry so much. She will be loved in the lower levels. The care facility is broken into units of ten children per Care Mother. The Mothers love all the children and she will grow up with care mates, who will look after her. I'm sure one of the older boys will become very protective, and she will fuss about his attention but be his staunchest supporter."

The woman stared at me as if I had sprouted wings. I didn't know what caused me to say so much. At least I didn't lie to her. Care mates could be very protective.

Instead of questioning me on how I knew so much, the upper sighed in relief. "What do you think they'll name her?"

"Hmm… She'll need a pretty name, but not too girly as I think she'll be a bit of a tomboy."

"Gillie? I always liked the name."

"A good choice."

We discussed Gillie's life, her toddler years, her schooling and her career.

"I think she might gravitate to working in the care facility. As a helper to start and then as a Care Mother," I said.

By this time, the upper's tears had dried. She smiled proudly. "Yes, I'm sure she will love the little ones and have enough patience for the active three-hundred-week-olds."

"And the nice man who works in recycling, you know, the one who made her those metal flowers?"

"Do you think he wants to be her mate?" she asked.

"There's not much time or material to make those petals for just anyone. He's interested."

We talked through Gillie's life from start to finish, including all her accomplishments and major life events. The woman fell asleep with a dreamy half smile still on her lips.

I remained by her bedside. Cog would be amused by my efforts to comfort an upper. No. Not amused. Proud. I liked Ella. She was a good sort, much nicer than Trella, and I hoped she managed to survive the next thirty hours.

Doctor Lamont woke me. I had been dozing in the chair. "Sorry," I said.

"No, I'm sorry. You had a hellish twenty hours and I left you to watch my patients."

"You need to sleep, too." Memories of the emergency replayed in my mind. "I don't know how you could be so rational with all the blood gushing, and being able to cut through her stomach...." My own stomach rolled and I had to put my head in my hands to stop the swirl of dots in front of my eyes.

"But you were fine during the crisis. I've had to step over interns who had passed out during surgery."

"Like I said, I didn't think about it."

Lamont pressed her fingers to the woman's wrist, checking her pulse. "Poor Doreen. She's in for a rough time. Losing a child..."

She stared at the wall, but her gaze peered into another world. "The loss lingers inside you, clinging like beads of moisture until rust forms and spreads. Eventually, the structure can't hold the weight and it collapses."

Her description had to come from experience. Not knowing what to say, I again let instinct guide my words. "I hope she finds another way to support the weight and keep the rust at bay. It would be a pity for her to live her life as an empty shell, when she has a mate and another child to care for."

The doctor snapped out of her reverie. "It would be, but words are easy. It's convincing the heart that's hard. Get some sleep, Ella."

★ ★ ★

I did as the doctor ordered and slept for the next eight hours. Feeling almost normal, I ate a large portion of a three-bean casserole Lamont had cooked. She had access to the same ingredients as the lower levels, but her concoctions tasted better.

After enduring a lecture to be careful, I climbed into the air shafts above level three. The tight duct was at once comforting and oppressive. An unfamiliar moment of panic washed over me. I ignored the flood of doubts and fears that soaked me. It was just like being in the surgery, if I stopped to think too much about what we planned to do, I would be unconscious.

The trip to Logan's barrack lasted twice as long as normal. My movements were slow and my muscles protested being used after such a long time. I paused every few minutes to listen and search for RATSS. The mechanical clicking of their metal rollers echoed through the vents and I managed to dodge two devices.

Logan waited for me by the heating vent near his bunk.

"What about your Pop Cop?" I asked.

"He thinks I'm sleeping." Logan grunted as he squeezed into the vent.

I led him to Domotor's room. It had been over a hundred hours since I'd been there and I hoped he was well.

Slumped on the couch, Domotor's drawn face relaxed a bit when he saw me sliding from the vent after Logan.

"Where have you been? What's going on? I'm a wreck, jumping at every noise."

Dark smudges under his eyes stood out in contrast to his pale face. His uncombed hair hung in greasy clumps. An overripe smell emanated from his body.

He noticed my expression. "I didn't want to be caught in the shower. I do have my dignity."

"Not to worry," Logan said. "I covered your computer trail

just in time." He aimed for the computer and pulled a chair close to the keyboard. "Trella, what are the passwords?"

For a moment, I felt as if he talked to another person and I didn't respond.

"Passwords?"

As if waking from a dream, I cleared my head and repeated the ones we had figured out. "We still have three unanswered, but at least we'll get some information."

"What about the teeth one?" Logan asked.

"Forty-one."

"I'll plug in the others first and see what happens."

Domotor struggled into his chair and wheeled it over to watch Logan. The images and numbers on the screen meant nothing to me. Trusting Logan would extract the needed data, I checked Domotor's food supplies. Low. He would need more and soon. With so many RATSS I doubted the kitchen scrubs would risk discovery by filling the air shaft again.

Perhaps I could raid the pantry when everyone attended the hundred-hour assembly. But I remembered I would either be in LC Karla's custody by then or perhaps I would be Outside. The strange thought of being somewhere else kept slipping away. With nothing to compare to, I couldn't even imagine it. To me, Outside resembled Inside with no Pop Cops and with more space.

I planned to touch base with Riley, and coordinate the opening of Gateway during hour ninety-seven. But first, I needed to uncover it.

After cleaning Domotor's washroom and bedroom as best as I could, I joined them. Huddled over the keyboard, Logan's eyes were lit with a childlike glee and even Domotor seemed thrilled. They turned to me with identical grins.

"What?"

"We know," Logan said.

"Outside. Look." Domotor pointed to the screen.

My stomach boiled as I peered at the image. Green and blue jumped out, but I blinked and the details became clearer.

"It's like hydroponics," Logan said. "But the plants are huge and the sheep's special grass is all over the place. Look at the ceiling, it's blue and goes on forever."

"Does anyone live there?" I asked.

"I don't quite know. The text states numbers and details for things like breathable air mixture, compatible food source, mineral deposits, drinkable ground water and something called wildlife. Which, as far as I could tell, are animals without any real intelligence."

"In order to obtain the information, someone has been to Outside." Even though thrilled with the news, I wondered how long ago the data was collected. Everything changed with time. "Can you find out when?"

"No. The information was pulled from various files and dumped together. A few sentences are incomplete, and the topic changes abruptly. Some of the files are damaged and I can only read about half of what's in them."

"It doesn't matter when," Domotor said, dismissing my concern. "Most likely it was before the Travas took control. Perhaps after the scouting mission, the Travas panicked, thinking they would lose power in such a big place. We know it's safe to go to Outside."

"And we know the code to open Gateway." Logan typed at the keyboard and numbers marched across the computer screen.

I committed the code to memory.

"Something else…" He pointed. "Colored buttons. Green to open. Red to close. Any ideas?"

"To get back to Inside," Domotor said. "There would have to be controls on Outside. Proof that no people live there or they would have opened the door by now."

He had a point.

Finally, Logan announced he had no more useful info. "Wish we had those last three passwords."

"What about the file with my birth week on it?" I asked.

Domotor glanced at me in surprise. "There's a file with your birth week on it?"

"And the hour of her birth. I forgot about that one." Logan's fingers flew and he hummed to himself. A white screen flashed and he paused for a second. "Uh…Trell, you'd better read this. It's from your mother."

I backed away. "She couldn't have… No way to know I would be involved… A trap?"

Domotor leaned closer to the screen. "No. She admits the chances of you finding this letter is little to none." He continued to read. "It's similar to a diary entry. Written more for herself than you, explaining what had happened. Interesting… A confession. Why didn't you tell me Kiana was the spy?"

I plopped on the couch. "A lot has happened since I last saw you."

"Do you want to know her reasons for—"

"No. Four people were recycled because of her. I've no desire to hear her pathetic excuses."

He frowned at me. "Someday you'll want to know."

"Then I will ask you. It's not important right now—she isn't one of the uppers who have agreed to help us."

Domotor brightened when he heard this, and I explained what I had been doing in the upper levels, but I didn't tell him Doctor Lamont's name or Riley's cousin. He knew of the others, but those two were new. Despite my conviction that Kiana was responsible for my father and Riley's mother's fates because she had spied for the Travas, Domotor had been the one to name them.

"Excellent news," he said when I finished updating him. "Just imagine, we'll open Gateway and usher out all the scrubs and uppers who want to go, leaving behind the Travas with no one to rule."

I laughed at the humorous picture.

After I escorted Logan back to his barrack, I borrowed a few supplies from maintenance, filled my tool belt and headed to the Gap. With visions of blue ceilings and grass rugs filling my mind, I didn't stop until I reached the outer wall near Quad G1—Gateway's location.

I removed my new flashlight and shone it on the insulation. The thick yellow foam rippled on the wall, and I couldn't see any marks indicating a doorway underneath. Starting at the southwest corner, I sprayed water from the floor to level two's support beams and worked my way to the left. Made from vegetable starch, the biodegradable foam dissolved and dripped. It didn't take long to realize two bottles of water wouldn't be enough. One meter thick foam had been sprayed onto the wall.

When the bottles were empty, I pulled the insulation off. The bottom layers were brittle and easy to break apart with my new screwdriver. Logan had said Gateway would be between three to four meters from the corner. I planned to clear at least five meters.

The air around me cooled as I worked. My breath made clouds, but the cold felt good against my sweaty skin. Foam piled on the ground, and I reveled in the effort.

Bits of foam clung to my student's uniform and hair. I stopped well past four meters. Panting in the icy air, I grabbed my light. The beam lit specks of floating insulation. My attention focused on the exposed wall as I swept the light across the surface.

Its appearance matched the interior walls—metal panels riveted together with support beams. No obvious doorway. I searched for a near-invisible hatch.

Nothing.

I drew in a deep breath. Once again, I scanned the wall, but this time I started from the corner and concentrated on each section in a systematic way.

Nothing.

Emotions soured, but I ignored them. We had coordinates and codes and pictures. I ripped another meter of insulation from the wall.

Nothing.

We had uppers willing to risk their lives and knew which colored buttons to use to return to Inside. Another meter piled on the floor. I choked on the dust, but pulled off another half meter convinced it would be here. It *had* to be. Otherwise, I would have made the worst mistake of my entire life. Believing before seeing. Another meter landed on the pile.

Nothing.

I lost track of how long I worked or of how many meters of wall I exposed or of how many times I scanned the wall. My body transformed into a machine with one task: find Gateway.

Eventually the fuel was depleted and the machine broke down. It was unable to complete its task. There was nothing to find.

twenty

I had no recollection of leaving the Gap, or the trip back to Riley's storeroom. My body felt insubstantial as if crushed into powder and reduced to a layer of dust to be sucked up by a cleaning troll.

Rooting under the couch, I pulled Zippy from his hiding place. Tufts of dust clung to his brushes. I hefted the troll, cradling his weight. The hunt for Gateway had been a whirlwind. A thrill of risks, and I had been swept up by the excitement. I had allowed myself to believe in something that didn't exist. Gateway.

Cog. I'd already decided to lie and tell him we found Gateway. It would give him a moment of joy before Vinco played with him again and the Pop Cops recycled him.

I resisted the urge to hide in the pipes. Instead, I sat in the storeroom, savoring an ill humor with the hope I could build up an immunity to it and form another metal layer around my heart. The first one was ill-wrought and had cracked with ease.

"What happened?" Riley stood over me.

I stared at him in confusion.

"You were supposed to report back to the infirmary hours ago and tell us the content of those files."

The files. I almost laughed. We'd been duped. Domotor had to be a Pop Cop spy.

"Riley, forget about the files. Gateway doesn't exist. It's all a big con. The Pop Cops planted those files and sent Broken Man here to see who they could get to fall for it. It's just a matter of time before we are arrested."

He rocked back on his heels as if slapped in the face. "Wait. You didn't say you were going to Gateway."

"Logan showed me a picture of Outside and I was…excited." I could have substituted *stupid*, *naive* or *brainless*.

"Really? What did Outside look like?" Even knowing Gateway didn't exist, Riley couldn't contain the excitement in his voice.

"Doesn't exist, remember? It was just a picture."

He sat next to me on the couch. If he wondered why Zippy was in my lap, he didn't show it. "Are you sure about Gateway? Were you at the right location?"

"I cleared at least six meters of insulation off the west Wall outside Quad G1. From the floor to the next level."

"Those files are old. Perhaps the coordinates are wrong."

"The age of the files is all part of the scheme."

"What about Logan? Is he part of the ruse?"

If Domotor duped me with ease, so could the others. "I don't know anymore. I guess those who don't get arrested are in on it." Karla and the Pop Cops must be enjoying the show. I wondered when they would spring their trap on us.

Riley wrapped his arm around my shoulders and pulled me close. I sank against him, breathing in his warm scent.

"Let's not jump to conclusions," Riley said. "You're suspicious of everyone. Domotor would have had to be a heck of a liar to convince you to help him."

"Deep down I wanted to believe. I probably saw what I wanted instead of the truth."

He rubbed my arm. "I don't know. It's a pretty complicated setup. The Travas don't have the imagination for it. Unless someone else is involved or something else is going on."

I straightened. "The Controllers?"

He frowned. "It's possible."

"Do you know who they are?"

"No. When I think about them in a logical way, I believe they don't exist. The Travas desire control of all systems, and I don't see them obeying orders from mysterious Controllers. I'm sure they invented them to have someone to blame when things don't go well. However, when I access the computer network, I feel like I'm being watched. That every time I go into the system I lose a part of myself, and when I'm done I have a horrible headache. Sounds silly. My dad says the pain is from eye strain."

"It's not silly. I wish I knew why someone went to all this trouble. Maybe Karla will grant me a last request and explain it all to me." Doubtful, but a girl could try.

"Don't say that."

"Why not?"

"Because we'll figure it out."

I didn't share Riley's optimism. Instead I checked the clock. Hour ninety-four. Six hours until Cog's final walk, until I...

No. I wouldn't think those thoughts. At least, not yet. Riley's arm remained around me. I set Zippy on the floor and turned toward him. My sudden desire to be closer to Riley drove out my scary future. Our lips met. A wave of heat rushed through my body as we kissed.

He pressed against me; his hot hands splayed on my back. Wherever our bodies met, tremors vibrated on my skin. I twined my fingers in his hair.

Too soon, Riley pulled away. "My break's over." Regret

flashed in his eyes. "I need to get back." He stood. "Don't do anything rash. Don't go anywhere. Please. You're safe here." He hesitated as if he wanted to say more, but instead, squeezed my arm then hurried away.

When the door clicked shut all warmth fled my body. Reality returned and time continued. My dreamy thoughts solidified and I planned my next move. I would have to find the perfect spot to approach Karla.

My head throbbed. I stared at the opposite wall, counting rivets. Twenty for each sheet of metal. No more, no less. The builders of Inside had never deviated from their plans. No creativity. No surprises.

However, the Pop Cops had managed quite the surprise with a fair amount of creativity. Impressive.

Time marched like Pop Cops on patrol. I located my scrub uniform balled up in a corner of the room. The musty-smelling fabric was stiff with dried sweat and blood, but I pulled it on anyway. No need to dress up for the Pop Cops. I covered the large hole and biggest bloodstain by ripping a part off the student's uniform and tying it around my waist. My goal was to get as close as possible to Karla and Cog before some other overenthusiastic Pop Cop arrested me.

I debated about bringing the microphone and receiver. Should I tell Jacy the bad news? He could be working for the Pop Cops. Yanking the earring from my lobe, I set it on Riley's desk with the button. No sense letting the Pop Cops find the technology on me.

Hour ninety-nine. Time to go. I glanced around the room, memorizing the details, and decided to write Riley a quick note. The words refused to come. I scrawled an inappropriate thank-you and an "I'm sorry for causing so much trouble for nothing" message.

Back into the air shaft, I proceeded to the lower level not

caring if RATSS spotted me. I reached the bottom without encountering a single one. Figures.

As I crawled through the duct, a strange droning noise vibrated the metal. It grew louder as I drew closer to the vent. Scrubs packed the hallway below. In a few places, scrubs stood three deep on each side, leaving a narrow space.

Pop Cops tried to get them to move, but stubbornness radiated from tight jaws and hard eyes. The hundred-hour assembly bell rang—a faint ring compared to the general murmuring. Again, Pop Cops demanded they report to their assembly locations, screaming and harassing the scrubs to no avail. I wondered how long it would be before they started stunning people. They seemed reluctant to pull their weapons. I wondered if they feared a panicked stampede if they started shooting.

I stayed in the duct until I found a location without Pop Cops. When I dropped to the floor, the closest scrubs jerked in surprise, but soon they beamed at me. The line of people shifted, creating an opening my size. Sliding into the spot, I swallowed, trying to push my heart back down to its proper place, but it refused to budge, choking me.

While waiting for a sign of Cog, my body felt as if it held too much water. My nose dripped and tears blurred my vision. I concentrated on the floor, counting the lines of rivets. If I couldn't see and was barefoot, I could probably navigate through the hallways of Inside by feeling the little bumps. At least, Inside's predictability would benefit the blind.

The sudden jolt of insight felt as if I'd just connected two live wires in my brain. I had the answer to question number three, *Your eyes can see, but mine don't work, yet I see what you can't. What am I?* It was the reason I couldn't find Gateway.

The noise level rose to my left, and Cog's head bobbed through the crowd. I gasped when he came into view. New bruises covered his swollen face, patches of blood soaked his coveralls and his hands were cuffed behind his back.

But the most astonishing aspect was his smile. He grinned at everyone.

I leaned out past the scrubs. Four Pop Cops led the way, pushing back the edges of the crowd, and four were behind him. Lieutenant Commander Karla wasn't there. Instead, Lieutenant Arno followed the procession.

I turned to a woman on my right, and stood on my tiptoes so I could talk into her ear. "Can you take a message to Jacy for me?"

She nodded. Her face pale and serious. When I told her the message about Gateway she gazed at me in frank astonishment.

"It's very important," I said. "Promise?"

When she promised, I stepped into the middle of the corridor. An angry frown replaced Cog's smile as soon as he spotted me.

"I found it," I yelled over the buzz and babble of many voices.

I knew he couldn't stay mad. His whoop of joy rang through the hallway. Everyone stopped talking. The silence became an eerie almost living presence.

The Pop Cops in front finally noticed me. They shouted and pulled their stunners.

Maximum damage, I thought and rushed them. The element of surprise was the only reason I managed to knock one of the Pop Cops over. I yanked his gun from his hand and stunned him.

"No one recycles Cogon!" I yelled, pleased the ad hoc battle cry rhymed.

Then everyone moved as if my shout were a signal. Scrubs overwhelmed the rest of the Pop Cops, taking their weapons and knocking them down. A short and brutal attack. I gaped at the unexpected turn of events.

The chant rippled through the lower levels. *No one recycles Cogon.*

It didn't take long for the scrubs to overpower the Pop Cops. A few scrubs were stunned, and little blood was shed on both sides. Cuffed with their own handcuffs, the Pop Cops huddled in the middle of the dining room. All the tables had been pushed back and scrubs surrounded Cog, slapping him on the back.

Cog organized teams to secure entrances. Every resident of the lower two levels had come to level one for Cog.

Understanding ripped through me as I watched them look to Cog for answers, for plans on what they should do next and for praise.

Broken Man wasn't their prophet, Cogon was the true prophet of Inside.

Karla made a huge mistake in wanting to parade him through the scrubs as an example. The Pop Cops had grown overconfident and now her lieutenant knelt with the rest.

After a few minutes, I pulled Cog aside.

"Can you believe this?" Cog gestured to scrubs nearby.

I had been surprised, but shouldn't have been. The signs had been there; I was too wrapped up in my own problems to notice.

"They think I know all the answers." He shook his head in amazement, then sobered. "We can't hold out for long. The uppers control everything but the food. All they need to do is send gas through the air shafts or shut off our air. Unless..." He shouted at one of the maintenance crew to install air filters in the ducts. "Now tell me everything about Gateway," he ordered me.

"Yes, sir." I dodged his playful swat, then told him how we discovered the location from the files. "I need to get a few supplies to be absolutely sure Gateway is there."

"I'll come along," Cog said.

"You can't fit through the shaft."

He laughed. "Trell, you're still thinking we need to sneak around. Hank," Cog yelled.

A large maintenance scrub hustled over to us. "What do you need, boss?"

"A hole."

Raiding a maintenance closet, we found the needed items and climbed through the air shaft. A huge section had been cut open, revealing the Gap above. Hank and his team muttered in amazement and wanted to ask questions, but the urge to hurry pulsed through my veins. The scrubs might have filters, but they wouldn't last without fresh air.

I raced through the Gap. Cogon kept pace despite his size. We stopped at the uncovered west Wall. I shone my flashlight over the exposed metal, counting to twenty.

Rows and columns of twenty rivets. Starting from the corner and moving right.

Twenty. Twenty. Twenty. Twenty. Twenty. No deviations. Twenty. Twenty. Twenty. No creativity.

Twenty. Twenty-two. I found the blind. A sheet of metal covering Gateway. I pointed and Cog pulled a chisel from his tool belt and removed twenty-two rivets from each side. The metal blind had been connected to the wall for so long, it remained in place despite the removal of the rivets. Inserting the edge of a crowbar Cog pulled with all his strength. Then moved to another spot.

The metal groaned and squealed and finally dropped down. A loud clang echoed throughout the Gap. We didn't care who heard it.

Behind the sheet was Gateway.

Wild joy shone on Cog's face. An ecstatic sizzle pumped through my veins. Gateway even appeared different than a regular door with its rounded corners and a black substance shoved into the crack between the door and the wall. The bulging substance ringed the entire door and was smooth and hard. When I tapped it with my fingernail, it didn't clang like metal but produced a solid thumping sound.

Cut from one piece of metal, the door also lacked a knob or latch. But a small computer screen had been installed next to it. I pressed my ear to Gateway. Nothing to hear, but the Hum. The icy surface sucked warmth from the side of my head.

I pulled away. Now I knew why Inside was always heated. Outside was cold.

"Do you know how to open it?" Cog asked with a reverent tone in his voice.

"I have a code. But the uppers will be alerted."

"Trell, there's been a rebellion in the lower levels. I think the uppers are probably a little busy helping the Pop Cops to restore order. Besides, I doubt we'll get another chance."

Good point. Steeling myself, I touched the screen. It grumbled and grunted as if I had woken it from a deep sleep, then it glowed. Squares with numbers shone from the display.

With my heart slamming, I typed in the number code and hit the enter button. For a moment, nothing happened.

Then a horrible sucking noise sounded and Gateway's door sunk in first before swinging to the side with a loud squeal of protest. Weak light emanated as a puff of stale air blew in our faces. We coughed.

Nothing jumped out. Water did not flood Inside. No unknown substance oozed through. No strange beings flew through. No voices called or cheered in welcome.

Only a small room waited within. I stepped in and flinched. Silence greeted me. I looked around. A light panel on the ceiling illuminated the empty, metal rectangle-shaped space, which had another Gateway. No screen was next to this new door, just a panel of oversize square keys lit from underneath with different colored lights. One red button remained unlit.

Cogon joined me. His face showed his disappointment until he spotted the other door. "Do you have another code?"

"No. Logan didn't mention this little surprise. We couldn't open all the files." One of the keys glowed green. "But he did say green to open and red to close, perhaps that was for this part." I pressed the green button. Nothing happened.

He stared at the lights. "Ten buttons with ten colors. Perhaps…" He pointed to the one on the far left. "This one is the number one. Assuming they're in numerical order, you can try the code for the outside door."

I pressed the first number/color and the light under it turned off. Then I inputted the rest of the numbers, noticing that none of the numbers repeated. Nothing except the remaining key lights turned off.

"Or maybe not," Cog said.

After a few seconds, the lights returned.

"Perhaps the numbers are in descending order." I tried again. Still nothing. "Or, the numbers start with zero and go to nine."

This time all the numbers darkened—except the green one.

"Green to open," Cog said, and pushed it.

The door behind us hissed closed. The green light pulsed. A sucking hydraulic noise sounded, but the other door remained shut. Cogon pushed on it to no avail.

I struggled to pull air into my lungs. No one knew the code to enter. We could be trapped in here. I felt light-headed and my insides bloated as if I had eaten too much.

Cog turned, leaning on the door. The panic on his face matched mine. He clamped his hands to the sides of his head as if holding his skull together.

Without a sound, the other Gateway opened. Pure black waited on the other side. A bone-killing cold reached us. White spots sparked from the blackness, but it was hard to know if they were real or not. Black and white spots swirled in my vision. My eyeballs felt as if they would burst.

My stomach dropped and spun as if I fell from a tall ladder. I glanced down to see my feet no longer touched the floor, but floated. Cog twisted and his body drifted past the door. He pointed.

The red key burned bright. Red to close. On the edge of unconsciousness, I reached for the button. But Cog was Outside. I needed to help him.

He gestured again, but I didn't press it.

Cog threw his hammer. It sailed toward me as he somersaulted backward. Then the darkness claimed me.

twenty-one

I would like to have said that I went to a better place. However, the skin-freezing cold woke me. Dumped onto the floor of the small room, I untangled my legs and stood. My skin felt stretched and saggy. I wanted to crawl under a heavy layer of blankets to press my body tight. Red fog tinted my vision.

The outer Gateway was closed, but the door to Inside was open. The panel of colored lights glowed brightly and I wanted to smash them into tiny bits. Cog wasn't with me and I doubted he'd made it through the door in time.

No way could he survive in that airless, weightless... void. But I had to try. No living with myself unless I tried. I punched in the first few numbers.

"Stop!" a most unwelcome voice ordered.

I ignored Lieutenant Commander Karla, getting in another two numbers before she stunned me. A wall of energy slammed into my body. My last thought was of Cog.

The next time I woke, my situation hadn't improved. Rows of black bars, the stench of unwashed bodies, excrement and fear and the hard metal bunk underneath me all clued me in. I was under arrest and incarcerated in the holding cells.

When Commander Vinco arrived with the LC at his heels, I wished I had floated away with Cog.

"Just so you don't think you'll be rescued by your scrub friends, we have secured the lower levels," LC Karla said. Her lips flattened into a pleased smile that didn't reach her eyes. "Do you want to know how?"

"No." The truth. The game had ended badly. Cog was gone. Outside didn't exist. Nothing was left that Trella cared for. Ella, on the other hand, planned to keep her mouth shut.

"You've been rather busy these past four weeks." Vinco sounded impressed. "A little scrub like you, causing so much trouble." He tsked. "Finding the portal and opening it. Of course you paid a price. I'm going to miss my stubborn sturdy friend." He pulled a knife from his belt. The edge gleamed in the sick yellow light.

My pulse reacted to the threat out of habit, but I remained in my reclined position.

"She had help," Karla said. "She couldn't have found the space around the levels, hidden Domotor, stolen from my office and stitched the knife wound on her hip by herself. She's not that smart."

"You underestimated me. Don't feel too bad—it's a common mistake." I waved my hand in a dismissive gesture.

Vinco crouched down to my eye level. "You *will* tell us where Domotor is and who helped you."

I couldn't believe they'd failed to find Domotor. The game might be over for me, but there were a few others still able to do damage. I repeated my vow to keep my mouth shut.

Vinco straightened. "Key?"

No keypads here. Bored inmates could find the code by trial and error.

He grabbed the ring of keys from Karla. The light jingle sent a vibration of dread up my spine. The snap of the cell door's lock increased the terror. By the time he stood next to me, my body shook.

A beeping sound emanated from Karla's belt. She cursed and toggled on her communicator. "What?"

Vinco paused and I hoped she would talk for a long time. But she flipped it shut and flashed me an annoyed frown. "I'm wanted elsewhere. Do you need me?" she asked him.

Yes, I thought. Need her.

"No. I'll show her what I can do first. Then we'll come back and ask questions."

"Fine." She turned on her heel and left.

The slam of the door echoed in the room. No blankets or pillows or anything soft to absorb the sound. I pushed up to a sitting position, thinking to fight or maybe even escape around him. Maximum damage.

But Vinco's reactions were as sharp as his knife. He grabbed my arms and pushed me back on the bunk. Using his weight to keep me down, he pulled my hands behind my head and through the bars.

The click slide of handcuffs snapped around my wrists, trapping my hands. Feeling completely vulnerable, I twisted. Fear pulsed through my veins, and I clamped down on a plea. I would not give him the satisfaction of begging for mercy. I would not whimper or utter a word.

He smiled in anticipation and proceeded to demonstrate with the tip of his knife just how much pain he could cause—a considerable amount.

True to his promise, he never asked me a question. Instead he remained quiet, taking pleasure in my screams. Screaming and yelling weren't weeping or pleading—a difference I clung to with a tiny bit of pride.

I lost track of time. Moments of burning pain mixed with excruciating pain and gaps of dull throbbing pain. Karla came and went. Vinco's knife danced on my skin.

They asked questions and I refused to answer, and we all settled into a routine. I disconnected from the fear and terror. Growing a metal barrier in my mind, I kept my emotions walled off. The visits tapered and my screaming sessions were further apart. Something was happening to keep the Pop Cops busy. Karla's insistence on knowing who I worked with grew more frantic.

The clang of a door roused me from a mindless stupor. I glanced around, but no Vinco. Confused, I raised my head and peered into the other cells.

The Pop Cops had locked up another person.

Riley stared at me with horror-filled eyes. I groaned.

"Are you all right?" he asked.

"What do you think?" I couldn't suppress my sarcastic remark.

"I think you look like something Chomper has chewed on and spat back out."

"Such sweet sentiment, lying to me to avoid hurting my feelings."

"At least you still have your sense of humor."

I let my head drop back onto the bunk. "How many have been caught?"

The silence pressed on me, but I didn't have the energy to look and decipher Riley's expression.

"Do you mean from the scrubs' revolt? They've been confined to the barracks and are only allowed to leave in small groups supervised by well-armed Pop Cops. No one's been arrested yet. I believe Logan and Anne-Jade are hiding with Domotor. Cog is missing."

I avoided the inevitable conversation about Cog. The rest was nice to hear, but not what I wanted. "I mean of the uppers. You, obviously, have been caught, but what about Doctor Lamont and the others?"

"Oh! I'm here for talking back to a commanding officer. Ten hours extra duty and ten hours in the brig."

Relief flowed through my skin, helping to calm the angry welts.

He continued, "No upper has been implicated. Karla's people have been so busy in the lower levels it took me three smart remarks to three different officers to get punished."

Shame Vinco wasn't needed below. But then his comment sunk in. "You *wanted* to get arrested?"

"Since I don't fit through the vents, it's the only way to talk to you. Logan and Anne-Jade have been busy." He huffed with amusement. "Anne-Jade's been wearing the Pop Cop uniform and delivering these devices—little anti-stunners shaped like belt buckles. It deflects the energy from the stunner somehow."

I smiled at his awe-tinged voice, but couldn't share his enthusiasm. Time to burst his bubble. "Riley, we opened Gateway. Outside is nothing. A great big black place of nothing. Cog is gone. He's out in the nothing. No reason to resist the Pop Cops. No escape from Inside."

Silence and more silence. Perhaps I shouldn't have been so blunt.

"Sorry to hear about Cog," Riley said. "I wish I could have met him. He sounded like a great guy."

"He was. The scrubs revolted because of him. Now they don't have him or Gateway."

"But they have you."

I tried to laugh, but it turned into a coughing fit. "So do Karla and Vinco. Don't think I can do anything for the scrubs, but keep my mouth shut and hope Vinco's knife slips." Slips into my neck and ends my time here. During our last session, I'd lost my grip on my metal barrier and almost told Vinco everything.

"You are the reason I'm here," Riley said. "If you remember, I didn't get involved to find Gateway. But to find a way to improve living conditions in the lower levels. I talked to Doctor Lamont and there is a way to even things out between uppers and lowers. The Force of Sheep is worried about being caught, but they're also motivated."

"Why?" I figured they would do what they had done before and lay low.

"Because of you."

"Me? You've got to be joking."

"You're right. I am. It's really because of Sheepy. How he risked his life for them, and how he showed them that scrubs are real human beings who care and want the same things in life. Opened their eyes to the fact the Travas are our mutual enemy."

"Sheepy's a great guy…er…sheep."

"He is. But he's going to be mutton chops soon if he doesn't fight back."

Energized I raised my head and glared at Riley. "Hard to fight back when I'm cuffed to the bars."

"Your legs don't work?"

"Vinco's built like a tank. Have you tried to resist him?" I demanded.

"Yes. If you remember, extra duty is being Vinco's sparring partner. Except he has a weapon and you don't." He rubbed his left forearm.

I remembered Riley's bloody sleeve. "Then you know how hard it is."

"I never said it would be easy. Giving up is easy."

I grumbled.

"Vinco isn't very smart. If you do decide to try resisting, there is a package for you in the heating duct right near the vent."

"Who—?"

"Logan rigged Zippy to deliver it to you."

"Hard to get it out with solid iron bars acting as a vent cover."

"Think about it," Riley said.

I grudgingly realized Logan would know about the bars and had probably packed the gift so I could pull it through. I wiggled my fingers. My hands felt swollen, and my wrists felt as if the metal cuffs had ripped off my skin.

"All you need to do is free yourself from those cuffs," he said as if commenting on the food in the cafeteria.

"The Force of Sheep don't really need me. You have Logan for the computer stuff and Anne-Jade building anti-stunners. In fact, by staying here I'm keeping Vinco and Karla busy for you."

"That's mighty nice of you. But don't you think you've suffered enough? Or do you still feel guilty for Cog's loss?"

I sputtered, fuming. "You act like I can just saunter out of here. I didn't ask to be tortured. If it were up to me, I'd have been Chomper's dinner hours ago."

He sighed. "It's going to be hard to tell Sheepy that Trella has given up. To tell him that fierce, spunky scrub I first met is gone."

I refused to comment.

"Poor Sheepy will be sad. He'll miss his best friend."

"He's a toy, Riley. He'll get over it."

He remained quiet for a moment. "You're right. He will recover. But you've gotten a lot of other things wrong."

Now it was my turn to sigh. Here we go again. "I don't have the energy to argue anymore. My throat hurts." Every word burned and my dry tongue kept sticking to the roof of my mouth. I rested my head on the bunk and closed my eyes.

"Then just listen to me. I'll tell you all the things you're mistaken about. First, you're not going to be able to resist Vinco much longer. Cog eventually broke. He's the one who named you and told Karla that Domotor was still alive." He paused, probably to let the news sink in.

No wonder Cog had been so frantic when I had visited him

the second time. But I couldn't blame Cog for anything. He suffered enough for me.

"Second, you're wrong about no one needing you. The Force of Sheep has been working to infiltrate the security systems, but they need motivation only you can provide. Doctor Lamont needs her intern back, and I need…"

I waited, but when he didn't continue, I looked up. He sat on the bunk in his cell with his face in his hands. We both startled when the heavy clang of metal sounded as the main doors to the holding cells were unlocked. For me, it meant Vinco returning for another dreaded session.

Riley jumped to his feet and stared at me through the bars. "Whatever I say to the commander about the scrubs and you is all a lie. Understand?"

A wedge of bright light grew between the doors.

"Yes." Before he could turn away, I asked, "What do you need?"

"I need you. I need to give you a proper kiss. I need you to be my mate." His words were a harsh whisper, but tenderness shone in his eyes. Nothing like the shock that must be in my own.

The door swung wide, slamming into the wall. Vinco eyed Riley with disgust. "What're you in for, boy?"

"Telling Lieutenant Arno to go screw himself, sir."

Vinco laughed. "That takes balls, boy."

"Well, I didn't know there was a scrub in the cells, sir. Otherwise I would have been nicer. Don't you think being so near one of them is cruel?"

I bit my lip, remembering Riley's words about lying.

"Worse than extra duty with me?"

"Yes, sir."

The commander chuckled again. "Okay, boy. You can work off the rest of your brig time. Ensign Hollis," he called, "release Mr. Ashon."

Another man entered and unlocked Riley's cell. Glad to see him free, I watched him leave, but all pleasant thoughts disappeared when the door shut and I was alone with Vinco.

He entered my cell and began his work. Jabbing me with the tip of his knife, I recoiled. With my pain-addled mind, I was surprised when a plan to escape formed. Not a great one, but better than being Vinco's playmate.

During a particularly intense bout, I shouted, "Enough. I'll talk." I tried to ignore the satisfied smirk as he drew back.

"I'm listening," he said.

"I'll show you where Domotor is hiding on level two. It's all I know, honest."

A doubtful, but interested expression creased his ugly face. "Tell me."

"Can't. The entrance is hidden. It's easier if I show you. You'll need to bring bolt cutters."

He considered and I tried to appear pathetic and weak. Not hard to do, considering I was pathetic and weak.

"Okay." Vinco unlocked my cuffs.

Burning pain shot through my arms as I moved them, sitting up turned into an effort of will. I rubbed my hands together, avoiding my blood-soaked sleeves.

"Come on." He jerked me to my feet.

I swayed and stumbled against him. He shoved me away in disgust. As I fell I grabbed his stunner from his weapon belt. Aimed for his chest. Pulled the trigger. A grunt of surprise and he collapsed on the floor with a wonderful thud.

The effort left me winded. After a few huffs of air, I stepped over Vinco's unconscious form and knelt by the heating vent. Nothing visible through the bars, I slid my hand inside. My fingers brushed cloth and I pulled a narrow bag from the duct. Tied with string, the sack contained a number of useful items—a sparkly metal cutter, Logan's decoder, bandages, a bladder of water and a handful of protein nuggets.

I ate the nuggets and downed the water. My stomach rebelled for a moment, but I kept the food down by pure force of will. I would need the energy.

Pulling off my mangled uniform, I wrapped the bandages around my arms, legs and torso. I stole Vinco's shirt. It fell to my knees. I also snatched his knife and stunner, leaving the kill-zapper on his belt.

Coated with diamond dust, the metal cutter sawed through the bars. I worked as fast as I could, but it still felt as if hours had passed. Every sound caused me to jump. Finally I finished the last bar and slid into the vent. Making sure I didn't leave a bloody trail, I hurried to…where?

Only one place to go—Doctor Lamont's. The warm air inside the shaft sucked at my energy. I used our storeroom on level four to switch to the air shafts and then to the Gap. The space between levels felt as it always did, hollow and unoccupied. I thought the Travas would have it filled with Pop Cops by now.

I dropped into Doctor Lamont's office, thumping hard on the ground. She showed little surprise when she came to investigate.

She bent over me. "Can you walk to the treatment table?"

Now that I had arrived, all my cuts throbbed and burned for attention. I nodded and she helped me stand, keeping a hand on my elbow as I wobbled to the table and collapsed on top of it.

Starting with my legs, the doctor unwound the bandages. She clucked and tsked and cleaned the cuts. I, in turn, cringed and winced and hissed in pain.

"Four need stitches, and that's just your legs." She crossed to her supply table and filled a metal tray with various instruments, including a needle and thread. "This first." Handing me a glass of water and a small white pill, she gestured for me to swallow it.

"What's it for?" I asked.

"Sleep. Unless you want to be awake when I stitch your injuries?"

I popped the pill into my mouth, wasting no time. After all the hours spent with Vinco's knife, I had no desire to feel metal sliding through my skin ever again.

It didn't take long for the room to soften and for shadows to gather in the corners of my vision. Soon a blanket of black settled over me as I slipped into a dreamless heavy sleep.

LC Karla's voice woke me. I nearly groaned aloud. My escape had just been a dream! But through slits in my eyelids, I discovered I still lay on the exam table. However, I had been wheeled into surgery. A sheet covered my body up to my neck. Blood stained the cover in the area around my midsection, and a mask rested over my nose and mouth. Some kind of soft cap held my hair.

Doctor Lamont argued with the LC beyond the double doors. "You can*not* go in there," she said. "You are not sterile and could cause a horrible infection."

"We have a dangerous scrub on the loose and you're worried about an infection?" Karla asked in amazement.

"I haven't seen this scrub. I told you no one is here but me and my patients. And Ella, of course."

"Why is she in surgery?" Karla demanded.

"Appendicitis. In fact, if I don't finish the surgery soon, she could die."

"Then you should want to cooperate fully with our search." The surgery doors banged open and Karla's voice sounded right next to me. "I'll be quick, Doctor, so you can return to your patient."

twenty-two

I lay still and kept my eyes closed. Karla's heavy footsteps sounded all around me followed by the clang of metal hitting metal.

Doctor Lamont pressed her fingers into my neck as if checking my pulse. "Do you want to search the *incision,* Karla?"

The sheet near my hips bunched as if she gripped it. I held my breath, terrified Karla would call Lamont's bluff, but at the same time impressed by the doctor's courage.

"I'm not amused. You should be offering your assistance to find this scrub. Remember your history, *Doctor.* Cooperation saves lives."

"Why should I cooperate? I don't have a child for you to hold over me anymore. You've seen to that."

Interesting. It explained why Lamont hated the LC so much.

"I'm sure I can find another you care for. Your intern perhaps? How long can she survive with a burst appendix?"

"Get out." Lamont's icy voice sliced as sharp as a scalpel.

"I've hit a nerve. Kiana, you're way too caring of others. No one will miss a few of them. We have plenty more below."

I wasn't sure of Lamont's reply because my thoughts reeled over Karla calling the doctor Kiana. But I was sure there had to be more than one person named Kiana in the upper levels. The lower levels had a number of scrubs with the same name. Plus the coincidence would be too great.

Of course the clues all added up. The doctor's queasy expression when I named the spy during the first Force of Sheep meeting. Her pointed glance with Riley's father. The fact she was a friend of Jacob's from their training days. But the odds I would be the one climbing around the pipes and getting involved in the search for Gateway and that I would find Riley were huge. Unless…

It wasn't a coincidence. Domotor had sought me out, claiming my reputation as Queen of the Pipes drew his notice. It had been a setup from the start.

I had lost track of Karla and the doctor. The room remained quiet and I risked a peek. No one. I waited and soon enough Lamont entered. Her flushed face and tight grimace softened once she saw me.

"Karla and her cops are gone. How long have you been awake?"

I pulled the mask from my mouth and sat. "Long enough, *Kiana*. Were you going to rat us all out at once or wait until I'd healed enough for Vinco to have fresh skin to gouge?" Wrapping the sheet around me, I tried to slide from the table.

She blocked my way, pushing me back. "Oh, no, you don't."

"You can't stop me." I struggled to sit up.

Kiana jabbed me with a needle. "Yes, I *can* stop you."

Liquid fire coursed through my veins, erasing all desire to fight. I wilted and dropped into oblivion.

I knew I hated examination tables for a reason. When I woke from my drug-induced sleep, I was strapped to the table and unable to move. A few of the cuts on my body pulsed with pain, but otherwise I felt all right. For now.

Voices murmured in the infirmary, and I wondered if I should call for help. Knowing my luck, it would be Karla and Vinco so I kept my mouth shut.

I turned my head at the sound of footsteps and was shocked by Riley's arrival. He looked ill at ease, tugging his shirt and glancing everywhere but at me. I closed my eyes to keep from crying. How many times have I been wrong? You would think I'd cease to be surprised.

"Ella, are you all right?" he asked.

"My name is Trella. My friends…" I swallowed. Yes, I had friends, damn it. "Call me Trell. How long have you been planning this?"

"Ah… She just contacted us. Doctor Lamont said she needed us to help you understand. Understand what?" he asked.

My eyes flew open and I gaped at him.

He gasped. "Is it about your eyes?"

"What's wrong with my eyes?"

"They're blue."

Alarmed, I asked "What the hell is going on?"

"I don't know!"

"He is owed an explanation, too," Jacob said as he entered the room with Doctor…Kiana following.

"So why isn't he strapped to a table?" Sarcasm rendered my voice sharp.

"Because he isn't full of new stitches," she said.

"What did you do to my eyes?" I demanded.

"I returned them to their original color to help disguise you. Riley said you might be an upper sibling. Since the reversal drops worked, you must be."

"Why would you bother? Is it going to make you feel better when you betray us?" I asked.

"Dad, what's going on?"

Riley's father sighed. "You both know about the Force of Ten and Domotor. What you don't know is exactly how the group was betrayed nearly eighteen hundred weeks ago."

"Nolan…my mate…" A hitch interrupted the doctor's words before she continued. "Nolan grew too confident. He had discovered the information about Gateway and Outside and was putting it into protected files when the Travas found out. He was…arrested and tortured but refused to name anyone else as an accomplice even when the Travas threatened me and our daughter."

I turned my head to stare at the wall, bracing for the rest of the story.

"I wasn't so strong. Lieutenant Commander Karla, who was an ambitious lieutenant back then, merely threatened to recycle my daughter and I blabbed. Told her about Domotor and agreed to spy for them to keep my mate and daughter alive. When the arrests were made, they…"

Silence. Then Jacob picked up the story. "Karla didn't keep her bargain. Father and child were recycled as well as three others. Riley, you should know Domotor named me as a member, but your mother convinced the Travas she'd used my port and was working alone."

"Why didn't you tell me?" Riley asked.

"She made me promise to keep you safe and to not put crazy ideas into your head. Ramla didn't want you to know." He huffed in tired amusement. "She knew any more attempts by the uppers would fail. Yet look at what has happened from a chance encounter."

I glanced at Jacob. He looked hopeful.

"Why don't you call yourself Doctor Garrard?" Riley asked.

"The name is too painful for me. After Karla recycled Nolan, I returned to my mother's family and used her name." She met my gaze. "I'm trying to amend my past deeds by helping you. I knew once you heard my real name, you wouldn't listen to me. That's why I invited Riley and Jacob here."

I mulled over their story, searching for hints of deceit. "I'm not so sure about the chance encounter. Domotor did seek me out in the lower levels."

"That's because you knew how to travel through the pipes," Riley said.

The others nodded as if this explained everything.

They didn't know I was Kiana's daughter. They didn't know I was alive. Still, the story seemed too pat. "But what about the loose vent cover in the storeroom? Someone had to sabotage it."

Riley flushed. "That's my fault."

We all stared at him and his cheeks reddened.

"Uh…I wanted to meet one of the cleaning scrubs, so I… I did push the couch underneath, but even though you missed it you didn't get hurt…well, not too bad, and…" At a loss for words, he finally stopped.

I glanced at them. But couldn't decide whether to trust them or not. Not like I had any other options at the moment. Although I planned to keep the information about my birth parents to myself. Even with my eyes blue, Kiana hadn't recognized me. For once I knew something the rest did not.

When I had healed enough for the doctor's approval, I entered the air shafts and headed toward Domotor's room. I brought as much food as Lamont could smuggle without raising any suspicions. The duct was free of RATSS because the scrubs kept the Pop Cops busy with small revolts.

Jacy relayed the details of the resistance to me through the earring/receiver. Interesting how the Pop Cops generated more problems when they clamped down harder on the scrubs. The scrubs also stopped working and cleaning. Dirty laundry spilled over bins in Sector B1, piles of fertilizer and items to be recycled grew into large mounds.

I arrived at Domotor's room without any trouble. The prophet sat on the couch surrounded by bits of metal. Anne-Jade and Logan worked together at the table. They all stared at me as if seeing a ghost.

Logan whooped and ran over to me. "You escaped!" He hugged me.

"Easy," I said as his arms brushed several healing cuts.

"We thought you didn't. What took you so long?" Anne-Jade asked.

"Overprotective doctor." I tried to explain about the uppers and the Force of Sheep, but they already knew more than I did. "What's been going on?"

"I'm getting good at traveling through the ducts," Logan said, "and Anne-Jade's been wearing the Pop Cop uniform so much the others are calling her Ensign Mineko." His brow creased. "They keep close track of the scrubs, it would make sense that they would keep even closer track of their own people."

"They're glad to have the extra help," Anne-Jade said. "Besides, just because the Travas have control of Inside doesn't mean they are smart enough to know all their weaknesses." She smiled with a predatory glint in her eye. "Weaknesses we can exploit to the fullest."

"But don't get too cocky," I said, thinking of my father. "The Pop Cops have, and see what's happening?"

"But it's all noise," Domotor said. "Travas control the computer systems. Despite these anti-stunners—" he flourished the metal piece in his hand "—another outright revolt will fail again. Although this time they might use poison gas instead of sleeping gas to subdue us."

"Won't happen," I said. "They need us."

"But what's to stop them from putting us all to sleep and then going around and kill-zapping the troublemakers?" Domotor asked.

Nothing. "Then we'd better get control of the computer systems. Logan?"

"It's going to take a coordinated effort from both uppers and lowers, but it's doable." He met my gaze. "And we'll need to get into the Control Room."

"Impossible," Domotor said.

"Why? We have one upper who works there," I said.

"All the overrides are there. One person isn't enough," Logan said.

I considered. All the high-ranking officers work there and they were all armed. Probably had extra guards, too. No way to walk through the door. Air duct seventy-two was the best way in, but we could be picked off as we dropped down.

"Logan, do you have any anti-kill-zappers?"

"No, but I have Zippy." He hunted under the table and pulled Zippy from a pile of metal. "I've added another feature. Toggle this switch—" he pointed "—and Zippy will emit a pulse that should knock out their weapons."

"Should?" I raised my eyebrows.

"I haven't fully tested it yet. And he only has a short range."

"What about the computer systems?" Domotor asked.

"They'll be fine."

A full-out rebellion would take a major amount of luck and coordination. The Tech Nos and Domotor looked at me, waiting. No one else would be able to organize both sides. I drew in a deep breath. We had the technology, the intelligence and the people—put enough sheep together and you have a herd, a force to be reckoned with. We needed a leader.

"Anne-Jade, how many of those listening and receiving devices do we have?" I asked.

"Four."

"We're going to need seven more all on the same frequency, plus all the anti-stunners you can make."

"We'll need more supplies," Logan said.

"Make a list, I'll contact Jacy." He should be able to find a few skinny scrubs willing to make deliveries through the air shafts.

I made my own mental list of all the steps we would need to take. A daunting effort. Sadness gripped my heart. I wished Cog were here to help. He would be able to motivate the scrubs.

Maximum damage. It was the beginning of the end. Either we would fail or not. At least we could say we tried.

The Force of Sheep planned to declare war on the Travas during week 147,006 at hour sixty-six. After eighty hours of planning, of secret meetings, of setting distractions and false trails and of assembling illegal technological devices, we were ready.

At hour sixty-five, I crouched in air duct seventy-two with Zippy, waiting for the signal. Takia worked at her station. Even through the vent I could feel her nervous energy, and I willed her to stop looking over her shoulder. The atmosphere throughout Inside had been charged. Those who didn't know what was about to occur, still sensed the keyed-up feeling of expectation. The Travas had tripled the number of Pop Cops on patrol.

Twice as many Travas had assembled in the Control Room. Both the fleet admiral and the admiral studied maps over the conference table in the far corner. I knew to expect one admiral, but not both. Surrounded by computers, the captain occupied the center of the room. I checked Zippy for the hundredth time. So much rested on the little cleaning troll.

Various stations called in their readiness. Riley and the rest of the uppers had changed their shift times and managed to be at their workstations. Domotor and Logan ghosted in the network. Doctor Lamont prepped for casualties. Anne-Jade, Jacy and his gang waited to overpower the Pop Cops on the lower levels and I prepared to spring a surprise on the Control Room.

Jacy's voice sounded in my ear. "We go."

Warning lights flashed in the Control Room's panels. Banks of computers lined three walls of the room, and uppers sat before them, leaving an open space in the middle for the captain's station.

"Call for help from Commander Vinco, sir," an upper called. "Scrubs are revolting."

The fleet admiral strode over to the captain. "Time to weed out the troublemakers, Captain," he said.

"Send reinforcements, alert the air controllers to prepare the poison gas canisters," the captain ordered. He typed on his keypad. "I've had it with these bothersome scrubs."

A spinning feeling of panic grew in my stomach.

"Sir? The air controller on duty just told me to blow the gas out my ass." Shock whitened the upper's face.

I suppressed a chuckle. Logan's voice sounded. "We're in."

All I needed to hear. I finished loosening the screws on the vent cover and pulled the cover inside the duct. No need to mask my noise as the upper workers reported one by one to the captain that the mechanical systems failed to respond.

"What do you mean not responding?" the captain demanded.

I lowered Zippy a few inches into the room and flipped the switch. No hum or spark, according to Logan the pulse would be silent. Still I would have felt better to at least see a flash. Trusting the technology, I yanked Zippy back.

The captain pounded on his computer. "Damn thing."

"Engage the override, we'll control the systems from here," the fleet admiral ordered.

My turn. I dropped down onto the fleet admiral. A few cries of alarm had alerted him, but all he had time to do was look up. We landed together in a heap. The stun guns from all the Travas aimed at us, but none of them worked. I wore one of Anne-Jade's anti-stunners just in case. Yanking my protected stunner from my belt, I neutralized the fleet admiral, the captain and the uppers working near the override controls.

It didn't take long for a flaw in my plan to become obvious. I needed more time to aim and shoot than I expected. The other uppers left their seats to join in the fray, grabbing for me. Takia remained at her post.

Outnumbered, it was a matter of time before I was unarmed. Stunned bodies littered the ground and a few uppers moved awkwardly with half-stunned body parts. Two men held my arms with tight grips. Not part of the plan. I was supposed to stun everyone and open the Control Room door from the inside.

The admiral remained by his station. He glanced at his stun gun in his hand, then tossed it aside. "Report," he ordered his team.

Except for the two holding me, the uppers returned to their posts.

"Override engaged, sir," an upper said.

"Lieutenant Commander Karla is at the door," Takia reported.

I suppressed a grin of triumph. The override would be knocked out as soon as the door opened and Anne-Jade, Jacy and his group stormed the room.

"Let them in," the admiral said.

Preparing to join in the fray, I braced for action. The double metal doors slid aside with a hissing noise.

My heart shattered and the men beside me grunted and supported me as my legs turned to liquid.

Lieutenant Commander Karla Trava stood at the door with Commander Vinco on her right side and Doctor Lamont, or rather Kiana Garrard on her left.

twenty-three

Speechless, I stared at my mother. Doctor Lamont's expression fluctuated between fear and hope as she scanned the faces in the room with a frantic intensity. She clutched something with both hands. When she met my gaze, guilty pain flared for a moment. I marveled at my own stupidity. Even when we knew she had betrayed the last group of rebels, she had conned us again.

Karla swaggered into the Control Room with a smug smirk. Vinco followed with ten Pop Cops behind him. One of them pushed Doctor Lamont into the room. The door hissed shut with a thump that crushed the remains of my heart.

"Report, Lieutenant Commander," the admiral said.

"The lower levels are secured, sir."

"Excellent work. How did you manage it so quick?"

Karla glanced at Doctor Lamont. "We had a few hours' notice."

"Well done. Braydon, send instructions to our men below and have them separate the leaders."

"Yes, sir," an upper called, typing at his computer.

Takia remained at her post. Her fingers rested on her keyboard, and I hoped she countered the admiral's order.

The admiral pulled his kill-zapper from his belt and advanced on me. "I'm going to enjoy weeding out the first troublemaker."

I shrank against my captors, but they held me tight. My heart trembled when he pressed the nozzle to my chest. Hell of a way to find out if Zippy worked and neutralized the kill-zapper.

"Stop," Doctor Lamont shouted.

The admiral paused. He frowned, turning toward the doctor. "Why?"

"She's the leader of this whole thing. She knows everyone involved. If you recycle her before you question her, you might miss a few troublemakers."

"Trella's proven resistant to torture," Karla said. "If you keep her alive, the scrubs will have someone to rally around." She scowled at Vinco. "Or she might escape into the pipes again."

He hunched his shoulders and ducked his head.

"She might become a martyr and you'll have more scrubs revolting," the doctor said.

"I don't care," the admiral said. His focus returned to me. "Clear." The men holding me let go. He pulled the trigger and I screamed. Nothing else happened. I swayed with relief.

My relief was short-lived. The admiral scowled, threw his weapon down and gestured for Karla's kill-zapper. She hadn't been here when Zippy had knocked the other weapons out. Hers would work.

Before he could press it against me, I smiled. "Go ahead. That one won't work either."

"She's bluffing," Vinco said. "If she's so confident, why did she scream before?"

I shrugged. "I was having a little fun." My voice remained steady despite my muscles turning to mush.

Vinco flashed his knife. "This will work." He grinned in delight.

Breathing was difficult, I sucked in air through my tight throat, trying not to gasp.

The admiral considered then returned Karla's kill-zapper. "It's too messy. Take her to the brig, Commander. Find out what she knows, but if you don't learn anything new, feed her to Chomper."

"Yes, sir!" Vinco snapped to action, striding toward me.

"Wait," Doctor Lamont said.

"Now what?" Annoyance creased the admiral's face.

She turned to Karla. "What about our bargain? You said *she* would be here."

"And she is." A nasty glee sparked in Karla's eyes. She pointed at me. "Meet your daughter, Kiana. Trella, or should I call you by your birth name, Sadie?" She rubbed her chin as if deep in thought. "I liked the name Trella. Guess I'm partial to *TR*s and *A*s." She shrugged. "Anyway, Trella, meet your mother."

Horror gripped Doctor Lamont's face, but she shook her head. "You're lying, Karla. It's too big of a coincidence." She uncurled her fingers. My pearl-handled comb lay across her palms. "I fell for it, too." The faint words just audible.

"Troublemakers tend to breed more troublemakers," Karla said. "Although, I must admit I was a bit surprised when I went digging into Trella's records. I knew keeping your child alive would come in handy sometime—she's your weakness. I suspect Domotor also did a little digging into the computer files and recruited her to his cause."

"No. I don't believe it. She looks nothing like me or Nolan," the doctor said.

"Really?" Karla cocked her hip, studying me. "With her

new blue eyes wide with fear, she looks exactly like Nolan did right before we fed him to Chomper."

A murmur ran through the Control Room as the others either agreed or disagreed.

"Touching as all this is, there is much work to be done." The admiral issued orders for the Pop Cops to carry the stunned officers to the infirmary. "Doctor, please make sure they are comfortable. Commander, take this scrub from my sight."

As Vinco's hand wrapped around my upper arm, I said, "This is just the beginning." It was a delay tactic, but the truth of the words knitted my heart together. Even though our rebellion failed, and we had been betrayed, I stood in the Control Room. A future effort might bring the scrubs even further.

I laughed. "You can try and weed out the troublemakers, Admiral, but you'll miss one or two and they'll multiply. Think about it. How do you think we managed to get this far? If I can take advantage of Karla's incompetence, then it's only a matter of time before others do the same."

The lieutenant commander yanked her kill-zapper and shoved it into my ribs. "Let's see if my weapon works."

Vinco released his grip.

"Hold on, Karla," the admiral said. "What do you mean by incompetence, scrub?"

"Look at what we accomplished. Domotor disappeared. We opened Gateway. I escaped the brig and have been living in the upper levels for a week. We infiltrated the computer system. And I'm in your Control Room and your captain is stunned. It was ridiculously easy to break into her office. The list of her incompetence is endless." I tsked.

She dropped the kill-zapper—the upside of my taunt. And wrapped her hands around my neck—the downside.

"I'm going to feed you to Chomper myself," she said, and then squeezed.

She cut off my air and I feared she would crush my windpipe. Groping for her belt, I found her stunner and pulled the trigger. A jolt ringed my neck, but her fingers kept the pressure on my throat. I dropped the stunner and pried them from my numb skin, I shoved her back into the admiral and they fell to the floor together.

Now I would go to Chomper happy.

I almost jumped a meter when Logan's chuckle vibrated in my ear. "*That* must have felt good," he said. "Wish I could have been there."

Jacy added, "We have regained control of levels one and two."

"Trell, stay with us," Riley said. "Once Takia can open the Control Room door, we'll send a rescue party."

Distracted by their voices, I had lost track of events in the Control Room. After a quick scan, my mind raced to plan a way to delay the inevitable. The admiral's red face failed to encourage me. Vinco helped him to his feet.

"Messy or not, silence the scrub," the admiral ordered.

Vinco advanced on me with his knife in hand.

"Overconfidence, Commander, will be your downfall," I said. Weak, but all I could come up with.

"And a sharp blade through your heart will be yours," Vinco replied.

Why didn't I hold on to Karla's stunner? I thought fast. "Actually time is against me right now."

"Time?"

The admiral answered. "She doesn't have any left. Finish the job."

Vinco raised the blade to slice my throat. Movement across the room caught my attention for a second.

"The admiral's wrong," I said. "What I meant by time was I didn't think I had enough of it to distract you. But I did. So I guess I was wrong, too."

Armed scrubs streamed into the room. Before the room erupted into chaos, a number of uppers had been stunned.

Vinco managed to dodge the initial blasts. With his knife still aimed at my throat, he lunged at me. I kicked him in the chest. Instead of cutting deep into the skin, his slash skimmed my neck.

Single-minded, he stepped closer. My back hit a wall, trapping me. He grinned with satisfaction as he pressed his blade under my chin. The steel bit into my jaw. Then strong arms yanked him from me and spun him around.

Riley gave him a mocking salute.

Vinco was amused. "Okay, boy. You first, then the scrub." He pounced.

Riley twisted his hips to avoid the knife thrust and knocked Vinco's arm aside with his hand. Vinco tried again and this time Riley grabbed Vinco's wrist, pulled him off balance and pressed a palm to his elbow, forcing him to the ground.

"Thanks for all those lessons, Commander," Riley said. "They've really paid off."

After the takeover of the Control Room, events blurred together. Lack of sleep and the stress of the previous eighty hours caught up to me. With my body aching from Vinco's attack, I blindly followed Riley back to the infirmary to have the cuts on my neck stitched. At this rate, I would use up all the thread.

The male doctor who had helped with Doreen was pressed into service while the others decided what to do with Doctor Lamont.

I woke hours later in the infirmary's extra bedroom. Searching, I found the doctor bustling about the infirmary, tending the others wounded in the fight.

"Go back to bed, Ella," he ordered.

I didn't bother to correct him. Trella, Ella or Sadie—at this

284 MARIA V. SNYDER

point I didn't care. Instead I said, "Every bed is full. You'll need my help."

He scanned the room. "Nothing serious, thank air. And only a few Pop Cops were recycled. You need your rest. Once things settle down, it's going to be…interesting around here."

I shuffled back to my room, thinking my task was complete and I'd leave the others to figure out the rest.

The second time I woke, Riley sat on the edge of my bed. He beamed as if he knew something I didn't.

"What?" I asked.

"You look much better." He smoothed a strand of hair from my face.

"I'm sure you didn't come here to tell me that."

"No, but it's nice to see. Especially after…you know… Vinco."

I shuddered at the memory of his wicked knife. Touching the tender area on my throat, I remembered how it could have been worse. "Thanks for saving me."

"Anytime." He flashed me another overly bright smile.

I pushed to a sitting position. "Okay, Riley, tell me what's going on."

"I found my brother."

"Wonderful. How—no, let me guess. You went to the lower levels with Mama Sheepy and found the man who still had Dada Sheepy."

"Yep. The Sheepy family is whole again. His name is Blake and he works in the kitchen." He beamed.

I squinted. "You have more news."

This time, he shot me a nervous smile. "I was hoping—" he pulled a necklace from his pocket "—we could make a commitment."

A brief pulse of fear shot through me. "You mean be mates?"

"No. At least, not yet. Our tradition is to give a gift as the first step. Sort of a symbol that we plan to see how well we get along." He laid the necklace in my palm.

A silver pendant swung from a thin chain. "A sheep?" I asked.

"I thought it appropriate, considering what has happened."

So much had happened, and Inside would no longer be the same. But the thought of Riley by my side sent a comforting pulse through my body.

"How do I accept?" I asked.

"You wear the necklace."

I marveled at the detail of the sheep. "Are you sure? You don't know everything about me—"

"I do know I felt as if my heart had been shredded when I found you in our storeroom, unconscious and bleeding. And leaving you with Vinco in the holding cells was the hardest thing I've ever done." He wrapped an arm around me and pulled me close. "We can take it slow. We have plenty of time."

He kissed me. A sizzle traveled through me that didn't stop when he drew back. My mouth tingled.

"Your answer?" he asked.

I kissed him, enjoying the sensation of happiness blooming inside me for the first time. Too soon, we parted.

"I'll take that as a yes." Riley unhooked the clasp of the necklace. "Another one of our traditions is for me to make the pendant myself, but I had help from Logan and Anne-Jade." He looped it around my neck then secured it, sweeping my hair out of the way.

I fingered the sheep. "Logan and Anne-Jade? Is it one of their gadgets?"

"Yes, but," he hurriedly added, "it's inactive. If you ever get into trouble and need help, you can squeeze the pendant and it will send a signal. We can trace the signal to your location and send reinforcements."

I laughed. "Do you really think it's necessary now?"

"I may not know everything about you, but I do know that if there is trouble, you'll be in the middle of it."

He stifled my squawk of protest with another kiss. After a while, I forgot to be mad.

The transition from the Travas controlling Inside to a more democratic method wasn't smooth. Even though each family elected a representative and each scrub "family" had a person attending organization meetings, many uppers still viewed the scrubs with suspicion and the scrubs in turn made planning difficult with their distrust and bitterness.

I had hoped to avoid all the political wrangling, but, since I understood both sides, I attended all the meetings to smooth relations. Even so, we had a long way to go. Overcrowding remained a problem, and a few people resisted the change in their lifestyles. Violence erupted on occasion, and Anne-Jade organized a security detail with members of all the families to keep the peace.

Being able to walk the hallways of the upper levels without worry felt liberating. Domotor also enjoyed his freedom from the hideout. He was busy preaching to everyone to be patient and understanding. All the Travas had been incarcerated for now. The Committee would decide their eventual fate. Doctor Lamont had been confined, too.

It was week 147,007, and I had received a message to meet Logan in the Control Room at hour ten. He had been camped out there since the takeover, using the computers to harvest lost information.

He hunched over a keyboard, muttering and humming to himself. I touched his arm and he almost jumped from his seat.

"Don't scare me like that," he said, waving a hand in front of his face.

"I'm sorry. Should I have bowed and announced my presence first? Have they coronated you fleet admiral yet?"

"Go ahead and be sarcastic." He swiveled back to the screen. "I'm not going to tell you—ow! Let go of my ear, I'll tell you."

I released his lobe. He rubbed it.

"Logan?"

"All right. I found the answers to those final three files and accessed the information. Outside is something called Outer Space. It's an airless and pressureless environment unable to support life."

Sorrow and guilt welled. If we just had waited, Cog wouldn't be floating out there. "Thanks for the reminder."

"Sorry. Ah…well, we are actually traveling *through* it. Seems it is so vast that it takes an incredibly long time to get from one planet to another."

"Planet?"

"As far as I can tell, a planet is the *real* Outside." He typed on the keyboard. The picture of the blue ceiling and greenery filled the computer's screen. "This is our destination. We've been heading there for the past 147,000 weeks."

"When are we scheduled to arrive?" But the answer popped into my mind. *It's the end and the beginning. What is it?* I looked at Logan.

"Week one million," we said together.

I groped for a chair. We had 853,000 weeks to go! My head spun as I sat. Eight thousand generations of people would be born, live and end in this metal cube before reaching the true Outside.

"There's so much to learn about our past and why we're here," Logan said. "I've just scratched the surface. The Travas tried deleting all the files, but they were protected by the system's safety guards and buried."

"The system's guards? What about the Controllers?"

Logan flipped his hand as if dismissing an underling. "No evidence of them. At least no indication that the Controllers are actual people. It's the system's operating parameters and fail-safes. Also certain directives have been programmed into it, which were set by the original designers."

"What directives?"

"Like the one about our population. Once we reach Outside, the designers wanted to make sure we had enough people to survive. These directives couldn't be changed or altered, so the Travas must have thought they were a divine message." Logan chuckled. "Anyway, it's amazing Domotor found those buried files, and was able to copy parts of them."

"It wasn't Domotor. He was the leader of the group, but Nolan Garrard was the first to find them."

"Then Garrard was a genius." Logan tapped a finger on his chair. "Speaking of Garrard, did you want to read your file?"

My file? It took me a moment to remember the file marked with my birth week and hour. "No."

"But it's important. Your mother explains her actions. You **need** to forgive her."

I glared at him. "She betrayed you, too. We almost lost."

"Almost. She didn't tell them *everything* about our plans. How do you think we rallied?"

"I don't care. She told them enough. Besides, Karla could have planted the information about my birth parents in the computer. It could be a complete hoax and she's not related to me at all."

"There's a way to prove or disprove the relationship," Logan said.

"How?"

"With your blood. Those vampire boxes do more than test for pregnancy."

Logan had overwhelmed me with information. I wandered around in a daze until I was needed for yet another Committee meeting. The uppers and lowers squabbled like children and

I wished to be back in the infirmary, helping the doctor. Or better yet, to be with Riley in our room.

As I let the discord roll over me, I decided I needed to be the Queen of the Pipes for a little while and not worry about blood tests and overcrowding.

Returning to the air shafts, I felt light and free. I explored more of the upper levels. With the constant threat of being caught by the Pop Cops, I had limited my forays above level four. Now, I climbed into the Gap and investigated the space between the pipes and the ceiling of Inside.

I felt as if there was a missing element. Air shafts and water pipes crisscrossed above the level. No laundry chutes or waste pipes—understandable since both of them go down to level one.

Climbing over a duct, I bumped my head on the ceiling and realized the missing element was foam. There was no insulating foam. I sat until the pain subsided.

Why wasn't there any foam? I shone my light on the metal panels, counting rivets. I lost track of time, but I didn't care, planning to search the entire ceiling.

In the northeast corner, I found a hatch. It resembled the near-invisible hatches that accessed the Gap, but it had a black rubber seal around it.

No keypad. No handle.

My body hummed with nervous energy. This door was different than Gateway. I should leave it alone and tell the Committee I had found another hatch. I *should* didn't mean I *would*. Gateway had another inner door, and I couldn't leave without seeing if this one did, too.

I pushed with my hands. Nothing. Putting more force into it, I tried again. A crackling sounded. I bent over and pressed my shoulders to the hatch, using my legs for added strength.

A slow sucking noise grew louder as I kept the pressure

on. Then it popped free. I staggered with surprise. The hatch banged down off to the side as darkness spilled from the opening.

I braced for the ice-cold nothing to rob me of air, but only the stale smell of dust reached me. I straightened, poking my head into the space past the doorway.

The semi-darkness stretched up to an impossible height and disappeared into black. It felt like Outer Space, but with stale air and walls. Faint bluelight climbed the sides. I hoisted myself onto the floor constructed of metal sheets riveted together just like the rest of Inside.

I walked along, shining my light. It was a huge empty space. At least, it was empty until my light lit stacks of metal sheets, pipes, equipment, barrels and I-beams. An amazing array of supplies.

In the far southwest corner were gigantic shelves. The shelves appeared to be half-completed levels. I counted them. Six. The space had room for six more levels!

No. A huge expanse loomed above the sixth one.

I knelt on the floor as understanding sucked my breath away. The builders of Inside knew the journey would be long and our population would grow. Above me was plenty of room for us to expand. No more overcrowding. No more restrictions on the number of children. We could have large families and privacy. I could have a family.

I pressed my forehead to the cold metal floor, trying not to pass out. My shaky hand found the pendant. I squeezed the sheep, sending the signal.

Riley, I thought, *bring reinforcements, we're going to need them.*

★ ★ ★ ★ ★

Acknowledgments

My thank-yous always start with my husband, Rodney. His support is critical to my writing and essential when I'm flying all over the place to attend book events. My children, Luke and Jenna, also get a thank-you for inspiring me and for not making me feel too guilty when I'm running around for my other job.

The entire story for this book came to me in a dream, including characters, plot twists and ending. That hadn't happened to me before and hasn't since. However, dream novels still need to be written, and I'd like to thank a group of Seton Hill University critiquers who looked at the first chapter and said, "You may have something here."

Thanks to Dr. Michael Arnzen, Venessa Giunta, Johanna Gribble, Sara Lyon, Kathryn Martin, Heidi Ruby Miller, Darren Moore, Sabrina Naples, Rachael Pruitt and Shara Saunsaucie.

A special thank-you to the original Tricky (the good one), Mike Mehalek, who came up with the cool title!

A big thank-you to those who read the first draft and helped with revisions—my editor Mary-Theresa Hussey, my agent Robert Mecoy, my critique partner Kimberly Howe, and Elizabeth Mazer. Also to all those at Harlequin Books who helped the book along the way (too many to count, let alone list), thank you all so much! The cover is dead-on perfect—a heartfelt thanks to the art department and all the talented artists and designers who helped with the cover.

No acknowledgments are ever complete without thanking

my mounting army of Book Commandos. They are spreading the word about my books in bookstores, in book groups, in libraries, in line at the grocery stores, throughout their families and online. You guys rock! A special thank-you for those who went that extra mile: Amberkatze, Lorri Amsden, Deborah Beamer, Linda Childs, Allison Leigh Davis, Michelle Deschene-Warren, David Hankerson, Michelle Haring, Kristy Kalin, Lexie, Holly Nelson, Lora Negrito, Rosemary Potter, Lee Ann Ray, Christina Russo, Rachel Smith, Michelle Staffa, Jenny Sweedler and Diana Teeter. Trella will want to recruit you all to the Force of Sheep.

OUTSIDE IN

To Mary-Theresa Hussey,
for her editorial excellence and extreme patience.
Thanks for the help, encouragement and smiley faces!

introduction

My world changed in a heartbeat. That's how it felt to me. As if one second ago, I was Trella the lower level scrub, cleaning the air and water ducts of Inside, and now I am Trella the victorious leader of the Force of Sheep rebellion. Yes the name sounds ridiculous, and I still can't believe we named a major life-changing event after livestock—or actually a stuffed animal—but it made sense at the time.

Why? Because I once thought my fellow scrubs were sheep, passive and content with the status quo. I was wrong and learned if you put enough sheep together you have a herd—a force to be reckoned with. A force that turned our world upside down and inside out.

Of course, it really didn't change in a second. It took six weeks, which in Inside time is six hundred hours (one hundred hours per week). But if I compared it to how long we've been living here in Inside—147,019 weeks—it's a mere four thousandths of a percent. And here's the kicker, we have another

852,981 weeks to go before we reach our destination. Mind-boggling!

Where are we going? Good question. According to Logan, our computer expert, our metal cube-shaped world is traveling through Outer Space. And since Outer Space is incredibly huge, it will take us a total of a million weeks to get to a planet where we can go Outside and live. We're not sure what exactly Outside is since many of Inside's computer records have been deleted.

According to our remaining records, another so-called "rebellion" happened around week 132,076 when Admiral Trava reported saboteurs had tried to destroy the computer systems with magnets, erasing all the historical files. But Logan says it's bogus and he suspects the Trava family deleted those files so they could rule the people of Inside.

Before that first rebellion, Inside was ruled by a Committee comprised of all the nine families, but the Trava family didn't want to share. Since they were in charge of security, they had the weapons and they took control. Each family had been responsible for the different systems that keep us all alive. Air, water, hydroponics, shepherds, recycling, the infirmary, the power plant and the kitchen. Yeah that's a lot, but when you're living in a big metal cube in the middle of Outer Space, you need every one.

The Travas separated the people into uppers and lowers (a.k.a. scrubs), and kept us confined to our levels (uppers on levels three & four, scrubs on levels one & two). They sowed the seeds of distrust and created the Population Control Police (a.k.a. Pop Cops) to make sure we all followed the rules. Their propaganda worked. The scrubs, including me, thought the uppers were living in big apartments with big families and cushy jobs, while we lived in overcrowded barracks with no privacy and were forced to clean and maintain the systems (after all, rust and dust are the twin evils of Inside).

It worked. The scrubs hated the uppers and the uppers hated us.

Now back to our rebellion. It started with an upper named Domotor. His first attempt at overthrowing the Travas failed, but he discovered the location of Gateway—the mythical Gateway to Outside—and saved the info on disks.

This is where I come in. Domotor hid his disks in an air duct above his rooms on level three. Later, Domotor recruited me to retrieve his disks and I did. This one event set off a whole heap of trouble for me. And my best and only friend Cog was arrested for covering for me.

Now I'm not going to detail everything that happened. If you want to know all about it, you can go to your computer and read through this file: ISBN-978-0-373-21006-0.

But I will summarize. I discovered the uppers didn't have it any better than scrubs, and I met one I really liked named Riley. He helped me, along with Logan and a few others, to find Gateway. Unfortunately when Cog and I opened it, we learned Outside was really Outer Space, a big black freezing nothing that sucked my friend out. Cog's very last act was saving my life.

So much for freedom in Outside. But the others didn't let the disappointment stop them. Riley, Logan and a few uppers—the rest of the Force of Sheep—still wanted to restore power to all the families. And we did. The Travas were arrested and a temporary Committee was formed.

Even with this new Committee, I knew it wasn't going to be easy to change our ways. And with four levels, Inside was still too small for our population.

I had a hard time sitting through meetings, so I escaped to explore the ducts every so often. Without having to worry about the Pop Cops, I could really search places I had only briefly passed.

And guess what? I discovered that Inside wasn't just four

levels high. There was a vast space above level four. Plenty of room for many more levels. We could spread out!

After this breakthrough, I thought Inside was done with trouble.

Too bad, I thought wrong.

one

My fingers ached as my leg muscles trembled. Beads of sweat snaked down the skin on my back, leaving an itchy trail. I clung to the almost sheer metal wall and breathed in deep. When my heart slowed to a more normal rhythm, I relaxed my right hand's grip and stretched for the next handhold—a short piece of pipe. Then I repeated the motion with my left, climbing another meter higher.

Far below, spots of daylight illuminated the half completed construction on level ten. Distant voices floated on the stale dusty air. I had passed the last of the bluelights. Nothing but blackness remained above me.

I cocked my head, sweeping the flashlight's beam across the wall in search of another pipe to grab. Logan had designed a special helmet equipped with a light to keep my hands free.

"Trella?" Riley's voice startled me.

I lost my grip. Falling, I cursed my own stupidity for not switching my earring/receiver off.

"I know you can hear me," he said with an annoyed tone. "Where are you?"

Getting one hell of a rope burn, I grabbed my safety line and squeezed to slow my fall. After what felt like a thousand weeks, I reached the end of the rope and jerked hard, biting my tongue. I swung, tasting blood and lamenting the slip. That had been the highest point I or anyone else had attained. Ever.

Riley grunted in frustration. "Trella, you can go exploring later. You're late for the Committee meeting. They're waiting for you."

He wasn't the only one frustrated. For the last twelve weeks, I'd been promised time to go exploring the Expanse. All my previous forays had lasted about an hour before I'd been summoned to another important meeting. This time, I had been determined to ignore everyone, only to forget about the receiver.

I had hoped to reach the ceiling of the Expanse, but the effort needed to re-scale the wall would be too much for my tired muscles. Resigning myself to yet another delay, I stopped my swing by dragging my hand along the wall.

The construction workers wanted to build a ladder up the side of the Expanse, install daylights and find the ceiling. But the Committee insisted they first finish the six new levels for the citizens of Inside to spread out. I agreed, yet my curiosity would not be satisfied until I knew the height of the Expanse.

Pressing the top button on my shirt, I said to Riley, "Tell the Committee I'll be there in an hour. They can start without me. They don't need me there to quibble over every minor detail."

"You're right," Riley said. "They need you when they quibble over the insignificant details, the worthless details and the waste-of-everyone's time details."

While understandable, his sarcasm was too harsh for someone as even-tempered as Riley. "What happened?"

"I can't get a work crew to fix the faulty wiring in level five. It's a mess, but they're too busy with level six. We've lived in those four levels for the last one hundred and forty-seven thousand plus weeks, it won't kill us to wait a few more."

Overcrowding in the bottom two levels had been insufferable, but now that the uppers and lowers were united, there should be more room. Except the uppers wouldn't consider any plans for the scrubs to move into their levels. They insisted it would be a wasted effort since the new levels would be ready soon.

"I'll see what I can do," I said. I transferred my weight back onto the wall and unclipped the rope from my safety harness. Climbing down two meters to the roof of level ten, I glanced up. Next time, I would need a longer rope.

By then, level six would probably be finished. I walked over to the access stairs. It was so nice not to squeeze between levels. But before I reached them, the construction foreman called my name.

I waited for him to join me and smiled in recognition of the burly man. "Hi, Hank, how's it going?"

"Lousy," Hank said. He had buzzed his gray hair to a stubble on his head. Holding a wipe board in one hand, he tapped the board with a marker. "I've a list of repairs for levels one to four, but no one will do them. And I'm losing construction people every hour."

"Losing how?"

"They take a break and never come back." My alarm must have shown on my face, because Hank rushed to assure me. "It's not like that. They're angry the uppers aren't doing any of the work. My crews are being difficult, showing up late, leaving early or not coming at all."

A passive resistance. Wonderful. "Why won't anyone fix the repairs?"

"Same reason. The uppers aren't doing their share."

I suppressed a sigh. The Pop Cops had threatened the uppers with exile in the lower levels in order to scare them into cooperating. They had thought life below would be nothing but hard physical labor. Since they had run all the systems in Inside, their jobs involved sitting in front of a computer, and telling the scrubs what to do. Changing their perception of the scrubs was still ongoing, and I believed would be one of the hardest tasks. But not impossible.

"Okay, Hank. I'll tell the Committee."

He looked doubtful. "That Committee can only agree on one thing."

"What's that?"

"To disagree."

I laughed, but Hank didn't. "Oh, come on. It's not that bad. We don't have Pop Cops anymore."

"Maybe we should."

Hank's words followed me as I descended to level three. He had to be joking. No one…well, no scrub—and Hank had been one for maintenance—would ever wish for the return of the Pop Cops. I dismissed his comment as being melodramatic and hurried to my room.

Since it had only been twelve weeks since the rebellion, I still slept in the extra room in the infirmary in Sector B3. It had been designated for the doctor's intern, but, so far, no one could handle the job. I wouldn't mind—a place of my own was a luxury I've never had—except I shared the suite's washroom and kitchen with Doctor Lamont. Also known as Kiana Garrard. Or as I liked to call her, the Traitor.

Unfortunately, I remained in the minority. The Committee had reviewed her actions during the rebellion. They decided she had been duped by Lieutenant Commander Karla Trava and her betrayal had minor consequences. Of course, the two infirmaries full of wounded from the revolt had nothing to do with their ruling. And the limited number of doctors hadn't been a consideration, either. Yeah, right and I was Queen of Inside.

The Traitor tended to a few patients in the main room of the infirmary. Which consisted of two rows of beds lined up along each side. Curtains hung from U-shaped tracks in the ceiling for privacy and a narrow path cut through the middle. A high counter full of medical supplies covered half the back wall. Next to the counter was another door that led to the Traitor's office, the exam room and the surgery. Beyond them was the apartment.

Without looking at her, I hurried past the beds, aiming for the far door.

"Trella," she called.

I paused, but kept my back to her.

"I have a surgery scheduled for hour sixty. I'll need your assistance."

"What happened to Catie?"

"She passed out when one of the construction crew came in with a bloody gash on his forehead that exposed the bone."

Closing my eyes, I suppressed the accusation that she purposely tried to gross out the people I found to help her. Yet another item for my long to-do list—find the Traitor an intern. "I'm busy. You'll have to find someone else to help." I glanced at the clock. Hour fifty-five.

"I can't train them in five hours, Trella. You have experience and an iron stomach. Plus…"

I waited.

In a softer voice she said, "Plus you're good. You have a natural talent that shouldn't be wasted. You must have inherited that from me."

Whirling around, I confronted her. "Now you decide Karla wasn't lying. Does thinking I'm your daughter help you with the guilt over betraying us? Am I supposed to feel special that you risked all we had worked for and *died* for because of motherly love?"

She stepped back in surprise, clutching a tray to her chest as if it were a shield. Her long hair—the same color as mine—had been braided into a single plait that hung to her waist.

I hadn't meant to be so nasty, but since the rebellion, she had never once acknowledged the possibility of our relationship, insisting it had been another one of Karla's twisted tricks. I agreed. Riley, though, had speculated that if she believed I was her offspring, then the enormity of what she had done would have overwhelmed her. He had tried to explain it, to help me see it from her point of view.

But a traitor was a traitor in my mind. No need to waste time justifying her actions. I had enough to do.

Despite my personal feelings, we did need her doctoring skills. "What about Doctor Sanchia?"

"Busy with his own patients and the scrub…the caretakers in the lower levels…" She hesitated.

A ripple of unease lapped against my stomach. "They refused?"

She met my gaze. "Not in so many words. They just won't answer my requests, and when I go down there, they ignore me or give me the runaround until I give up and leave."

Dark circles, new wrinkles and streaks of white hair aged her. She appeared older—closer to fifty centiweeks than forty.

"How critical is the surgery at hour sixty? Can it be delayed?" I asked.

"It's Emek's appendix. If I don't remove it soon, it will burst and kill him."

"All right, I'll help you. For *Emek's* sake." I headed to my room. My thoughts returned to the Committee. They would need to investigate why the lower care workers were ignoring requests for help.

My palms stung as I washed up. I had forgotten about the

rope burns. Grabbing a tube of antiseptic, I rubbed it on the abrasions. Abrasions? I needed to find another place to sleep before I started spouting medical lingo like a pro.

Riley's father had offered to move from their apartment, but it was too soon for us to go that next step. Since the rebellion, Riley and I had little to no time to get to know each other better. I touched my silver sheep pendant—a gift from Riley. Perhaps I could live in our storeroom and spend more alone time with Riley. Only a few members of the Force of Sheep knew of its existence. Which made staying there even more appealing.

The Committee met in the large conference room next to Inside's main Control Room, both within Quadrant G4. I had argued for the new levels to be built in a different configuration than the existing levels without success.

With so many changes happening so fast, the Committee thought a new design would just confuse everyone. So level five resembled levels one through four—a three by three grid, like a tic-tac-toe board. The four corners were labeled Quadrants and the middle sections were Sectors. Starting from the top row on the left, the first Quadrant was A, then Sector B and Quadrant C. The middle was Sectors D, E and F and the last row had Quadrant G, Sector H and Quadrant I. Just add the level number and any idiot could find a location.

I arrived at the meeting two hours late. Slipping into an empty seat beside Jacy, I glanced around the long oval table. The Committee had been comprised of one representative from each of the nine upper families and one leader from each scrub area like hydroponics and waste-water. Eighteen in all. Since an even number could cause problems when members voted, a nineteenth spokesperson had been added.

Despite repeated requests that I become the nineteenth member, I refused, preferring to be a part of the Committee as a consultant only. Less responsibility. Riley had been asked next, but he'd quipped that the Committee didn't need both him and his father and he'd claimed that he would be more useful as support personnel.

They finally elected Jacy.

After my initial surprise at his appointment, and, when I thought it through, it made sense. He had taken over the organization and leadership of the rebellion when I had been captured by the Pop Cops. Plus he was well connected through his network of people in the lower levels.

I leaned close to him. "What did I miss?"

"They're trying to decide which group can move into level five."

"Group?" That was new.

"Once all six new levels are completed, the Committee thinks the nine families can share five levels and the scrubs, broken into groups by areas, can live in the other five."

"That won't work."

"I know and you know, but try and explain it to those eighteen." He swept his hand out. "They're still thinking in terms of uppers and lowers."

Which reminded me. "Are you aware of the labor strike?"

Jacy stared at me with a guarded expression. "Yep."

"How do we get the workers back?"

"By having the uppers get their hands dirty for once."

And Jacy just proved he also thought in terms of uppers and lowers. If I was being honest, I did as well. That was the problem. But I couldn't figure out a solution.

Why should I? I'd done my part and found Gateway, led the rebellion and discovered the Expanse. The multiple scars on my arms, legs and torso from Pop Cop Commander Vinco's knife proved I had sacrificed for the citizens of Inside.

I had also lost my closest friend, Cogon. He had acted more like a brother, and I missed him so much my insides felt rusted and brittle. Cog would have loved organizing the construction crews. He'd have insisted on perfection before moving on to another level.

Slouching in my chair, I let the Committee's voices roll over me. They didn't need me. The Committee would take us to the next stage.

After listening to the sixth scrub area representative list the reasons they should be the first to move into level five, I willed the clock to move faster. These meetings were a waste of my time. I could be spending these hours with Riley. The session went on and on. Assisting the Traitor with surgery grew more appealing with each minute. I lasted until hour fifty-nine.

"I'm outta here. I'm helping the…Doctor Lamont," I whispered to Jacy.

"Will you be back before the vote?" he asked.

"Why? Nothing I say changes their minds." Frustration and weariness welled, but I swallowed them down.

"You've given up, Trell. That's not like you."

"Sitting in endless meetings for twelve weeks isn't like me either. I'm a big picture girl." I tried a smile, but Jacy kept his frown. I made a sudden liberating decision. "Tell the Committee I'm resigning as a consultant and going back to what I do best."

Shock, anger and censure warred on Jacy's face. His lips moved for a moment before he spoke. "And what do you do best?"

"Explore. We have no idea how high up the Expanse's ceiling is. What if I find another hatch at the top? There could be another Expanse filled with supplies. That's just as important as arguing over who gets to move into the new levels first."

I left before he could respond. For the first time since the rebellion, I strode through the bland white corridors of Inside feeling light as air. I couldn't wait to tell Riley!

My good mood dissipated once I arrived at the infirmary

and spotted Emek's colorless face. Grimacing with pain, he clutched his sheets in tight fists. He wouldn't respond to my questions. His skin felt cold and clammy. The Traitor wasn't in the main room so I raced to the back.

She prepped for surgery. "You're early."

"Emek looks bad. When's the last time you checked on him?"

Pushing by me, she ran to him. I caught up to her as she probed the skin below Emek's waist with her fingers. He screamed.

"His appendix has burst." She kicked off the brakes on the bed. "Move!"

I helped her roll him into surgery and we transferred him to the operating table. Then she issued rapid-fire orders. The experience, which usually passed by in a blur of blood and frantic activity, slowed this time. Even with the emergency, I anticipated her needs a few times and handed her instruments without being asked. Despite my resistance, I was learning.

As she worked to save Emek's life, I no longer viewed her as the Traitor, but as Doctor Lamont. According to Doctor Sanchia, Lamont was the best diagnostician in our world and a skilled surgeon as well. More reasons she was here and not locked in the crowded holding cells with the Travas.

After sewing up Emek's incision, Lamont told me to dress the wound as she adjusted the anesthesia. It didn't take us long to finish. I wheeled him into the recovery room, which also served as the examination room.

Once the new levels were completed, the infirmaries on levels two and three would be combined into one large medical facility, spanning two grids. This had been an easy decision for the Committee. A shame they all weren't.

Keeping an eye on his vital signs, I stayed with Emek until he stabilized. When he roused, we moved him to a regular bed in the main room. I ensured he was comfortable, helped him sip a glass of ginger water, then tucked him under a blanket as he drifted off to sleep.

I turned and met Lamont's measuring gaze. She had watched me, but instead of commenting on my nurturing instincts, she checked Emek, nodded and returned to the operating room to clean up. Knowing the importance of a sterile area, I helped. We worked in silence, but the tension between us wasn't quite as thick. When the surfaces gleamed and the place smelled of antiseptic, I tossed the dirty rags into a special medical bag and sent it down the laundry chute.

"You did well," she said. "Thank you."

I grunted a reply, heading to my room. The rush from the emergency surgery fizzled and exhaustion soaked into my bones.

"There's a package on your bed from Logan," Lamont said as I pushed open the door.

Good thing she had mentioned Logan's name. Because if I hadn't known he brought it here, I would have assumed it was from Lamont. Then I would have carried it to Lamont's office and smashed the thing to little pieces. Instead, I set the vampire box on the table. The device had been used by the Pop Cops to test the scrubs for illegal drugs and pregnancy by taking blood samples. It could also settle the issue of my birth mother, determining if Lamont was indeed my parent. It had been Logan's idea to use the box.

I stretched out on the bed. Staring at the ceiling, I wondered why Logan sent it now. He knew I had no desire to prove the relationship. Lamont hadn't acknowledged me—that was proof enough. Guess I would need to visit Logan and ask him.

Eventually I drifted to sleep. Floating in a sea of blackness and surrounded by nothing, I strained to reach solid ground. But my body thinned. My arms turned translucent. My legs disappeared. I dissolved into a void.

Sound and touch returned with a vengeance. A roar woke

me. The noise rattled the floor and my bed lurched so hard it tossed me across the narrow room. I slammed into the wall along with the table. The vampire box clipped my forehead as it shattered against the sheet metal.

Loose items spun around and knocked into me as if the contents of my room had been stuffed into one of the huge laundry dryers and turned on.

The bluelight died, plunging me into darkness. Then it all stopped. I ended up sprawled in a heap on the floor amid a pile of debris. Dazed and confused, I stayed still, trying to clear my head.

Then the silence hit me. As familiar as the beat of my own heart, the Hum had always rumbled throughout Inside. A comforting constant noise noticed more on a subconscious level than noted on a conscious level.

The Hum meant the power plant was doing its job, producing electricity and heat, keeping us alive.

Silence meant the opposite. Until that moment, I hadn't known true terror.

two

In the blackness of my room, I untangled from the heap and stood. A wave of dizziness hit, spinning me back onto the ground. Pressing my fingers to my temple, I touched a tender spot covered with a sticky wetness—blood. I probably had a concussion.

Unable to trust my legs, I crawled, shoving aside debris as I moved toward the door. Or so I hoped. In the darkness, direction was hard to determine.

My hand touched a round dome, and I picked up my exploring helmet with a cry of triumph. Funny how the small things become important in an emergency. I donned the helmet, toggling on the light.

I faced the wrong way and the room was a mess—no surprise. A thick glass splinter jutted from my right forearm—a surprise since it didn't hurt. Of course once I stared at the blood welling from the wound, pain shot up my arm. Basic first aid instructions that I'd learned when I lived in the care facility replayed in my mind. I left the glass in place.

The crushed innards of the vampire box crunched beneath me as I reached the door. Despite my refusal to use the box, the damn thing had still gotten my blood via the glass shard.

I stumbled through the door and illuminated another disaster area. The sitting room appeared as if a giant had upended all the furniture. I checked Lamont's bedroom. It mirrored mine, but at least she wasn't trapped under debris.

The sudden understanding that whatever had shaken Inside most likely caused major injuries and maybe death, cleared the confused fog from my mind in a microsecond. Energized, I wove through the carnage of the apartment. Ignoring the disaster area that used to be her office and exam room, I reached the patient area.

I swept the light around the broken beds. Emek waved a bloody hand from underneath a pile. Digging through the debris, I uncovered him.

"What happened?" he asked.

"No idea. Are you injured?"

"I woke up on the floor."

"Any pain?"

"Don't think so."

I righted a bed, returned the mattress and helped Emek lie down. A groan sounded across the room. I followed it to the other patient. She had a gash on her cheek, but I couldn't find any other injuries.

"Is Doctor Lamont all right?" she asked.

"I haven't seen her," I said.

"She was right here before…"

What to call it? The Big Shake? Then the thought of Lamont being one of the casualties sent panic, fear and…grief?…shooting through my heart. It triggered another horrible possibility—Riley. He could be hurt or worse.

My first impulse was to run to his apartment and check on him, but he could be anywhere. The ten-hour shifts had ceased after the rebellion and no other schedule had replaced it yet. Once I settled my out-of-control pulse, I decided to stay here. Riley knew my location. He would come to me. If he could.

I searched the infirmary and found Lamont unconscious and bleeding from a nasty gouge on her head. Something like relief flowed through me, but, if asked, I would deny the feeling. After I hefted her into a bed and bandaged her wound, I worked to get ready for the inevitable arrival of the injured.

As I rushed to clean up, redlights came on. I skidded to a stop. Redlights? That was new. And creepy. I'd never seen it before or even heard stories from the old-timers. In Inside, bluelights stayed on for sleeping or in temporarily unoccupied areas. Daylights brightened occupied rooms and work places. Darkness stayed in places like the Gap between levels, and closed rooms. In the Expanse, there had been a couple rows of bluelights in the Expanse, marking the walls.

I switched off my light and removed the helmet. The eerie red glow gave enough illumination to see, which meant I had little to no time before my "guests" showed up.

At first, they trickled in, coming in pairs or by themselves, seeking medical treatment. The trickle transformed into a stream then a deluge. I recruited those who had carried friends. We divided the injured into three groups—bad, really bad and dire. The first two groups were taken next door to Quad A3—a common area. The last stayed in the main infirmary.

Then the emergencies arrived. Panicked, I flipped the switch that called Doctor Sanchia even though I knew he would be swamped with his own problems up on level four. I tore through the piles on the floor under the supply cabinets, searching for smelling salts to wake Lamont.

When I found them, I broke the package open and waved it under her nose.

She jerked away, but opened her eyes. "Trella? What—"

Her eyes cleared as I rushed to explain. By the time I finished, she was on her feet and issuing orders. Every able-bodied person was pressed into service. She took one look at the glass shard in my arm and yanked it out.

"Wrap it for now. We'll deal with it later," she said.

The hours blurred together. It seemed complete and utter chaos was but a moment away, yet somehow Lamont kept us on track. I sewed stitches until my fingers turned numb. Set bones until my arms ached. The bandage around my forearm dripped blood, but I had no idea if it was mine or not.

At one point a mechanical voice boomed. Everyone froze for a second as an announcement played. "Citizens of Inside, please do not panic."

Too late.

"All life support systems are fully operational," it continued. "Please remain at your posts. Those off-duty, please remain in your barracks and apartments. Anyone with medical experience is asked to report to the infirmaries on levels four, three and two. More information will be relayed when available."

We all stared at each other for a moment. Who was speaking, the computer or one of the Committee members? Before the rebellion, only the Travas had made announcements. However, nothing like this had happened when the Travas held power.

Just like the redlights, the mechanical voice was probably an automatic safety measure. After another minute of stunned silence, activity resumed and I gave up keeping track of anything.

But all through the frantic hours, bits and pieces of what had happen started to emerge. From half caught conversations and comments, I learned the power plant had caused the Big Shake. The plant occupied Quadrant C on all four levels. And the most severely injured were from Sectors B, F and a few from E. All shared a wall with Quad C. Which explained why the infirmary—Sector B3—had been in such disarray.

At some point, the daylights returned, which meant we had power again. Eventually, the flow of patients eased and dribbled. I filled a tray with glasses of water and handed them out. A numb exhaustion had soaked into me, muting my emotions and slowing my reactions.

For the first time since the…accident, I saw faces. Before I had focused on the injuries. But now I searched for those I recognized.

Half of me was relieved not to see Riley among them, but the other half was terrified that his lifeless body was in the pile on level one, waiting to be fed to Chomper. Other horrible scenarios danced through my tired mind. His body hadn't been discovered yet. He clung to life in level four's infirmary. He was trapped, pinned under a heavy piece of machinery.

I reached for another glass, but my tray was empty. Staring at the ripple pattern on the metal, I tried to remember what I should do as I swayed. Strong hands grabbed my shoulders from behind and guided me to my room. The bed had been cleared and the hands encouraged me to lie down.

My weak protests were ignored. Unable to resist, I collapsed onto the mattress and through a slit in my heavy eyelids, I saw Doctor Lamont. She pulled a blanket over me. And the touch of her lips on my forehead was my last memory.

Familiar voices woke me. They argued. I tried to produce the energy to care, failed and rolled over to return to sleep. But my mind wouldn't cooperate. It mulled and tugged until it plucked the proper memory from the depths, exposing it in a series of images. The Big Shake. The injured. Beds filled with people. Blood everywhere.

I lurched to my feet and ran from my room. My sudden exit surprised the two people on the other side of my door. Not caring I almost knocked Lamont down, I flung myself into Riley's arms.

He squeezed me as I clung to him. Questions poured from my mouth. "Are you all right? Where have you been? What happened?"

"I'm fine. I've been helping Doctor Sanchia. Logan—"

I pulled back. "Is he…" The word stuck in my throat.

"He'll be all right." Riley swept my sleep-tousled hair from my eyes. "He looks better than you." He rubbed his thumb lightly over the cut on my forehead. "This needs a few stitches. Want me to sew you up?"

I studied his face and realized he was half serious. "Doctor Sanchia let you suture wounds?"

"He didn't have much choice. We were swamped with people." Riley feigned nonchalance, waving a hand dismissively. "It's just a needle and thread. I've repaired rips in Sheepy before so I was more than qualified." Humor sparked in his blue eyes.

My mouth formed an automatic smile whenever I thought of Sheepy and his mother. The stuffed animal family had a special place in my heart. "I hope Sheepy and Mama Sheepy weren't damaged."

"They're fine. I checked on them before coming here. I do have my priorities straight," he teased.

I swatted him on the shoulder and he winced. Yanking his collar down, I exposed a fist-sized purple bruise.

He peeled my fingers from his shirt. "It's okay. No broken bones."

"How did you get hurt?" I asked.

"I was inspecting the wiring on level five with Logan and the floor just heaved, tossing us across the room. He hit his head, but it's a minor concussion."

"Heaved?"

"An explosion happened in the power plant and we stood directly above it," he said.

"Does anyone know what set it off?"

"No. That's for another week." He straightened his shirt

and smoothed his black hair. Since the rebellion, Riley had let it grow. It smelled of shampoo. "Right now attending to the wounded and finding missing people is the main concern."

"Have you slept?"

He nodded to the couch. "I arrived just after you went to bed. I didn't want to wake you, so I showered and slept here. I've been helping Doctor Lamont."

Which reminded me. I stepped away from him, glancing around, but Lamont had left. "I should…"

Riley stared at me in horror. Not my face, but my clothes. Dried blood stained almost all the white fabric, which had stiffened.

"Relax, it's not mine."

He pointed to a wet patch on my forearm. "And that?"

"Just a cut. I need to shower and—"

Unwinding the tattered bandage, he exposed the gash. I hissed in pain when he touched it.

"Come on." He grabbed my hand and pulled me from the apartment.

Patients recovering from their injuries lay on the floor in Lamont's office and in the exam room. Only a thin walkway remained free. At the examination table, Lamont finished with a young girl. The girl's mother, who hovered nearby, swept the girl into her arms and carried her out.

"Since you refused to get some rest, you might as well do Trella next," Riley said to Lamont.

He had been more forgiving of her betrayal. Which didn't make sense to me. His mother had been recycled when he was little because of her. Well, not directly. But with Lamont spying for the Pop Cops, the Force of Ten had failed. The consequences had been high. My father—if Karla Trava had been telling the truth about me—Riley's mother and two others had been recycled.

Lamont claimed she had spied to protect her daughter, Sadie, which would be me if Karla's word could be trusted. Except Karla said she recycled Sadie along with Lamont's husband afterward. The lesson that should have been learned—don't trust Karla or her word.

Yet when the rebels were on the verge of winning, Karla told Lamont her daughter had really been living in the lower levels as a scrub. Once again Karla threatened to harm Sadie unless Lamont helped Karla stop the rebellion.

How could such an intelligent woman fall for the same trick twice? When Karla had pointed to me as the long lost Sadie, Lamont had refused to believe her. It had been too coincidental. And I agreed.

"Sit up on the table," Lamont said to me.

I stared at her. Deep lines of exhaustion etched her pale face. She moved as if she'd shatter at any harsh sound.

"You're in no condition. Go to bed before you do more harm than good." I snapped my mouth shut before I said "again." As a doctor, she might be one of the best, but as a decent, reliable person, she failed.

"But your arm—"

"I can do it."

"One handed?"

"Riley will help. We'll keep an eye on everyone for you. If there's an emergency, we'll wake you." I gave Riley a significant look.

Understanding my hint, he released my hand and led Lamont back to her bedroom.

I sorted supplies. Since the majority of the injuries from the accident had been cuts, we were low on sutures. I would need to restock them.

"Why did she listen to you and not me?" Riley asked when he returned.

I shrugged. "She thinks I'd be a good doctor."

"Like her?"

"Don't start." I almost growled at him.

He kept pestering me to test my blood. I couldn't make him understand that the result wouldn't change my opinion of her.

"We're running out of supplies. Has anyone opened all the crates found in the Expanse?" I asked.

"Not yet."

"Somebody should go through the crates and inventory them."

"Good idea, you should bring it up at the next Committee meeting. Oh, wait." He smacked his head as if remembering something. "Since it's a good idea, it will be promptly ignored."

"They have a ton of decisions to make. Just give them time to sort everything out."

"You're defending them?" Riley cupped my cheek. "Are you feeling ill? Headache? Fever?"

I swatted his hand away. "I'm serious."

"And this change in opinion is due to…"

"I realized they have a tough job and I shouldn't be so critical. Especially since I'm no longer a part of the Committee."

He gaped at me. "What did you just say?"

"I resigned. They don't need me. I'm going to explore, and now I'll have time to go through those crates."

"I think that's a bad idea."

"What? Inventorying the crates or exploring?"

"Resigning."

"Why? I'll have more time for…Sheepy. I'm sure he misses me."

"Sheepy can wait. You're the voice of reason. You've seen both sides."

"They don't listen to me. I'm too young."

"You led the rebellion."

"And almost all the people who were involved are on the Committee—Domotor, Hana, Takia, Breana, Jacy and your father. If you really think about it, I started it, but Jacy, Anne-Jade, Logan and the rest finished the rebellion. This is the same thing. The Committee has it covered. I'm just in the way."

Riley tried to argue, but I didn't want to dwell on how useless I was in those meetings. I handed him the antiseptic and pointed to the gash on my arm. He grumbled, but helped to clean and then suture the cut. Although a bit awkward, he didn't balk when it was time to pierce my skin with the needle. That part tended to unnerve potential interns. I shouldn't be surprised. He had assisted Lamont with surgery in our storeroom when a Pop Cop had knifed me. Maybe he should be the one to train with Lamont.

When he finished tying the last stitch, I examined his handiwork. Yet another scar on my arm. Between Vinco's knife and my various injuries, I resembled one of those striped tigers listed in the computer files. A wild animal we had left behind. Why we left, I'd no idea, but I was sure Logan's efforts to find the original files for Inside would be successful. Then we would know everything.

After Riley and I finished checking on all the patients, I showered and changed into clean clothes. Since I no longer traveled through the air ducts and pipes, I wore the comfortable light green V-neck shirt and pants Lamont and the other caretakers wore. Yes, I realized the irony, but since I was only 1.6 meters tall, only a few uniform types fit me—unless I wanted to wear the student jumpers. And I wasn't about to go around Inside wearing my air scrubbing uniform or the surgery whites—a special white fabric worn during an operation that allowed the blood stains and other fluids to be easily bleached clean.

After my shower, I returned to the infirmary and organized the mess left by the Big Shake. Riley went to search for his father. Their rooms were located in Sector E4, catty-cornered to the power plant, but he wasn't too worried.

"He didn't come to the infirmary on level four," Riley had said. "I doubt he's hurt, but I want to make sure."

As I worked, people stopped by to look for loved ones and to visit the injured. Everyone seemed dazed, and I wondered how long it would take them to recover.

Hana Mineko arrived to record the names of the injured. She carried a portable computer—one of Logan's new devices. Not only a member of the Force of Sheep, she had also been involved with Domotor's first effort to regain control of Inside from the Trava family. Now she was a member of the Committee.

Her black curly hair, usually fixed in an intricate knot, hung in messy clumps. Dirt smudged her cheek and scratches marked her petite nose.

When she finished, I asked her how bad it was.

Pressing a few buttons on her computer, she said, "So far, I've listed five hundred and three…" Hana glanced at my forehead. "Make that five hundred and four injured and sixty-six to be recycled."

My heart lurched and I put a hand to my chest. "That many are going to Chomper? Are you sure? The blast wasn't that strong."

"The number is unfortunately accurate and bound to increase slightly. It could have been worse," Hana said. "The explosion happened between levels four and three. The hardest hit areas were Sectors F3 and F4, which houses apartments for the uppers. If the blast had been in the lower two levels, the scrub barracks in Sectors F2 and F1 would have been in the line of fire, and thousands would now be waiting for Chomper." She swept a hand, gesturing to the far wall of the infirmary. "Another piece of luck, the energy went south. If it had gone west, this place would have been torn to bits. You and Doctor Lamont would be waiting for Chomper. And if it had blown to the east or north…"

Horrified, I stared at her. "Was it strong enough?"

"To punch a hole to Outside?"

A disaster that would cause the end of our world. "Yes."

"We don't know yet. Maintenance is looking into it."

At the start of week 147,020, another announcement played. It had been thirty hours since the accident—looking at how much we'd done in the meantime, thirty hours seemed an impossibly short time. The mechanical voice—which I had been correct in assuming was the computer's automatic safety system—informed us maintenance had bypassed the damaged sections of the power plant and operations had resumed. Once again electricity and heat were being generated and we would be up to full capacity in a matter of hours.

A new voice, sounding like Hana, requested helpers to assist with cleanup in Sector B4. One of the water storage tanks had ruptured. I imagined rust growing on the walls and floor of B4, spreading like a disease.

During the week, the infirmary emptied as people healed. About midweek, I finally had a few hours to myself. I decided to inspect the damaged areas, starting with Sector F3.

In the back of my mind, I knew the force of the blast had been significant. But to see a huge jagged hole, crinkled metal and scorch marks was a whole other experience. A number of apartments had been destroyed. Wires hung to the floor and water dripped and pooled. The ceiling had been peeled back, exposing the Gap between levels three and four.

Using the buckled metal wall, I climbed up into the Gap. At this location, I could stand, but normally I would have to crouch in the one and a half meter space. The damage to level four resembled level three, except the floor had been ripped apart instead of the ceiling. The water pipes and air conduits that crisscrossed this space looked like broken toys.

Climbing higher, I found Logan in the plant's main Control Room on level four. He pounded on a keyboard, muttering and cursing to himself. A white bandage covered his left temple and eyebrow. Dark purple and red bruises colored his left cheek.

"How bad is it?" I asked him.

He jerked. "Where the hell did you come from?"

It took me a moment to respond. Riley had said Logan looked better than me, but I'd slept since the explosion. Logan's haggard oval face and bloodshot eyes told me it had been a long time since he'd rested.

"Where else would I come from? Outer Space?"

He grunted and his focus returned to the computer screen.

"I'm fine. Thank you for your concern. However you look like Chomper's been chewing on you. When's the last time you've eaten?"

"No idea. What time is it now?" Logan cursed and slammed his fist down.

I pulled his chair away from the console.

"Hey!" He braced his feet, trying to scoot back.

"No." I swiveled him to face me. Nose to nose, I gave him my best scowl. "You need food and sleep."

"But—"

"Inside has power and heat."

"But—"

"Whatever you're working on will still be there when you return."

"But—"

"You can't think straight without rest."

He clutched the chair arms as if I had threatened to pick him up and carry him to the cafeteria. No need. I would roll his chair if I had to.

His words rushed out in a panicked burst. "But this is important!"

I straightened and crossed my arms. Keeping a stern expression, I said, "This had better be good."

Logan's wild gaze flicked to the door and back to me. "Promise to say nothing?"

"I can't."

"For now. Just for now. Until I confirm it."

"Logan, you're starting to worry me."

"Promise to keep quiet for now?"

"Okay, okay. Now spill."

Once again he checked the door. He pointed to the top button on his shirt. "Is your microphone off?"

"Yes." I almost screamed the word at him.

"The power plant wasn't the only system to be damaged by the explosion."

"All the systems were affected by the electrical outage. Why is this a secret?"

He rubbed a hand over his face. "We didn't even know this system existed until ten weeks ago."

"Oh. An *Outer Space* system?"

"Yep. And not a minor one like Gateway. This one is called the Transmission. In simple terms, it takes a portion of the energy produced by the power plant and transmits it to Outer Space, pushing us toward our destination. With me so far?"

"Yeah. It's moving us through Outer Space."

"Right. Except the explosion wrecked it. Without the Transmission operating, we can't go faster or slow down or maneuver."

"And why is that so upsetting?"

He raked his fingers through his brown hair. "Outer Space isn't empty. There are massive objects called Planets, huge projectiles with names like Asteroids and Comets, and dense balls of burning gas named Suns. If we don't crash into one of them, all these things exert a force that can either slow us down, push us off course or trap us. In other words, we're dead in the water."

three

"Are we in any immediate danger?" I asked Logan.

"I don't think so."

"Think?"

"Sorry, some well-meaning scrub interrupted me before I could finish my calculations," he teased, but his humor didn't linger.

"Can we fix the Transmission?"

"I don't know. The maintenance scrubs didn't perform the routine cleaning and upkeep on it. I've a terrible feeling the Travas had been in charge."

Not good. Since Inside had a limited number of holding cells, most of the Trava family had been confined to their quarters in Sector D4.

"Can I go back to work now?" Logan asked.

"You can finish your calculations," I said.

"You're not going to leave, are you?"

"Nope."

I stood behind him as his fingers flew over the keyboard.

After twenty minutes Logan whistled in relief, relaxing back against his chair.

"Good news?" I asked.

"We're not about to crash into anything in the next four weeks." He turned and met my gaze.

"But?"

"We might be on a collision course."

"Might?"

Logan gestured weakly to the computer. "I need to search through the data…"

"Not now. You need to eat and sleep." I cut off his squawk of protest as I yanked him from his chair. Marching him down to the uppers' cafeteria in Quad G3, I stayed with him while he ate. Then I escorted him to his little suite next to Inside's main Control Room. The small cluster of rooms had been used by the captain so he would be nearby in case of an emergency.

We didn't have a new captain yet, but Logan came close. With his technical knowledge and familiarity with the computer systems, he had his fingers on the pulse of our world.

Since the rebellion, the uppers kept doing their jobs, monitoring the life-support systems. I realized the scrubs hadn't. They didn't want to clean and perform the mindless tasks anymore. I didn't blame them, but those tasks were vital to our existence. How could we convince them?

I tucked Logan into bed. "Don't leave until you've had a few hours of sleep. Do you understand?"

He gave me a tired salute. "Yes, sir."

As I headed to the infirmary, I mulled over the problem of dividing up the work. No brilliant idea sprung to mind. I wondered how the people had done it before the Travas took control and separated us into uppers and lowers. Logan had discovered hidden files about the history of our world. Perhaps our ancestors had found a perfect balance. They must have had a system worked out. Once this crisis was over, perhaps Logan could cull this information from those files and show it to the Committee.

I stretched as far as I could, groping for the next handhold. It remained just out of my reach. Resting my sweaty forehead against the cool metal, I let the disappointment roll through me. At least I had gone an additional five meters higher than my previous climb. I would have to find another path to reach the top.

Sliding down the rope, I returned to the half-completed roof of level ten. Work on the new levels had ceased until the power plant repairs were finished. I was used to the sounds of construction and the bright daylights, so the Expanse felt desolate. I walked the perimeter of the completed section, shining my light over the metal wall, looking for another potential route to the Expanse's ceiling.

Hank had suggested I use magnets to climb. A great idea, except I needed a way to hold on to the magnets, and they couldn't be too strong or I wouldn't be able to move them as I climbed. He offered to build me a set, but I couldn't ask him now. Hank was one of the few who volunteered to help clean up the mess from the explosion and to repair the damage. Even though it'd been over a week, the work progressed at a slow pace.

When I found a promising place to climb, I marked the spot with paint. My shift started at hour ten and I needed to change. I hurried back to my room. Riley waited for me in the sitting area. He sat on the couch, but didn't look relaxed as he rolled my earring/receiver between his finger and thumb.

"Forget something?" he asked.

"No. I left it here." Wrong answer. I braced for the lecture.

"Out exploring without it?"

"It's distracting." I pointed to the transmitter pinned on my collar. "I can still call for help. And I have my pendant." The necklace Riley had given me always hung around my neck. If I squeezed the little metal sheep, it would broadcast a signal, reporting my location.

"What if I or Logan needed *your* help?" He studied my expression. "Didn't think of that, did you?"

"I'll take it with me next time. Okay?" I held my hand out for the earring.

Riley dropped it into my palm. "Promise?"

I swallowed my retort. Riley's overprotectiveness grated on my nerves at times. For more weeks than I could count, I had climbed all over Inside without any way to signal for help and without any trouble either. Cogon had warned me of the danger, but I had ignored him. Good thing, too. Without my knowledge of the ducts and my ability to travel through them, our rebellion wouldn't have succeeded.

"I promise," I said, rushing past him.

"Where are you going?" he asked.

"To change. I'm late." I closed my door on his reply and switched the drab gray overalls the recycling workers wore for my skin-tight climbing clothes.

When I returned to the sitting area, Riley blocked my exit. "Late for what?"

I gestured to the ceiling. "My shift. I'm helping to repair the ductwork between levels three and four."

His shoulders drooped. "Oh. I thought we could—"

"I'm done at hour sixteen. I'll meet up with you later." I slipped around him and waved.

"It's always later, Trella."

I rounded on him. "This is important."

"And so is exploring and the Committee meetings before that, and—"

"I quit the Committee to spend more time with you. I wasn't counting on an explosion. But I'll remember to factor that in for the future." I mimed writing on my palm. "Riley first, emergencies second. Got it." I saluted him, rushed from the room and almost plowed into Lamont.

She said, "Trella, I need—"

"Find someone else," I said. "I can only do so much."

My anger cooled as I reported for work. I regretted my nasty comment to Riley. He had been putting in long hours, too. One of a few. The same handful of faces kept volunteering. Each time, they looked more and more exhausted.

During my shift, we fixed air shaft number fifteen. A small accomplishment, but that didn't stop us from cheering.

After I organized the tools for the next group, I found Logan and his sister, Anne-Jade, arguing in the corridor near the power plant.

"…force them. I'm not a Pop Cop," Anne-Jade said. Her dainty nose was identical to Logan's as well as the light brown color of her long hair. It hung past her shoulders in a shiny cascade.

The family resemblance was unmistakable, and I wondered if they were fraternal twins. They've always known they were related—a rarity among the scrubs—perhaps they knew who their parents were.

I hung back and waited for them to notice me.

"We need more people. I don't care how you get them," Logan said.

Anne-Jade fiddled with her belt buckle. She wore a modified Pop Cop uniform. The silver stripes down the sleeves and pants had been removed as well as any rank insignia. Her weapon belt held a stunner only, and the symbol representing Inside—a cube with the capital letter I on the front side—had been stitched onto her right collar.

After the rebellion, Anne-Jade had volunteered to organize a security force comprised of both uppers and lowers.

"What about the Trava family? They're not doing anything but taking up space. And we could *force* them to help," she said.

"No." I jumped into their conversation. "They can't be trusted."

"To do what?" she asked. But she didn't let me answer. "We have all the weapons and lock codes. I can post guards. It won't be hard to do."

By the thoughtful hum emanating from Logan's throat, I knew he mulled over her suggestion. Between the two of them, Anne-Jade had all the common sense. As Tech Nos, they had needed to hide their activities from the Pop Cops. When they had built their illegal technology, she disguised their gadgets as everyday items. Those devices had played a critical role in winning the rebellion.

Sensing her brother's agreement, Anne-Jade added, "And we can inject tracers in them. So even if they climb into the pipes to escape, we can track them."

"Tracers?" I asked.

She grinned. "Tiny little bugs that are injected under the skin. They emit a signal we can pick up."

"What's to stop them from cutting it out?" I asked.

"They won't know it's there. We'll use vampire boxes, but instead of taking blood samples, we'll inject the tracer. They won't know the difference. At least the civilian and lower ranked Travas won't suspect anything." An impish spark lit her greenish-brown eyes.

"Why not the upper ranks?" Deemed too dangerous, this group had been incarcerated in the holding cells.

"Because it was their idea," she said. "I found notes on the project in Commander Vinco's office. Although his tracer was twice the size of ours."

Logan corrected his sister. "It was four times the size. Humongous. The scrubs would have panicked, thinking the lump on their arms was a tumor."

I marveled over their skills. "How do you make your devices so small?"

"When I was experimenting with a circuit board, I—"

"You can tell her later, Logan," Anne-Jade interrupted. "I need to know if you want me to schedule the Travas for repairs."

"Do you have enough tracers?" he asked.

"Enough for a small group. Once we know if they'll work, I can make more."

"Then go ahead. Keep me informed."

Logan's grown-up, decisive tone surprised me. He usually deferred to her opinion.

As Anne-Jade turned to leave, I said, "Wait a minute. Shouldn't you get permission from the Committee first?"

"No," Logan said. "They put me in charge of the repairs. And time is critical."

Using Travas to rush the repairs didn't sit well with me. Perhaps the Committee could entice people to help by offering them first choice of the living space in the new levels. It was a good idea, which meant it would be ignored along with all my other ideas. Riley had called me the voice of reason, but the Committee remained deaf to me.

I returned to the infirmary, slipped past Lamont who was preoccupied with a patient and took a long hot shower. Half expecting Riley to be waiting in the sitting room when I finished, I felt a pang of disappointment over the empty couch. After donning my comfortable green shirt and pants, and weaving my wet hair into a single braid, I debated between food, sleep and Riley.

Riley won. I switched on my button microphone and turned it to Riley's frequency. "Hi, Riley. Where are you?" I asked.

No response. I tried reaching him two more times before giving up. He must be asleep. I heated a bowl of soup. The kitchen was another reason I stayed in Lamont's suite. So nice not to fight the crowds in the cafeteria.

Unfortunately my enjoyment ended when Lamont entered. I tried to ignore her, but she sat next to me and clanged her plate on the table.

I glanced up, catching her staring at me. "What?"

She didn't flinch. Her frank appraisal sent warning signals. Ever since the explosion, Lamont's confidence had grown. Not as a doctor, she had never hesitated when working, but in her interactions with me. Before, her guilt made her uncertain around me, which it should. She was a traitor after all. Her actions during the rebellion had almost gotten me and my cohorts sent to Chomper.

"What?" I asked again.

"If you plan to keep living here, you have to help me in the infirmary. If you don't want to work for me, then you need to move back into the barracks."

I gaped at her.

"The extra room is supposed to be for an intern," she said. "Off-hour emergencies are harder to respond to if I have to wait for my assistant to come from another level or Sector." She leaned forward and her voice softened. "I've been thinking about Karla's claims about you."

Snorting in disgust, I stood.

Lamont jumped to her feet and blocked my path. "You're not running from me. Not this time. Sit down or I'll—"

"What? Strap me to a gurney again?"

"If that's what I have to do to get you to listen to me, then I will."

A hard determination settled on her face as if her skin had turned to metal. The woman was serious. She seemed to have two separate personalities, Kiana and Doctor Lamont. I was facing the Doctor right now.

"You can't. Not when—"

She brandished a syringe and a "try me" stance.

I stepped back, bumping into wall. Damn. "Where did…" She had planned this little chat.

"Sit down."

If she knocked me out, I could have her arrested for assault. But would Anne-Jade's new Inside Security Force (ISF) even charge her? Probably not. Especially not since she proved to be invaluable after the explosion.

Unwilling to make this easy for her, I crossed my arms, sat and glowered. "I'm listening."

"Good." Lamont remained on her feet with her weapon pointed toward me. "For the last 1,430 weeks my heart has ached for my daughter and husband. And yes, I betrayed all of you just for the slim chance to hold Sadie in my arms again. Karla knew my weakness. And she had the comb I had hidden in Sadie's diaper. It was wrong, and stupid, and I regret it. But I can't change the past. All I can do is atone for my mistakes. Karla might not have lied about you. Why would she send a hundred-and-two-week-old to Chomper? I'd like you to take a blood test."

I surged to my feet. "No blood test."

"It would settle the question once and for all. And if you're Sadie, you can stay here."

"But if I'm just plain old Trella, I need to leave?"

"No. You're still welcome to be my intern and stay."

"I'm not interested in being your intern or your daughter." As I brushed past her, I braced for the needle's prick. Would she stoop to knocking me out and testing my blood? Not yet. Unharmed, I hurried into my room and stopped. I wore my pendant, earring and transmitter. Besides my tool belt and moccasins, there was nothing here I needed.

Changing back into my air scrub uniform, I buckled my belt, secured my mocs to a loop, climbed up to the air vent, opened the cover and entered the air ducts. I wasn't about to give Lamont another chance to trap me. After securing the vent, I followed the familiar twists and turns, deciding which way to go.

The abandoned controller's room in Quad C1 remained empty. Domotor had hidden in there during the rebellion, but it was next to the power plant and the heat and dirt made it less than ideal. However, it did have a small kitchen and bathroom.

Despite the amenities of the controller's room, I headed toward the storeroom on level four. The place where I first met Riley. It had a comfortable couch—all I needed. I'd eat in the uppers' dining room in Quad G3, and use the scrub washrooms on level two. It'd be just like old times. Well, without the constant fear, which was a bonus.

And just like the past, I'd have to use the air ducts to get to the storeroom. Since the room was located deep within Sector D4, I couldn't use the hallways. I wanted the room to remain forgotten by all but a few people, and Sector D4 was patrolled by the ISF to keep the Travas in their quarters.

When I reached the room, I peered through the vents. The bluelights were on, and I couldn't spot any signs of recent activity. Opening the vent, I swung down and dropped onto the couch. Dust puffed and I sneezed. The daylights snapped on, triggered by my motion. Riley hadn't disconnected the motion sensor and I wondered if my entrance would signal him.

By the film of dust on all the furniture, I knew Riley hadn't been here since the rebellion. I tried to contact him again. No response. Perhaps he was still mad at me.

I cleaned the room as best as I could. Finally exhausted, I switched back to bluelights, dumped my tool belt in a corner, curled up on the couch and fell asleep.

The sudden brightness of the daylights woke me. I stared at my surroundings for a few seconds in confusion until I remembered my location. According to the clock, it was hour twenty-five of week 147,021. Riley leaned on the door to the hallway, but his posture was far from relaxed. His black hair hung in his eyes, obscuring half of his expression.

I sat up and pulled my legs in close, making room for him to sit down.

He didn't move. "What are you doing here?"

"Lamont kicked me out. It was either this, the pipes or the barracks."

"Dad and I have a couch." His flat tone held no emotion.

I sensed I trod on thin metal. One wrong word and it would buckle underneath me. "Last I heard, your brother had claimed it."

"Blake moved back to the barracks weeks ago. He couldn't stand the quiet."

Which made sense. Growing up in the lower two levels, we had been assaulted by the constant noise of the other scrubs. For most of the scrubs, the clamor soothed and comforted. For me, the racket grated and drove me into the pipes, seeking privacy and distance from the noise.

"I tried to contact you a couple times," I said in my defense.

"I know."

Not good. "Riley, I'm sorry for getting angry. I'll skip my next shift and we'll spend time together."

His muscles relaxed just a bit. Progress.

"Why did Doctor Lamont kick you out?" he asked.

"She gave me an ultimatum." I told him about the argument.

As I talked, he moved away from the door and closer to me. "I'm surprised she didn't tell you to leave sooner."

"Why?"

"You're nasty to her at every opportunity. And I suspect the only reason you stayed there is to make her suffer for her actions during the rebellion. Her guilt was probably why she put up with you as long as she did."

I wanted to correct him, but I suspected he was right. "I like helping the patients." Weak.

"You could have interned with Doctor Sanchia." Riley sat next to me.

"I wasn't that nasty. More like grumpy and a little surly."

"Sorry, but no. Nasty is the right word." He held up a hand to stop my protest. "Consider your refusal to take a blood test. She still grieves for her daughter and you could ease her pain."

"What if I'm not Sadie?"

"Then she'll know Karla lied and there's no hope."

"Wait a minute. Karla could be telling the truth and Sadie is living in the lower levels right now."

"Doctor Lamont already tested every girl born close to Sadie's birth week. All fifteen of them. No match. You're the last one."

Oh. "Are you going to counter all my comments?"

"Yes."

"Why? Her betrayal could have sent us all to Chomper, including your father."

"You keep forgetting, she didn't tell Karla *everything*. Her information made it difficult for us, but we won." He ran a hand through his hair, pulling his bangs from his eyes. Riley stared into the past. "Besides, if Karla had offered me the chance to see my mother again, to hug my mother and tell her I love her… I would have been mighty tempted. And you had been ready to exchange your life for Cogon's. Remember? Lamont's actions aren't as despicable when you look at it that way."

I grumbled, but couldn't respond. He had a point.

"Will you at least think about it?"

"I will. Later." I scooted closer to him and he hooked his arm around my shoulder.

"Do you want to stay with us?" Riley asked. "You'll have a shower close by."

I glanced around the storeroom. "Eventually I'll want to,

but right now this place is…comforting and familiar. Do you understand?"

He smiled and I realized just how much I missed his smile. This was the first time in weeks that we had complete privacy.

"Yes, I do. And so does Sheepy. He was just reminiscing about those hours we spent in here with you before the rebellion." Riley turned to me. "In fact your uniform is bringing back those memories of the first time I met you." He trailed his fingertips along the slippery material of my arm as he cocked his head, considering. "Something's not quite right."

Reaching around with both hands, he pulled my hair from its braid. His touch sent shivers through me. When he finished, he mussed my hair. "There, that's better. Now you look like the wild scrub that fell into my life."

"Because *you* loosened the vent's screws."

"Best. Decision. Ever." He combed his fingers through my hair and laced them behind my neck, pulling me in for a kiss.

Heat burned inside me as he deepened the kiss. I snaked my arms around his shoulders and pressed against him. The thin material of my uniform chafed and when he tugged at the zipper along the back, I broke our kiss long enough to whisper an encouragement for him to keep pulling. Reclaiming his lips, I worked on unbuttoning his shirt.

He peeled the top of my uniform down, exposing my breasts. One of the benefits of being on the smaller side—no uncomfortable support garment. His surprise at encountering nothing but smooth skin lasted mere microseconds, before his thumbs sent tingling waves through me.

This was farther than we've ever explored before, but I wasn't about to complain. I yanked his shirt off and ran my hands along his muscular arms. He abandoned my lips to nibble on my neck, pushing me back so I reclined on the couch.

"Trella, are you there?" Logan's voice squawked from my earring. I groaned in annoyance and was about to switch it off when Logan said, "Trell, I need you at the power plant's control room now." Logan's panic rang loud and clear.

Riley pulled away. Concern creased his forehead.

I fumbled for the transmitter clipped onto my uniform. "What happened?" I asked.

"Sabotage."

four

All tingly warmth fled my body. "Sabotage?" I asked. "I didn't feel—"

"Come to the control room, and I'll explain," Logan said.

"Why can't you tell me now?"

"This frequency isn't secure."

The click from Logan switching off sounded in my ear. I met Riley's resigned gaze. He buttoned his shirt. I pulled up the top of my uniform and zipped it.

"Promise me we'll continue this…conversation later." Riley's mournful tone made me smile.

"That's an easy promise to make."

I glanced at the air vent in the ceiling. Riley's broad shoulders would never fit. Gesturing toward the door, I asked, "Did anyone see you come in here?"

"Nope."

"The corridors should be patrolled by ISF officers."

"They are. I told them I was checking the wiring. As soon as they lost interest in me, I ghosted down our hallway."

"Ghosted? You've been hanging around Logan too much."

"I'd rather be…exploring with you." He ran his hands down my sides and rested them on my hips. "There may be other surprises under your jumpsuit just waiting to be discovered."

I slipped from his grasp and stood. "Key word, waiting."

He groaned. "If Logan's exaggerating, I'll pound him."

Picking up my tool belt, I clipped it into place. "Can you leave here without being seen?"

"Yep."

"Great. I'll meet you in the control room." The ladder I had used before leaned against the far wall. I set it up under the air vent and climbed. Before I pulled myself into the duct, I caught Riley staring at me. "What's wrong?"

"Nothing. Just wondering."

"About what?"

"If you'll keep your promise."

"When have I *ever* broken a promise?"

"What about leaving the Committee?" he asked.

"I didn't promise them anything, just offered to help."

"I didn't mean the Committee members, but the people of Inside. By freeing them from the Travas' control, you promised them a better life."

"First off, the Force of Sheep freed them, not me. And second, they have a better life. No Pop Cops, grueling work schedules and we'll soon have plenty of room. How could you possibly see that as breaking a promise?"

"There wouldn't have been a rebellion or the Force of Sheep without you. You started everything and you need to finish it."

Words jammed in my throat. How could he think I didn't finish it? I shook my head. "We can argue about this later. Logan's waiting for us." Before he could reply, I slid into the air duct, heading toward the control room.

Riley's voice followed me, echoing through the metal shaft.

"Logan called *you*, Trell, not *me* about the sabotage. Think about that."

As I traveled in the duct, I dismissed his comment. It was a matter of semantics, nothing more.

I arrived at the control room and took a few seconds to see who worked below. Logan sat in front of a computer, frowning at the monitor. Riley hadn't arrived. No one else was in sight.

The noise from opening the air vent should have alerted Logan to my presence, but the poor guy jumped a meter when I landed behind him.

"Would you stop doing that?" he asked. "You're going to give me a heart attack."

"You knew I was coming." I studied him. He still had bags under his eyes, but he no longer looked as if a hundred-week-old could knock him over.

Logan flinched when the door opened, but relaxed when he spotted Riley. Something had him rattled.

"Time to explain," I said.

He typed on the keyboard for a minute. The screen changed to tables and charts that meant nothing to me.

"The explosion in the power plant was caused by sabotage," Logan said.

"That's—"

He cut me off. "It's the only explanation. My first clue was the location of the blast. Damage to the plant itself was minimal, but it hit the Transmission in the perfect spot."

"The Transmission?" Riley asked.

Logan glanced at me. "Didn't you tell him?"

"You made me promise not to." I shot Riley a look. "And I *keep* my promises."

"Oh. Well you could have told him," Logan said.

"Then next time you swear me to secrecy, you need to include that exception." I quickly explained the Transmission to Riley. "Did you fix it yet?" I asked Logan.

"No."

"What about being on a collision course?" Riley asked.

"We should have plenty of time to avoid it. As I was saying, the Transmission's controls were damaged, but not the equipment. Repairs should be easy if we knew how the controls worked."

"I could look at it for you," Riley offered.

"It couldn't hurt," Logan said.

"How do busted controls lead you to sabotage?" I asked.

"Second clue is this." He pointed at the screen.

Riley bent closer, but I wasn't going to try and decipher it. "And?"

"Operating data for the plant right before the explosion," Riley said.

"And?"

"All the machinery was operating within normal parameters," Logan said. "There is nothing here to warn of an impending explosion. No spike in power, no jammed valves, no fire or anything unusual."

"But the computer might not have registered it in time. Did you examine the plant?"

"Of course. Went over it with a couple of the supervisors. They're equally puzzled about the cause."

"But that isn't enough to suggest sabotage," Riley said.

Logan uncovered a glass container. "Final clue. At the explosion site, I found an oily residue coating the walls, and pieces of a timer and switch. And before you try to explain them, I tested the residue and it's a flammable substance not found anywhere in the power plant. It's used in the recycling kilns on level one."

Riley picked up one of the twisted hunks of metal from the container. As he examined it, a shocked horror filled his eyes. "This could detonate a bomb."

A bomb. Spoken aloud, the words slammed into me. Someone had set off a bomb, killing people on purpose, risking all our lives—thousands of people. I let the stunned outrage roll through me. It took me a few minutes to pull my emotions together and think.

"Who did this? Why?" I asked.

"Who would have to be someone who knew about the Transmission, and had enough knowledge to make and place the bomb so it didn't blow a hole to Outside," Logan said. "As for why, I can only guess. Since the Transmission was the target, either someone doesn't want us traveling through Outer Space or someone wants to get our attention."

"Do you think they will make demands or threaten to damage another system if we don't comply?"

"I've no idea, Trell. This is all new territory for me."

"If they plan to make demands, it should be sooner rather than later," Riley said. "Actually, if they do contact Logan or the Committee, we might be able to find out who they are."

"Have you informed the Committee?" I asked Logan.

"No."

"Why not?" I demanded.

"I just connected the clues. And this information needs to be handled with care. Knowing we're dealing with a saboteur gives us an advantage. If nothing is said, maybe the person will relax and give himself away."

"And if word gets out, there could be panic," Riley added.

"This is too big. The Committee needs to know."

"Nineteen people can't keep a secret. It's statistically impossible," Logan said.

"What if the saboteur makes a demand?" I asked.

"The Committee will know then, won't they?"

I huffed in frustration. "You need to tell someone," I said.

"I did."

"Besides us."

"I think that's unwise."

"Do you have any suspects?" Riley asked.

"Don't encourage him," I said.

"He's right and you know it."

"I can pull together a list of all those who know about the Transmission for you and Trella," Logan said.

"Us?"

He ignored me. "Anne-Jade is still trying to find out which Travas worked on the Transmission equipment. Once we have those names, I'll add them to the list. It's doubtful the Travas pulled it off, but one of them could have given the information to someone who isn't under constant surveillance."

"I can talk to the maintenance scrubs, see if they know more than they're letting on," Riley offered.

"Are you going to tell Anne-Jade?" I asked.

"Of course. She can be trusted."

Still not convinced we were doing the right thing, I knew when I was outnumbered. "We're going to need Jacy's help. He has kept his network of contacts."

"Is he trustworthy?" Riley asked. "He's on the Committee."

Remembering how he had bartered and traded for services and favors, I said, "I'll talk to him."

From the air shaft, I searched for Jacy among the Committee members' offices in Sector H3. Each of the nineteen had been given a small space and computer to use when they weren't sitting in meetings. Using the ducts had been a cowardly act on my part. I didn't want to encounter any of the other members. I didn't want to be questioned about why I left or guilted into returning.

Jacy's office was empty. I debated waiting or leaving a note. Neither appealed to me, so I found a vent in the main corridor between Sectors and dropped down. He could be in the uppers' dining room next door in Quad G3, but my skintight jumpsuit would draw everyone's attention. Since I needed regular clothes anyway, I headed down to the laundry in Sector B1 via the stairs in Quad I.

When I reached level one, I almost tripped. Huge mounds of glass, metal and clothing filled most of the floor space. The recycling plant in Quad I1 remelted glass and metal and turned clothing back into thread. Usually a busy place with scrubs sorting and carting items to the kiln or the furnace or to Chomper, only a few people worked among the piles.

I put my moccasins on, but was still careful to avoid the sharper objects as I skirted the heaps. The recycling scrubs were required to wear thick boots for a good reason.

After the mess in the recycling plant, the condition of the laundry room failed to surprise me. Bins overflowing with soiled garments and uniforms had been lined up. The line snaked around the room. Rows of washers and dryers stood silent and unused. The bins for clean clothes were empty. One person loaded a washer. Another folded clothes. A few picked through the dirty bins, searching for sizes. Otherwise the place was empty.

I crossed to the lady shoving sheets into a washer. She wore the drab green jumper that the scrubs wore when off-duty.

"Where's everyone?" I asked. By necessity, the laundry had the most workers in the lower levels.

She shrugged. "Not here. If you want clean clothes, you have to do them yourself."

"How long has it been like this?" I asked.

"Where've you been?" The woman paused to look at me for the first time. "In the upper levels, I'd bet." She swept her hand out. "The laundry scrubs stayed for a few weeks, but none of the uppers came down to help them. Eventually they stopped. They're not washing the uppers' clothes. We're all supposed to be equal, but as far as the scrubs are concerned nothing's changed."

I bit back my reply about the lack of Pop Cops patrolling

the hallways and kill-zapping dissenters or about not having to report to the hundred-hour assemblies. Instead I said, "You have to be patient. It's going to take some time to get everyone organized. And we outnumber the uppers ten to one."

"So? Can't a few come down and help? How hard can it be?"

Opening my mouth to respond, I closed it. She had a point. But it wasn't like the uppers sat around doing nothing. Yet another problem for the Committee to address.

The woman waited for my reply.

"The Committee—"

"Has caused more problems than they solved. This is a big ship, right?"

Confused by the change in topic, I said, "Sort of, but—"

"We had a captain, right?"

"Captain James Trava. But he was relieved of duty. All the Trava officers were." We also had an admiral and a fleet admiral. Although I didn't know why since one ship didn't equal a fleet.

"So? Appoint another."

I smiled. "Just like that?"

"Why not? Can't be any harder than taking the Travas out, right? Unless you're afraid?"

My humor died. "I'm not afraid of anyone."

"I don't doubt that, young lady, but I wasn't talking about a person."

"Then what—"

She poked a finger at a bin half hidden behind the washers. "You'll find clean clothes in there. They're too small for most of the scrubs." Scooping up an armful of clothes, she added them to the washer. Conversation over.

I sorted through the uniforms and jumpers. Finding a few shirts and a pair of pants the kitchen scrubs wore, I tucked them under my arm. The nearest washroom was in Sector E1, which also housed the barracks, along with Sectors D1 and F1. Bluelights lit the rows and rows of bunk beds stacked three high.

Unlike the laundry and recycling areas, many scrubs lounged in the barracks. Some gathered in groups, others slept despite the noise and a few played cards. The place was packed and the stench of them nearly knocked me over. I hurried to change my clothes in the washroom, but as I dashed through the barracks on my way out, I spotted a number of ISF officers patrolling the barracks.

I felt as if I had just slammed into a wall. Why were they here? The scrubs didn't like their presence either. They threw snide and nasty comments at them, mocking and taunting them. Horrible. I wondered if Anne-Jade knew what was going on down here. Or was she like me, avoiding the lower levels? I hadn't been on levels one or two in weeks and I didn't have a good reason either.

Sick to my stomach, I paused in the corridor and breathed in the clean air until my heart slowed to normal. Going with a hunch, I braced for another assault on my senses as I entered the barracks in Sector D1. Jacy used to hold court in a corner.

Not as bad as E1, there were less people and ISF officers. Also the general mood seemed stable and not as tense.

Sure enough, Jacy and a few of his followers huddled together. When I approached they broke apart.

"Hello Trella," Jacy said, but his tone was far from welcoming. "What's the emergency?"

"There isn't one. Why would you think that?"

"You're here with the scrubs so it must be something big."

I ignored his snide comment. "Did you mention what's going on down here to the Committee?"

"And just what is going on?" He acted innocent.

"The piles in recycling and the dirty laundry. How no one is doing their jobs."

"Of course."

"And?"

"And nothing. It's not a high priority. The Committee thinks once the extra levels are completed and the scrubs get more space, everyone will be *happy* to return to work." His sarcastic tone implied otherwise.

"Is it the same for all the systems?"

"Except for maintenance and security, they're busy and productive. Why? Do you care now?"

I laced my hands together to keep from punching Jacy. "Okay, tell me. What should I be doing?"

He jerked as if I surprised him. "Truthfully?"

"Always."

"Disband the Committee. Appoint a few people to be in charge."

I laughed. "Is that it? And here I was ready for something that would be hard to do."

"You asked." He kept his expression neutral.

"I don't have the power to appoint people. I'm just a—"

"A scrub?"

"No. A citizen of Inside. I've done my part. It's time for other people to step in and set up a better system. I wouldn't know the first thing about running a society."

"Uh-huh." Jacy leaned against a bunk. "And you're here because…"

"I need to talk to you."

"So talk."

I glanced around. There were too many people nearby who seemed interested in our conversation. "Some place private."

He frowned with annoyance then snapped his fingers at his men. They cleared a wider space around us. Impressive.

"Better?"

"Yes." But I hesitated. His hostility worried me. Plus he acted like he had before the rebellion—as if we were enemies.

Yet he had been a key member, rising to the occasion and being invaluable. I suppressed my doubts and asked him if he knew or heard of an expert in explosions.

He whistled. "You think someone damaged the power plant on purpose?"

Trust Jacy to put the pieces together so quickly. "Let's just say I'd like another opinion."

"Uh-huh. And what if this *expert* is the one you're searching for?"

"There is always that possibility."

He tapped his fingers on the bunk's metal support beam as he considered my request. "I do know one scrub that would be regarded as an expert, but you need to do something for me in return."

No surprise. "And that would be…"

"Remember those microphones you planted for me in air duct seventy-two?"

"Yes."

"I need you to plant more in another air duct."

"Why?" I asked. "The Pop Cops are gone and you should know everything that's being decided from the Committee meetings."

"Let's just say I like another opinion. Deal?"

"Yes, I'll plant the mics for you." But I didn't say *where* I would.

"Good. I'll get them to you soon."

"And that expert?"

Jacy grinned. "His name is Bubba Boom and he works for maintenance."

"You got to be kidding me."

"Nope. He probably had a real name when he was born, but his care mates gave him that nickname at a young age. Bubba Boom can set fire to anything, and he loved setting off little explosions. Drove his Care Mother crazy, burning up various things in the care facility. He was the youngest scrub to be a member of the fire response team since he's equally adept at extinguishing fires."

He sounded familiar. "Is he the guy who rigged that container of casserole to explode?"

"Yep. He had to help the kitchen scrubs clean green goo from the walls and ceiling for a week."

I remembered hearing about his pranks. My care mates used to delight in telling the stories, but I had never learned his name. By the time I graduated from the care facility, he had stopped his mischief. "Did working for the fire response team settle him down?"

"Nope. The Pop Cops took care of that."

Understandable. Vinco could convert anyone after a couple sessions with his knife.

Hank worked on repairs to the pipes below the blasted section of the power plant between levels three and four. He shouted orders and the others rushed to follow them. A few faces weren't familiar and I hoped that meant more of the lower level citizens had volunteered. My optimistic assumptions burst when I spotted a number of armed ISF officers nearby.

Anne-Jade didn't waste time. She had mentioned using Travas for the repairs a mere twelve hours ago and here they were.

When Hank took a break, I asked him about Bubba Boom.

He chuckled. "I haven't heard that name in a long time. We just call him Bubba and he's up on level four welding the ruptured water tank."

I thanked him and headed for the water storage tanks located in Sector B4. When I entered, the humid air reminded me of hydroponics except there was nothing living growing here—only rust. The spilled water had been cleaned, but not before some of it had dripped down to the infirmary.

The crackle and hiss of a torch sounded in the corner closest to the explosion. Sparks flew, pointing out Bubba even though he wore a metal shield over his face. He worked on a long crack along the seam of the metal tank. Wearing gray maintenance coveralls streaked with dirt and peppered with holes, his large frame reminded me of Cog.

Looking at the damage to the tanks, I wondered how Cogon would have reacted to the explosion. He would've been angry and upset and I would have had to force him to take breaks. He'd have every single person of Inside helping until the damage was repaired, and they would have been happy to do it for him.

Not for the first time, nor for the last, I thought it should have been me, not him that floated away into Outer Space.

I waited until Bubba finished before I cleared my throat, letting him know I was there. He pulled off the shield, revealing messy light brown hair that seemed to stand on end. Sweat trailed down the sides of his face and freckles sprinkled his cheeks and nose. Close to my age, I figured he couldn't be more than a hundred weeks older than me.

"Need something?" Bubba Boom asked.

Going with the second opinion ruse, I asked him if he had a chance to see the point of the blast.

The edges of his mouth dipped as a guarded expression covered his face. "Everyone in maintenance has looked at it. I wondered when one of you would start asking about it."

"One of us?"

"Committee upper."

"I'm not…" Correcting him would be a waste of time. Since Lamont had changed my eye color back to its original blue, I had difficulties convincing people I had been raised in the lower levels like them. "Are all your colleagues wondering or just you?"

Again he masked his emotions. "Just me."

"And you didn't say anything to Hank?"

"No."

I waited.

Wiping the sweat off his chin with his shoulder, he jabbed the torch in my direction. "I knew this would happen if I said anything."

Just in case he decided to attack me with his torch's white-hot flame, I planned which tool I would grab from my belt. Hopefully, my outward calm remained. "This?"

"Stop with the dumb act. You figured out a bomb set off the explosion, you talked to Jacy, and now I'm your primary suspect."

Guess I needed to work on my investigative skills. Even though I wasn't an expert in reading people, I noted the edge in his voice when he said Jacy's name. "You would have looked less guilty if you reported your concerns to Hank."

He shrugged, but there was nothing casual in the movement. "Force of habit. I've learned to keep a low profile." Bubba Boom absently rubbed his hand along the bottom of his rib cage.

"If you didn't build that bomb, who did?"

I surprised a laugh from him. "I don't know. And if I did, I wouldn't tell you."

"Why not? You like welding up ruptured tanks? Sanding out rust spots and re-painting the walls? What if he sets off another one? What if someone you care for dies in the next blast? What if he blows a hole to Outside and—"

"Impossible."

"Which one?"

"Damaging one of the Walls. We measured them, they're two meters thick."

"How?"

"Cogon's Gateway. That inner room between the doors is as wide as a Wall."

Interesting and good to know. "My other points are still valid. There might be another explosion."

"And I still wouldn't squeal on a fellow scrub."

"You do know the Pop Cops are no longer in charge, right?" I didn't wait for his answer. "The worst thing we'd do is incarcerate the saboteur. He wouldn't be fed to Chomper. And he wouldn't be tortured into submission either."

A stubborn tightness hardened his gaze.

I couldn't say when I decided he wasn't guilty; it was an internal instinct. "You think I'm an upper."

A slight confused nod.

"My clothes and eye color gave me away."

"Yes."

"Do you think being called an upper is better or worse than my old nickname of Queen of the Pipes?" I asked him.

He stared at me.

"I like Queen of the Pipes better. It doesn't have any prejudices or wrong assumptions associated with it. And the best thing, the Pop Cops didn't give me that name. I earned it. Just like these…" I pulled up the bottom of my shirt, and showed Bubba Boom the line of round scars that followed the edge of my rib cage where Commander Vinco had gouged out my skin. "And if I knew the bastard who was blowing holes in *our* home, he wouldn't need to worry about Chomper. Oh no. He'd need the ISF to protect him from *me*."

Bubba Boom's Adam's apple bobbed as he swallowed. "Or she would need protection. Even the Queen of the Pipes can make wrong assumptions."

I smiled. "Never said I was perfect. And I'm not going to accuse an innocent."

He held up a hand to stop me. "I didn't get a chance to fully examine the blast site. Did you find any shrapnel that looked like it didn't match any of the surrounding equipment?"

"Shrapnel as in pieces of the bomb?"

"Exactly."

"Yes."

He set his torch and mask down. "Okay, I'll look at the site first, and then I'll need to see what you found."

I followed him to the blast location. He squinted at the damage, ran his fingers along the scorched marks, sniffed the wreckage, and sorted through the rubble. Filling his pockets with odd bits of metal and wires, he straightened and asked to see what we had collected.

The control room was empty when Bubba Boom and I entered. I showed him the pieces Logan found. He set every-thing out on a table, including the fragments he had gathered. Arranging and turning the bits, he scrutinized each one.

Logan arrived, but I hushed his questions. He stood next to me as we waited for Bubba to finish.

"This doesn't look familiar," Bubba said. He held the biggest chunk up to the light.

"Not one of yours?" Logan asked. His tone was almost nasty—very unusual for him.

"I stopped building these. You know that better than any-one," Bubba said.

These two had a history. Wonderful.

"The Pop Cops aren't around. You could have returned to your old ways."

Bubba Boom huffed in exasperation. "You're still mad at me? I never told the Pop Cops about you and your sister. *That* was more important than the fact I stopped helping you design your little gadgets."

"Those gadgets—"

"Logan, that's enough," I said. "He agreed to assist us with finding the bomber."

Giving me an odd look, Logan said, "How did you find out about him?"

"Jacy."

Logan and Bubba exchanged a glance.

"What?" I demanded.

"A distraction?" Logan asked him.

"Could be."

Fear sizzled up my spine. "Another bomb?"

"No," Logan said. "More like keeping you busy and away from the real culprit."

"Why would Jacy do that?" I asked.

"Don't know," Logan said. "He's hard to read."

"Anything that doesn't have numbers scrolling across it is hard for you to read," I teased.

"Real funny. At least I didn't fall for Jacy's disinformation."

"Not quite," Bubba Boom said.

"What does that mean?" I asked.

"Just because I stopped playing with fire, doesn't mean I ignore what's going on around me." He held up a twisted piece of metal. "I recognize this."

five

"Do tell," Logan said.

I swatted Logan on the arm. "Cut it out." He acted like a two-hundred-week-old, and I wondered if he had looked up to Bubba Boom only to be disappointed when the man caved in to the Pop Cops.

"There's a couple of scrubs," Bubba said. "I wouldn't call them Tech Nos as their devices are rudimentary, but they've gotten together and built a few incendiary apparatuses."

"Could they be responsible for the damage in the power plant?" I asked.

"Possible. One of them works in the waste-water treatment plant, the other in hydroponics. As far as I know they've only set off a couple stink bombs. One time they cleared everyone out of Sector E2 due to the stench." He smiled at the memory. "They also helped keep the Pop Cops occupied while you were busy rebelling."

Which meant Jacy knew about them. "What are their names?"

Bubba Boom squinted at the warped metal in his hands. He turned it over and over. "What if they're innocent?"

"Then we keep searching. We're not like the Pop Cops," I said.

"Really? Then why are there ISF goons patrolling the barracks all the time?" he asked.

"Because of the fights," Anne-Jade said from the doorway. "They're not working so they're bored. Nine times out of ten boredom leads to trouble. We did our share of proving that theory didn't we, Bubba?"

A wide grin spread on his face, matching Anne-Jade's. "We sure did," he said.

Logan's displeasure deepened. "As much as I'm not enjoying this little reunion, we need the names of the two stink bombers."

Bubba Boom met Anne-Jade's gaze. "Promise me you won't do anything rash? That you will be one hundred percent sure they're guilty before you arrest them?"

"When have I ever done anything rash?" Anne-Jade asked.

He gestured to me. "When you risked *everything* helping her."

"That wasn't rash," she corrected. "Risky, dangerous and suicidal, but not rash. We studied the situation carefully before offering our assistance." She winked at me. "Stubborn scrub almost turned us down, but it worked in our favor."

Bubba Boom tapped the metal piece against his leg as he considered. "All right. Kadar works in waste management, and Ivie is one of the gardeners in hydroponics."

"Thanks," I said. "Can you keep our…suspicions quiet for now? I don't want people to panic."

"Sure." He hesitated and glanced at Anne-Jade before leaving the control room.

"He's full of sheep's manure," Logan said. "A woman named

Ivie who just happens to work in hydroponics. Come on, how dumb does he think we are?"

"At least he didn't say Crapdar," I said.

Logan laughed. "Close enough."

Anne-Jade frowned. "I think he's telling the truth."

"You would," he said.

"What's that suppose to mean?"

Before they could launch into an argument, I asked Logan, "Can you look up those names in the population records, see if they do exist?"

"I don't have the time, but you can do it. It's easy," he said.

I tried to object, but Anne-Jade said, "I need you first."

Her tone didn't give me a warm feeling. "For what?"

"None of the Travas will tell *me* who worked on the Transmission."

Cold fingers gripped my stomach as I braced for the rest of her news.

"However, ex-Lieutenant Commander Karla Trava is willing to cooperate. But she'll only negotiate with you."

"Do I want to know why?"

"I think it's obvious," Anne-Jade said. When I failed to respond, she added, "Gloating over our problems for one, and just being difficult because she can. Plus she sees you as her ultimate enemy. If it wasn't for you, she would still be in command of the Pop Cops."

"Does she know I don't have the authority to grant anything she asks for? That I would need the Committee's approval?"

"Yes. And that may be part of the gloating."

"Wonderful," I grumbled. "Do I have to talk to her in the brig?"

"No. We'll bring her to my office and secure her, then give you two privacy."

This kept getting better and better. "When?"

"Now."

The thought of negotiating with Karla Trava sapped my energy. I rubbed my hand over my eyes.

Logan said, "Trella, each second we stand here brings us closer to a collision. We need to fix the Transmission."

"All right." Let the fun begin.

Anne-Jade had commandeered half of Karla's office in Quad A4, including her large desk and multiple computers. The other side held two smaller worktables for her lieutenants. The room remained almost the same from when Karla occupied it. Weapons and handcuffs hung from the side wall, Remote Access Temperature Sensitive Scanners (RATSS) lined a shelf and a bench with chains and cuffs bisected the area.

The couch had been removed and a variety of high-tech devices filled the long table. Anne-Jade's little receivers and microphones made the Pop Cops' communicators look clunky and old.

While Anne-Jade and her lieutenants fetched Karla, I paced the room. I automatically noted all the points of escape—two air vents in the ceiling and four heating vents near the floor.

When the door banged open, I steeled myself for the encounter. Sitting on the edge of a hard metal chair, I fidgeted with the buttons on my shirt. Wedged between the two ISF officers, Karla's smirk didn't waver as they cuffed her to the bench. She had twisted her long blond hair up into a knot on the top of her head. Her gaze swept my face and clothes, sparking amusement in her violet-colored eyes.

Now that I knew the doctors could change a person's eye color, I wondered if Lamont had tampered with hers.

"We'll be right outside." Anne-Jade handed me a stunner. "Just yell if you need us."

The door shut with a metallic clang that vibrated in my heart, matching my rapid pulse.

Karla laughed. "Still afraid of me?"

"Don't flatter yourself. It's disgust and not fear on my face. You reek of the brig."

"And you should know, having spent many hours there."

"Yes, I spent about thirty hours in your custody before I escaped. You're up to…what? Fourteen hundred at least and counting. Big difference."

Her humor faded. "We underestimated you. Something that won't happen again. But who could blame us? Look at you. Leader of a rebellion and you're still a scrawny little scrub."

"What did you expect?"

"Better clothes." It was my turn to laugh, but it died when she said, "And more power. You risked your life for them, yet you have to beg for the Committee's permission to do anything."

"Unlike you, I'm quite content with my role as support personnel. I never desired power, just freedom," I said.

"Uh-huh. And do you have your freedom?"

"Of course."

She opened her mouth, but I cut in and said, "Let's skip the small talk crap. We need the names of those who know how to repair the Transmission. What do you want in exchange?"

A sly half-smile teased the corners of her mouth as she leaned back, crossing her legs. "We never had that type of trouble when we were in charge. I think some of the scrubs miss us. And when you combine unhappy scrubs and bored prisoners, you can get an explosive reaction."

I studied her. Was she guessing about the sabotage? And was her comment a hint of more problems to come? Either way, a quick negotiation didn't seem likely.

"Should we recycle all the Travas to avoid any more trouble?" I asked.

She shrugged. "You obviously need a few of us to help with unexpected repairs, but this indecisiveness over what to do with us will only cause more problems. Which I'm more than happy to sit back and watch."

Anne-Jade had been right about her desire to gloat. "Thanks for the tip," I said. "But I'm here to get names and not a lecture."

Annoyance flashed in her eyes before she returned to acting casual. "Fine. In exchange for fixing the Transmission, we want the people in the brig to be released to our quarters, and we desire trials to determine degree of guilt in your warped little minds. There is no reason the entire Trava family should be confined."

I hated to admit this, but she had a point about the Trava family. However, releasing the upper officers from the brig would be a mistake.

Karla waved her hand as best she could while cuffed to the bench. "Run along to the Committee now and deliver my request like a good little scrub."

I couldn't suppress my grin as I toggled on my button microphone. Repeating her demands to the Committee, I waited as they discussed them. She rested her hands in her lap in an attempt to disguise the fury pulsing through her body, but her rigid posture betrayed her. I slid back in my chair, relaxing.

As expected the Committee was willing to review each family member's actions prior to the rebellion to determine degree of guilt for each, but they refused to move the brig prisoners. I relayed this to Karla.

"Next?"

She scowled and my heart stuttered for a few beats—an automatic response.

"My terms are not negotiable," she said.

My temper flared. This had been a waste of time. "Then we're done." I stood to leave.

"You *have* to fix the Transmission." Karla's voice held a bit of panic. "The survival of our world depends on it."

I pressed a finger to my ear as if listening to a message. "The Committee is willing to include those in the brig in the review process."

"No. We want out of the brig."

Keeping my hand near my ear, I cocked my head and furrowed my brow. "Okay, then you'll be taken out of the brig and sent to Chomper."

Shock bleached her face. "That's not what I meant. What about the repairs?"

It was hard not to snigger over her reaction. "I'm sure once the others see how we cleaned out the brig, they'll be more cooperative."

Her hard stare burned like acid on my skin, but I kept my face neutral.

"You're lying," she said.

"Doesn't matter if you believe me or not." I strode toward the door.

"Wait," she said.

I paused but didn't turn around.

"I'll tell you the names if you do a review for all the Travas, including those in the brig."

Glancing over my shoulder, I said, "All right."

I rummaged for a wipe board and marker and returned to Karla. "Don't lie," I said. "If the names are wrong, you'll be the first to be sent to Chomper. I'll do the honors myself."

Karla rattled off three and I wrote them down. I didn't recognize any of them, but I hadn't been expecting to. Without saying goodbye, I left the office. Anne-Jade waited in the hallway.

"Well?" she asked.

I handed her the board.

She whistled. "Last I heard, the Committee was waiting for a counter-offer. What happened?"

"She pissed me off."

★ ★ ★

Feeling rather satisfied over my meeting with Karla, I changed into my climbing clothes and returned to the Expanse. I found the mark I had left on my last trip. The safety equipment hung nearby, so I strapped it on and made another attempt to reach the ceiling.

The new route looked promising and, after finding plenty of handholds, I climbed higher than ever before. I rested at twenty-three meters above level ten. Craning my head back, I shone my light up into the blackness. Still no ceiling. Logan had found a few diagrams in the computer system, and from them he estimated Inside's height to be about seventy-five meters, which would put it about two meters above my head. Either the computer or Logan had been wrong.

I yanked on the safety line and guessed I had another couple meters before I was literally at the end of my rope.

When I felt strong enough, I continued and discovered why meter seventy-five was mentioned in the computer. A bottom rung of a ladder started at that point. I grabbed the wide cold bar, hoping the rung would hold my weight. The smooth and rounded shape fit nicely in my hands. And my light illuminated the ladder, which continued up with more rungs disappearing into the darkness.

I climbed on the ladder another meter, confirming the metal hadn't rusted or deteriorated with time. Squinting, I shone my light higher, but the ceiling still remained out of sight. However, I thought I spotted a dim gleam of a reflection. Wishful thinking or my imagination, it didn't matter. It was enough to justify my decision to unhook my harness from the safety line.

Despite the cold, sweat soaked the fabric of my uniform. I rubbed my moist palm on my arm before grasping the next rung. Continuing up the ladder with slow and careful movements, I tested each rung before allowing it to bear my weight. In the silence of the Expanse, my breath sounded loud and mechanical. My heart thudded with urgency as it reminded me of the danger. One slip, and…I wouldn't think about it.

Instead, I focused on keeping a tight grip and my balance on the rungs. Concentrating so hard on my hands and feet, I bumped my head on the ceiling. I clung to the ladder in surprise, and when my muscles stopped trembling, I scanned the flat expanse of metal over my head. Finally!

I checked the altimeter. Inside was eighty meters high, which meant we could build six more levels for a total of sixteen. Wow. That was mind-numbing. I hoped our systems could service all those levels. And what about keeping them clean and in good condition? And when did I turn into such a worrier?

Eventually, someone would need to explore the entire ceiling. Logan had read about another Outer Space Gateway in the computer files. By the way he described the file system, it had sounded as jumbled as the infirmary's supplies after the explosion. Between the Travas' attempts to erase files and the sheer amount of information, Logan had said—with his usual glee over a technical challenge—that it was an utter mess.

With one last look upwards, I steeled myself for the descent and stopped. Moving the beam of light slowly, I searched for the almost invisible indentation I thought I spotted from the corner of my eye. I swept the beam back and forth over a square meter-sized section. When I was just about to give up, the light skipped over a line.

I found a near-invisible hatch! Pleased over my discovery, it took me a few seconds to understand the full ramifications of my find. Above each of the four levels we have been living in, was a near-invisible hatch to the Gap between levels. This meter and a half space housed pipes and wires and room for someone like me to move between levels without being seen.

I had thought I reached the ceiling. But the presence of a near-invisible hatch meant there was *something* on the other side.

six

Something on the other side. I repeated it in my mind in order for the logical side of my brain to catch up. No black rubber ringed the hatch, which meant it wasn't a Gateway to Outer Space. There could be another Expanse and room for additional levels. I laughed, but it sounded strained and metallic as it echoed. I had thought sixteen levels incomprehensible.

Only one way to know for sure, I hooked my legs through the rungs on the ladder to anchor my body. Stretching my hands up, I felt for the release.

The pop-click reverberated through the bones in my arms. I pushed the hatch. The metal groaned and creaked, setting my teeth on edge. A dusty stale smell drifted down.

When the opening was big enough for me to fit through, I shined my light inside. The ladder continued another meter before stopping. Odd shapes decorated the wall. Taking a risk, I climbed into the space. The floor seemed solid so I stepped down, but still held on to the ladder just in case.

The good news—the floor didn't disintegrate under me.

The bad—a strange tingle zipped through my foot and daylights turned on.

Blinded by the bright white light, I squeezed my eyes shut. Even through my eyelids, the harsh brilliance stabbed like a horrible migraine.

It felt like hours before my vision adjusted.

When I could finally see, I saw a giant monster.

I screamed and hopped onto the ladder before logic took control. The huge thing was a thing, not a living breathing creature. It didn't move. No sounds emanated. No lights shone from it. It appeared to be made of an odd black metal without rivets.

Unable to stifle my curiosity, I stepped closer. About nine meters tall and a hundred meters wide, it was too long for me to guess with any accuracy. A colossal sheep without a neck had been my initial impression. Or a long sock filled with round balls. Or glass balls all stuck together in a rectangular shape.

Either way, the whole oddity rested on eight thick metal legs with massive wheels. The head—for lack of a better word—had two large glass panes for its eyes, which reflected the daylights set into the ceiling. If the roof above this strange level was indeed the ceiling for Inside. At this point, I wouldn't be surprised to find yet another level and perhaps a whole other society living above us.

I ringed the structure and spotted its tiny twin right next to it. Not as scary as its super-sized brother, the smaller…what to call it? A lamb? A bubble thing? It appeared to be a conveyance of some type.

Once the shock of my discovery wore off, I realized that the room I stood in was indeed a room. Inside was approximately two thousand meters wide, by two thousand meters long. This area was a fraction of that size. In fact, my body's internal sense of measurement suspected the room's dimensions equaled one

Sector or Quadrant—six hundred and sixty-six point seven square meters. One ninth of a level. Or to convert it into Inside's designation system so it matched the levels below, this area would be Quad G17.

Which meant, there was potentially four Sectors and three more Quadrants in this level. Did that mean eight more bubble monsters? I shuddered, sending a horde of goose bumps across my skin. Feeling as if I would float away, I leaned against the bumpy wall.

Remembering the patterns and symbols covering its surface, I straightened to examine them. The pictures and diagrams made as much sense to me as one of Logan's computer screens.

I walked along the walls, seeking a doorway. The strange markings continued, filling every centimeter without a break on three of the four walls. In the middle of the north wall, which would be shared with Sector D17, was a Gateway outlined in the familiar black rubber seal. But this one extended almost to the ceiling and was at least two hundred meters wide. Big enough to fit the bubble monster. In the northwest corner, sheets of the black metal had been stacked. I touched the smooth surface. It felt like glass, but seemed too thick. Prying the first sheet up, I expected it to be heavy. But it peeled away with a staticky-crackly sound. It weighed nothing compared to metal or glass. And the edges drooped like cloth, but not cloth. It reminded me of a slice of Outer Space—black, cold and weightless.

The floating dizziness returned full force. I dropped the sheet, and sat on the floor, holding my head in my hands. Discovering the Expanse paled in comparison to this find.

And then a thought stopped my heart. Should I tell the Committee? The rapid pace of changes in our society had been overwhelming to the majority of the people. Some even had trouble accepting the Expanse and new levels. And what about the saboteur or saboteurs? If they were upset over the fact we traveled through Outer Space to an unknown destination, what would they do when faced with this new discovery?

Perhaps we needed to deal with our current problems before I added more to the mix. I returned to the ladder and climbed down below the floor, replacing and resealing the near-invisible hatch. I wondered about the daylights and hoped they would turn off.

I had no memory of the rest of my descent other than the tricky maneuver of reattaching my harness to the safety line.

By the time I returned to the storeroom, it was hour thirty. Only two hours had passed since I had left Karla and gone exploring. It seemed as if weeks had come and gone.

I perched on the edge of the couch's cushion and tried to decide between showering and sleeping. But each time I forced my thoughts to the matter at hand, the image of the Bubble Monster reclaimed all of my attention.

When Riley arrived an hour later, I hadn't moved. He sat next to me and I collapsed against him. Should I tell him?

He wrapped his arm around my shoulders, supporting me. "You look like you had a close encounter with Chomper. What happened?" he asked.

I opened my mouth, but the words jammed in my throat.

"Logan told me you talked to Karla Trava. If she upset you, I'll…"

Wrenching my thoughts away from my discovery, I focused on Riley, looking up at him. A hard stubbornness radiated from his blue eyes and the muscles in his neck strained.

"You'll what?" I asked.

"I'll put her in the same cell with Vinco and smuggle a knife to him."

"Although she tried, she failed to unnerve me. But it's so sweet of you." I tapped my chest. "Nothing says you care for me better than offering to torture my enemies."

He grinned. "No sense doing things halfhearted. And to think, some girls have to endure listening to poetry."

"Poor things." I tsked, but couldn't stop a smile.

Riley stroked my cheek with his fingers. "That's better. Now you have some color in your face. Did something go wrong with searching for the bomber?"

Glad to have a topic I could handle, I said, "No. Jacy sent me to a guy named Bubba Boom." I held up a hand to stop his snort of disbelief. "Just wait, the story gets better." Telling him about the stink bombers, I filled him in on what I had learned.

He fiddled with a piece of ripped fabric on the couch's arm. "Not much to go on. You can use the computer in my rooms to research the names Bubba Boom gave you. Logan assigned you a ten-degree security clearance so you can access the entire network."

"Why would he do that? I barely know how to use the computer."

"You're kidding, right?" Riley stared at me as if I had told him Sheepy could talk.

I ignored his question. "Your computer is fine. I also need a shower. Is your dad working? I don't want to bother him."

This time Riley gave me a slow conspiratorial leer. "What a coincidence. I need a shower as well. Good thing my father's busy for the next couple of hours and you have a promise to keep."

Taking different routes to Riley's rooms in Sector E4, I figured my path through the air ducts would be quicker than his through the corridors. But when I reached the vent for suite number three-six-nine-five, he waited below, standing on the table.

I opened the cover and dangled my legs. Riley caught me around my waist and I slid down him the rest of the way. He didn't let go when my feet touched the table. Dipping his head closer to mine, he kissed me for a long time.

When he tugged at my uniform, I pulled away. Breathless for a moment, I sucked in a few deep breaths.

"Are you sure your father won't be back soon?" I asked.

He answered with the metallic trill of my zipper unzipping. Cool air caressed my sweaty back. A nervous shiver raced over my skin. His lips found mine and his hands stroked my exposed back. Heat from his touch burned all the doubts away.

When he began to pull the fabric of my jumpsuit down, he paused. "Shower?"

A big step, but my heart beat its approval. And the desire to see him naked and soapy overrode all logic. I imagined cold reason melting and steaming away in a puffy cloud.

We left a trail of clothes to the washroom. Warm water, the scent of soap and slippery skin made for an exhilarating combination. I worried about the ugly scars crisscrossing my torso, arms and legs, but no hint of disgust or pity darkened his expression.

He wiped the water from my eyes. "You're beautiful. I—"

I covered his mouth with mine, afraid to hear him utter words I couldn't repeat back to him. Grabbing the soap, I worked it into a frothy lather. I explored the hard ridges of his stomach, the smooth lines of his back and his nice grabable butt as we kissed under the spray of hot water.

His hands were equally busy and quite distracting. And when his lips moved to my neck, I lost all track of time and location. However, Riley kept an eye on the clock in the washroom, and he stopped way too soon with a sigh.

"Dad's due in a few minutes. Although…" He trailed a finger along my ribs. "He wouldn't just barge in here. He'd think I was alone in the shower so we could continue."

"And what happens when we both come out?"

"He would grin like an idiot, beaming with happiness."

I pushed Riley's hand away before it could move any lower. "No. I'm not ready for your father to get any ideas."

"Too late. He's been full of ideas ever since I started talking about an intern named Ella." Riley pulled me close. "The rebellion distracted him, but he's back to being way too nosy about our relationship."

"He needs one of his own."

Riley dropped his arms and turned off the water. "It would be nice, but he says my mother was the only one for him, and he hasn't met anyone who drove him as crazy as she did." He grabbed a couple of towels and handed one to me.

"Drove him crazy in a good way or bad?" I dried my body and wrapped the towel around my torso.

He paused as if struck by an amazing notion. "He always said both good and bad, but I never really understood how it was possible…" He met my gaze. "Until now."

I looked away and rummaged for a comb. My question had almost been in jest, and I didn't want to start a serious discussion. The knots in my hair resisted the comb's efforts, but I managed to smooth them out. I braided my hair without drying it. A certain amount of patience was required to dry it first. Patience I didn't have. Never did.

Glancing at Riley, I watched him run his fingers through his wet mop before he dressed. I never cared about my appearance prior to meeting Riley, and he'd seen me at my worst. So why would I waste precious time to fuss over my hair? I studied my reflection in the washroom's mirror. A stranger stared back. Even after fourteen weeks, my blue-colored eyes still seemed like they belonged in another face. The blue had been my original color; otherwise, the reversal drops wouldn't have worked.

According to Domotor and a few others, I had my father's eyes. They also claimed my father was Nolan Garrard. Unlike Lamont's name, his didn't make me cringe. In fact, I would be proud to be his daughter. Even though the Force of Ten's attempt to change our world failed, his final defiance by saving those ten files had been vital. Without them, we wouldn't have found Gateway. And their existence impressed Logan—hard to do when it came to technology.

Perhaps settling the matter of my birth parents wouldn't be so bad. So what if Lamont's my mother? It's not like I'd be forced to live with her or to forgive her. Nothing would change.

I hurried to dress before Riley's dad returned. Riley already sat at the computer in the living area. The apartment had one bedroom, a washroom, a small space for the computer, a table and couch. Posh accommodations from a scrub's point of view, but still not the huge suite of rooms I had imagined when the Pop Cops kept us from going above level two.

Riley typed for a few minutes before relinquishing the chair. "I logged you on. You'll need to pull up the population records to search for those names."

Reluctance kept me from claiming the seat. "Can't you look them up for me?"

"Sit." He pointed. "You need to learn how to access the computer files."

Not happy, I plopped in front of the screen. He leaned over me as he explained how to navigate the network. I might look like Nolan Garrard, but I didn't have his knack with computers.

After more than a few frustrating minutes, Riley almost growled at me. "Think of the network as a map of Inside and the files are stored in different Sectors and Quadrants. In order to find the right file, you need to know the location."

"But what if it isn't there? Logan said—"

"That the files had been jumbled, but I'm used to them that way. If I can't find what I'm looking for, I request a search."

"From who?"

"The computer."

"Oh. Like from the Controllers in the network?"

"No. Yes."

I turned my head to see him. He squinted at the screen as if in pain.

"Which one is it?"

Riley ran a hand over his face. "We learned that the Controllers are really just an operating system. It connects all the information in the network, lets you know if you can do something or not. It protects certain areas. And it will search for files and tell you where they are." He swept his arm out. "Everything in Inside is all connected to the network. Technically, I could run all the systems from one computer."

This fact seemed to impress him, but, considering the recent sabotage, it scared me. "What happens if the network breaks down?"

"It can't."

"Why not?"

"There are backup systems and everything has been saved in protected files."

"But what if they're compromised as well?"

He dismissed my concerns. "Won't happen. And you're trying to distract me so I don't teach you how to navigate through the network."

"I'm not. I'm just worried another bomb might blow apart the network."

"Don't worry, there are many safeguards in place. Unless you want me to have Logan explain—"

"No! I trust you."

He clutched his hands to his chest. "She… Gasp… Trusts me! Call for medical aid stat!"

I swung at him, but he grabbed my wrist and pulled me to my feet.

Snaking his arms around my waist, he said, "We need to celebrate this momentous occasion."

"What are we celebrating?" Jacob Ashon, Riley's father, asked from the doorway.

I pushed Riley away to greet his father. But the damage had been done. He grinned at us like an idiot. Joy beamed from his brown eyes as his gaze went from Riley's wet hair to mine. I suppressed a groan.

"We're celebrating Trella learning the computer system," Riley said.

The wattage from his grin dulled a few kilos. His slightly disappointed expression reminded me of Riley. He had his father's solid build, sense of humor and mannerisms, but, according to Jacob, Riley's black hair, blue eyes and stubbornness had been inherited from his mother, Ramla Ashon.

She had been another casualty of the failed Force of Ten rebellion along with Nolan Garrard, Blas Sanchia and Shawn Lamont. Four brave souls who would be honored with a plaque or memorial along with Cogon once our world settled back into... What? Not like we would return to life before. I guessed just when our society settled into a new routine.

"Oh," Jacob said, then recovered his brightness. "Don't teach her too much. She tends to leave a wake of trouble behind her, and I don't want to spend hours trying to decipher the carnage."

"Not funny," I said, plopping back down in the chair. The diagram of file names on the screen hadn't gotten any more understandable with Riley's explanation.

Riley attempted another round of frustrating instruction before giving in and swapping places with me. I paid attention for a few minutes, but soon lost interest. As he worked, I studied Jacob. He straightened the mess of wires and gadgets Riley had strewn about the room, collecting them into a neat pile.

Jacob had been thrilled to be reunited with Blake, Riley's younger brother. Having to send a child to live in the lower levels must be difficult especially since Jacob reveled in the whole family experience. I wondered if Blake's decision to return to living in the barracks upset him. If I did test my blood to determine if Nolan and Lamont were my parents, I knew Jacob would be happy. Despite Lamont's first betrayal costing him his wife, and the second one almost killing his son, he stayed friends with her. Crazy.

"…paying attention, Trella?" Riley asked.

"Uh…"

"You're impossible. Here's the file you need." He stood. "*You* can search through it."

Back in front of the computer, I scanned the directory of names with birth weeks, barrack locations and other stats listed next to them. The file contained all the lower level scrubs. All eighteen thousand and change. Ugh.

As I scrolled down the page, Riley asked his father why he was late.

"I visited your brother," Jacob said. "The Committee heard rumors of the kitchen workers threatening to cook only enough food for themselves. I thought I'd check into it and see if I can resolve the issue."

I tuned out their conversation, glad I no longer had to deal with the Committee's problems. Concentrating on the list, I thought there must be a reason why the names had been put in this particular order. It wasn't alphabetical, by barrack location, birth week, by Care Mother or by care unit. At the end of the stats for each were the same letters: AS.

When my name jumped out, I stopped. Did AS mean air scrub? I didn't recognize the other names with AS, but I hadn't learned the names of my fellow workers either. After I scrolled a few more pages the AS turned into a CS and I found my Care Mother's name in that section.

The list had been organized by work area and they had been alphabetized. I quickly bypassed the other workers until I reached the hydroponics scrubs. Sure enough, Ivie was listed. After I wrote down her stats on a wipe board, I found Kadar and copied his as well.

They had been care mates. No surprise. They were also a few centiweeks older than me, putting them closer to Cog's age. And they slept in Sector D1, Jacy's barrack. I tapped the marker against my teeth. This information didn't mean anything other than they existed. Bubba Boom could have picked their names at random.

To really find out what's going on, someone would need to follow those two around. I couldn't do it as I was too recognizable with my blue eyes and small stature. The best way would be to recruit someone not in Jacy's network and who I could trust.

"Trella?" Riley interrupted my train of thought. "Did you hear what's going on in the lower level kitchen?"

I turned. "A little. I found those names, and I think we—"

"There might be a food strike. Don't you care?"

"Of course I do, but your dad and the Committee know about it. They can deal with it. Plus they have Blake to…"

Riley crossed his arms. A danger sign. "To what?"

"To warn them." And he would be perfect to spy on Ivie and Kadar for me. "Does Blake come up here often to visit?"

"Why?" When I hesitated, he said, "I recognize that look. Tell me what you're planning."

By the tension rolling off Riley, I knew to tread carefully. "We need a reliable person to keep an eye on Ivie and Kadar for us. I thought Blake cou—"

"No. You're not putting him in danger."

"It won't be that dangerous."

"What if Ivie and Kadar are the bombers and they notice Blake's interest in them? He could be their next target. Besides, he'll be needed to report to the Committee about the food situation. Trella, you've got to keep in mind the big picture, not just the next thing you want to do."

The big picture. I almost laughed, remembering what I had said to Jacy about being a big picture girl. Drawing in a deep breath, I held it along with a sarcastic reply. My search for the saboteurs was important, but I suspected his ire went deeper than the recent kitchen crisis, and I had no energy to fight with him. The climb to the ceiling of the Expanse had sapped my strength.

Instead, I swiveled back to the computer screen. Not sure how to log out, I picked up the wipe board. Before I could stand, a bright whiteness flashed on the monitor, erasing the list. Then it faded to black. It seemed odd, but when I glanced at Riley, his attention remained on me.

I stood and waved the wipe board. "I'll find someone else to help me with my problem." Hurrying toward the door, I had almost reached the handle when he called my name.

"Who are you going to recruit?" he asked.

"I'm sure Anne-Jade knows a trustworthy person. I'll see you later." I slipped out of the room before he could say anything else.

When the door clicked shut, I leaned against the hallway's wall and considered my next move. No one was in sight. The corridors in the upper living sectors never had much traffic and they tended to be a bit of a maze. I was already on level four and Anne-Jade should be working in her office in Quad A4. Pushing off the wall, I headed to the right and froze.

Gray smoke rolled along the thin carpet. I recovered from my shock and ran, following the clouds. They thickened and blackened as I drew closer to the air plant in Quad I4. Halfway there, the shrill fire alarm sounded, assaulting my ears. Soon shouts and shrieks joined in the cacophony.

The smoke blocked my vision as it stung my eyes. I dropped

to the floor and crawled to the entrance of the plant. The heat reached me first. Then I gawked at the fire. Erupting from the units that housed the air filters, flames licked at the ceiling. Water rained down from the sprinkler system, the streams hissed and steamed on the hot metal, but nothing sprayed from the nozzles directly over the air filters.

A few workers ran past me, emptying the room. About to do the same, I spotted a figure sprawled on the floor near the control panel. His legs draped over pieces of a broken chair. It looked as if he had fallen backwards. Dead?

I strained to hear any sounds that meant the fire response team had arrived, but the roar of the blaze dominated. Then he rolled to his side and I saw his face.

Logan.

seven

What the hell was Logan doing in the air plant? His shoulders shook as he coughed and I realized the flames burned closer to him. It didn't matter why. All that mattered was saving him.

I ripped two strips of fabric from the hem of my shirt. Lying on the floor, I pulled myself toward him as if I squirmed through a tight air shaft. When I encountered the warm puddles of water from the sprinklers, I rolled, soaking my clothes and dipping the strips in them. I tied one around my nose and mouth.

Logan's lips moved, but I couldn't hear what he shouted. Blisters peppered his face. He squeezed his eyes closed as another coughing fit racked his body.

Sliding as fast as possible on my belly, I finally reached Logan. He jerked in surprise when I touched him. At this distance, the heat from the fire was almost intolerable and breathing was all but impossible.

"It's Trella," I yelled in his ear. "Can you walk?"

He clutched my arm. "Yes, but I can't see!"

"Here." I wrapped the other strip around his face to filter the smoke. "Stay low and keep—" Hot air choked me. Thick black smoke engulfed us and stung my eyes. A brief thought that perhaps I should have waited for the fire response team flashed. But the air cleared for a nanosecond and I tugged Logan toward the entrance.

We crawled, rolled and stumbled. The heat intensified, evaporating the water from the sprinklers before it reached the floor. The hot metal seared our skin. Halfway there, Logan collapsed and I yanked him another meter before I joined him.

Air refused to fill my lungs and my throat burned. Blackness danced in my vision, swirling with white sparks. It reminded me of the brief glimpse I had of Outer Space before Cogon floated away. Except then it had been ice cold and this time it was my turn to drift off.

A blast of water hit me, rousing me and rolling me over. Strong arms peeled me from the floor, carried me. Voices yelled and admonished, but I had no breath to respond. Tucked against my rescuer's chest, I stared as the walls of Inside streaked by.

Then the familiar curtains of the infirmary surrounded me. I was laid on a bed as a mask covered my nose and mouth, forcing cool air down my lungs. I sucked it in despite the sharp pain in my throat. My skin felt like the flames still licked at it. The small prick in my arm a mere nuisance in comparison to the rest of my body.

Only when the dizziness started did I realize what the prick meant. Too late to resist, I let my world spin out of control. It wasn't a new feeling. Not at all.

At least when I woke, the pain was gone. But the mask remained—a good thing since my lungs strained to breathe. My arms and legs had been wrapped in bandages. Soft white gloves covered my hands. Faces came and went as I drifted in and out of consciousness. I recognized Lamont's frown, Riley's worry and Bubba Boom's scowl. I understood the words *painkillers, idiot, brain damage, reckless* and *growing skin grafts*. But I didn't see the one face I worried about or hear the one voice I wanted to hear or heck, I'd even settle for someone mentioning his name. Logan.

Without him, Inside would be lost. Besides the high-ranking Travas, he alone knew how to run this ship. The captain in all but name. I suspected he had been the primary target of the fire for just that reason. I tried to yank the mask off to ask, but Lamont slapped my hand and threatened to inject me with a sedative if I touched it again.

Hours or weeks later—hard to tell—I woke into the quiet stillness of bluelights. They shone through the fabric of the privacy curtains. I no longer felt as if a person made of solid metal sat on my chest so I removed the mask, but kept it close just in case.

Sheepy was tucked in next to me. Smiling, I moved him so he wouldn't fall on the floor as I struggled to sit up. The effort winded me. I sucked a few deep breaths from the mask. Moving with care so I wouldn't make a sound, I slipped through the overlap in the fabric. I paused to let my eyes adjust and my legs solidify under me. The clock read hour ninety-two, which would mean I had been out of it for sixty hours. Losing hunks of time just had to stop, I felt as if I spent more time in the infirmary than anywhere else.

A robe hung over a nearby chair as if someone suspected I'd be creeping out of bed—Riley probably. Wrapping it around my shoulders, I scanned the other beds. A couple of patients slept in the next two, but the third had also been isolated from the room by the curtains. Logan's, I hoped.

I shuffled-stepped—all I could manage with my bandage-wrapped legs and tight skin—over to the hidden patient.

Ducking under the curtain, I almost fainted with relief. Logan slept in the bed. Or at least I think he was sleeping. Bandages covered his eyes and a mask rested over his nose and mouth.

He tugged it away from his face. "Who's there?"

"Trella," I whispered.

Logan reached with his free hand and I took it in mine. He also wore the special white gloves. "Thanks," he said.

I shrugged, but realized he couldn't see the motion. "I just got you closer to the door. Someone else did the true life saving." And I would need to find out his name. "Besides, you'd have done the same for me."

"Probably." His smile didn't last long.

"What's the damage?"

"Ten air…filter bays. The computer—"

"I meant you."

"Oh. Burns over fifty percent—" he puffed "—of my body." He pressed the mask to his face and inhaled deeply for a few minutes. "Lost my vision…but it might be…temporary."

Horror swept over me and I squeezed his hand. "Might? That's vague."

"Doctor Lamont…will know better…in time."

"How much time?"

He shook his head. "Don't know."

I waited as he drank in more of the oxygen-rich air flowing from the mask. "I have a million questions, but I'll ask you them later. Just answer this one. Do you think the fire was an act of sabotage or an attack aimed at you?"

"Both."

The news inflamed the burns on my skin, sending a hot surge of fear. "Why aren't you surrounded by guards?"

"He's protected," Anne-Jade said. She poked her head in between the curtain's overlap.

I jumped. "How long have you been listening?"

"I've been here the whole time."

"Why didn't you say something sooner?"

She smiled. "I didn't want to interrupt."

"Yeah right. You were hoping to overhear something juicy."

Parting the fabric, she stood next to her brother's bed. Anne-Jade glanced at him and then me. "And just how much juice do you think I could get from a couple of overcooked mutton chops like yourselves?"

Logan's laughter turned into a coughing fit.

"Okay. Point taken. Who else knows about the attack?"

"The Committee has been informed of both sabotages and the attempt on Logan's life."

She gripped the rail on Logan's bed as if a great weight rested on her shoulders. All humor fled her eyes and I realized she teetered on the edge of exhaustion.

Even though I was reluctant to ask, and I could probably guess the answer, I had to hear it from her. "And the Committee's response?"

"Lockdown and search of all levels."

Now I had to grab the rail or risk falling to the floor. We had come full circle. Instead of Pop Cops policing the lower levels, we now had ISF officers. They would confine everyone to their barracks until they could do a thorough search for evidence. At least, they included the upper levels.

Anne-Jade said, "Do you have any better ideas? We can't let them keep blowing and burning up vital life systems. We also brought Ivie and Kadar in for questioning."

"How did—"

"We found your wipe board in the hallway outside the air plant. I remembered the names from our discussion with Bubba Boom."

"But you don't have any proof they're involved. Just his suspicions."

"Doesn't matter. There could be another explosion or attempt to get to Logan or you."

"Me? Why would they—"

"To prevent you from discovering any more surprises. They're still reeling from the fact we're in a big ship and we have all this extra room to spread out."

Good thing I'd kept the bubble monster to myself.

Anne-Jade then asked me how I had gotten to the air plant so fast. "Did someone ask you to meet there?"

"No." I explained about leaving Riley's, but omitted the fact I had been going to find her. Any chance to discover what Ivie and Kadar had been up to had been ruined. And if they had been working with anyone, it would be impossible to find out now.

"A lucky coincidence," Anne-Jade said. She smoothed Logan's hair. "By the time the fire response team arrived they could only go a few meters into the plant. If you hadn't dragged Logan closer…"

"Who pulled us out?"

"Bubba Boom carried you and Hank from maintenance grabbed Logan."

"How's the plant?"

"Bad. Smoke spread throughout Inside and made a bunch of people sick. Half the air filters are burnt to a crisp. The air workers are rigging up a temporary cleaning system, but it won't last long. When you're feeling better, they're going to need you to help install filters in the air ducts. It's another temporary measure."

Logan lifted his mask again. "Plant fire also…a distraction."

"And a lure to get you in harm's way," Anne-Jade said.

"No. A distraction from…computer."

Dread twisted and I wished I had stayed in my bed. "What's wrong with the computer?"

"Compromised."

My chest felt as if my body had gotten stuck in a tight pipe. "How bad?"

"Don't know…I need to…see."

I considered. Besides the burning from the smoke, my vision hadn't been affected by the heat. "Logan, was there an explosion in the air plant before the fire?"

"No. Light exploded from—" Another coughing fit seized him. "From…the computer monitor. It burned…my eyes."

Anne-Jade and I shared a horrified look.

"Who could…?" I couldn't even say the words.

"I could," Logan said.

"Who else?" his sister demanded.

"A few…of the Travas. Maybe Riley." He drew on the mask for a few breaths. "Domotor. Trella's father."

"Nolan's been fertilizer for over fifteen centiweeks," I said, dismissing him.

"According to…Karla Trava." He shrugged. "She didn't recycle you—"

"We don't know that for sure." I squelched any and all hope. It was ludicrous. "Besides, he would have revealed himself after the rebellion."

Another shrug. I mulled over his list. Not Riley and I doubted Domotor, so that left the Travas. "Are there any working computers in Sector D4?"

Anne-Jade scowled at me. "Do you think I'm an idiot?"

"We disabled them," Logan said.

"Could they have hooked them back up?" And before Anne-Jade could snap at me, I added, "They don't have anything else to do. And you and Logan made a number of amazing devices just from recycled parts so it's a valid question."

She scratched her arm absently. "I guess it's possible. I'll have a team go in and check." Huffing in annoyance, she slid her hand under her sleeve and rubbed harder.

Logan reached out blindly and touched her arm. "Stop it. Doctor Lamont said…to leave it…alone or it'll get infected."

"But it itches," she said between gritted teeth.

"What happened?" I asked her.

She pushed up her sleeve, revealing white bandages like the ones on Logan and my arms. "I donated skin so the Doctor could grow my brother a new coat."

Logan smiled. "I'm covered with girl germs…don't tell Riley."

"Maybe you'll be smarter now," she quipped. "I'd like to think you will appreciate having a sister more, but I doubt it."

I remembered he had said he had been burned on over fifty percent of his body. "He needed skin grafts from you to live. Didn't he?"

"Yes. I matched his skin type, which doesn't always happen with siblings."

Glancing at my own bandaged arms, I wondered how badly I had been burned. I met Anne-Jade's steady gaze.

"You weren't as bad as Logan, but you needed skin grafts to survive as well," she said.

She shifted her stance as if challenging me to ask her who donated skin cells for me; either that or she prepared for a fight. I didn't have the energy to deal with either so I said goodbye and shuffled back to my bed.

The effort to visit Logan had exhausted me. Grateful for the flow of clean air, I inhaled large lung-filling breaths from my mask. Funny how I had taken something as vital as breathing for granted—not paying it one bit of attention until it had become a problem.

The next time I woke, the daylights brightened the infirmary and half of my curtain had been pushed back. Lamont rolled a small table toward me. Stocked with clean bandages, salve, a bowl of water and a sponge, I grimaced in anticipation. She planned to change my dressing and clean the burns.

Hour two glowed on the clock. Another ten hours lost to injury. Another week gone. We were now on week 147,022.

Lamont tried a smile, but thought better of it. She kept her tone and mannerisms all business. Doctor to patient. "How are you feeling?"

"Like I've been stuffed into an oven and twice baked."

Amusement flashed on her face. She tucked a long strand of her hair that had escaped her braid behind her ear. Wearing her light green shirt and pants, she looked ready for surgery. "You know I need to—"

"Just get it over with...please."

With deft fingers, she peeled the bandages from my left arm, starting at the wrist. "You might not want to see your skin. It's not fully healed yet and will look like..."

I waited.

"Raw meat. But it will return to normal healthy skin. I even removed the scars on your arms and legs from...before."

"You can do that?"

"It's considered cosmetic surgery. I normally wouldn't do it for arms or legs. Faces, yes. But since you needed so much skin already..."

"Oh. Thanks."

Without the dressing the air stung my skin. I braced for the touch of water and it didn't disappoint, feeling like liquid fire as it ran down my arm. I hissed in pain.

"Do you want a pain pill?" she asked.

"No...thank you. They make me sleepy and I've slept enough." Why was I being so polite? *Because this woman saved your life.*

I kept that thought in mind as she changed all the bandages. My extremities fared the worst. When she finished my bedding and gown were soaked, and so were her sleeves. She pushed them up to help me switch to a clean bed and I froze.

White bandages peeked out from under the wet fabric on both of her arms. I stared at them, knowing what they meant, but not wanting to really believe it. Finally, I pulled my gaze away and met hers.

"You were going to die," she said. "We needed to find you a match."

eight

"And you matched my skin type?" I asked.

Struggling to keep her professional demeanor, Lamont nod-ded. Impressive considering I stood less than a meter from her. The fact we matched meant I was her daughter. The daughter she had thought had been fed to Chomper over fifteen hundred weeks ago. Alive and…not quite well, but living and breathing.

How would I feel if Cogon returned from Outer Space and he hated me for leaving him out there? Thrilled and awful at the same time.

But I couldn't get the image of her standing with Karla Trava in the main Control Room out of my mind. She had searched all the faces in the room and didn't recognize me. Shouldn't a mother recognize her own daughter no matter how old she was? Plus the fact that she had been there with Karla in the first place, cooperating with her, endangering thousands of people for her own selfish desire.

However, if I was being fair, I endangered everyone with our rebellion. Was I being selfish as well?

Too confused to say anything but thanks for the skin cells, I collapsed on the clean bed and closed my eyes. Too much of a coward to meet her gaze.

Riley visited me around hour ten. He smiled and sat on the edge of the bed. "How are you doing?"

"Great. I'm ready to go. Do you think your dad would mind if I sleep on your couch?"

"Nice try. But you're not leaving here until Doctor Lamont gives you permission." He took my hand gently in his. "Did you even stop and think about the danger to yourself before you rushed in to save Logan?"

"No time. I hope you didn't come here to lecture me."

"Actually, I came to see how Sheepy is doing. He doesn't like sleeping in strange places." Riley picked up the stuffed sheep and smoothed his gray fuzzy hair made from real sheep's wool. The little toy had been sharing my pillow.

At my age—1,535 weeks or 17.5 years in the old time—it seemed silly to lavish so much affection on a toy. But with a limited amount of playthings available while growing up in the care facility with nine others, and the all-work-and-no-free-time structure of my upbringing, Sheepy filled a void.

"Sheepy's been keeping me company," I said. "Thanks."

"He does have an ulterior motive," he said with a sly smile.

"And that would be?"

"Spying on you. Making sure you're listening to the doctor's orders and not… What's that?" Riley put Sheepy up to his ear as if listening to the toy. "Not staying in bed? Bothering Logan?" He tsked.

"Anne-Jade really needs to learn the difference between her job and basic friendship." I grumped. "I don't suppose she has any suspects for the attack on her brother?"

"She's questioning the two stink bombers, but that's all she has right now." He fiddled with his shirt. "Inside has been locked down. It's worse than when the Pop Cops had been in charge."

An outrage on her behalf surged through me. I struggled into a sitting position. "She's dealing with a very different type of rebel than the Pop Cops ever did. We didn't blow anything up, or kill any innocents or set fires. The only people to get hurt were our own and a few Pop Cops."

He refused to meet my gaze. "There has to be a better way."

"I'm sure she's open to ideas. Have you talked to her?"

"I would if I had one. I'm more of a support person." He finally looked me in the eye. "You're the one who has the knack for coming up with new ideas."

I flopped back. Not *this* again. Time to change the subject. "What have you been doing since the fire?"

Pressing his lips together, he swallowed his obvious ire over my dodge. "Once I knew you and Logan would live, I've been checking the computer network. Logan said it had been compromised, but I've yet to find evidence."

"Did Anne-Jade search the Travas' rooms?"

"Yep. None of the computers they found were connected to the network."

Interesting word choice. I asked, "Do you suspect they have a hidden connection?"

"It's possible, but not probable. I think we have another person or persons with Logan's ability to ghost through the network. He or she would be all but impossible to catch."

This conversation felt familiar, and I wondered if eighteen weeks ago, Karla Trava had a similar discussion with her lieutenants. The arrival of Lamont to check my vitals was a welcome distraction. Although she declared they were all strong, she remained vague about when I'd be able to leave the infirmary.

When she went to check on Logan, Riley raised his eyebrows. "You were…civil to her." He sounded surprised.

"With my tendency to end up as her patient, there's no sense being nasty. Besides, everyone else seems to think she's okay."

"Oh no. I'm not going to believe you'd be influenced by others. That's not the Trella I know. Are you sure it isn't because she saved your life?"

I shrugged. "Well…it helps."

"Uh-huh. And how about the confirmation that she's your mother? Did that help?"

"Not at all."

"Whew! I was beginning to worry the fire had burned more than your skin," he teased.

Glad to see Riley smile, I relaxed. Too often lately, our conversations had transformed into…not fights, but arguments. Right before the fire, he had accused me of not caring about Inside, and I had… A memory pulled on the edges of my thoughts.

"The scrub file," I said.

"What?"

"White light flashed on the screen probably the same time Logan was attacked. Then it erased the list."

He leaned forward. "Are you sure?"

"You might be able to find evidence of tampering in that file if it is still there. Or perhaps where those files are stored."

"It's a starting point." Energized, he kissed me on the forehead, tucked Sheepy next to me and left the infirmary.

Happy to contribute to his search, I squirmed into a comfortable position. But it didn't take long for me to miss him and wish for something to distract me from the sting of my injuries. Perhaps I should ask for a painkiller.

I scanned the infirmary for Lamont and spotted Jacy. None of his goons accompanied him. Guess he felt safe visiting a half-burnt scrub. That or he didn't want to make an impression on the two ISF officers stationed next to the door. Now why did

I automatically think scrub? Whenever I saw him, he always reminded me of the time before the rebellion. Even though he helped, I always wondered why. Jacy's life had been better than most under the Pop Cops' control.

He swiped his bangs from his eyes and sat in the chair next to my bed. "You look terrible," he said.

"Gee, that really cheered me up. Thanks for visiting."

He flashed a grin. "You do know the Committee is unhappy with you. Don't you?"

"I figured they weren't keen about us keeping our suspicions to ourselves."

"Keen is such a…mild word."

"Jacy, if you keep trying to scare me, I'm going to have Lamont toss you out of here."

Not bothered by my threat, he shifted into a more comfortable position. "Just trying to warn you."

"How about you tell me who's been endangering our world instead?"

He tapped his fingers on his leg. "Wish I could."

"You're lying. You know—"

"Nothing." The word tore from his mouth as if it hurt him to speak it. "I *used* to have eyes and ears in every Sector and Quadrant. But my sources turned blind and deaf after I joined the Committee. I have a few loyal supporters, but not enough to discover who set off that bomb in the power plant."

I studied his expression. He seemed truly disgruntled, but it could be an act. "If you didn't know, why did you tell me Bubba Boom's name then?"

"You asked for an expert. You didn't ask for a suspect."

True.

Jacy pulled a small bag from his pocket and tossed it on my stomach. I couldn't open it with the gloves on. When Lamont had changed them earlier, my palms were still raw.

"Your part of our bargain," he said, pitching his voice lower. "I need you to plant them in air duct seventy-two, ninety-five and eighty-one."

His list of ducts targeted all the critical areas of Inside—the main Control Room, Anne-Jade's office, the brig and the Sector full of Travas. I hefted the bag, calculating how many microphones might be inside.

"That's three different shafts. You only gave me one name," I said.

"I told you I don't—"

"I don't need names. How about locations?"

"Locations of what?"

"If you could have eyes and ears in the lower levels again, where would you want them?"

His expression smoothed as he caught on. "Sector F1, waste handling and maintenance."

I waved the bag of mics. "Why not ask me to install these there?"

"Because the scrubs didn't know about the Transmission, and they don't necessarily know Logan's the brains of our operation, so I think they're just following orders. Besides, I have a limited number of mics."

"Well, it may be a week or more before I can install these," I said. "It depends on Lamont and how much help the air plant workers need."

"Let me know when they're in place." He stood, but paused. "I also suspect the explosion in the power plant and the fire in the air plant were done by two separate groups."

Double the trouble. Wonderful. "Why?"

He spread his hands out. "A gut feeling. Before the rebellion, I've dealt with many scrubs that broke the laws, and they get comfortable with one method or one type of defiance and rarely move beyond that. A bomb and a fire are two different methods."

"But the results were the same."

He studied me a moment. "No they weren't. Think about it."

Jacy had given me plenty of information to mull over. The explosion had targeted the Transmission, which only a limited number of people knew about. It affected our travel through Outer Space and killed many. To me, the sabotage screamed a message that someone wasn't happy about our situation and wanted to be noticed. I wondered why they hadn't made any demands yet, or announced the reason they damaged our world. Perhaps the Travas engineered the explosion and didn't want the Committee to know they still had connections with…who? Uppers or scrubs? It didn't matter.

The fire had targeted Logan. Most Insiders knew he was a member of the Force of Sheep, but only a few were aware of his brilliance with the computer network. No one was killed, and I wondered about the timing of the fire. The attack on him felt more intelligent and part of a greater plan. Unfortunately, I couldn't fathom why anyone besides the Travas would desire the problems that would be caused by Logan's inability to access the network.

Even though I failed to solve anything, I understood the logic behind Jacy's two-group theory. I played with the cloth bag of microphones, turning it over and over, and listened to them clink together. Jacy had been quick to mention those three areas when I had asked him where he'd like eyes and ears. Two of them made sense. Scrubs filled Sector F1, and the waste-handling workers had the worst jobs. They would desire change. But maintenance didn't fit with the others.

Why not? Jacy had mentioned maintenance before. I searched my memory and remembered his comment about how maintenance and security were the only systems working.

Busy and productive had been his words. Which was opposite to the two things that led to trouble—bored and destructive.

I changed tactics. Chasing the reason those two systems kept working despite all the chaos, I found the answer. Anne-Jade and Hank. They led their people, and they weren't on the Committee but reported to them. And then I considered "their people." A mix of uppers and lowers. Riley and a bunch of his cousins helped Hank all the time. Anne-Jade had recruited from both as well.

What did all this mean? Perhaps one of the uppers working in maintenance wished to cause trouble. And one of Jacy's ducts crossed over Anne-Jade's office. He could suspect the uppers working in those two areas—that would be one group. The waste-handling scrubs and those living in Sector F1 could be the other.

But which one was which?

My restless agitation inflamed all my burns. Before I helped myself to a pain pill, I visited Logan again. He no longer needed a mask—a good sign. I said his name in a soft voice in case he slept.

"Done with all your visitors?" he asked.

"I only had two."

"Two more than me," he grumped.

"You had lots of visitors, but they were all quiet."

"Oh real funny. Tease the blind man." But a grin tugged at the corners of his mouth.

"Any better?"

"I've gone from seeing nothing but white to seeing large black spots on white. Doctor Lamont's pleased voice indicated this is a step in the right direction."

"Good. At least your hearing has improved. Did you hear what my visitors said?"

"Most of it. Except for Jacy's last bit. What jingled and what does he want you to do?"

I told him.

He whistled. "Cheeky of him. He'd be privy to more than he should. Are you going to plant them?"

"I promised to in exchange for information, but didn't agree to where I put them. It just doesn't feel right. We shouldn't have to spy on our own people."

"True, but I think bugging the Trava apartments and brig is a good idea," he said. "Before you plant them, ask Riley to get the frequencies from them. We might as well listen in, too."

"Should we tell Anne-Jade?"

"Not yet."

"Is that wise?"

"Probably not, but I'll blame the pain medicine and say it clouded my thoughts if she finds out."

"Good luck with that, I've seen her mad and it's not fun." Her new profession suited her. As soon as she had donned that stolen Pop Cop uniform, she'd fit right in. Then I remembered. "Logan, do you have any mics not being used?"

This time his smile broadened. "I have a few stashed in my room. Take what you need."

The itch drove me insane. Every centimeter of my arms and legs felt as if tiny invisible bugs crawled over my skin. Lamont claimed it was part of healing. If given the choice, I preferred the pain.

Riley visited, but he seemed distracted and never stayed long. I endured another fifty hours as a patient. Finally Lamont released me at hour sixty-two with so many instructions on how to care for my newly healed skin, I almost jumped back into bed. Almost.

"Are you staying with Riley?" Lamont asked as she packed a few meds and a salve into a bag for me.

"No." I carefully pulled on the shirt and pants she had brought me. The curtains had been closed; otherwise I would have flashed the ISF officers. Logan's vision had improved, but he still had another week in here at least.

"The barracks?" Surprise laced her voice.

"Don't worry about it."

She stopped and pierced me with her doctor stare. "You need to sleep in a clean environment for another week. No pipes or air shafts or—"

"I know."

Lamont touched my arm. No longer in doctor mode, she said, "Stay in my extra room. No strings attached."

"What if you find an intern?"

"At this point, it's highly unlikely, but if I do, then we'll wheel an extra bed into the sitting room. Once we move to the medical center on one of the new levels, we'll have plenty of space."

I considered. "Does no strings mean if I have a gaping wound, you won't try to stitch it up for me?"

"No. I'm still your doctor. It means I won't try to...mother you."

"Okay, I'll stay."

She nodded as if I just agreed to take my pills on time and pushed the curtains back.

"Doctor?"

Lamont tightened her grip on the fabric and wouldn't meet my gaze. "Yes?"

"Thanks."

I contacted Riley through my microphone. His terse reply indicated he was in the middle of something and would catch up with me later. Heading up to the main Control Room in Quad G4, I planned to fetch those mics from Logan's room.

The double metal doors failed to hiss open when I approached. Odd. A mechanical voice asked for identification.

I said my name and they parted just wide enough for a large ISF officer to poke his head out.

"What do you need?" he asked.

"For you to get out of my way," I said.

He didn't move. "Only authorized personnel are allowed in unless you have a reason for being here. I'm sure *you* understand the need to protect the critical equipment and personnel inside the Control Room."

Was that a slam? In an icy voice, I asked, "And *you're* the protection?"

"Yes. No one gets by me."

"Uh-huh. Tell Takia I'm here."

"She's at a Committee meeting."

Figures. "Fine. I'll come back."

As the door clanged shut, fury simmered in my blood. I understood the need for security, but to prevent *me* from entering was borderline paranoid. No, not borderline, but outright paranoid. I was the last person the Committee had to worry about.

Or was I? I alone knew about level seventeen, and there weren't many places I couldn't get to. Actually there was no place I couldn't get to. Scanning the hallway as I walked away from the Control Room, I found a perfect heating vent. And the beauty of the heating system was the vents were all close to the floor—easy to access.

I had left my tool belt in our storeroom so long ago it felt like a centiweek instead of a week and a half. In a pinch, the thin flat disks of Jacy's microphones worked as well. Most of the vents popped on and off, but the ones on the fourth level had screws as well. I wiggled into the shaft and pulled the vent back in place.

Warm air flowed around me as I swam toward the Control Room—pulling with my arms and pushing with my feet. It was harder to do with regular clothes and a pocket full of mics. Plus my skin burned with the added friction.

The familiar smell and hum reminded me of when I had slept in the heating ducts. Combine that with muscles that had been doing nothing but lie in a bed for the last hundred and thirty hours, and the trip turned into an endurance test.

Finally, I reached the Control Room. Through the slats of the vents, I saw legs of seated workers and rows of computers. Bypassing them, I found Logan's rooms. In no time, I popped open the vent and tumbled into his small living area. The captain had occupied this space when he was on duty but not needed. I imagined problems had been few and far between until Domotor recruited me.

Glad to have room to stretch, I glanced around. No surprise the place was a mess of computer parts, wires and gadgets. It took me longer than I hoped to find his stash of mics. Pocketing them so I was balanced, I debated about returning through the heating system. The bigger air ducts would be easier to navigate, but I would have to climb to the ceiling. My newly healed skin hadn't liked my recent activities and I doubted I had the strength to scale the wall.

Instead, I walked from Logan's rooms and through the control center. Most of the workers just nodded a greeting unperturbed. A few seemed surprised. The oversized ISF officer's glare could have burned a hole in sheet metal. But he didn't try to stop me.

I waved to him as the doors opened for me to leave. "Guess I should change my name to No One, since *no one* gets by you." It was not a mature thing to do, but I never claimed to be an adult. And I never could resist a challenge.

Tracking down Riley proved to be a challenge as well. I found him at his old workstation, banging on the keyboard in irritation. He monitored electrical usage and since the power plant produced all the electricity in Inside, his station was located in the office next to the plant's control room.

"Not now, Trella. I'm—"

"Busy. I know. I'm starting to understand how you felt when I attended back-to-back Committee meetings."

My comment earned me a glance and a brief smile.

"This is critical. The computer…" He slammed a fist on the keys. "Damn it. There goes another one."

"Has the network been compromised?" I peered over his shoulder.

"Sort of. Files are just disappearing as if they never existed."

"Is that possible? I thought—"

"Lousy son of a Trava!"

White light filled the monitor. Without thought, I covered Riley's eyes with my hands and dipped my head, blocking mine with my upper arm.

After a few seconds, Riley pulled my hands down. "It's okay. I think." A strange hitch cracked his voice.

I peeked. White still dominated the screen, but big black letters shone from the center. Squinting at them, I read: *All access denied by order of the Controllers.*

nine

I blinked a few times, but the words remained on the screen. *All access denied by order of the Controllers.* "Please tell me it's a joke," I said to Riley. "Or Logan's idea of a sick prank."

"Wish I could. But this is the third system that has disappeared."

A dizzy weakness swept over me. "Critical systems?"

"Not yet."

"Yet?"

"I can't stop it. Takia and a few others tried as well."

"Does the Committee know?"

"Yep. They've been getting kicked out, too. Mostly informational systems and not mechanical or life systems."

Good thing. "Can Logan bypass the Controllers?"

"I would think so. Why else would they have targeted him?" Riley swiveled around to face me. "We need to find who has hacked into the network."

"How?"

"I don't know. I need to talk to Logan and maybe Anne-

Jade. She might have a few ideas." He rested his elbows on his legs and put his forehead into his hands. "It wasn't supposed to be like this."

"What?"

"We reclaimed our freedom and we have all this room to spread out and grow. Yet some group is hijacking the network and blowing holes in our world. Why? Why are they destroying when they could be building levels and using their computer knowledge to help Logan?"

I knelt down, pulled his arms away and met his gaze. "Because of fear. Fear of the unknown. Fear of change. Fear of the Committee's decisions."

"Fear can be a big motivator." Riley tucked a loose strand of my hair behind my ear. "Did you think our new life would be like this when we were fighting the Pop Cops?"

"No. I thought we'd be lying on that big green carpet under that huge blue ceiling in Outside relaxing."

He laughed, but sobered. "We won't ever see the real Outside. We have to make the most of what we have Inside. We can't let fear ruin it."

"You've convinced me. Now you only need to convert nineteen thousand others," I joked.

But he wasn't amused. "No, Trella. You're not convinced. If you were, we wouldn't have half these problems."

An icy chill zipped through me. "So I'm to blame for half of these new problems?" I kept my voice even despite my desire to scream at him.

"No." He slid off the chair and knelt in front of me so we were eye to eye. "I didn't mean it that way. It's just you gave up too soon."

"Gave up what?"

"Power. You handed it over to the Committee without thinking about how the Insiders would react."

"The Committee members are Insiders. And they have more experience."

"This is all new to *everyone*."

I balled my hands into fists, tapping them against my thighs. "Yes, but they're older and more knowledgeable. All I know is the internal structure of Inside. Good for moving around unseen and planting mics, but little else." My knuckles knocked against my pants' pockets. The discs inside jingled.

"Planting mics for whom?" Riley asked in concern.

Glad for the change of topic, I told him about Jacy's request. I pulled a handful from my pocket. "Can you get the frequencies from them? Logan wants us to listen in too."

"Where are you sticking them?"

I listed the areas Jacy requested. "But I'm not bugging the Control Room or Anne-Jade's office. And I have extras to plant for us."

Riley sat back on his heels as if bracing for bad news. "Why?"

Explaining Jacy's theory of two groups, I speculated that one of the groups had to be connected to the Travas. "The Pop Cops had moles in the lower levels, spying on the scrubs. They could still be loyal. Perhaps by listening in, we can discover who sabotaged the power plant."

He considered. "I doubt the network hackers worked in the lower levels. With the degree of complexity it needed, I believe there could only be a few suspects with that ability. And the people I'm thinking of are all uppers."

His obvious sincerity didn't stop my instant ire over his statement. "Logan broke into the network and reached the highest levels without a port. He's not an upper so why are you assuming only they could sabotage the files?"

"That's a valid point. Why are you getting so defensive?"

"I'm..." I had been about to protest, but realized I had overreacted. "It was an automatic gut reaction. The Pop Cops had brainwashed us to believe the uppers were superior in every way."

"You know that's not true."

"Knowing and believing are sometimes hard to combine."

While Riley discussed the network problems with Logan in the infirmary, I showered then slept. When I woke, Riley had left a wipe board listing the frequencies of all the mics next to Sheepy.

I reported to the air plant at hour seventy to assist with the clean up and repairs. No surprise to see Hank there, barking orders and organizing workers. Pleased to see so many helpers, I waited until he finished instructing a team before claiming his attention.

"You're in high demand," I said to him with a smile. "Do you even have time to sleep?"

"Sleep? What's that? A new type of casserole?"

I would have laughed, but the craters under his eyes proved he and sleep were strangers.

"You have a big crew now. Can't you take some time off?" I asked.

My comment had the opposite effect. Hank's mood soured. "Yeah, lots of scrubs being forced to help."

"What do you mean?"

Hank shook his head in a slow way as if he couldn't believe I had to ask. "Where have you been, Trella?"

"In the infirmary, growing new skin."

"Oh. Sorry. I forgot." He ran a calloused hand over the stubble on his face. Dirt and ash stained his coveralls. "The Committee and ISF have commandeered hydroponics and the kitchen. If the scrubs want to eat, they have to work two hours for each meal."

I noted Hank's use of the word commandeered. Even

though the Committee was desperate for aid, they had mis-handled the situation. In theory Hank should be on their side. He bore all the stress of having to make repairs with a limited crew. They should have asked him how to recruit workers.

"Any work or just repair work?"

"Any. Laundry, recycling, kitchen duty, waste handling... All the jobs that need to be done. Repair work actually counts double—one hour for one meal—because of the critical time-sensitive nature of them."

"Did they set the same requirements for the uppers?"

"What do you think?"

Damn. "But to be fair, the uppers are still doing their jobs. It's just—"

"None of the scrubs has a clue what their jobs are. I know, and the scrubs on the Committee understand, but the rest of them believe all the uppers do is sit in front of a monitor and type every so often. No one is taking the time to explain it to the scrubs." He swept a hand out, indicating the flurry of activity around the air filter bays. "At least there has been one positive thing to all this. I've a few uppers who don't mind getting their hands dirty and they're putting in long hours right beside the scrubs."

The situation felt sickly familiar. "Who's keeping track of a person's hours?"

"The ISF or as we'd like to call them, the Mop Cops."

"Do I want to know what that means?"

"Things are a mess right now, and they're trying to mop it all under the bed and pretend it's not there."

Hank had a point, but I didn't believe the Committee and Anne-Jade had been blind to the mess, just overwhelmed.

I asked for my assignment and Hank sent me to the foreman. He eyed my skin-tight climbing suit and tool belt, handed me a stack of air filters, and listed the air ducts to install them in.

Glad to be productive, I set the filters inside the shafts. The magnets along their edges made the installation easy. The best part, I could plant the mics as I worked. The worst, my new skin protested the activity. And my muscles hadn't returned to full strength. I lasted four hours, which equaled two meals. I found the ISF officer and made sure to report my time.

Over the next twenty-five hours, I installed filters and mics in four-hour shifts. During the last four hours of the week, I planted one of Logan's mics near the air vent above Sector D1 where Jacy tended to hold meetings with his people. An unhappy murmur drifted through the shaft over the barracks.

I slid east over the bunk beds in the barracks in Sectors D and E. With the buzz of voices below, I doubted anyone even heard me. As I crossed into Sector F1, snatches of loud conversation reached me.

"…did you see the piles of laundry?"

"…the air still smells bad. It makes me nauseous."

"…idiots…we need a better Committee."

"…I saw Meline and Bo behind the dryers. They're finally together."

"…still haven't seen Kadar. I bet they tortured him and fed him to Chomper."

"…uppers have it sweet. We outnumber them…can bribe a few Mop Cops, get weapons…"

I froze, then backed up to the last vent, listening to the man.

"…I heard that Tech No is out of the picture and the computers are going crazy. Perfect time to attack. We'll force the uppers to be scrubs and live in their posh apartments. Then feed the Committee to Chomper."

The man's voice grew louder and I strained to see who spoke.

"What about that little scrub who started this whole mess?" a woman asked.

"I heard the Committee's upset with her. Maybe we could…" He lowered his voice.

I pressed my ear to the vent as he mentioned something about recruiting. My tool belt clanged on the metal, but I doubted it was loud enough to be heard amid the general noises below.

Without warning the cover popped free. In the seconds that followed, I caught a brief glimpse of a man then hands grabbed my shoulders and yanked. I fell onto the top bunk a meter below.

It was a soft landing, and I rolled over to my back. The man who had pulled me from the air shaft straddled my hips. He seized my wrists, pinning them to the mattress with his weight. I struggled to no avail—he outweighed me by forty kilograms. Finally, I stopped, but my heart kept up its fast tempo.

"Hello little bug," he said. His smile seemed more amused than sinister. "Do you know spying on others isn't playing nice?"

"Get off me."

"Not until you explain what you were doing up there."

"I was installing air filters so we can all breathe clean air. Let me go."

His round face was close to mine. He had light brown eyes with tiny flecks of yellow, a mustache, and short brown hair. Another man's head and shoulders appeared beside the bunk. He gripped the safety rail, probably standing on the bed below us. "Hey, Sloan, Wera said you wanted—" The scrub noticed me.

"Help me," I said.

"Uh…what's going on?" His voice almost squeaked.

"I caught me a blue-eyed bug," Sloan said. "She *claims* she was installing air filters and is even wearing an air scrub uniform. Can you check the duct for me?"

"Uh…sure." He climbed up to the vent and poked his head in. "It's too dark to see."

I huffed in frustration. "There's a flashlight in my tool belt."

Sloan shifted back so his friend could reach it. Now his weight rested on my upper thighs and wrists.

"There's a filter…don't know if it's new or not." His voice echoed slightly.

"What color is it?" I asked.

"White."

I met Sloan's gaze. "It's new, otherwise it'd be gray."

"Then why did you stop over my vent when I started talking about bribing the Mop Cops?"

"I had to fix my tool belt, it slipped. You heard it bang."

He studied me and I kept my innocent expression.

"Hey! Look what I found." The friend held the microphone I had planted above the vent. Damn! I had hoped he wouldn't look directly up. He rolled it around his palm. "I think it's a mic."

"Care to change your story?" Sloan asked.

"I didn't plant that. Someone else must have."

But Sloan didn't believe me and recognition flashed in his eyes. "You're *that* scrub. And as I recall, your little group of uppers used those mics to listen to the Pop Cops."

"So? It's probably left over from before. Let me go or I'll scream for help."

"Go ahead and yell, no one in here will care. Cain, check her belt for more of those devices."

A cold and clammy fear spread through my muscles as Cain fumbled through my tools. He found the bag with the remaining few mics.

Sloan's grip tightened as anger shone on his face. "Traitor." He let go of my left wrist and slapped me across the cheek.

Pain exploded as my head whipped to the side. Tears welled. Sloan shifted off my legs. And before I could react, he shoved me with his feet. I slammed into the rail opposite Cain. With another push from him, I went up and over, falling off the bunk.

The landing knocked the breath from me. I curled into a ball and gasped for air. My shoulder hurt. Sloan's loud voice carried over the general din, informing everyone in the barracks about me.

No time to recover. Legs surrounded me on both sides and I suffered two hard kicks to my back. When one clipped my head, I feared for my life. I rolled under the bunk. Too narrow to provide any protection, I kept rolling, hoping to outdistance the scrubs chasing me. Bunk, walkway, bunk, walkway, bunk, walkway.

Yells followed me. The floor vibrated with the rush of so many feet. As I drew closer to my goal—the far east wall, I noticed a line of scrubs waiting along that last walkway. Damn. I couldn't stop and I couldn't change my trajectory. Or could I?

Taking the biggest risk of my life, I paused under a bunk. The scrubs chasing me climbed over and through the bunk without checking underneath. I knew there would be stragglers, but I couldn't wait too long. Changing direction, I rolled the opposite way toward the west wall. Yells erupted.

But after I reached an empty walkway, I jumped to my feet and ran toward the south wall. It didn't take long for them to catch on, but I had a bit of a head start. I poured every bit of energy into my short legs. Feet pounded behind me. I yanked a screwdriver from my belt.

No heating vent was in sight so when I reached the wall, I dove under a bunk and rolled again until I found one. I popped the cover off and scrambled inside. A hand grabbed my ankle, tugging me back. I stabbed the screwdriver into the hand. It released me as its owner swore loudly.

The heating vent would not provide a safe haven yet. I

slid, squirmed, pushed and pulled. Voices shouted and echoed. Once I felt certain I'd escaped, I stopped. I had reached the connector shaft that led into waste handling in Sector H1.

Sweat-drenched and huffing for breath, I lay there. As my heart slowed and my muscles quit trembling, my other injuries demanded attention. My shoulder, wrists and hip ached. Sharp pain stabbed my back anytime I breathed in too deep. Overall I felt like I'd been shoved through a pipe too small for me. However, every stab of pain reminded me of my luck in getting out of there alive.

I didn't blame Sloan and the others for being angry. But I wondered if he had said those things about attacking the Committee because he heard me in the duct or if he had meant them. If I hadn't gotten away, would they have killed me? I rubbed my cheek. It still burned from the slap. Sloan had called me a traitor and by the fury in his gaze, I guessed that yes, they would have easily vented their anger on me.

Eventually, I continued into waste handling and exited the shaft at the first opening. I had no energy left to travel through the ducts. Leaning on the wall, I scanned the plant for scrubs from Sector F1. No one appeared to be searching for me. The regular plant workers milled about the equipment.

Emek spotted me, smiled and approached. "Haven't seen you down here in a long time. Did you come to check up on me?"

"Yes. I'm making sure you're fully recovered from the surgery."

He inspected my appearance. "How nice." Yet his tone implied he didn't believe me. "Rough trip?"

"Yep. Installing air filters is hard work, I better get back." I pushed off, but just then Rat raced into the plant like he'd been chased by an angry mob. Or it just could be my imagination.

"Emek! The scrubs in…" Rat slid to a halt when he spotted me talking to Emek. Two bright red splotches stained his cheeks and his short brown hair stuck up as if he had run his fingers through it.

"Don't keep us in suspense," Emek said.

"The scrubs in Sector F1 are rioting. They're fighting with the ISF officers, claiming the Mop Cops are spying on them."

Emek pierced me with his scowl. "Did you know about this?"

I suddenly wished to hide under the covers of my bed. "The riot? No."

Rat's gaze jumped from Emek to me and back. "I heard Trella's name."

Emek groaned. "Do the ISF officers need help?"

"Yes."

"Go get the rest of the crew, Rat. They're cleaning out the secondary sludge tanks." He hooked a thumb, pointing toward another room. Rat dashed off.

"Do you need an escort back to level three?" he asked.

"No thanks. I'm fine."

He raised one eyebrow. "Are you sure? You look—"

"I'm sure."

Rat returned with a dozen people on his heels. They sprinted out the door. Emek's gaze followed them.

"Go help the ISF officers," I said.

"No one's in the plant right now so you can use the small washroom in my office before you go."

"Thanks." I shooed him away.

Tucked into the northeast corner of the plant, Emek's neat office seemed very organized. When I considered the raw sewage that flowed into the plant, it made sense for him to have his own washroom. It always amazed me how the machinery and bacteria transformed crap into fertilizer and cleaned our water. Plus the process produced a special gas that was pumped into the power plant to be used as fuel.

I glanced at my reflection in the mirror. Dirt smudged my face. Clumps of dust clung to my hair. My bottom lip was swollen and bloody. And a bright red handprint covered my left cheek. I cleaned up as best as I could, braiding my hair. In my haste to escape I hadn't noticed how dirty the barrack's floors were.

Dirt and rust harmed our world. They weren't as bad as sabotage, but they could do plenty of damage.

I left Emek's office. The hum and whoosh of the machinery sounded louder without the workers. I debated between the risk of walking the hallways or the effort needed to climb into the air shaft. Scanning the ceiling for an accessible vent, I spotted one over the digester, which had a ladder up its side. Perfect.

Halfway up the ladder a clang sliced through the mechanical drone. I hoped it meant the riot had been quelled. Leaning to the side, I peered around the digester. One man, wearing an off-duty green jumper crouched next to the gas collector. No one else had returned.

I waited a few seconds to see if the others would arrive. The man kept glancing over his shoulder. Then he pushed something under the collector, straightened and hurried off.

Odd. Did he come back from the riot just to fix the machine? About to shrug it off, I paused, remembering all of Emek's men wore dark blue coveralls.

Sliding down the ladder, I rushed over to where the man had been. Nothing looked out of the ordinary, but I wouldn't know. I unhooked my tool belt before wiggling under the collector. Yet another unique view of my world. At least the space was cleaner than under the barracks. The irony wasn't lost on me.

I peered up. Hoses, wires, pipes and a strange device wedged between the pipes. The device had a short fat pipe about twenty centimeters in diameter and sealed on both ends. On top of the pipe were two glass containers of liquid. Between the containers was a metal box with a digital display. Each time the four numbers flashed they were one less.

Understanding hit me as hard as Sloan. I'd found a bomb.

ten

I gaped at the bomb's display, watching the countdown with a numb horror. Three thousand and fifteen, three thousand and fourteen… When it reached three thousand, I did the math and fumbled for my microphone, switched it on and turned it to Riley's frequency.

"Riley, find Bubba Boom and bring him to the waste-handling plant now. There's a bomb that's going to explode in forty-nine minutes!"

Staring at the bomb, I debated. Should I move it? Where? Every place in Inside had critical equipment. And people.

I slid out from under the collector. The adjoining Quads should be evacuated as well as the infirmary and care facility filled with children directly above the plant. I checked the clock. Five minutes past hour ninety-nine. The bomb was set to detonate at the very beginning of week 147,023.

There was enough time to evacuate, but I couldn't leave. What if Bubba Boom arrived while I was gone? Instead, I paced and worried and second-guessed myself, sending out a call to Riley every ten lengths.

When Emek and his crew arrived, I rushed over. Not caring that they seemed upset to see me. My words tumbled out in a flood as I explained about the bomb. Emek quickly grasped the situation and he organized three teams to evacuate the Quads and Sector H2. Since the explosion would be so close to flammable gases, Emek told them to go to Sector E1 and H3 if they had time. Rat volunteered to find Bubba Boom in case Riley slept through my calls. He still hadn't answered any of them.

I showed Emek the bomb. He barely fit under the collector. Another worry flared in my chest. Would Bubba Boom fit?

"Should we move it?" I asked.

"No."

"How much time left?"

"About thirty-five minutes." He pulled himself out and stood. "I wonder why the bomber left it with so much time. Could this be a distraction?"

"I hope not. Perhaps he wanted enough time to be far away. He did wait until everyone left the plant and probably figured no one would find it. Plus he didn't know I was here since I came through the heating ducts."

"After causing problems in Sector F1." Emek crossed his arms, clearly unhappy.

"If I hadn't been here, we wouldn't know about the bomb." I snapped at him.

"True. Although you being here to witness it seems too coincidental."

"But who would know I'd be here? I didn't know I'd be here. I was supposed to be in the air ducts, installing filters."

"Perhaps someone saw you come in and he placed it here at this time to throw suspicion on you."

"Why would I plant a bomb and then tell everyone about it? That makes no sense," I said, outraged by his suggestion.

"So starting a riot made sense?" Emek asked, but his stern expression had softened.

"Nothing has made any sense since the first explosion!" I paced again. "Where are Bubba Boom and Riley?"

"If Bubba Boom was in Sector F1, then we'll have to find someone else who's an expert with explosives."

"Why?"

"The ISF had to gas the entire Sector, putting everyone to sleep. They're looking for you so you can identify the trouble-makers before they wake."

Lovely. I'd go from traitor to snitch. Getting blown to bits didn't seem so bad.

When Bubba Boom finally arrived with both Riley and Rat right behind him, the tight band around my chest eased a bit. Emek showed Bubba Boom where the bomb had been planted.

"Why didn't you respond?" I asked Riley.

"I did." He touched my earlobe. "Your receiver is gone." Blood dotted his fingertips.

"Oh." I must have lost it in Sector F1.

Then Riley cupped my chin and turned my head. "Who slapped you?" Anger flared. "I'll kill him."

"Don't worry, I'll take care of him."

"What happened?"

"She started the riot in Sector F1," Emek said.

I shot Emek a sour look as Riley rounded on me, demanding an explanation.

"We have more pressing problems," I said, gesturing to Bubba Boom as he knelt next to the collector. "A bomb. Remember? I'll tell you later."

Since Bubba Boom was too large to fit underneath, he used

a mirror to read the display. The counter read nine hundred seconds, which meant we had fifteen minutes.

Riley insisted everyone else leave, including me.

"I need Trella to stay," Bubba Boom said. "She's the only one who fits underneath."

Riley closed his eyes for a moment. "Fine, then I'm staying too." He shooed Emek and Rat out the door.

As Bubba Boom inspected the bomb with his mirror, I pulled Riley aside and whispered, "There's no reason for you to stay."

"You've been trying to get yourself killed since Cog's death. At least this time I won't have to wait for news or wonder if you'll survive your injuries. If this thing blows, we'll both go."

"I'm not trying to kill—"

"I think I know how to disarm it," Bubba Boom said.

"Think or know?" Riley asked.

"It's a basic mixing design. The glass containers are filled with two stable chemicals. When the counter reaches zero, it removes the barrier between the liquids. They'll pour into the bigger pipe and mix together, creating a highly explosive combination. The counter will then create a spark and goodbye half of waste handling." Bubba Boom met my gaze. "As long as the bomber didn't get cute with the wiring, it should be easy to disarm." He handed me a pair of wire cutters.

Once again, I wriggled underneath the collector. Ten minutes left. My guts twisted and knotted with each second that disappeared.

"Pull the counter gently away from the pipes to expose the wires behind it," Bubba Boom instructed.

My hands shook, but I eased the box out from where it was nestled between the glass containers. I moved the mirror so he could see.

"Interesting."

"Good or bad?" Riley asked. I recognized the tight tension in his voice.

Bubba Boom ignored him. "Trella, I need to see where the second wire on the left ends."

All the wires were covered in black. I pointed to my guess. "This one?"

"No. One over. That's it," he said when I touched the next wire.

Running a finger along it, I followed it until the end and repositioned the mirror. I rubbed my sweaty palms on my uniform.

"Well?" Riley asked.

"I'm thinking."

"Eight minutes left," I said.

"Not helping. Riley, I need a wipe board to draw out the circuit."

"Emek's office," I called, remembering the neat stack of them on the corner of his desk.

The desire to scream at him to hurry lodged in my throat. His pounding feet faded then returned. Through the gap in the machinery, I watched Bubba Boom draw on the board. Riley peered over his shoulder. Dark gray sweat stains covered his gray shirt and strands of damp hair clung to the side of his face.

Bubba Boom instructed me to move the mirror a few more times. He discussed the circuits with Riley as they figured out how to cut off power. I clamped both hands over my lips to keep quiet. The need to urge them to move faster filled my mouth and pushed against my teeth.

Finally Bubba Boom told me to cut the wire I had traced for him. I placed the wire in the cutters and drew in a deep breath.

"Stop!" Riley yelled. He argued with Bubba Boom. "Trell,

you need to cut that wire and the one on the other end at the exact same time," he said.

I found the other wire. "This one?"

"Yes," Riley said.

"No," Bubba Boom said. "He's wrong. Cut only the wire I told you."

"No, don't. I'm right, Trell. He's going to get us all killed."

My fingers refused to work. Who to trust? Bubba Boom, the explosives expert or Riley, the electrical expert. Less than two minutes left. I listened to Bubba Boom and cut his wire.

The numbers stopped counting down, but they flashed red. The box started to beep.

"Break the glass on one of the containers," Bubba Boom yelled. The beeping increased its pace. "Now!"

"Avert your face," Riley shouted.

I rested the wire cutters on the glass with the clear liquid. Turning to the left, I covered my face with my arm and then struck the container as hard as I could. The glass shattered. Shards rained as the chemical splashed on my chest and stomach.

Yanking me out by my ankles, Riley picked me up, threw me over his shoulder and ran toward the shower in Emek's washroom. Shoved under the cold spray, I caught on and helped Riley tear off my chemical-soaked uniform. He ripped his shirt off and we scrubbed our skin, removing the last traces of the acidic substance before it could burn holes into our bodies.

I shivered and hugged my chest. "I've been wanting to take another shower with you," I said. "This wasn't quite how I imagined it."

His lips quirked into a brief smile, but it didn't reach his eyes. And it disappeared just as quick. Turning his back on me, he grabbed a couple of towels, handing me one without looking at me.

I dried off, then wrapped the towel around my body. Riley's shirt lay in a heap on the shower's floor tangled with my ruined uniform. They needed to be disposed of properly so I stuffed them into a hazardous waste bag.

"Trella, I…can't do this anymore," Riley said.

Cold dread stabbed me. "Do what?"

"Me and you…us." He gestured between us with both his hands.

Shivers raced across my skin as I realized Riley wasn't just angry at me for trusting Bubba Boom over him. This ran deeper.

"Trella, you have no qualms risking your life for Inside, sweeping in to save people, yet you don't want to stick around and deal with the cleanup. You'd rather let others come in and decide how to organize our world. It's frustrating and terrifying for me. I keep hoping the Queen of the Pipes will return and put a stop to all the Committee's nonsense. Only you can help them focus on the real issues." Riley dropped his hands. "Plus you don't need me. You've been pushing me away since we won control of Inside. Since you accepted my pendant."

"That's not true," I said.

"Really? How about when you discovered the fire in the air plant? I was right around the corner. You could have easily turned on your mic and called me to help, but you didn't."

"There wasn't any time," I tried, but knew by his cold expression he thought it was a lame excuse. "I called you when I found the bomb."

"You ordered me to fetch Bubba Boom. If he had his own receiver, I doubt you would have bothered and we would be having this conversation in the infirmary while you once again grow new skin. Every time I try to get close to you, Trella, you turn to someone else. You only need me to clean up after you. You don't trust me. I'm sorry, but I can no longer be with you. It's too…painful to watch you self destruct."

Did he believe I cut the wrong wire on purpose? Shocked over his announcement, I couldn't form a coherent response.

Riley left Emek's office and the waste-handling plant, ignoring Bubba Boom and Emek who waited for us.

Before they could question me about Riley or before I could fall apart, I asked, "What about the bomb?"

"Crisis averted." With a chagrined expression, Bubba Boom said, "Riley was right. Both wires should have been cut."

"I got that," I said, letting sarcasm edge my tone. "Do you know who built it? Who planted it?"

"I don't recognize it. I'll take it apart and see if I can learn anything."

"Did you get a good look at the man?" Emek asked me.

"Just his back and the side of his face. Short brown hair. No facial hair. Average build. Between 1,800 and 2,200 weeks old."

"That's a big help." Emek's turn to be sarcastic.

I bit back a nasty reply. "Now what?"

"The Committee's looking for you. And Anne-Jade wants to talk to you," Emek said. "I'm surprised she isn't here now."

The thought of being questioned by Anne-Jade and the Committee made diffusing a bomb seem like a pleasant task. Then I remembered the ISF wanted me to finger Sloan and his friends, which I was loath to do. Add that to Riley leaving me and all I craved was to curl up in a little ball in the quiet solitude of an air duct.

Rat fetched a set of clothes for me from the laundry. He had grabbed the green shirt and pants that the infirmary workers wore. I dressed in Emek's office. Anne-Jade's voice pierced my haze of exhaustion. She waited for me beyond the door.

Glad I had taken my tool belt with me, I strapped it on, placed Emek's chair on his desk and climbed into the air shaft. Once again I was avoiding confrontation. I didn't go far. Dropping down into the middle of the recycling plant, I scattered a group of workers. I apologized and headed straight for the stairs. Others had also clumped together and from the bits of alarmed conversation I caught, they discussed the evacuation and bomb.

News of the attempted bombing could either work in our favor or ignite panic. If everyone kept an eye out for unusual activity and strange devices, it might stop the bomber from trying again, which would be good. Panic would bring nothing but trouble and more destruction.

I reached the infirmary without encountering any ISF officers. Unfortunately Lamont took one look at my face and accosted me.

"Trella, what happened?"

"It'd be easier to tell you what didn't happen," I said.

She swept my hair from my face and, for a second, I wanted to press her hand against my cheek. "I need to put a suture in your earlobe." Inspecting my face, she frowned. "Who hit you?"

"Did you hear about the riot?"

"Of course. I needed to be ready in case there were injuries. Were you caught in the riot?" She tried to keep her tone professional, but alarmed concern dominated.

"Sort of. I…uh…started the riot."

Lamont paused. "You're serious."

"Yep."

"Do you want to talk about it?"

"No."

"All right. Come back to the exam room and I'll fix your ear."

As I followed her, I passed Logan's empty bed. "Where's Logan?"

She waited until I sat on the examining table before saying, "He's in protective custody."

"Arrested? The riot was *my* fault. Not his."

Her eyebrows rose, but she smoothed them. "He's not in the brig. With all the troubles, Anne-Jade felt he'd be better protected in a more secured location."

Lamont filled a needle and approached. I flinched away instinctively.

She stopped. "It's lidocaine. If you'd rather not—"

"Go ahead. Numb my earlobe please. I've had enough pain."

"Little pinch and I'm done."

Compared to the slap, falling to the floor, being doused with an acidic chemical and Riley breaking up with me, the pinch barely registered.

As she prepped the sutures, I tried to focus on something besides myself. "What about Logan's vision? Isn't he under your care?"

"I can't do anything more for him. It's just a matter of time."

"Will he regain his sight?"

"His progress is promising, but I can't guarantee it."

"Do you know where he is?"

"No." Lamont looped two stitches to close the tear in my lobe.

By this time, I could have fallen asleep on the exam table. Lamont trailed behind me as I headed toward my room. I stopped at the threshold. She hovered, rubbing her hands together. I had spent enough time with her to recognize her anxiety.

"No mothering. Remember?"

Although she didn't look happy about it, she nodded.

"I just need to sleep for about a hundred hours. If anyone comes looking for me, can you tell them I'm not here?" I asked.

"Even Riley?"

My hands shook. Doubtful he would be looking for me. "Yes."

"Okay, I'll keep everyone out."

"Thanks." I collapsed onto the bed, crawling under the

covers and muffling my sobs. Eventually, I would seek out Anne-Jade and tell her everything about the riot.

Too bad she found me first.

Startled from a deep sleep, I stared at Anne-Jade through puffy eyes. Confusion clouded my mind and her words failed to make sense. I rubbed my face in an effort to focus. My cheek throbbed.

"…hear me?" she asked. Grabbing my arm, she yanked me from the bed. "Do you even know how much trouble you're in?"

I swayed on my feet, but straightened real quick when I spotted her two lieutenants standing behind her. "I—"

"No excuses, Trella. I have orders from the Committee to arrest you."

Wide awake now, I said, "But—"

"You had your chance to explain down in waste handling, but you chose to run away."

"I—"

"Running is an act of a guilty person. I had no choice. Yuri, secure her." Anne-Jade stepped back to let Yuri closer.

With nowhere to go, I could only appreciate the speed in which Yuri slapped a handcuff onto my left wrist, spun me around and snapped the other cuff onto my right. With my arms pinned behind my back, my sore shoulder ached.

"Anne-Jade, the cuffs aren't necessary," I said.

"I disagree. Let's go."

She gripped my arm, propelling me forward as if I would resist. With a lieutenant in front of us and one following, they marched me from my room. Lamont hovered in the sitting area. Hour three shone on the clock.

"You could have at least waited to call Anne-Jade until I got more sleep," I grumped at Lamont.

"Give us some credit, Trell," Anne-Jade said. "No one called us. You weren't that hard to find."

True. If I had known she'd arrest me, I'd have slept in the ducts. She'd been to our storeroom and the small control room where we had hidden Domotor. That was back when I could trust her. I needed to find a new hiding place. The image of the bubble monster sitting on top of the Expanse filled my mind. No one would find me there.

Our little parade entered the lift and went up to level four. When the door swished open, a horrible possibility struck me. I resisted Anne-Jade's pull.

"What?" she asked.

"You're not taking me to the brig, are you?" I couldn't keep the panic from my voice. The thought of being there with Karla and Vinco, even in separate cells, caused me to sweat.

"It's up to you. The Committee has a number of questions for you. If you refuse to cooperate, they'll send you to the brig to think over your decision."

We bypassed Anne-Jade's office and walked down the main corridor to Quad G4. Inside didn't seem so big until I was handcuffed and stared at by every single person we passed in that hallway. The time it took us to reach the conference room off the main Control Room felt like hours.

My relief to be out of the public's eye disappeared in a heart-beat when I faced the nineteen Committee members. They sat around the long oval conference table. Domotor's wheelchair faced the front of the curved end. Scanning the faces, I did a quick calculation. Five members gave me encouraging nods, twelve people wore a variety of unhappy expressions from pissed off to mildly annoyed, one wouldn't meet my gaze—Riley's father—and one kept his face blank—Jacy.

Anne-Jade pushed me into the empty chair at the end opposite Domotor. I perched on the edge since my hands were still cuffed. She stood behind me as if I might try to escape or harm someone. I would have laughed, but I couldn't miss the heavy tension that filled the room. The lines of strain, dark circles and signs of fatigue were the common denominator from all eighteen members. Jacy wasn't giving anything away, and that scared me more than anything else.

Domotor took the lead. It was a good sign as he had been one of the encouraging nodders. The mics sat on top of the bag on the table. Computers were another new feature on the table. Each member had a small monitor in front of them.

Domotor started asking me questions about the riot.

I was honest to a point. Admitting I planted the mics, I got a little creative with why. "I hoped to overhear the saboteurs." Which was the truth.

"Why didn't you and Logan tell us about them?" Domotor asked.

I noted the lack of Anne-Jade's and Riley's names. They were both aware of the sabotage and failed to inform the Committee. Funny, I had been the one to argue to tell the Committee. "The evidence was circumstantial. We didn't want to accuse anyone without proof." Also true.

"Where did you plant these mics?" he asked.

"The air shafts about Sectors E1 and F1." I pointed my chin at the mics. "I planned to do more, but was…interrupted."

"She means caught," Anne-Jade said. "The scrubs in Sector F1 heard her in the air shaft."

"I haven't climbed through the ducts in weeks. I'm a little rusty," I said in my defense.

A few Committee members smiled at my play on words. I wouldn't go as far to say I was winning them over, but it was better than nothing.

Anne-Jade wanted to know who pulled me from the air shaft and incited the riot.

"I started the riot. It all happened so fast, I didn't get a good look at him." Just because I protected the bastard who slapped me, didn't mean I would forget him. Oh no. I owed him a visit. I just didn't need the scrubs to think I was an informer as well as a traitor.

The questions then turned to the bomb in waste handling. Those I answered with complete honesty. Jacy relaxed back in his chair. His gaze contemplative. Probably wondering why I hadn't told them about his request to plant his mics over sensitive areas. Right now they assumed Logan provided the mics. I'd like to say I had a grand scheme in mind, but at this point, I operated on pure instinct.

When all the questions had been answered, Anne-Jade escorted me out to the main Control Room so the Committee could discuss…I wasn't exactly sure what.

We waited near the door. "Thanks for not mentioning me," she said in a quiet voice. "I owe you one."

"Great. Take off these damn cuffs," I said.

"Not until the Committee gives me permission. Sorry."

I stared at her. "Come on, it's me. You *can't* be happy with how they're running our world."

"Do you really think I like being called the Mop Cops?" She balled her hands into fists. "I worked so hard to *not* be the Pop Cops and look what happened. Bombs, computer failure and someone tries to kill my brother. It's a mess and I wouldn't even know how to fix it at this point." Anne-Jade punched the wall. The Control Room workers glanced at us as the loud bang vibrated. "It's our fault, you know." She rubbed her knuckles absently. "The Force of Sheep gave them the power. It seemed like a good idea at the time."

It did. I mulled over what had happened. Why did the Committee fail? Then I remembered where they sat at the conference table. All the uppers sat along the left side, then Domotor, Jacy and the rest of the scrubs on the right side. Jacy had known the problem all along and so did I, but I'd hoped it would work itself out. That the uppers and scrubs would play nice together and forget all the Pop Cop propaganda.

But they remained divided. And all the current problems just drove them further apart, which didn't make sense. With saboteurs threatening all our lives, we should be banding together, not sitting on opposite sides.

"Trell, you have that look. What are you planning?"

"Maybe we should take the power back and start again," I said, thinking a new smaller Committee could have people like Hank who viewed our world as a whole and not two groups.

"Too late."

"Why?"

"Because someone else beat you to it."

eleven

"Are you saying the Committee no longer has the power to make decisions?" I asked Anne-Jade.

"Yep. They're just following orders. And so am I." A look of self-disgust creased her face.

Even though I feared the answer, I asked, "Who is issuing these orders?"

"The Controllers. They have hijacked the computer network, shutting down access to all but a few people. If the Committee doesn't do as they say, they'll erase the programs for running vital systems."

"But that would hurt them as well."

"They're in the network, Trell. They don't need air or water. Just electricity."

"Anne-Jade, you know better. Logan said they were an operating system. Nothing more."

"Well, Logan is blind and the Committee has him locked away somewhere. So as far as I'm concerned, I obey their orders." She rubbed her face.

A sudden surge of outrage consumed me. "I can find Logan for you."

"Not from the brig."

Surprised, I gaped at her. "I answered all their questions."

"And the Controllers will tell them what to do with you."

"I haven't been involved with the Committee in weeks. Why would the Controllers consider me a threat?"

"You planted those mics. You helped diffuse a bomb. Those aren't the actions of someone who is uninvolved. And the last thing they want is for *you* to be involved."

My head spun with all the information from Anne-Jade. It seemed like an elaborate joke and I expected Anne-Jade to laugh at me for falling for it. But her shoulders dropped and worry filled her eyes.

"Don't let the Committee know I told you all this," she said.

"I won't."

We were summoned back into the conference room. I noticed the vampire box on the table right away.

I endured a lecture about planting the mics on my own and how I should have come to the Committee right away. No surprise.

"Since you no longer wished to be a consultant to the Committee," Domotor said, "we insist on your cooperation to stay out of our affairs, and to keep out of the air shafts, the Gap and the Expanse. Failure to comply will result in your incarceration in the brig."

Big surprise. How did they plan to enforce… The vampire box. A cold wave of dread swelled in my chest as I remembered those tracers Anne-Jade had invented. She must have told the Committee about them.

Domotor met my gaze. His gray eyes held an impotent anger. "You're also confined to level three and are hereby designated as Doctor Lamont's intern."

Another shock. While I enjoyed helping patients, being forced to was another matter.

"Do you agree to all these conditions?" Domotor asked.

"What happens if I say no?"

"The brig."

I thought so. No choice. I agreed.

Anne-Jade removed the handcuffs and shoved my right arm into the vampire box. The pricks in my forearm just below my wrist stung more than usual. I wiped the blood on my shirt.

"A tracer has been implanted into your arm," Domotor said. "If you stray from level three for any reason, we will be informed. Should you be tempted to remove the tracer, we will also be alerted. The device monitors temperature."

Damn. He had read my mind. With access to the medical supplies, removing the device would have been easy. However, body temperature was approximately thirty-seven degrees centigrade while Inside's ambient temperature was kept at twenty-two degrees centigrade.

The meeting ended and the Committee members either milled about or filed out. Returning to my seat, I had to wait for Anne-Jade to escort me to level three. She discussed the lockdown with Takia. No one spoke to me. Jacy remained in his seat, studying me. I ignored him. Let him wonder.

After most of the others had left, Jacob Ashon approached me. By the uncomfortable stiff-armed way he stood, combined with his queasy expression, I knew this wouldn't be pleasant.

"Trella, I...uh. I'm sorry things didn't work out with Riley." He cleared his throat, then his words rushed out. "It's best if you make a clean break and forget about him." True. And that's when the full realization of no longer being with Riley stabbed me deep into my heart. Unable to utter a sound, I reached behind my neck and unfastened the clasp. Hooking it back together, I handed the pendant to Jacob.

"I didn't mean...you don't need..."

"Give it to him…please."

Jacob's fingers closed around it. The edges of my vision blurred as black and white spots danced in front of my eyes. I closed them and inhaled deep, calming breaths, concentrating on that simple act only.

When I opened my eyes, Jacob was gone along with Jacy. Anne-Jade tapped my shoulder, gesturing me to follow her. I did.

The trip back to the infirmary occurred without incident. Lamont spotted me, but she continued to wrap bandages around a patient's hand.

"Do you want to inform the doctor about your assignment or should I?" Anne-Jade asked.

"Feel free." I kept walking.

"Where are you going?"

Annoyance spiked. "To my room. Do I need to file a request with the Committee first?"

"In triplicate."

I turned and made a rude gesture. She laughed. I couldn't help but grin. It lasted a microsecond. All memory of it was erased when I entered my room.

Sheepy was gone.

Sitting on the edge of my bed, I stared at the cuts from the vampire box. I ran my finger along the skin, but couldn't feel the tracer buried inside. If I hadn't been there, I would never have believed if someone told me that helping diffuse a bomb would send Riley and Sheepy away.

I lay in bed, curled under the sheet. Action was required. Plans needed to be made. A tracer to trick. I couldn't let the Controllers or the Committee ruin what I had worked so hard for. What Cogon had died for. I hadn't wanted the responsibility. No. If I was being honest, I had been…or rather was still terrified of the responsibility. And despite what Anne-Jade had said, it wasn't too late.

But for now, I needed to grieve for the loss of the world I had imagined with the Committee in charge. For the loss of Riley. And Sheepy.

Lamont woke me. "An ISF officer is here to check on you."

"Why?" I blinked. Her presence had triggered the daylights.

"You haven't moved in eighteen hours."

An impressive amount of sulking time.

Standing behind Lamont, an ISF officer nodded to me. "Just making sure you're okay," he said.

"Yeah right. You're more worried I've found a way to fool the tracer," I said.

He dropped the pretense. "AJ warned us not to underestimate you."

"AJ?"

"Anne-Jade."

"Cute. Yet you still waited eighteen hours."

"The doctor's word was sufficient until she also became alarmed as well."

"Guess I was tired." I stretched my stiff muscles—the downside of being inactive for so long. However, my shoulder no longer ached, the swelling in my cheek had gone down and scabs covered the two cuts—the upside.

"You should shower and eat. When you're done, I need help with a couple patients," Lamont said. She shooed the ISF officer out as she left.

Ah, the glamorous life of an intern. I pushed the covers back and padded through the sitting area to the kitchen. Rebel that I was, I ate first then showered. Sad and pathetic.

The water cleared my mind. I considered how to bypass the tracer as I helped Lamont with routine tasks. Rolling clean bandages, I figured I needed to find a way to keep it at a constant thirty-seven degrees and to move it around, but only on level three.

Inserting it into another person would work. The next time Lamont has surgery, I could slip it in. Except as soon as the patient left this level, the ISF would pounce on the poor un- suspecting person. Avoiding the brig was imperative.

I could use the newborn warmer, parking it in my room when I wanted to explore. But if it didn't eventually move, the ISF would be suspicious. Absently, I reached to play with my pendant only to encounter smooth skin. The jolt of pain reminded me of when Vinco's knife had found a sensitive spot.

I wrenched my thoughts back to my current problem. The warmer could work if I moved it around the infirmary, wheeled it to the cafeteria and other areas on level three. Searching the patient area, exam room and surgery, I couldn't find it.

"Looking for something?" Lamont asked when I exited the surgery.

"The newborn warmer."

She gave me a rueful smile. "Confiscated by the ISF."

Damn. "What if we need it?"

"They'll bring it back only when I have a newborn. We do have a few pregnant patients, but they're not due for weeks."

So much for that idea. Again I grabbed for the pendant without thinking.

Lamont noticed the gesture. "Did you lose your necklace in the riot?"

"No. I lost it diffusing the bomb."

"Bomb?" Her voice squeaked. "The one found in the waste- handling plant? You were there? But I thought the riot…"

"I had a busy week."

She stared at me for a few seconds. "I can only imagine." She gestured to my neck. "Is Riley upset that you lost it? Is that why he hasn't come around?"

Normally, I would have snapped at her, telling her to mind her own business. But I couldn't produce the energy. Instead I had a moment of weakness and told her about the choice I had made when disarming the bomb.

She drummed her fingers on the exam table. "I think I would have done the same thing. This Bubba Boom is an expert in explosives after all."

"Yeah, but it was a wiring problem. That's Riley's area of expertise." I rubbed the spot where the tracer had been inserted. "Riley thinks I have a death wish. He may be right." I stared at the floor. "Ever since Cogon floated away...I keep thinking it should have been me. He wouldn't have been afraid to guide us through all these changes. He would have united the uppers and lowers by now. Sabotage and riots would never have happened if Cog was here."

"And what would killing yourself accomplish?" Lamont asked. When I didn't answer, she continued. "It won't bring him back. Cogon is gone. And from a purely medical point of view, you don't have a death wish. If you did, you wouldn't have fought for every single breath in those first critical hours after the fire. Your skin wouldn't have healed as fast as it did."

Even though I hated to admit it, she had a point. And damn it. I felt a little better. Looking up, I was going to thank her, but she had her doctor's purse on her lips as if reviewing a diagnosis in her mind.

"Who also has Cogon's way with people?" she asked.

"Hank from maintenance. Emek's people love him. And Riley. He's been able to work with both uppers and scrubs."

"Then you need—"

I waved my arm. "I can't do anything. Remember? I'm stuck here."

"Let's pretend you don't have the tracer. What would you do first?"

"I'd find Logan, rescue him and set him up at a computer terminal to bypass the Controllers."

"What if he can't see?"

"Then I'd find someone who knows enough about computers to sit next to him and be his eyes."

"Riley?"

"No. He's good, but not Logan good." I considered.

"Your father was Logan good." Pride filled her voice.

I waited for the pain and anger to flair inside me, but only sadness touched. However, his name reminded me of another. "Domotor would be perfect."

"Would he agree to help?"

I remembered his anger. He couldn't be content taking orders from the Controllers. "Yes."

"Then it's an excellent plan. Let's get started." Lamont headed for the surgery, pushing through the double doors.

Curious, I followed her. "But—"

She handed me two syringes. "I think a local anesthetic should be enough. Grab the lidocaine and alcohol wipes." Then she collected a few other supplies—sutures, scalpel and long curved tweezers.

Understanding hit me hard; I grabbed the operating table to steady myself. "You realize the risk you're taking?"

"There's no risk to me. You're the one who will be in danger of being thrown into the brig. And you'll still need to work here so you're visible to others. Otherwise, they'll get suspicious."

"You'll have to stay on level three."

She shrugged it off. "I'm always here anyway."

The final concern was mine alone. Could I trust her? No. But she offered the only possible solution. If I wanted to make Cogon…and Riley proud of me, I couldn't give up.

With the two of us working together, it didn't take long to remove the tracer from my arm and implant it in Lamont's.

The device had only been exposed to the ambient air for a second.

Just to be sure, I stayed and worked in the infirmary for the next six hours. Then we went to the cafeteria in Quad G3 with the intent to eat and then stock up on food for our kitchen.

Riley's brother Blake worked behind the counter, serving soup. His resemblance to Riley sent a flash of pain across my heart.

I wondered what he was doing up here. "New job?" I asked him, trying to sound casual.

"Same job, new location." He shrugged then tilted his head to the people sitting at the tables. "Change of scenery. Change is good. Right?"

"Uh…yeah." I wondered what he was implying. Was he glad Riley and I were no longer together? Hard to tell. I didn't know Blake that well.

After our excursion to the cafeteria I took a brief nap, then changed into my skin-tight uniform. As long as Lamont stayed in our suite or in the infirmary the ISF shouldn't suspect anything.

I climbed into the air duct, grinning.

The Queen of the Pipes has returned.

There weren't many hiding places in Inside. I doubted the Committee knew the locations, but I didn't want to leave anything to chance so I ruled them out right away. They had probably taken him to an empty apartment. Since I had been confined to level three, I suspected he would be on level four. The Travas filled Sector D4, so that meant I had to search Sectors E4 and F4. Doable in the time I had.

I tried not to think about apartment number three-six-nine-five in Sector E4 as I carefully traveled through the air shafts and peered into rooms. At least there weren't any air filters to bypass.

After the rebellion we discovered that scrubbing air shafts and water pipes had been one of the jobs created purely for busy work. With a simple programming adjustment, the trolls cleaned the shafts and pipes without a scrub minder. Which worked well for me now.

When I reached Riley's apartment, I paused for only a moment. The empty living area and bedroom matched the hollow feeling in my heart. I didn't see Sheepy and wondered where he was. Moving on, I finished searching Sector E4 and crossed into F4.

I found Logan in a small room in the far northeast corner of Sector F. Sprawled on the couch, his arm covered his eyes. His space also had a bed, refrigerator and a tiny washroom. The computer station had a screen, but no keyboard or box.

No guards, but I checked the hallway to make sure. A complex series of locks had been installed on his door. And when I returned to the air vent, I noticed the thick bolts securing it. What I worried most about were microphones and other sensors.

The air shaft was free of any sensors, and knowing Logan, any sensors within his reach would be dismantled by now.

So taking a chance, I said his name.

He sat up and squinted. "Trella?"

"Up here," I said.

He jumped to his feet and whooped. "I knew you'd find me!" No microphones then. "Come down! It's safe."

"I can't." I explained about the bolts. "Next time I'll bring my diamond wire."

"Oh." He dropped back onto the couch. "I can't escape anyway."

"Did they inject you with a tracer?"

"Yep. Nothing like having your own technology bite you in the ass. If you see Anne-Jade can you punch her in the face for me?"

"She didn't lock you in there." I explained about the Controllers.

"The Travas have a link into the network," he said right away.

"That's what I thought. How's your eyesight?"

"Better, I can see about a meter so I can read the monitor if I had a working computer."

"Could you fix the damage to the network?"

"Of course. First thing I did when we gained control of the computer systems was to secure backup in case something like this happened."

I considered his problem. "You can't leave, but I can bring you what you need. Will you be able to hide it when your keepers come to check on you?"

"I should with proper warning." He surged to his feet, excited. "I have a sweet little sensor you can install in the ceiling of the hallway, and I'll need—"

"Slow down, Logan. Remember it's me. Start with the most important and we'll work from there."

He listed several items and I determined how many trips I would need.

"Zippy can pull the skid I rigged," Logan said in excitement. "Then you can bring more."

"Where's Zippy?" I hadn't seen the little cleaning troll since the rebellion.

"Under the bed in my room."

Ugh. Too close to the Committee for my comfort, but almost all the gadgets he needed could be found there, including the computer.

"Okay, Logan. I'll be back with your supplies, but it may be a while." I used more time to locate Logan than planned so I hurried back through the shafts as fast as I could without making noise, which wasn't very fast at all.

At least I arrived in my room without encountering trouble. It was hour thirty-five. I changed my clothes and joined Lamont in the exam room. She helped an elderly man down from the table.

"I'm not sure when your ears will stop ringing, Ben," she said. "You were close to the blast and are lucky you didn't lose your hearing." Lamont handed him a bottle of small white pills. "Try these, one pill every ten hours. They might help."

He thanked her and shuffled through the patient room.

She watched him go then said, "When we move to a bigger place, I'd like a separate waiting room for walk-ins."

"You should be the one to design it," I said. "Do you know how to use the blueprint program?"

"No."

"Here, I'll show you." I went into her office and sat at the computer. The blueprint program was the only one I used. After the rebellion, Hank had me draw out the layout of the Gap between levels.

"You might have trouble," she said. "Something's wrong with the network. I can't access patient records right now."

I wondered why the Controllers would block them. No idea, but the program I sought popped up without hesitation, and I demonstrated to Lamont how easy it was to draw lines and type in labels.

I surrendered the chair to her. She caught on pretty quick. "This is fun."

Her comment reminded me of my trip through the shafts. I asked her if she had any problems while I was gone.

"Not really," she said.

"That's not an answer."

"One man stopped by to talk to you, but I said you were asleep and he said he'd come back later."

"ISF?"

"No. Big guy with freckles. Kind of cute."

Bubba Boom. I wondered why he came by.

"No trouble from him," she said. "But what if the ISF comes by and you're not here?"

That could be a problem.

"I need a way to contact you," Lamont said.

I touched my earlobe, but remembered I'd lost my receiver in the riot, and the microphone on my uniform had been thrown into a hazardous waste bag. "I'll see what I can find."

"Did you locate Logan?"

"Not yet." I lied, but thought the less she knew the better.

I spent the rest of week 147,023 fetching supplies for Logan. Sneaking into his room next to the main Control Room caused my pulse to race. And even though I had been here two times before, I still sweated.

This last trip was for me. I had planted all those mics and they remained in position. Why not listen in? Logan had a device I could use. I also picked up a set of communication buttons and receivers for me and Lamont. Logan would program them so no one could overhear our conversations.

Back in the duct, I used Zippy to haul the supplies. Round with cleaning brushes and a vacuum, he rolled along, pulling the skid. The noise hadn't bothered anyone so far. I'd encountered a few other cleaning trolls in the air ducts.

I reached Logan's without incident and opened the vent. The diamond wire had sawed through the bolts and we had rigged them to appear as if they still secured the vent. I dropped the supplies I brought to him, then swung down. He had managed to disguise most of his new toys. I hoped his keepers wouldn't check under his bed or under the couch.

"Who brings your food? ISF?" I asked him.

"No. The same two guys. Uppers, but not part of the ISF and I would know. Anne-Jade had me check into the background for all her officers to make sure they were trustworthy." He chuckled. "They're armed with stunners, but they have no idea their weapons won't work in here."

"Any luck?" I pointed to his computer. It looked the same, but according to Logan, he had installed all the important components behind the screen and the keyboard could be hidden before all the locks on the door were opened.

"No. They have built a wall around the important systems. I'm trying to find a way to slip inside without anyone noticing, but it's been difficult." He rummaged in the cushions of the couch, pulling out a long glass tube. It resembled a light bulb. He handed it to me. "A Trava computer in Sector D4 has to be connected to the network. Use that to find which one."

"How?"

"Get as close as possible and if the tube glows green, you've found it. Then…" He knelt next to his bed and reached under the mattress. Logan tossed me a small box. "Insert that into Zippy's undercarriage and he should be able to knock out that computer."

"Like when I used him to disable all the weapons in the Control Room?"

"Yep." He straightened and wiped the dust from his pants.

"Why not use a stronger pulse and hit all the computers in Sector D4 at once?"

"It's too risky over a large area."

"But after the computer's zapped, you'll be able to take back control?"

"Don't see why not."

Between sleeping, working for Lamont and searching Sector D4, I didn't have much time for listening to the mics or for implementing the other part of my plan—talking to Hank and Emek. I tried to think of a better way to organize my time.

Logan picked up the button mic I had brought and fiddled with it. He snapped it onto my uniform. "All you have to do is turn it once to the right and it'll go to this receiver only."

Dropping a small earring into my palm, he grabbed the other mic, adjusted it and gave it to me. I placed the set into my tool belt.

When he handed me the other receiver, I went into the washroom. The cut on my earlobe had healed, but a tiny hole remained. It wasn't big enough, but it was better than nothing. I pushed the receiver through my earlobe in one quick motion. It stung and I guess I could have waited until I returned to the infirmary and used lidocaine. Oh well. Waiting had never been one of my best traits. And looking at my reflection in the mirror, keeping my hair neat seemed to be another impossible task.

I contemplated cutting my hair as I untangled my messy braid. The knots in my hair resisted my fingers and I couldn't find a comb. When I peeked out to ask Logan, he sat cross-legged in the middle of the room with one of his gadgets nestled in his lap. I noticed how he squinted and brought objects up close to his eyes.

The computer beeped. He hopped up and sprinted to the monitor. "Someone's coming," he said.

My cue to leave. "See you later." I crossed the room and climbed up the wall to the open shaft.

"Trella, wait."

"Why?"

"It's not my keepers. Look."

I glanced over and almost lost my grip. On the screen was a moving picture of Anne-Jade and Riley walking down the hallway. They kept peering back over their shoulders as if worried someone followed them.

"Wow, Logan, that's amazing! How did—"

"They're here to rescue me," Logan said. He grinned, but an instant later alarm replaced his excitement. "If they mess with the locks, we're done. They're wired to set off an alarm if not opened in the proper order. You have to stop them!"

twelve

"What's the proper order?" I asked.

"No time and it doesn't matter." He waved his arm.

The tracer. How could I forget?

"Hurry," he said.

I pulled myself into the air shaft and crawled the short distance to the hallway in front of Logan's locked door. Anne-Jade's hushed voice drifted up. Without hesitation, I popped the vent open and dropped down almost on top of them.

They both jumped back in surprise. Anne-Jade pulled her stunner. I braced for the sizzle slap of the weapon, but she lowered it.

"Trella?" Her shocked expression didn't last long. "What are you doing here?" she demanded. "How—"

I held up a hand. "If you try to open Logan's door, you'll set off an alarm."

"How—"

"He can't be rescued anyway. He has a tracer."

"Really?" Anne-Jade didn't sound convinced. "Yet you managed to circumvent the tracer in your arm."

I noticed she didn't put her weapon away. Although I felt Riley's gaze burning on my skin, I resisted glancing at him. "What I did won't work for him."

"I already anticipated the tracer. We're planning to cut it out," she said.

"And alert the Controllers?"

"We have a safe place to hide him," Riley said.

Now I met his gaze. Even though my insides twisted— I missed him more than I realized—I kept my voice even. "You'll still alert the Controllers, who will be on guard. Right now they think Logan isn't a threat."

"Think?" Anne-Jade asked.

"He's been busy."

"I'm assuming so have you," she said.

"I'm not at liberty to say."

"Why not?"

I glanced at her weapon. "You still haven't put that stunner away. And I don't know if you're going to arrest me or not."

The tension in the hallway pressed against my skin.

"They've been using Logan to force my cooperation," she said. "If I had him somewhere safe—"

Logan's door swung open. He poked his head out. "Get in here before someone sees you."

We hurried inside and he closed the door. Wires hung down from below the knob. Anne-Jade rushed to her brother, wrapping him in a hug. Not wanting to intrude on the siblings, I inspected the wiring by the door.

"Interested in electrical circuits now?" Riley asked. The tone in his voice bordered on sarcasm, but could be teasing.

Looking at him was too painful so I traced the loops of wires instead. "Yes. I thought I'd try electrocution next. Since a bomb, a fire, Vinco's knife and a brief encounter with Outer Space didn't kill me."

"There's not enough juice in those. You'll just get a nasty shock. The best place to get electrocuted would be in the power plant."

"Thanks for the tip."

He huffed. "Trella, what are you doing here?"

"Visiting Logan."

Riley stepped in front of me. "You know that's not what I meant. Why are you helping him? You didn't care what the Committee was doing before. Why now?"

I stared at his chest. "I always cared."

"You didn't act like you did. You let—"

"Everyone down. I know. It's because I cared too much."

"That doesn't make sense."

Now I met his gaze. "I didn't want to screw it up. It was terrifying to have the entire population of Inside counting on *me* to make our world a perfect place. It was too much responsibility. Too much to expect me to suddenly know exactly how to combine a society that has been divided and brainwashed for so long."

"What changed?" He whispered the question.

"They *ordered* me to stay away."

He laughed.

I punched him in the stomach. "I'm serious."

"I know, but you have to admit, it's funny."

"What's funny?" Logan asked.

Riley gestured to him and Anne-Jade. "This. Us. Trying to find a way to bypass the Controllers… Again."

"That's easy," Logan said. "Trella's gonna find the active computer in the Trava Sector and disable it."

Unease rolled through me as I remembered when Anne-Jade had commented that the Pop Cops' downfall had been due to overconfidence. Lamont had said the same thing about my father. His confidence had made him cocky and sloppy, leading the Pop Cops right to him.

"And then what?" Anne-Jade asked.

"We regain control of the network and start over with a new Committee," Logan said.

"What about the saboteurs?" I asked.

"We're close to finding them, and there haven't been any more attempts," Anne-Jade said.

"Was it the stink bombers? Ivie and Kadar?" I asked.

"No. They taught a bunch of maintenance scrubs how to build bombs. The suspects sleep in Sector F1. I just need to narrow it down." She peered at me as if I were one of the bombers.

Logan shooed us out so he could repair the locks before his keepers came to check on him. "They usually come every twenty hours, and the new week starts in thirty minutes."

Anne-Jade and Riley headed back through the corridors, while I climbed into the air shafts.

Before Riley left, he shot me a significant look. I mulled over what he tried to communicate to me as I crawled through the ducts. Did he want to talk about us? Or just about the situation? At least he knew I had realized my fears and acknowledged my mistakes.

I returned to the infirmary to make an appearance. My mind remained on the task of finding the live computer in the Trava Sector while I disinfected the examination table.

"…see you. Trella, are you listening?" Lamont asked from the doorway.

"Sorry. What did you say?"

"That Bubba Boom is here. He's waiting out in the patient area."

I peeked past Lamont. No missing the big uncomfortable man who tried to stay out of everyone's way, but ended up in the wrong place each time.

Curious, I joined him. "You wanted to talk to me?"

Relief flooded his features and he smiled. His pleasure at seeing me was a nice change of pace. Plus he reminded me of Cogon.

"Is there somewhere private we can go?" he asked.

"Sure. Come on back." I led him through the exam room and to our sitting area.

He settled on the couch and I perched on the edge of the chair.

"What's going on?" I asked.

"I examined that bomb." Bubba Boom shifted with unease, focusing on his hands in his lap. "I think I know who built it."

"Why aren't you telling Anne-Jade?"

"It's complicated." He laced and unlaced his fingers together.

"One of your colleagues?" I guessed.

He glanced up. "Yeah. And…it's hard. He works with me sometimes. But…I don't want him to damage any more systems."

I waited, letting him work through the logic.

Taking a deep breath, he said, "It's Sloan. He's getting everyone in Sector F1 riled up and has been talking about forming a resistance and storming the upper levels."

I'd never forget that name, but it seemed a little too convenient. "Sector F1 was rioting at the time."

"Exactly. They planned it as a distraction."

Which made sense, yet they didn't know I would be in the ducts. "But I started the riot."

"Yes, but how did Sloan know you were there?" he asked.

"He heard me in the shaft."

"You? The Queen of the Pipes?"

"My tool belt banged the metal. I'm out of practice."

Bubba Boom shook his head. His shaggy hair puffed out

with the motion. It reminded me of when Cog had decided to grow his hair as long as mine—what a mess.

"If you had spent any time in the barracks, you would know it's too noisy in there to hear anything, let alone a bump in the air duct. Sloan knew you were coming."

"How?" I still wasn't convinced.

"Jacy rigged the bag of mics he gave you with a little sensor, tipping Sloan off."

The bag I no longer had. "Why would Jacy set me up? I was supposed to be helping him."

He leaned forward. "Supposed to be? There you go. Jacy doesn't take kindly to people who lie to him or double-cross him. He makes the Pop Cops seem nice."

I scoffed. "You're exaggerating. Jacy helped with the rebellion."

"Of course. All so he can get more power." His cheeks flushed, causing his freckles to almost disappear.

"No. He doesn't even have enough people to maintain his information network."

"Because they're all afraid." He sagged back against the cushions. "Why would I lie? I'm gonna tell all this to Anne-Jade."

"Good." Confusion tugged. I thought I could trust Jacy.

"You need to know Jacy isn't your friend. He hoped the angry mob in Sector F1 would send you to Chomper."

An icy finger of fear touched the back of my neck. I rubbed my cheek, remembering the fury in Sloan's gaze.

Bubba Boom scooted closer to me. "Be very careful." He rested his warm hand on my knee. "I know you're confined to level three, but you shouldn't stray from the infirmary. When I save someone's life, I expect them to stay safe."

"Which time? Helping to diffuse the bomb or rescuing me from the fire?"

He laughed. "Maybe I'm expecting too much from you."

I swatted him on the arm. "Well, thanks for both."

"Anytime. In fact, I think I should visit more often just in case you need saving again." His hand inched up my thigh.

Oh no. Just when I thought I might have found a friend who wasn't incarcerated or the head of ISF, I thought wrong. And I really didn't need another person keeping track of me. I moved my leg away. "Don't worry. As you said, if I stay close to the infirmary I should be fine."

His good humor died. "I thought you and Riley…"

News traveled fast. "We did, but I'm not ready to get involved in another…friendship. Besides, with all the troubles and sabotages, it's best if I just concentrate on helping Doctor Lamont for now."

He studied me as if I was a complicated explosive device, seeking weaknesses. I resisted the urge to squirm. Instead, I stood and said, "Make sure you tell Anne-Jade about Sloan and Jacy." I held my breath. Would he take the hint?

Bubba Boom ambled to his feet and grinned. "Okay. I'm willing to wait until everything is mended. I'm sure all these troubles will soon settle down." He gave me a mock salute and left.

I collapsed back into my chair. My mind swirled. Between his accusations about Jacy and advances, I had no idea what to think. The thought of being close to another man… No. I couldn't even contemplate it without my skin crawling.

Why could I run into a burning room, climb up sheer walls, diffuse a bomb and defy the Committee without hesitation, yet be terrified to admit my feelings for Riley? My own fear had really screwed up not only my life, but Inside's potential for peace and harmony. I hoped it wasn't too late for all of us.

The glass tube didn't glow during my first sweep through the Trava Sector. I had covered about half of the Sector before I needed to return to the infirmary for my shift. Lamont had created a schedule in keeping with the intern ruse. It worked, except I spent my free time crawling through air and heating vents searching for an active computer.

And as the hours passed, I felt more pressure to accomplish something. Anything besides how to determine if a wound was infected or not. Halfway through week 147,024, I completed the fourth and final sweep through the Trava Sector. Still no results. However, by spending so much time in the ducts above the Travas, I learned a few things.

One—they were dangerously bored. Two men had pulled apart a heap of computers to build a couple of hand-held devices. They could be weapons or a way to communicate, I had no idea. But my glass tube didn't glow so it wasn't a link to the Controllers.

Two—they planned to escape and release their comrades in the brig.

Three—they wanted to regain control of Inside and protect something or somebody. Which didn't make sense to me. They already had control. So why didn't the so-called Controllers tell the Committee to release all of the Travas?

My agitation grew and the tension in Inside filled every space. Fights broke out and a number of riots erupted. Anne-Jade's ISF officers were swamped and many were injured.

When she stopped by the infirmary to check on Yuri, I pulled her aside and informed her about the Travas' plans.

"They can have it," she snapped. "Nothing is getting done besides the repairs to the air plant, and everyone has reverted to acting like the Pop Cops are back. They're keeping to themselves and not helping despite the food rationing."

"And the Committee—"

"Does nothing! They're too afraid. I wish the Controllers would just lay it on the line and tell us what they want."

Interesting strategy. "Is the Transmission working?" I asked.

"No. The three Travas who Karla named had no clue how to work it."

"If the Transmission isn't fixed, eventually it won't matter who has control."

"You don't need to tell me, but the Controllers don't seem worried about that."

Odd. "What about Hank? Can he fix the Transmission?"

"He's busy with the air plant repairs. And trying to help us find the saboteurs."

"Did Bubba Boom tell you who they are?" I asked.

"Yeah. But the five of them disappeared when we tried to arrest them."

They could have been tipped off. "There aren't many places to hide."

"You think? Such stellar intellect, I'm going to promote you to captain."

"No need to be nasty."

Anne-Jade rubbed her eyes. Exhaustion had etched deep lines into her face. "Sorry. I don't have the manpower to search those places. If it wasn't for Hank's offer to keep an eye out, Sloan and his cohorts could be lounging in the dining room without having to worry about the ISF."

"At least with them on the run, there shouldn't be any more attacks."

"One good thing," she said.

"One thing at a time." Which reminded me of my task. "Anne-Jade, I know you're swamped, but can you search the Trava Sector for the active computer? I've done all I can through the shafts and came up with nothing."

"We do regular inspections. Too regular from what you've told me." She sighed. "I think it's time for a surprise visit."

"Take the glass tube with you. It should pick up anything that is hidden." I hurried back to my room and retrieved the detector and Zippy for her.

She raised her right eyebrow. "You keep Zippy in your room?"

"In case I need him. Can you bring him back when you're done?"

Anne-Jade left muttering about smoke damaged wits. I had told her the truth about Zippy, but not the entire reason I kept the little cleaning troll near my bed. He's been with me through some tough times. And he filled the void left by Sheepy.

At hour sixty, Anne-Jade returned with Zippy and the glass detector. Although her surprise inspection had netted her an interesting and scary array of illegal devices, weapons and contraband, she didn't find a computer linked to the network.

Which meant another person or group were the Controllers. Not good. Two hours later, I hurried over to Logan's room.

Faint voices rolled through the shaft as I neared his vent. I slowed, keeping as quiet as possible as I slid the final meter. Logan's aggravated tone was easy to recognize. The other two sounded calmer and were harder to discern.

"…long are you going to keep me here?" Logan demanded.

"…safe…saboteurs…life," a man's voice said.

"I'll stay in the Control Room. No one can get in there." Logan's anger rang clear.

"…rebellion…easy…"

"That's because we were all helping her. Besides, Trella's not a danger to me, you unrecyclable idiot. She's my friend."

More murmuring and I strained to hear the rest. The voices stopped and the door clicked shut. Metallic snaps and clangs followed before silence filled the room. I waited a few minutes until I was certain Logan's keepers had left, then I dropped down to the floor.

Logan stared at the closed door, hugging his arm to his chest.

"Logan, if you want to leave here, just say the word and I'll find you the perfect hiding place."

He spun around. "No worries, I'm fine. I just have to whine and complain to my captors or else they'll suspect I'm up to something. Did you hear my little tantrum about being bored to death?"

"No."

"Too bad, it was quite the performance." He crossed to his computer and pulled the keyboard out from its hiding place. Tapping a few keys, the screen lit up and displayed the picture of the hallway. The two guards walked down the corridor.

Still impressed by the moving pictures, I asked, "Do I even possess the rudimentary knowledge to understand how you invented a device that sees?"

He puffed up his chest. "No. You need to be a genius like me."

"I'm glad your sense of self worth hasn't changed," I teased.

"If you must know, I found the information and schematics in the computer. It's called a Video Camera."

"I remember them now. They were all over Inside, and a room full of computer screens for watchers to keep an eye on everyone. But I thought they were all destroyed."

"Those were. They were about fifteen centimeters long, by five centimeters wide, by three high. Bigger than mine, easier to spot and to smash."

"You can't blame them. It's creepy having someone spying on you."

"Not that different from the mics we're using."

"I disagree. It's a big difference." I shuddered.

Logan shrugged. "I was hoping to make more of these, but…" He closed his eyes and touched his eyelids with his fingertips, smoothing the skin as if he could wipe the injury away. "There are a few Video Cameras pointed toward Outside. They hadn't been damaged by the riots. I'd show you the pictures, but access to them has been blocked. Too bad, as they're really fascinating."

Another shudder shook my body. "No thanks. I've already seen Outside and I'm not fascinated at all." *Horrified* would be my word of choice. To rid myself of the image, I studied the screen. "The big guy on the left seems familiar," I said. "Too bad I missed their faces."

Logan's fingers danced on the keyboard and the men walked backward, disappeared and appeared again, but this time facing forward. They continued to walk backward for a few steps, then froze.

"How's that? Or do you want them closer?"

"That's good." I leaned forward and peered at the monitor. "The guy on the left reminds me of…someone. I've seen him before, but I can't place him." I hoped his name would eventually click.

In the meantime, I updated Logan on the search for the computer linked to the Controllers'. "Not in the Trava Sector. Where should I look next?"

He drummed his fingers on the edge of the keyboard. "Every Inside computer is suspect now."

"That's…" I couldn't even calculate a number.

"Two thousand, four hundred and nine computers."

My emotions warred between being impressed by Logan's memory and astounded by the sheer number of computers. "I couldn't—"

"Impossible to check them all." His fingers tapped again. "Did you bring the detector with you?"

"No."

"Next time you come, bring it along. I might be able to adjust it to hone in on the Controllers' signal over a wider area." He then added a number of other items he needed me to fetch for him.

★ ★ ★

Heading back to the infirmary through the air shafts, I concentrated on remembering Logan's list. When Doctor Lamont's voice sounded in my ear, I almost hit my head on the top of the shaft.

"Trella, Bubba Boom is here and he insists I wake you," she said. "What should I do?"

I fumbled for the button mic. "What's so important?"

"He wouldn't say."

Curious. "Tell him you woke me and I'll be out in a couple minutes. I'm almost home."

"Okay." She clicked off.

It wasn't until I had swung down into my room that I realized I had called the infirmary home. I really needed to return our world to a more normal state before I started calling Lamont Mom.

Changing into my green long-sleeved medical uniform, I pulled strands of my hair from my braid to appear sleep tousled. No need to act tired—sleep remained a low priority.

Bubba Boom wasted no time with hellos. He took my hand and pulled me from the infirmary and out into the hallway.

"Let go." I yanked, but he wouldn't release me. "What's going on?"

"I'll tell you in a minute." He kept his quick pace through the corridors.

The few people we passed gave us either curious stares or smirks, or ignored us. Bubba Boom dropped my hand as soon as we reached a quiet corner.

"I know you don't believe me about Jacy." He held a finger up before I could interrupt. "He's in his office and you should see for yourself who he's been…collaborating with."

"Why can't you tell me?"

"Better this way." He pointed to a vent above our heads.

"This will take you over the Committee members' offices in Sector H3."

"I'm not supposed to go into the air shafts. The tracer—"

"Isn't that accurate. It'll appear as if you walked through the Sector. You need to hurry before he finishes his meeting."

I glanced up. The vent was in the middle of the ceiling. "I'll need a boost."

He squatted down, holding his hands out. "Stand on my shoulders."

I kicked off my mocs, grabbed his hands for balance, and stepped onto him. He stood with ease and steadied my legs. The vent was within reach and I pushed it open. As I squirmed into the duct, I marveled at Bubba Boom's strength and height. He didn't appear to be that tall, but I doubted even Cog could boost me that high.

"I'll wait here for you," he called.

It took me a few minutes to get my bearings and head in the right direction. Despite Bubba Boom's suggestion to hurry, I slowed as I crossed over the Committee's offices. Bluelights glowed from most of them. No sounds or voices drifted, but that didn't mean no one was below.

The bright square of daylights reflecting off the metal duct marked Jacy's office well before his voice reached me.

"...don't know...she...problem," Jacy said.

Two almost-familiar male voices answered him, and I crept with care for the last two meters. The front half of Jacy's desk and two sets of legs facing it were visible from my vantage point. I strained to match the voices with faces and names.

"All your plans sound feasible, but you need to repair that Transmission before you can do anything else," said an authoritative and scary voice. Why scary? I searched my memories.

"We tried," Jacy said. "Karla sent us a trio of idiots."

"No surprise. She was having fun with that little scrub. *I'll* send you the right people."

I tucked that tidbit away for now.

"How do we get them past Hank?" asked the third man.

My hand flew to my cheek. I couldn't forget that voice. Sloan. Bubba Boom was right. Jacy had set me up!

"He has people in the power plant all the time," Sloan said.

"How long would they need?" Jacy asked.

"A couple hours at most," Authoritative and Scary said.

"We'll stage a distraction. If they wear the maintenance coveralls, they'll blend right in," Jacy said.

While Jacy working with Sloan was a bad thing, fixing the Transmission wasn't. I guessed Jacy had used the sabotage and the attack on Logan as a distraction so he could grab control of the computers and therefore Inside. It would make sense that he'd want to fix the Transmission once he gained power.

"What happens once the Transmission is repaired?" Sloan asked.

"We implement your plan," Authoritative and Scary said.

That comment supported my mutiny theory. Sloan and the other man stood and each shook Jacy's hand over the desk. I willed the unknown man to turn left to leave instead of right so I could see his face.

For once, I had my wish. I caught a glimpse of his beak of a nose and black mustache. His features were familiar. An upper, but not one I'd seen more than once or twice.

I chased the logic as I traveled back to where Bubba Boom waited. Scary had been one of my initial reactions, which meant I must associate him with a frightening event. Perhaps he had been a Pop Cop. But from the commanding tone of his voice, he was used to giving orders. Unfortunately, I knew most of the higher ranked Pop Cops. The answer slammed into me.

The other man was Captain James Trava.

thirteen

As soon as I pulled the vent open, Bubba Boom appeared below. I hung down. He grabbed me around my waist and lowered me to the floor.

He stared at me a minute before releasing me. "Now do you believe me?"

"Yes. How did you know about the captain?"

"Hank never trusted Jacy, and one of our guys found a maintenance panel that had been tampered with in Sector D4."

"Maintenance panel?"

"There're these covers on the walls that blend in and are easy to remove in case you need to get to the pipes and wires inside. It's better to pop off a panel than cut a hole in the wall. The Travas have been using the one in Sector D4 to sneak in and out."

"But there are ISF officers all over the place."

"Not up here. Heck, anyone wearing an upper's shirt and pants can stroll around levels three and four without any problems."

Sounded familiar. I had traveled the halls of the upper levels without notice when the Pop Cops had been in charge. Why? Not enough Pop Cops and people who kept to themselves too scared to get involved. Same thing, different names. There had to be a way to break that cycle, to unite us. The answer eluded me.

We headed back to the infirmary. I mulled over the information.

Jacy could no longer be trusted so everything he had told me should be considered a lie. The biggest threat to Jacy and Captain Trava was Logan. Even though it had been for the wrong reason, the Committee had actually done the right thing when they put Logan into protective custody.

As we neared the infirmary, Bubba Boom asked me to accompany him to the dining room. Since we needed to make plans, I agreed. I poked my head into the patient area to inform Lamont. Because of the tracer, she had to tag along, but she claimed it was a good idea.

Bubba Boom had been quick to hide his frown, but she noticed and said, "Don't worry, I won't sit with you two."

No one spoke as we turned south toward Quad G3. My thoughts still sorted through all that I had learned in the last few hours. Lamont filled her tray and joined a group of friends while Bubba Boom and I found an empty table as far away from everyone as possible. My plate contained a greenish-colored casserole, but I had no memory of scooping it.

I watched my mother. She appeared relaxed and when she smiled it changed her whole face, reaching all the way to her eyes. I realized she hadn't been happy in a very long time. Which should seem obvious, but I held no memory of her ever showing any joy or peace even before she betrayed us.

What was different? Her daughter was alive and despite her tendency to downplay the risk, she put herself in considerable danger by carrying the tracer for me. I thought about what I'd done without hesitation for my friends.

I'd been willing to sacrifice myself for Cogon. Would I have done it for some stranger? While I'd like to think I would, if I was truly honest with myself, the answer would be probably not. And why were we strangers at all? We lived in a giant metal cube. Granted, the Pop Cops had separated us, but if we went back far enough, we were all related to one of the original nine families.

A little zip of understanding jolted me. Could the solution to our problems be that simple?

"...look. Should I be worried? Trella?" Bubba Boom waved a hand in front of my face.

"Sorry. I was just..."

"What?"

"Thinking."

"I already figured that out." He tilted his head toward Lamont. "Are your deep thoughts about your birth mother?"

"Yes, but they don't help the situation with Jacy. Do you know what they're planning?"

"No. We've just connected him to Sloan and the captain recently."

"We?"

"Me, Hank, Phelan, Kren and Ange. The maintenance soups...supervisors."

"Aren't you a little young to be a soup?"

He shrugged. "After the rebellion, not many people were willing to step up and take charge."

Guilty of the same thing, I played with my food. At least I realized my mistake.

"We think Jacy and his cohorts are trying to hack into the computer network," he said. "It hasn't been working right the past two weeks. And if they gain control..."

"They already have."

Bubba Boom's expression flickered in surprise. "How do you know?"

Time to decide. If I wanted to fix the mess, I needed Bubba Boom's and Hank's help. They had already figured out a few things on their own. I explained to him about Jacy's group using the mythical Controllers to give orders to the Committee and Anne-Jade. But for some unknown reason, I didn't tell him about Logan.

"You've been confined to level three. How did you find out about all that?"

An interesting question. He didn't seem too upset about the Controllers, but he did suspect something wasn't right. "I'm allowed visitors."

He studied me a moment. "If they truly have the network, there's nothing we can do."

But Logan could. I hoped. "At least Jacy and the captain plan to fix the Transmission. That gives us one less problem to worry about."

I surprised him again. "When?" he asked.

"I don't know. But I think you should give them a predictable time when Hank won't be nearby so they don't have to create a distraction. And it will also give you an opportunity to see who else is involved." Spoken like a true Pop Cop. They had enjoyed baiting and trapping as many scrubs as possible in their schemes.

"But without control of the computers, it won't matter if we know who's involved or not," he said.

"We might be able to reclaim the computer systems."

"Might? Do you really think we have a chance?"

"I've done more with less."

He laughed. "So you're asking us to trust you."

"Yep."

"I'll talk to Hank. He's been saying we need to start over so I'm sure he'll agree to give you all the help you'll need."

★ ★ ★

Logan was thrilled to hear the Transmission might be repaired. He gave me one of his new tiny Video Cameras to plant so he could watch when they started working on the machine. Between my supply runs, he spent his time building gadgets. And I spent my free time with Bubba Boom. Since Hank and his crew had agreed to assist me, Bubba Boom acted as our go-between.

Modifying the glass tube detector, Logan returned it to me. Since I didn't have the time to sweep all the Sectors and Quadrants in Inside to search for the active link to the Controllers, I passed it along to Hank and his crew to check them.

"You want to start doing what?" Lamont asked me.

"Using the vampire boxes," I said again. It was hour fifteen during week 147,025, and the last fifty hours of traveling back and forth to Logan's had been physically draining. I perched on the edge of the examination table while Lamont sorted through her supplies.

"Why?"

"The files with all the blood test data are…unavailable, so I want to do tests on everyone."

Lamont stared at me as if I displayed symptoms of a high fever. "What do you want to test for?"

"Family bloodlines."

"Why?"

"I think it'll help us regain a sense of community. Instead of being the uppers and lowers we can be the Ashons and Minekos. Then each family can vote for a representative to be in the Committee of nine. But I think we still need a captain. Someone like Hank."

"Or you," she said.

"I don't have any technical knowledge of the ship."

"You don't need it. You have Logan, who you trust. A captain can't do everything, that's why she has a support staff of trusted people."

"The people of Inside might not be too happy to see me in that position."

"You have good ideas. When you get us on the right track everyone will be happy."

She had a lot of confidence in me. I waited for the familiar twist of fear in my stomach, but nothing happened. At least the thought of people relying on me didn't scare me anymore. Instead, it gave me a push of motivation. Much better.

"The only problem with using the vampire boxes is we can't put the results in the computer, and we don't have enough wipe boards," I said.

"Then we'll do it the old-fashioned way." Lamont gestured to the white metal walls. "They're just giant wipe boards and we'll have plenty of space."

I laughed.

"Do you want to test everybody? Even those who know their family names already?"

"No. Just test the people in the lower levels. Will the boxes be able to tell which family they belong to from the blood sample?"

"The families have been mixing together for the last 145,025 weeks in the lower levels. It might be hard to find a clear match. We could do hybrid families like the Ashekos?"

"That would give us too many groups. I'd like to keep the numbers small. If possible, pick the dominate family and tell each person his or her family name."

"And if I can't?"

"Pick a family. Preferably one that is short on members."

Lamont grinned then sobered. "One last problem. I can't leave level three."

"I'll have to send them to you."

"All eighteen thousand? How?"

"I'm not sure. Maybe Bubba Boom or Hank will have a suggestion."

But I didn't have a chance to ask them because soon after I finished my shift for Lamont at hour twenty, a series of loud metallic clangs rolled through Inside. The walls and floor shuddered with each, clearing the shelves and tripping anyone standing, including me. I had been in my room debating between sleeping and visiting Logan.

It wasn't as severe as the Big Shake. More like Little Trembles.

I joined Lamont in the exam room.

"You think it was another bomb?" she asked.

"I hope not, but unless a piece of machinery malfunctioned there aren't many other ways to cause that much movement." And then I remembered Jacy had talked about creating a distraction. Bubba Boom had assured me Hank had changed his schedule and eliminated the need for a distraction. Perhaps Jacy suspected an ambush. Otherwise, it meant Jacy risked all our lives just because he could.

Helping Lamont prep for casualties, I worried about my friends. I would have liked to search for them, but already a few injured people had arrived.

I felt better when it became obvious that most of the injuries were minor. Cuts, bruises, a few broken arms and legs, a couple concussions and a number of sprained ankles and wrists. Nothing like the overwhelming deluge after the Big Shake. And no burns.

Sometime during the next ten hours, Bubba Boom stopped by. He had a small cut on his arm, but wouldn't let me clean and bandage it.

He waved away my efforts. "It's fine."

When I asked about the others, he said, "I haven't heard of any fatalities." He pulled me outside and a few meters away from the infirmary. He lowered his voice. "The Transmission blew again. Jacy's Travas either overloaded it by mistake or incompetence. Or they did it on purpose."

"I heard them say *fix*."

"Maybe that meant *fix* it so it won't run again."

"That bad?"

"It's a mangled mess. We won't know for a week or more."

I wondered if Logan had watched the Travas with his Video Camera. Hank and Bubba Boom still thought he was in protective custody. They hadn't asked how I would bypass Jacy's Controllers, but at least they hunted for the active link.

"Any news about the link?" I asked.

"Nothing. And we'll have to postpone the search until we can figure out what to do about the Transmission."

Just what we needed—more delays. Jacy was bound to clamp down on our freedoms soon and release all the Travas. It still puzzled me why he hadn't by now.

After the last of the injured had been seen and I had slept for over eight hours, I climbed into the ducts and visited Logan.

He pounced on me as soon as I dropped down into his room.

"I've been calling you for hours," he said.

"I turned my receiver off so I could get some sleep. Sorry. Are you hurt?"

"No." He twisted the bottom of his shirt, coiling it tight.

"What's wrong? Did you see what happened—"

"Of course! I saw it all and I've been dying to talk to someone about it." He paced and twisted. "I'm bored."

I glanced at all his half-completed devices. "No. You're lonely. I should stop by more often."

He waved my comment away. "I'm sure you were busy." He sprinted to the computer and tapped a few keys. "Come see what happened before the Video Camera died."

The screen showed the long cylinder and control panel for

the Transmission. Bluelights glowed in the empty room. Then the daylights flooded as three men dressed in maintenance coveralls approached the control panel. Logan pressed a key and the men moved super fast as they went back and forth from the panel to the machine.

"They worked on the Transmission for about an hour," Logan said. "Here's where it gets interesting."

Their actions didn't make sense to me, but there was no missing the bright flash just before the panel exploded. The men flew back and the screen turned dark.

"The energy pulse blew the Video Camera." Logan swiveled around to me.

"Did they cause the explosion?"

"No. I studied that whole hour and it appeared to me they were repairing the damage from before."

"What happened then?"

"The panel must have been rigged to blow when they reached a certain point."

"Rigged by who? Did you see anyone else work on the machine?"

"No. The booby trap was in place before you installed the Video Camera."

Booby trapped prior to the explosion? It didn't make any sense. Everyone wanted the Transmission fixed. I pointed at Logan's screen. "That first explosion set off a bunch of others."

"Overkill, for sure. One was enough to obliterate the controls. Can you place another Video Camera in there for me? I'd like to see the extent of the damage."

"A mangled mess, according to Bubba Boom."

Logan sniffed. "I'd still like to see it for myself."

"Okay."

He gave me another Video Camera and a list of supplies. I climbed into the air shafts and crossed to the power plant. The Transmission was located in the southeast corner and the damage to the floor and walls from the first explosion hadn't been repaired yet.

Finding an intact shaft was difficult, but I switched to the heating ducts, and managed to circumvent the open areas. As I drew closer, the sound of an argument reached me. Strained, worried and upset voices shouted at each other. I doubted anyone heard the replies if there were any.

I peeked through the vent. Most of the Committee members gathered around a hole in the middle of a control panel. The metal had been peeled back as if a giant fist had punched through the panel. Black scorch marks streaked along the sides and water dripped from everything. At least the sprinkler system had doused the fire. Unlike the fabric in the air filters, there wasn't much here to burn. It looked bad, but not quite the mangled mess of Bubba Boom's description.

Hank and a few of his crew stood together, enduring the ire of the Committee members. I waited until they left and placed the Video Camera just below the vent.

I returned to the infirmary and helped Lamont change bandages and feed patients. The follow-up care wasn't as interesting to me as the initial treatment. Surgery fascinated me, but I'd be happy to let someone else take charge of a patient's recovery. All part of my impatience. Another aspect of my personality that led me into trouble.

A few hours into my shift, Domotor wheeled himself into the infirmary. Three shades past pale, his haggard expression regarded me with desperation. I yelled for Lamont and ran to him, asking him to list his symptoms, checking his pulse.

He gave me a weak smile. "I'm fine."

"Are you sure?"

"Well…I'm physically as fine as possible considering the broken back."

Lamont arrived with her scanner. "What hurts?"

"My ego. Apparently, I don't look well."

She paused. "That's putting it mildly."

"Nothing a good meal and ten hours of sleep won't cure, Kiana," he said.

I winced at the use of her first name. It had been so long since I heard it. To me, that name equaled pain. They pretended not to notice.

"Are you here for a checkup then?" she asked.

"No. I need to talk to Trella. Do you have a few minutes?"

I glanced at Lamont. She nodded and returned to work, giving us some privacy.

"Here?" I asked.

"If you'd be so kind as to wheel me over to the dining room, we can talk there."

Interesting how no one wanted to talk in the infirmary. I wondered if someone had planted a microphone here. Perhaps it was due to the patients. Lying around with nothing to do, they would enjoy eavesdropping on our conversation.

Domotor remained quiet as I pushed him to Quad G3, helped him fill his tray and found an empty table far away from those who eyed us with curiosity. Blake wiped off tables, ignoring us, but I had the strange feeling he'd been keeping track of the people who shared my table. I wondered if Riley had asked his brother to keep an eye on me. I hadn't seen Riley since our conversation in Logan's room.

While I pushed my food around my plate, Domotor attacked his food as if he hadn't eaten in weeks.

"If you need a break from Committee business, I know a little place in Quad C1 where no one would bother you," I said. "You'd probably eat more often, too."

He laughed. "Tempting, except for the black dust and roar of the power plant."

Domotor finished his meal. He wiped his mouth with a napkin, but kept the cloth clutched in his hand. A little color had returned to his face. No spark lit his blue eyes. Even during the worst moments of the rebellion, he'd never looked this bad.

"What's wrong?" I asked.

"Everything. But first tell me how you bypassed the tracer in your arm."

Was he guessing? Or did he know? I kept my expression neutral. "I didn't bypass the tracer." The truth.

"You can tell me. I'm no longer on the Committee."

A sinking feeling of unease stroked my stomach. "Why not?"

"There is no longer a Committee. The Controllers have taken over Inside."

"But the computer—"

"They have the network and all system controls. Except the Transmission's."

"All systems?" Fear swirled and I fought to keep from grabbing the chair's arms in panic.

"Yes. If they decide to cut off our air, we're dead."

"Did they release Karla and Vinco?" Funny how I was more terrified of those two than the threat of suffocation.

"No."

Surprised, I asked, "Why not?"

"The Controllers are *not* the Travas."

"Not all of them," I said. "Jacy's in charge, but he's working with them."

Domotor laughed. "Jacy? Where did you hear that?"

"I have my sources."

"Well your sources are wrong."

"Really? Then who are the Controllers?"

"Outsiders."

fourteen

"Outsiders." I repeated the strange word. "You think the Controllers are Outsiders? How… Why…" The concept was so outrageous, I couldn't say more.

"Logan isn't the only one who is good with the computer, Trella," Domotor said. "I've been trying to find a way around the Controllers since they showed up. I managed to isolate a small part of the network, and I traced where the link is coming from. It's not from anywhere in Inside."

"Are you sure? Jacy—"

"He could be helping them. It wouldn't surprise me. That boy's an opportunist."

"Do you know what the…Outsiders want?" I asked.

"To come in."

I felt as if I had drifted into Outer Space—unable to breathe as ice stabbed deep into my bones. "Can they?" My voice squeaked.

"Yes, they can and will."

No wonder he looked so haggard. "Maybe it would be a good thing. They could be in trouble or need our help."

"Then why didn't they ask? They infiltrated our network, they ordered us to lock down our people and they told us they're boarding. Not the actions of a friendly group."

"Can we stop them?" I asked.

"I've been trying, but since this last explosion they've shut down all access. I can't get into my isolated system."

My head spun. "Why are you telling me all this?"

"You need to give this…" He handed me a small round disk. "To Logan." Domotor studied my face. "He needs this disk to get to the isolated system. I know you've been visiting him so don't lie to me and say you can't. This is vital to our world."

"What can Logan do that you can't?"

"Work his magic, get control back and stop the Outsiders from coming in."

"What if he can't?"

"Then we're all at the mercy of the Outsiders."

Logan didn't mince words. "Holy crap, Trella, this is bad." He had inserted Domotor's disk into his computer and had been typing away.

"How bad?"

"We're screwed." He tapped the screen with a fingernail. "No wonder we couldn't locate the link. I never considered an Outside source."

His fingers flew over the keys as he murmured and cursed under his breath.

"But now that you know what's going on, you can stop them. Right?" I prodded.

"No can do."

My knees refused to hold my weight. I sank into a nearby chair.

He pushed back from the computer. "We're blocked out of

everything. Domotor isolated an area, but I would need an untainted computer to access it."

"Untainted?"

"One that hasn't been hooked into the network."

"What about the computers in the Trava Sector?" I asked. "Anne-Jade said they were cut off from the network."

Logan fiddled with the ends of his hair. He hadn't bothered to cut it while in protective custody. "It would depend on when those computers were unhooked. If the Outsiders had already gained access, they won't work."

"How do we get you there without anyone knowing?"

His face lit up. "I rigged a device that feeds off the heat from the lamp. It'll keep the tracer at a constant temperature."

"If we wait until right after your keepers leave, we'll have about twenty hours before the game is up."

I considered the steps needed to get Logan to Sector D4. After I scouted out a computer, he could travel through the air shafts with me. However, what would we do with the Travas in the room?

Time to pay Anne-Jade a visit.

"You want to borrow what?" Anne-Jade sat behind her desk and blinked at me as if she could clear me from her vision.

I had waited until the ISF office emptied of her lieutenants before dropping in on her. Keeping close to the heating vent in case one of the others returned, I repeated my request. "A stun gun, Anne-Jade. Not a kill-zapper. I need it to help Logan." And when she didn't answer, I added, "Trust me."

"Stun guns can kill if set high enough."

"I know." Cogon had killed a Pop Cop by accident because the Pop Cop's gun had been set to maximum. "Can't you lock it at a certain level?"

She crumpled. There was no other way to describe it. One second sitting straight and being stubborn, the next a defeated slouch. "You have the worst timing." Anne-Jade spun her monitor around so I could see it. The white screen had a row of black letters that read, *Collect all the weapons Inside and lock them in the safe, including your own.*

"Is that—"

"Yes. Orders from the Controllers."

"Do you know they're not—"

"Yes. And they know exactly how many weapons we have because our inventory was in the computer."

"But if you're locking them—"

"The floor of the safe has a weight sensor in case anyone decides to try to steal anything."

My mind raced. "Then add in extra weight. You can't lock up all the weapons! That's suicide."

"I don't have much time." She pointed to the bottom of the screen. A small clock counted down. She had less than an hour. "If I don't do as they say, they'll gas Sector D2."

"Sleeping gas?"

"I wish."

I sorted through the potential problems. "If I find you the weight, will you loan me a stun gun?"

"Sure."

Anne-Jade gave me the approximate weight of each weapon. While she called in her officers, I returned to the air shafts.

As I slid through them, memories of other panicked scrambles through the tight shafts replayed in my mind. I had hoped never to be in this situation again. In order to put a positive spin on my rushed descent to level one, I considered this trip practice. If the Outsiders did gain entry into our world, we would have one advantage of being in familiar territory.

The best place to pick up items of various weights was in the recycling plant. I peered through the vents, searching for a pile away from the bustle of activity and near a vent. Part of me was glad to see people working to recycle the large amount of waste that had collected during the last six weeks, but the other half worried one of the workers would recognize me. Too bad I didn't have time to don a pair of the drab gray overalls and boots.

A few people picked through a couple piles as if searching for something so at least in that regard, I wouldn't be calling attention to myself. I spotted a mound of broken glass items. They would be heavy enough to stand in for the weapons.

Easing from the air shaft, I dropped to the floor with a light thump. My heart added its own thumping that I swore the entire recycling plant could hear. A couple people glanced over, but resumed working. Careful of where I stepped, I tried to keep the glass pile between me and the others.

I filled my bag with a hefty amount—enough, I hoped, for three or four weapons. The beauty of taking glass was Anne-Jade could break off pieces if they didn't match the weight. Tying the bag to my belt, I climbed the wall, using the rivets. In the recycling plant, the air vents were at the top of the walls and not in the ceiling.

When I reached the vent, I pulled my body in. Except before I could draw in my legs, a hand clamped around my ankle and yanked.

I used my elbows to stop my fall. With the lower half of my body dangling from the vent, I glanced down. Sloan held my ankle and gave me a smirk. Damn.

"Come on out, little bug," he said. "You aren't supposed to be down in this level. You're a bad little bug that's about to get squashed, and not by Chomper."

The graphic image propelled me into action. I kicked back with my other foot. My heel connected with his eye. Not hard because of my awkward position, but it doesn't take much force to temporarily damage a person's vision. He yelled and let go of my ankle. I didn't hesitate to haul the rest of my body into the shaft.

His curses followed me, echoing in the thin metal duct. The good news, I escaped. The bad, Jacy would soon know I had bypassed my tracer. Although with the Outsiders poised to enter Inside, I doubted anyone would care about me.

By hour fifty-nine, I returned to Anne-Jade's office. Through the vent, I spotted a wall gaping open. It was the door to the safe. I had never noticed it before, which made sense.

A line of very unhappy ISF officers relinquished their weapons. One of Anne-Jade's lieutenants kept track of the number. I was about to squirm into a comfortable position to wait when I noticed the stun gun. Light from the office illuminated the dial. It had been set to level five intensity—enough force to stun an average-sized man. I tucked it into my belt and left the glass for Anne-Jade.

I needed to swing by the infirmary to gather a few supplies before going back to Logan's. Lamont found me stuffing a syringe, tweezers and sutures into a cloth bag.

"Are you here to help me?" she asked.

"No."

"What's going on, Trella?"

I hesitated.

"I think I've been more than understanding and patient with all your trips these last two weeks, but something zapped the computer and Domotor's face…" She shivered and wrapped her arms around her torso. "I figured you already found Logan. Did he get into the network?"

I considered what to tell her. "Logan's working on it and I'm helping him." I added about the Controllers disbanding the Committee.

A crease of concern lined her forehead as she watched me as I finished packing the bag.

"I can see you're spooked. What else is going on?" she asked.

"I'd rather not say." It was an honest reply.

"You're being smart. I shouldn't have asked and I don't want to know. Because if someone threatens to harm you, I'll do or say anything to protect you. Go on. I'll cover for you."

"Thanks."

"You will warn me if I need to prep for casualties?"

If the Outsiders come in, there could be panic and injuries. "Yes."

"Good. Now shoo."

I arrived at Logan's room a few minutes after his keepers had left. So far, they kept to their twenty-hour schedule, which meant Logan and I had that much time to find him an untainted computer.

Over the next hour, I learned a few things about Logan. He hated needles, he vomited at the sight of his own blood and he acted like a baby when it came to pain. Removing the tracer turned into an unexpected ordeal. I wished for Lamont's cool confidence that surfaced whenever she dealt with a difficult patient.

Finally, Logan and I crept through the air shafts. Unused to any physical activity since the fire, he moved slowly and we took frequent breaks. Plus he babied the arm with the sutures. At this rate, it would take us hours to reach Sector D4.

Despite my impatience, we arrived at the edge of the Sector. Locked wire mesh air filters blocked the duct that led into the Travas apartments. I had encountered them before when sweeping for the active link so it didn't take me long to unlock them.

I left Logan behind so I could scout for a computer. Looking for an apartment with only a couple Travas living there, I also wanted one close to where Logan waited. I found a small one-bedroom apartment with three male Travas. They played cards on the table right below the air vent. It was almost perfect.

I grabbed the stun gun from my belt and flipped the safety off. Easing open the vent, I aimed at the farthest man and pulled the trigger. As the loud sizzle slap filled the room, the pulse of energy hit him in the torso and he jerked. The chair toppled backward. Before he hit the floor, I had stunned the second man.

The third spotted me. He jumped to his feet and dashed toward the washroom. I dropped to the table, aimed and caught him before he reached the door. Stunners overloaded a body's nervous system. When directly hit with a pulse, a person lost all feeling in his body and couldn't move for a couple hours or more, depending on the intensity. If hit on the arms or legs, then it just deadened that extremity. I had been hit below the waist and it had numbed both my legs and hip area.

I hurried back to Logan and led him to the apartment. Logan ignored the three men and aimed straight for the computer, loading Domotor's disk into it. With nothing to do, I straightened the cards and moved the guys into more comfortable positions.

The couch looked inviting, so I sat on the end, tucking my legs up under me. It had been only fifteen hours since I last slept, but the pace had been nonstop. I rested my head on the couch's arm.

A weight settled next to me and I startled awake. Logan slouched beside me.

"Well?"

"No luck. Everything's blocked."

"What about Domotor's isolated system?"

"I can retrieve data from it, but I can't get into the executable files. The ones that run the systems."

"What type of data?" I asked.

"Useless stuff like the population control stats, fuel data, hydroponic fertilizer mixtures and sheep feeding times."

"Useless to you, but not to those workers."

"True," Logan said.

Checking the time, I calculated how long we had until the Travas recovered. Hour sixty-five. They would get feeling back soon. And we had fifteen hours until Logan's escape was discovered.

"Let's get out of here."

"Do you want to see the Outsiders?" he asked.

I almost fell off the couch. "How?"

"One of the isolated systems is the Video Cameras pointed to Outside. I took a quick look to confirm my suspicions."

My brain stumbled over his words. I felt as if I was always the last person to know. "Just tell me, Logan."

"I studied the damage to the Transmission. Bad, but not five explosions worth. One did the job. So what were the other four trembles? I guessed the saboteurs used the blast at the Transmission to cover the Outsiders attaching to Inside."

"Attaching?"

"Yep. They have to line up and attach to Gateway in some way or risk being exposed to Outer Space." Logan returned to the computer.

I stood behind him as the screen turned black. Then the view changed and spots of dim daylights illuminated a bumpy rectangle made out of black metal…a bubble monster! I had forgotten all about them in the craziness of the past few weeks. Eight long arms hooked onto an otherwise smooth metal wall…Inside. At least, I had been correct in assuming the monsters were a conveyance. Small comfort.

Logan pointed to the arms. "When these clamped on, they caused those tremblers. I'm guessing they attached two at a time. See this?" He tapped on a spot on the belly of the monster. "That's their Gateway. Even though they're moving slow, they'll link theirs up with ours soon."

"How soon?"

"Depends on them. They have control of our computer. We're completely unprepared and nothing can stop them."

"Thanks for staying optimistic," I said.

Maybe we weren't as unprepared as Logan thought. I wondered if those bubble…ships in the top level could stop them. Would they have weapons or could we use those arms to pull the Outsiders off? No idea.

I helped Logan back into the shaft and followed, closing the vent behind us. With no closer options, I led him to Riley's storeroom.

The room had an abandoned feel to it. Or was that just my heart?

Logan plopped on the couch. Dust puffed and I sneezed.

"This is just temporary. Once we figure out our next move, I'll find you a better place to hide," I said.

"There is no next step. The Outsiders will come in. The end."

"Unacceptable. Try again."

He groaned and massaged his forehead. "I'd think better without these headaches."

"I can bring you painkillers."

"I know. I only get them when I've been straining to see too long." He sagged back against the cushions. "I could go back to my room. All my stuff is there, and I have a shower."

"And that solves our problem how?"

"At least it doesn't add to it."

We sat in silence. I felt useless with my limited computer knowledge. Besides knowing how to turn it on and off…

"Logan, what would happen if we turned the network off?"

"Nothing. You can't just switch it off. It's impossible." He straightened. "I see what you're getting at. Hmm…" Drumming his fingers on his chin, he got that distant mind-crunching look on his face. "We could disconnect each life system and operate them manually. Except…"

"What?"

"We don't know how to operate those systems manually."

"Aren't there instructions?"

"Even if we could access the computer, there aren't any instructions on the network. After the damage to the Transmission, I searched for them and found nothing. Which makes sense. If something happens to the network, you don't want your operating instructions lost as well."

"Would they be written down somewhere? Or on disks?"

"Ink on a wipe board would fade over time and I couldn't find any disks with the information. Unless they're packed away in one of those storage boxes in the Expanse."

His words triggered another memory. "What would these instructions look like?"

"Diagrams and schematics. Mostly visual step-by-step guides. Why?"

"Like some of the symbols that show up on your computer screen?"

"They would be similar."

The walls of the top level of Inside had been filled with diagrams. "Uh...Logan... How do you feel about heights?"

Logan didn't have a chance to answer because Lamont's voice squawked in my ear. "Trella, where are you?" A nervous tremble tainted her voice.

"Level four. What's wrong?"

"I have a medical emergency and need your help," she said with a slight quaver.

Warning signals rang in my head. "Who's sick?"

"Emek's appendix is about to burst."

Which would be a medical marvel since we removed his appendix weeks ago. "Is he stable?"

"No. He won't last *two* hours. I'm stunned by how fast his vitals turned critical. You have to hurry or we'll lose him."

Damn! "I'll be right there."

Logan raised his eyebrows, inviting me to explain. How do I tell him two people had forced my mother to call me so they could ambush me when I returned to the infirmary? He would insist on coming along and I couldn't risk him.

"I need to go help Lamont," I said instead. "Will you be okay here or do you want to return to your room?"

He considered and I almost screamed at him to think faster.

"I might as well go back. No sense tipping them off about me. It's just a straight shot over to my room, isn't it?" he asked.

"Yes. Head east, you're the very last vent." I scrambled up the ladder, but paused as a horrible thought struck me. What if my "rescue" ended badly? No one would know about the Expanse's ceiling.

"Logan, just listen." I explained about level seventeen at the top of the Expanse, describing the symbols on the walls and the Bubble Monsters. "If I disappear, get Anne-Jade and climb up to the near-invisible hatch. I left the safety line tied to the ladder and I doubt anyone's noticed."

"Wow, Trella. How long have you known about this?"

"A few weeks. I've been busy fetching *your* junk."

He smiled. "And you didn't inform the Committee?"

"Probably a bad decision at the time, but now I'm thrilled I kept it quiet."

"Me, too. How long should I wait?"

"Ten hours. That'll give me enough time to help Lamont and sleep. But if the Outsiders enter, don't wait. I'm assuming you can contact your sister?"

"Of course. I have this sweet little device—"

"Tell me later." I entered the air shaft. As I hurried over and down to the infirmary, I replayed Lamont's exact words in my mind. She managed to give me quite a bit of information. Two ambushers, armed with stun guns and they waited in the exam room.

I slowed as I reached the ducts over the infirmary. Looping over the patient area, surgery and exam room, I noted how the two men had positioned themselves on either side of the door to our suite. Lamont had been strapped down on the exam table. White medical tape covered her mouth, but she had the best view of the air vent.

Potential rescue scenarios raced through my mind. I could find Anne-Jade and a bunch of ISF officers. Except they were unarmed and these two not only had stunners, but the one on the right side carried a kill-zapper. Who else could I trust? Logan might have some gadget… Zippy!

Sliding over to the vent above my room, I lowered myself down and grabbed Zippy from my bed. I hefted him up and into the shaft without too much noise. Hopefully, they'd think the few thuds meant I had returned.

I tucked Zippy under my arm so he wouldn't rub against the metal shaft. Back at the exam room, I removed the cover with care. Lamont's eyes widened and she gestured at the men with her head. I nodded and put a finger to my lips before lowering Zippy just enough so he cleared the shaft. Flipping the switch, I hoped he would do his silent electronic pulse thing.

Once I pulled Zippy back, I swung through the vent and dropped to the floor. I had the element of surprise and a stun gun. In the second it took for them to react, I shot them both. The sizzle slaps rang, but they didn't fall down.

The man on the left pointed to his belt buckle. "Anti-stunners." He aimed his weapon at my chest.

I flinched but nothing happened. Good job, Zippy. Then I realized it was me against the two of them. I bolted toward the patient area. And I would have escaped, too.

Except one of them yelled, "Stop or we'll hurt Doctor Lamont."

Damn. I turned. The right-side goon held a scalpel to Lamont's throat. Her angry eyes aimed a clear signal at me to keep running. They were probably bluffing, but I couldn't take that chance. Not with her life.

"Drop your weapon," Right Goon ordered.

An odd request considering I couldn't hurt them with it. I placed it on the floor and Left Goon picked it up. Before I could even say a word, Left Goon stunned me with my own gun. The sizzle slap hit me in the middle of my chest, knocking me back.

fifteen

As the pulse from the stun gun traveled through my body, it left behind a stinging pain as if thousands of needles jabbed into me. The numbness followed, but it seemed slower. Eventually I couldn't move, or think clearly, or talk. Voices reached me, but their words were jumbled. My vision blurred and I was unable to focus on one person or thing. I'd never felt so helpless and uncaring at the same time.

Encased in something white, I sensed movement. I concentrated on the sounds around me. After a while, I heard the washers slosh and spin. Then the hum of the power plant dominated as the laundry noises faded.

The crunch and clink of the recycling plant grew louder and I smelled the hot, sweet scent of the glass kilns. The light changed to bluelights and all sounds were cut off.

The white material disappeared. The two goons talked and my view changed to a lower point. They fussed with things around me, then left.

Time passed until pain pricked my feet, then sizzled up my

calves. Sensation returned with agonizing slowness. When the effects of the stun gun finally wore off, I felt relief that the fuzziness had lifted from my mind. It was quickly followed by panic.

I sat in a chair, but my wrists were clamped to the armrests with metal cuffs. A hard ring bit into my ankles, and I guessed they were cuffed to the chair's legs. My waist was strapped in, as well. The chair wouldn't move when I squirmed. I considered screaming for help, but the walls had been sprayed with insulating foam, which scared me more than being secured to a chair.

Taking deep breaths, I calmed my terrified thoughts and focused on the positives. I hadn't been recycled. I wasn't in the brig with Karla and Vinco. And Logan knew about Inside's top level. What else?

I glanced around in the dim bluelight. Shelves full of metal parts lined two of the walls and half of the wall with the door. A storage closet for maintenance was my first impression, but this chair didn't fit. And the worktable filled with half-completed gadgets meant this could be where the goons had built the anti-stunners.

I looked for air and heating vents, but didn't find any. That would explain why I didn't know about this room. It also meant the only way out of here was through the door. A gap under it let in daylights and air.

It didn't take a genius to guess Jacy had ordered my abduction. Although I was unclear on the *why*. Sloan obviously had informed him of my visit to the recycling plant, so Jacy knew I had tricked my tracer. Why would that goad him into doing this?

A couple of hours later I still didn't have any answers. Or food and water. My stomach grumbled. Finally, the door opened and my two goons and Jacy slipped inside the room, closed and then locked the door.

Clearly unhappy, Jacy studied me for a while.

I stared right back. "What's going on?" I demanded.

"You tell me. What have you been up to?" he asked.

"I helped lance a boil—that was gross. I stitched a patient's hand, I disinfected every surface of—"

"Stop playing around, Trella. You know what I mean."

Like I would tell him. "This isn't the right way to ask me, Jacy."

His scowl deepened. "I needed to get you away from the infirmary and Bubba Boom."

"And you couldn't have asked me to meet you somewhere else?"

"Would you have come?"

"No." A wave of pure exhaustion swept through me. "What do you want, Jacy?"

"I need to know what you and Logan have been doing for the last few weeks."

He knew about Logan. Not good. "Why would I tell you?"

"Because we're on the same side."

I made a show of looking at my restraints. "Is this how you treat all your cohorts or am I just that special?"

"I know Bubba Boom fed you a bunch of lies. I didn't real-ize what he was up to until too late. And I couldn't think of another way to make you listen to reason," Jacy said.

"So you attack me and tie me to a chair and I'm supposed to believe *you're* the voice of reason?"

"Yes."

I laughed at the pure ridiculousness of the situation. "Save your speech, Jacy. I saw you with Sloan and James Trava. I heard you plotting."

"Did you hear the entire conversation?"

"Doesn't matter."

"Yes, it does."

"Fine. I heard the last ten minutes or so."

"And Bubba Boom told you about the meeting, right?"

"Yes, but don't try to twist it back to him. You *were* with Sloan and Trava."

"For a good reason. We—"

"Jacy, I'm not going to believe anything you say. So there's no sense trying to convince me." As soon as the words left my mouth I realized my mistake. I had messed up any chance to pretend to believe him in order to get out of here. I could blame my lack of sleep or the side effects of being stunned, but sheer stupidity was the culprit.

"All right, Trella. We'll do this the hard way. You're usually pretty smart so I'm going to give you time alone to think about everything that has happened." Jacy conferred with his goons before leaving.

Right Goon crouched in front of me and rested his hands on my legs as if balancing himself. A sudden surge of fear flooded my body as I met his gaze. A hideous thought surfaced. Would Jacy's men resort to… Unable to even consider it, I shied away from that terrible scenario.

"I suggest you tell him what he wants to know," he said.

"Why?" I was proud my voice didn't shake.

"Because he's going to get our world back." He stood and left with the other man.

I remembered to breathe when they didn't immediately return. But the muscles in my legs still trembled from the goon's touch.

In order to pass the time and distract myself from my dry throat and empty stomach, I considered Jacy's argument. The meeting with the captain and with the bomber had been pretty damning. What other evidence did I have?

Sloan. He pulled me from the duct and we started the riot. Why? To empty the waste-handling plant of workers so one of his buddies could plant that bomb.

But Bubba Boom disarmed the bomb...well...sort of. It didn't matter how it had been stopped, just that it did stop. And Sloan knew right where to find me in the air shaft. Or did he? My tool belt had clanged.

Jacy wanted to plant those mics above the Control Room and Anne-Jade's office. Which made sense if he was worried about what the Committee was up to. Except he was on the Committee so why would he need to bug those areas unless he was more concerned about the Controllers?

And the whole situation with the Transmission hadn't added up either. Everything I learned about Jacy had come from Bubba Boom. Then again, Jacy had cuffed me to a chair in a locked room. And time remained critical. What if the Outsiders came in?

Logic remained on Jacy's side if he told the truth, but I just couldn't trust him. As the time passed and I grew hungrier, thirstier and stiffer, my inclination to believe Jacy diminished with each minute.

When the door finally opened, I wished I could strangle him. He slipped in with Sloan and another goon. A visit with Sloan—now my week was complete.

He approached me warily, which, considering the circumstances would have made me laugh, but I glared at him.

"Did you think it through?" he asked.

"Yep."

"And?"

"I've decided I'd wrap my hands around your neck and crush your windpipe first."

"Not helping, Trella."

"That's the point."

He sighed. "I'd hoped my involvement with the Force of Sheep rebellion would have earned me some of your trust."

My gaze flicked to Sloan. "Why did he pull me from the shaft?"

"At first, I was just playing around," Sloan said. "I heard you up in the duct. I planned to let you go, but when I found out about those mics…I lost it. It was like the Pop Cops all over again."

"Captain Trava?" I asked Jacy.

"We need to get the Transmission fixed. He knew the right people and he knows the Controllers are not… They're…"

"Outsiders," I said.

"I should have known you'd already have that figured out. Who told you—Bubba Boom?"

I kept my mouth shut.

"James Trava is helping us. He knows what Inside can do. How fast we can travel, how to maneuver our world. It's probably too late, but something had to be done!" He pulled in a few breaths as if to calm down. "That's why I need to know what you've been up to. You could be compromising our efforts."

He had explained the two inconsistencies, but still. "I'm not."

"What about Logan?"

"You should know better than me. He's in protective custody by order of the Committee."

Jacy stepped toward me, balling his hands into tight fists. I feared he would strike me.

Instead, he uncurled his hands and tapped his fingers against his thighs. He looked at Sloan. "Last try?"

"Don't bother. She doesn't believe you, boss. We don't need her. She can stay in the Pit until we have the situation under control," Sloan said.

The Pit? That didn't sound good.

"I would, except we *do* need her. Go." Jacy cleared a spot off the worktable and sat down.

"Is he bringing food and water?" I asked, trying to keep my voice steady.

"No. But if this doesn't work, I'll make sure you're fed."

"Nice of you," I said with a flat tone. "Since we're having this lovely chat, did someone rescue Doctor Lamont?"

"Yes. And Bubba Boom, Hank and a bunch of the maintenance workers have been searching for you ever since, causing us trouble. That's why it took so long to get back here."

"Too bad." Sarcasm laced my words. And when the silence lengthened, I asked about the Pit.

Before he could reply, the door opened. I braced for their "last try" by clamping my lips tight. But when Riley stood there with Sloan, a little yelp of surprise escaped me.

Riley turned on Jacy. "What's this?" He gestured toward me. "You said you were going to *talk* to her. Let her go. Now!"

Not what I had been expecting. Maybe Riley's anger was part of the ruse.

"She thinks we're the saboteurs," Jacy replied mildly. "How was I supposed to get her to sit down with me for a nice conversation?"

I noted the use of "we're." Nausea rose in my empty stomach.

"That's why I wanted to be the one to convince her," Riley said.

"You're needed elsewhere. We're running out of time." Jacy jumped to his feet. "This has been a total waste of precious time. Sloan, take her to the Pit. We'll manage without her. Riley, are the wires in place?"

"Not yet."

"Then go. Get it done. They're already attached to us. Sloan'll deal with Trella."

Riley didn't move. He met my gaze. "Did Logan find a way around the Outsiders?" he asked.

I might not trust Jacy, but despite Riley's belief, I did trust him. I should have trusted him with the bomb, and I should have tried to figure out what he'd been doing all these weeks. But my own hurt feelings had kept me away from him. Now though, if Riley thought Jacy's gang was doing the right thing, then I had no qualms. "No. Not yet. We think we have one last chance, but it would require a coordinated effort from a bunch of people."

Jacy and Riley exchanged a look.

"I have the manpower," Jacy said. "We can combine our efforts?"

That last bit sounded like a question. "I thought your sources dried up when you joined the Committee."

"Things have changed."

Riley knelt in front of me. "Will you help us, Trell?"

Looking into his eyes, seeing the concern on his face, I couldn't resist him. "Yes."

Free at last, I stood and rubbed feeling back into my muscles. "What do you need from us?" Jacy asked me.

"We have to confirm that our plan can work first, and then we'll need a few workers we can trust from every system."

"Okay, I'll find you three for each. Is that enough?" Jacy asked.

"Yes."

He nodded and turned to leave.

"Jacy, you said you needed me. What do you want me to do?" I asked.

He glanced at Riley. "You might as well tell her everything. Then get back to those wires."

Riley gave him a mocking salute. "Aye-aye, Captain."

Jacy smiled and left the room.

"Can you tell me in the cafeteria?" I asked. "I'm starving."

"No," Sloan said. "You'll have to be rescued by mainte-nance. I'll go get everything set up and come back for you." He shot me a sour look before leaving.

"I have a feeling I'm not going to like this," I said.

"I don't like it at all, but it's our best chance," Riley said.

"Just start from the beginning." I sat on the table in the place Jacy had cleared. No way I would sit in *that* chair again.

"Here's the condensed version. Bubba Boom is working for the Outsiders. He built those bombs and attacked Logan. We don't know how he contacted them, and we don't know who else is helping him. We suspect Hank, but have no proof. Jacy and I are trying to bypass the Outsiders by building another computer network independent of the existing one. Then we'll switch controls over to the new network. But we can't do that if Bubba Boom is just going to hijack the new network. We need to know more."

I connected the logic. "You want me to get closer to Bubba Boom and find out how he is communicating with the Outsiders?"

"You've been hanging out with him so...yeah." He didn't look happy about it.

"He's supposedly helping me with finding the active link to the Outsiders. And searching for Sloan and company. But he doesn't know about Logan."

"That's good."

"Yeah. I guess he wanted to make sure I didn't join Jacy." Fooled me big time. Why was I so easily convinced? Perhaps because I had lost faith in my own judgment.

"He did save your life," Riley said.

"So did you. I'd never have washed off the chemical so fast."

He shrugged. "If you had trusted...never mind."

I grabbed his arms and forced him to look at me. "I *do* trust you. I would have told Jacy to go recycle himself if *you* hadn't come in here. I didn't trust *myself*. I now know I made a mistake by listening to Bubba Boom. A big...huge mistake and I paid dearly for it." I huffed. "That's why I didn't want to be in charge. What if I make another wrong decision?"

"Then we'll deal with it. I'd rather have you make a mistake then have Outsiders tell us what to do."

"Are you sure? I've made some doozies."

"I'm positive. Besides, you're not the only one to mess up. Jacy screwed up your recruitment, I've done and said things I regret and your mother has had a couple lapses in judgment. Hopefully, Bubba Boom and the Outsiders will make mistakes that we can take advantage of."

He made me feel better, but I didn't fully agree with him. "You shouldn't have anything to regret."

A sad smile touched his lips. "I regret my harsh words. I regret my anger. "

"You shouldn't. I needed to hear those words and to be woken up to Inside's problems. Although, I don't have a death wish!"

"I know. Just voicing my frustration. You'd dash off to the rescue, but couldn't see Inside needed more rescuing." His smile reached his eyes this time. "If I only knew to tell you to *not* get involved, it would have saved us a lot of trouble. Plus, Sheepy's been miserable these last few weeks."

Sloan returned. "The room's ready. Let's go," he said to me.

"What's going on now?"

"I'm gonna lock you in a maintenance closet, we'll tip off Bubba Boom to your location and he'll sweep in for the rescue," Sloan said.

"You can tell him Jacy didn't trust you and wanted you out of the way. Try to get…close to him. Convince him you're on his side." Riley's queasy expression said more than his words.

I stepped closer to him and lowered my voice. "If you could change one thing, what would it be?"

He pulled the sheep pendant from his pocket. A question filled his eyes. I held out my hand. Riley placed it in my palm and I curled my fingers around the necklace, pressing the metal into my skin.

★ ★ ★

The trip to the maintenance closet with Sloan was part of the ruse. After giving Riley time to return to his wires, Sloan grabbed my elbow and pulled me along a few corridors in level one. We passed a bunch of people who ignored us. I was supposed to look scared—not hard to do considering I was with Sloan.

He shoved me into the closet. Only two meters wide by two meters long, the closet's shelves had been filled with mechanical parts. Sloan closed the door and turned on the light. No vents.

Sloan pulled out a roll of tape. "Turn around."

"Excuse me?"

Spinning me around, he yanked my wrists behind my back and taped them together, rolling the tape a few centimeters up my arms. He pushed me down to the floor, and did the same to my ankles.

"It's gotta look real," he said, but a perverse little smile played on his lips.

Being small may be beneficial when climbing through the ducts, but it sucked big time against Jacy's oversized goons. I needed to get my stun gun back.

"Did Jacy tell you to do this?"

"No. I really don't like you. Figured this is a little payback for not trusting us scrubs enough that you had to place a microphone over our barracks."

He ripped off another section of tape and slapped it over my mouth. My head jerked back and a stinging pain radiated over my jaw. I didn't know how or when, but I silently vowed that I would retaliate in some way.

"I hope it takes your boyfriend a long time to find you." He clicked off the light and locked me in the dark.

sixteen

After I concocted a list of creative ways to pay Sloan back, I squirmed into a more comfortable position. Sloan had my arms pinned too tight for me to bring my hands forward.

Should I try to escape? From my brief glance of the parts and supplies on the shelves, I figured I could find something sharp enough to cut through the tape. If this were indeed a real abduction, then I would try my best to get free.

Getting up on my feet was harder to do than I expected. Once stable, I hopped over to the light switch. Or rather to where I thought the switch was located. I bumped into the door, then rubbed my cheek on the cold metal wall to find the light. It was too high for my hands to reach, but I managed to flick the tab up with my shoulder.

I inspected the shelves, and discovered one positive aspect of my imprisonment. Sloan had taped my wrists so that my palms touched. If I found a sharp object, I could grab it with my fingers and saw through. If he had turned my wrists the opposite way, I wouldn't be able to manipulate an item as well.

I also searched for sharp edges jutting from the shelves that I could rub the tape against. The metal bins on the left side contained nuts, bolts, rivets and washers. Tubes, electrical connectors and rolls of wire filled the bins along the back wall. Finally on the right wall, I found a pile of nails. Long pointy nails.

Turning around, I tried to pick up a couple, but the bin was just high enough that even up on my unsteady tiptoes, I could touch it, but not get to the nails. Instead, I grabbed the bin and yanked.

I fell forward, landing on my knees. Nails rained down on my legs and bare feet. Sloan would regret his little payback, I promised. At least I had plenty of nails to use. And after a few awkward tries, I succeeded in keeping the nail in my hands long enough to poke it into the tape. When I added in being light-headed from lack of food and water, I realized a quick escape wouldn't be in my future.

Time ceased to have any meaning and by the time the doorknob twisted and the keypad beeped, I'd only ripped a little bit of the tape. I sagged to the floor in exhaustion.

The door flew open and Bubba Boom was next to me in a heartbeat. "Are you all right?"

I nodded. He pulled out his penknife, and cut through the tape on my wrists and ankles. I winced as he peeled it away from my skin.

He touched the one on my mouth. "Do you want to do it or should I?"

I pointed to him.

"On three?"

Again I nodded.

"One. Two." He ripped it off.

I yelped. My lips burned and tears stung my eyes. "No three?"

"Sorry. I thought that would be better."

A sticky residue from the tape coated my cheeks, wrists and ankles. "That's okay." I touched his arm. "Thanks."

He gave me a shy smile. "You certainly keep a guy hopping." Bubba Boom freed a few strands of my hair that had stuck to my cheek, and tucked them behind my ear. "Doctor Lamont's on the way."

"I'm fine. Just starving."

He took my right hand in his. Turning my wrist, he traced the tiny scar on my forearm. "We would have found you sooner if you hadn't taken the tracer out."

"We?"

"Hank and the others. And Doctor Lamont. We've all been searching for you."

"Did she rat me out about the tracer?"

"No, but we figured it out pretty quick." He grew serious. "Who locked you in here?"

"Sloan."

He nodded as if expecting that answer. "Who were the two guys who took you from the infirmary?"

"Jacy's goons. I don't know their names."

"Do you know why they grabbed you?"

"I think Jacy found out about my tracer. He wanted to know what I had been doing and I wouldn't tell him. It's obvious he's up to something and he thought I'd figure it out and cause trouble."

"So he made a preemptive strike," Bubba Boom said.

"Sounds like—"

"Trella!" Lamont rushed into the room. She dropped her medical bag and wrapped me in a tight hug. Her muscles trembled.

Stunned, I didn't move.

"I've been so worried!" She pulled away to look at me. "Are you all right? If they've hurt you, I'll dismember them without antiseptic and feed them to Chomper one tiny bit at a time."

Impressive. All I wished to do was slap Sloan a few times.

"Can you walk? I want to do a full scan right away." Lamont checked my pulse.

"I'm fine. Just really thirsty and hungry." I appealed to Bubba Boom. "Can you come with me to the cafeteria?"

But Lamont wouldn't take the hint. "I'll come along. You haven't eaten in at least twenty-six hours. You'll need to be careful about what you put into your stomach."

"Twenty-six hours? Are you sure?" That seemed too long. I wondered if Logan had been successful and what was going on with the Outsiders.

"Oh yes. I felt every one of them." Lamont thumped her chest. "You were stunned and, since you're small, it probably knocked you out for ten to twelve hours."

Funny, I didn't remember being unconscious. I'd been stunned before and hadn't blacked out.

Bubba Boom helped me stand. The room spun for a moment and my knees considered buckling. He put his arm around my shoulders, steadying me before we headed to the cafeteria.

Our ragtag group caused quite the stir in the dining room. At this point, I didn't care. Lamont fetched me a tray of food. Then everything blurred together as if a part of me had already fallen asleep. Gulping water, eating, returning to the infirmary and being tucked into bed by Bubba Boom combined into one long dream.

Before leaving, he kissed my forehead. I slid my hand into my pocket and clutched my pendant as I slipped into a deeper sleep.

When I woke, I took a long, scalding hot shower. Lamont descended on me as soon as I finished, ordering me to eat a large bowl of her special soup. I needed to visit Logan, but she wouldn't let me leave until I agreed to a full physical.

I stifled the desire to argue and remind her of her promise

not to mother me. Her medical request bordered on overprotectiveness. However, it had been nice to know people had been upset by my abduction and had been looking for me. Before I had gotten involved in the search for Gateway, I could have died in the pipes and only Cog would have cared.

"Aside from some bruising, a couple strained muscles and slight dehydration, you're in good health," Lamont said.

I jumped down from the examination table glad to be done.

"Do you really need to leave so soon?" she asked. "You should rest and rehydrate."

"There's too much going on right now. I'll rest later," I said.

I debated if I should climb into the shafts or not. Almost everyone in Inside knew about the tracer. Deciding not to risk being seen in the wrong place by the wrong people, I returned to my room.

Lamont trailed after me. "Trella, wait."

I turned. She hovered in the doorway, uncertain and vulnerable. Not Doctor Lamont, but Kiana Garrard. Interesting how she morphed from one to the other. At least I had some warning that this wasn't medical.

"You understood my clues, right? You knew there were two armed men waiting to ambush you."

"Yes. That's why I dropped in from the ceiling and tried to stun them." I still needed to get my gun back from Jacy.

"Why did you come? You could have saved yourself twenty-six hours of suffering. You had to know they wouldn't hurt me, and yet you came anyway and ended up turning yourself over to them."

Ah. A good question. Did I have a good answer? Was it because she was my mother? Or because she was an excellent doctor? Or because I was the reason she had been targeted in the first place? How about all of the above?

Riley's comment from the maintenance closet replayed in my mind. "It's what I do. I guess you could say it's my role or job. Rushing to the rescue, and doing what I can so others don't suffer." I spread my hands, trying to find the right words. "I don't really think about it, I just react and hope for the best." I shrugged. "Worked so far."

"You shouldn't have risked yourself for me, Trella."

"A moment of weakness." I smiled. "A mistake even. Everyone is entitled to make a few mistakes."

Logan slept on the couch. His arm covered his eyes and one foot dangled off the edge. I dropped down. The light thud woke him. Before I could say a word, he hopped up and embraced me.

"Trella! You're here," he said with glee.

"Even though I'm not as smart as you, I do know where I am."

"I feared the worst. No one could find you. Anne-Jade had all her ISF officers searching."

"I wasn't in any real danger. And I'm sorry to have kept you in suspense, but no one had time to stop by here." I explained about Jacy and Riley's plans to build a separate network. "Riley's stringing wires as we speak."

"Ooh. I like! Why didn't I think of that?" He bounced on his toes as his gaze turned inward.

"Because it's been me, you and Anne-Jade, while Jacy has recruited a bunch of people."

"True."

"What about your idea?"

He stopped bouncing. "When you said I should climb the Expanse, you didn't explain there wasn't a ladder."

"The ladder starts about seventy-five meters up, but there are lots of things to hold on to."

"That's assuming I have the strength to hang on and pull myself up the Wall. I don't know how you did it, but I didn't make it past twenty meters before my legs and arms turned to mush."

"What about Anne-Jade?"

"She was too busy, and I thought it would be less suspicious for one person to be up there. Besides, I doubt she would have climbed much farther." He plopped back onto the couch. "Is there another way up there?"

I considered. "I could rig a pulley to the end of the ladder and hoist you up."

Logan bent over and pulled a wipe board out from under the couch. "You'll need more than one wheel in order to lift my weight." He wrote a list of supplies on the board and drew a little diagram of how to hook them together. "This should work as long as the pulley is securely attached to the ladder."

I studied his diagram. It didn't appear to be too complicated. Hank could put this together in no time. Except Hank wouldn't like us exploring in the Expanse. I had a difficult time believing Hank was behind all the sabotage. He was Cog's right-hand man and good friend. Perhaps he wasn't involved. And perhaps I was kidding myself.

Why did I have no trouble accepting Jacy's involvement with the Outsiders? No answer. My head spun and I sat next to Logan. The trip to his room had taken me twice as long as normal. I had to keep stopping to catch my breath.

"Are you all right?" Logan asked.

"Just a little dizzy."

"Me, too. I'm not sure if I'm sick, but I keep having these dizzy spells."

That seemed odd. Lamont had also commented on feeling light-headed. "Since when?"

"A few hours after you rushed off to help the doctor. Do you think something's wrong with the air plant?"

"Could be. Last I heard, it was working even though not all the air filter bays have been repaired." A strange thought floated to the surface of my mind. "Logan, do you know what's going on with the Outsiders?"

He gestured to the computer. "I managed to get into a few subsystems. It's frustrating as hell, like putting my toe in the water, but not being able to jump in!"

"And?"

"Oh. Their vehicle is still attached, but I think no one has opened Gateway yet. I don't understand why they haven't."

"Maybe our air isn't right for them? Maybe the people who want them to come in have to adjust it slowly or risk hurting us?"

"Pure speculation. Maybe they're waiting for us to be told about them. Can you imagine if they just showed up? Massive panic."

"Then why aren't their cohorts spreading the word?"

"Maybe they plan to sneak in? Get a sense of the situation first?"

Too many unknowns at this point, guessing would be a waste of our limited time. "You're right. It's all conjuncture. We need more data."

"That's my girl." Logan slapped me on the back. "Spoken like a true Tech No!"

Unfortunately, in order to get more data, I would have to get closer to Bubba Boom. I'd rather be getting reacquainted with Riley. I checked the power plant's control room on level four, the air plant and maintenance in Sector B2, but couldn't find Bubba. He might be sleeping. I didn't even know what barrack he lived in. Actually, I knew very little about him.

While climbing around level four, I had placed the wipe board with the pulley diagram in Riley's bedroom, hoping he could make one and pass it to Jacy. Since I'd run out of places to look for Bubba Boom, I returned to the infirmary to help Lamont.

People filled the patient area. Lamont moved among them, handing out cups of water and white pills. Hair stuck out from her braid and she moved as if walking through a thick stew.

"What's going on?" I asked her.

"Headaches, dizziness and nausea," she said. "And a few patients have minor bumps and bruises from passing out. Everyone's blaming the air plant."

When I had poked my head into the plant, the air filtering machinery appeared to be working. However, a number of maintenance workers had been repairing one of the air scrubbers. "How can I help?"

"Can you wrap Jenna's sprained ankle? She twisted it when she stumbled down the stairs."

"Sure." I grabbed a roll of bandages and crossed to the girl with a bag of ice on her ankle.

We worked for a few hours as a steady stream of people from level three came in. My energy dropped faster than normal. And a couple times, I needed to stop and catch my breath. I worried that the Outsiders might just be slowly killing us all, which added to the low-simmering panic in the pit of my stomach. At any moment, it felt as if the terror would erupt into a full boil.

Bubba Boom arrived. He appeared upset, and I asked him if he was feeling sick.

He glanced around the full room. "No. I heard you were *all over* Inside, looking for me."

One of the maintenance workers must have spotted me. I rubbed my eyes. It was getting harder to sneak around Inside when everyone recognized me.

"Did I hear wrong?" he demanded, but somehow I sensed he already knew the answer.

"No. I wanted to ask you about Jacy and Sloan. And the air plant."

"Did you consider the danger? It's not safe for you to be

running around without a couple bodyguards. Do you want Jacy to grab you again?"

Ah. The reason for his anger. "No. I just—"

"Let's go for a walk."

We headed west toward the common area in Quad A3. The hallway was empty and the few people in the area sat listlessly on the couches and armchairs. Stranger than the emptiness was the quiet. So used to the constant babble of voices, I felt as if every word I said could be heard by everyone.

We sat on a couch in the corner. I willed myself not to sit as far away from him as possible, but still left a half meter between us.

"Jacy's goons caught me in the infirmary so I'm not—"

"You are now. Since you returned, we've had people in there to protect you."

"I didn't see anyone."

His anger deflated a bit. "You're not supposed to."

"Oh."

"Can you at least understand why I would be upset?"

"Yes. I'm sorry."

"You're lucky word didn't get back to Jacy. Must be all these headaches."

"Are you getting them, too?" I asked.

"No. Not yet, anyway."

"You're one of the few who isn't sick," I said. "Is the air plant malfunctioning?"

"No."

"How can you be sure? Everyone's been complaining."

Bubba Boom studied me as if trying to decide what to tell me. "Did Sloan or Jacy say anything to you about the net-work?"

"No. All they wanted was information."

"About what?"

"What I've been doing these past few weeks."

"What exactly have you been doing when everyone *thought* you were in the infirmary?" he asked. "You still haven't told me how you know so much."

Damn. I decided to stick to the truth as much as possible. "I've been searching for Logan."

"And?"

"I haven't found him yet."

He relaxed a bit more. "The information?"

"I've been spending a lot of time in the air ducts, so I've overheard quite a bit."

He considered. "Trella, I need to know who you believe. Me or Jacy?"

"You, of course! Jacy—"

"Was part of your rebellion. You were friends."

Interesting word choice. Your rebellion. I acted confused. "Not since you told me about him and Sloan and the captain. Not since he locked me in a storage closet, leaving me to die of thirst because he's too much of a coward to finish me off. Where are he and Sloan anyway? Shouldn't the ISF arrest them?"

"The ISF won't touch Jacy. Plus Anne-Jade has enough problems right now. We plan to deal with them." He took my left hand in his. "They both *will* suffer for hurting you."

"We?"

He drew in a breath and let it all out at once. "Me, Hank, our core crew and…the Outsiders."

I jerked as if surprised. "Outsiders? Who are—"

"They're from the Outside and they're angry about your rebellion. They have taken over the network, not Jacy."

"They're mad at me?" No need to fake the tremor of fear in my voice.

"No. Not at you." He rushed to assure me. "They're un-happy that our society has gotten out of control. Soon they will come Inside and fix everything!" His eyes glowed with conviction.

"Really? They're coming inside?" I pretended to be stunned. Then I leaned closer as if suddenly enthusiastic. "Will they repair the air and power plant?"

"Yes, and put our society back in order. No Committee, no ISF, no scrubs or uppers, they're going to fix it all."

"How?"

"By returning our society to its original configuration."

"Original as in Pop Cops?"

"No. As in the Outsiders once again being our Controllers, making the rules, enforcing the rules and the rest of you can return to work. I'll be one of their chosen liaisons."

Sounded like the Pop Cops, but I knew better than to argue with him. "When are they coming?" I asked instead.

"Soon. We have to prepare for them. And that's where you come in."

"Me?"

"Yes. You're a natural leader, Trella. You united everyone to fight the Pop Cops. They told us to convince you of their benevolence. They want you to get everyone excited about them. That's why Jacy wanted you out of the way. He knows about the Outsiders and is trying to prevent them from coming inside."

"Oh." A twist I hadn't been expecting. "Did they contact you?"

"Not me. Hank. He's believed that the Controllers live Outside and have been instructing us on how to live better lives. Though his beliefs were shaken a bit when you found Gateway and it lead to Outer Space and not to them. He's been searching the computers since your rebellion. He never gave up faith that they existed.

"All that nonsense about the Controllers being operating parameters and fail-safes was just that. Nonsense. When you think about it, there had to be a higher authority than the captain and admirals. The Travas followed the Controllers' rules, and we should have as well. A mistake that Hank and I are going to fix. And now you can help us." He leaned toward me. "We're not going to let Jacy win. We're going to have an ordered society again, but this time you and I and Hank and all our supporters are going to be the leaders."

Bubba Boom closed the gap between us. He wrapped his arms around my back and drew me in for a kiss.

For a second, I froze. Then, remembering my mission, I returned the kiss. It wasn't the same as when I had kissed Riley. Riley's zipped through my body, leaving a trail of fire in its wake. Bubba Boom's made me nervous. I wouldn't be able to do more than kiss him, and I hoped I wouldn't have to.

When he broke off, he pulled me tight to his chest. "Unlike Hank, you understand," he whispered in my ear. "Understand what it's like to be at the mercy of another. To suffer and be forced to make a choice between your friends."

"Are you talking about Vinco and the Pop Cops?"

"Yes. He wouldn't stop until I told him who the Tech Nos were, but I kept Anne-Jade's and Logan's names to myself, giving him the others. Every time I close my eyes to sleep, I see all their faces. Your mother understands as well."

I hadn't thought of it that way. Karla had threatened to recycle her husband and daughter if she didn't cooperate. She had named friends in order to protect them...me. And then we were taken from her anyway. She had lost everyone.

Bubba Boom released me. "That's why we need Controllers. They won't torture or trick people."

"Do you know why they wish to come in?"

Again his face shone with a fervent glow. "We're their lost children. We have run away and made a mess of things. They've been trying to catch up to us, but Inside is faster than they are. But not anymore. We've stopped accelerating so they could join us."

That's why the Transmission had been targeted twice. "Then we better prepare everyone for their arrival." I tried to sound like an avid believer.

His smile encompassed his whole face. "I knew you were smart. Hank said you'd be impossible to convince, but the logic is hard to ignore." He stood. "Come on, we have lots to do."

I hurried to keep pace with him as he headed back toward the infirmary. When we arrived in the crowded patient area, he said, "Go and get your things. I'll talk to the doctor."

"Why?"

"You can't stay here. It's too dangerous. We have an extra room for you and you'll be protected at all times."

Which also meant *watched* at all times. Not much I could do without blowing my cover. I collected my meager possessions. When I returned, Bubba Boom was talking to Lamont.

My mother met my gaze with a question in her eyes. I got the impression all I needed to do was signal her in some fashion and she would prevent him from taking me from the infirmary. Half tempted to see what she would do, I almost nodded in encouragement. But the need to find out all I could stopped me. Instead, I kept my expression neutral.

"Trella, can I have a word in private?" she asked.

"Uh. Sure." I turned to Bubba Boom. "Be right back."

Lamont led me to her office and shut the door. She motioned toward the chair and I perched on the edge. Remembering how Domotor and Bubba Boom both avoided talking to me in the infirmary, I guessed Lamont's office probably had a hidden microphone somewhere inside.

"I understand he rescued you and saved your life, but don't you think you should wait a few weeks before staying with him?" she asked.

"That sounds like a mother's question and not a doctor's concern," I said.

She stiffened as pain flashed in her eyes. "You had a rough week. You're not fully recuperated."

"I'll be fine. In fact, I can rest better surrounded by Bubba Boom and his colleagues. There's no way Jacy can get to me there." Unable to leave her without a better explanation, I took a wipe board and marker from her desk and wrote, *It's not what you think. This is part of a plan.*

"Oh. Well…then…I just wanted to make sure you considered your health. You'll come back if your headaches get worse?"

"Yes." I erased the words from the board and wrote, *Thanks.*

Bubba Boom led me up to level five. Although it had been completed before the first explosion, the Committee hadn't had time to decide who should move in. Bluelights lit the hallways and our footsteps echoed. The layout of the new level matched all the others so when he stopped in front of a set of double doors, I knew we were close to Quad A5.

He turned to me and took both my hands. "This is the new headquarters for Inside. All the system controls are now here." Letting my left hand go, he knocked on the door.

A thin hidden panel opened and eyes peered at us before the doors hissed apart. Bubba Boom didn't hesitate. He strode in like he owned the place, towing me along like a prized possession.

The area resembled the main Control Room in Quad G4, but it wasn't finished. Computers and half-completed manned stations sprouted exposed wires. Desks and diagrams were drawn on the walls. Lots of general activity and buzz of voices that ceased the moment we entered.

My heart paused as I glanced around. A feeling that I had just made the biggest mistake in my entire life overwhelmed me.

I expected to recognize a bunch of the maintenance crew. I also knew a few uppers and a couple scrubs.

I expected to see Hank. And expected he would be the hardest one to convince of my newfound faith. Hank jumped to his feet and barreled toward us clearly upset. No surprise there.

I didn't count on Karla Trava sitting with a group of uppers around a small conference table. But as much as her presence upset and surprised me, she wasn't the reason my heart tore a hole in my chest, fleeing for its life.

Two…beings wearing strange white reflective suits stood near a bank of computers. They had round silver metal heads with black tubes that ran from their chests to small tanks on their backs.

The Outsiders had come in.

seventeen

Even though they were shaped like us—two legs, two arms, hands, torso and, I guessed, a head—I backed away from the Outsiders. Bubba Boom stopped me. "It's okay, Trella, they're just wearing protective suits. They look just like us, and these two men are here to help us get ready for the others."

Men? Their silver heads reflected like a mirror. Hank's broad shape alone covered half of the one's on the left.

"Are you out of your mind?" Hank asked Bubba Boom. "Why did you bring *her* here?"

"She understands. I was right about her."

Hank snorted. "You're a fool."

It was time for me to convince Hank. I forced my gaze away from the strange Outsiders and met his. "He isn't a fool. *I'm* the foolish one. I thought once we gained control of Inside, my job was done. A mistake I plan to fix. I'm here to do it right this time. To get us back on track."

Hank stared at me as if he could read my thoughts. I suppressed the urge to squirm under his intense scrutiny. "Cogon told me you didn't believe in the Controllers. And you never stopped to consider our beliefs before you carelessly announced they didn't exist." He stepped closer to me. "The Controllers are just system safeguards and directives from our ancestors, you and Logan said. Do you know how upsetting that was?"

He didn't wait for my reply. "Do you even understand that when you told the scrubs Outside was not the paradise they believed in for thousands of weeks, but some airless void, you destroyed their hope of ever reaching a better place?"

"I do now."

"Too late! The damage's been done. I never gave up hope. I kept searching for them. I knew they wouldn't abandon us." He swept his hand out. "And here they are. Just like us. On a journey through Outer Space to find a home. And now I don't have to play nice with the Committee or you."

I glanced at Bubba Boom. "If everyone believes the Controllers are our leaders, then why did you say you needed me?"

"Because there are many like you who don't believe. And who trust your word," Bubba Boom said.

"But all you need to do is show them proof." I gestured toward the Outsiders. They moved closer. Their gait awkward. And so did Karla Trava. Oh joy. Two nightmares within easy reach.

"We don't want to spark a panic. They accepted the Committee because you endorsed them, so they'll accept the Outsiders as our Controllers as well."

Such confidence that I didn't deserve. Hank had been right about me. I hadn't considered the ramifications of my discoveries. But I did know taking out the Pop Cops had been a good thing.

"Why is Karla here?" I asked Bubba Boom.

"The Travas have been cooperating with the Controllers long before your rebellion. She helped us when they contacted us."

"Did the Travas know they're from Outside?" I asked.

"No," Karla said. "We believed they were intelligent beings living inside the computer network. The reality is far more logical."

"How did you get out of the brig?"

Bubba Boom answered. "Anne-Jade. All this time Logan's been under our…protection, not the Committee's. We have control of the life systems as well. Anne-Jade won't risk her brother's life. She cares too much to refuse us."

"I think Trella does, too," Hank said. "And I'm not convinced of her change in heart either."

Bubba Boom pulled me close as if to protect me. "She was taken by Jacy. Sloan tried to kill her and she understands."

"Understands what, exactly?" Hank asked.

"I understand that we need something to unite us," I said. And this I believed one hundred percent. Except my thinking skewed to uniting us as Insiders and not as servants to the Outsiders. "And I believe the Controllers will help and not hurt us."

Hank turned to Karla. "What do you think?"

"I think you should recycle her right away," she said. "She will ruin all your plans. She should *never* be trusted."

Bubba Boom's grip on my hand tightened. "I trust her. And Cogon loved her like a sister."

"And look how that worked out for him," Karla said.

Hank chewed on his lip. "I'll let the Controllers decide. Come with me."

It was a good thing my heart had already run away, otherwise it would have exploded in my chest from the sudden surge of terror.

Bubba Boom pried my hand from his. "It'll be okay. Just tell them the truth." He nudged me toward Hank and the Outsiders.

They waited for me to join them. I followed them into

another room. When the door hissed shut, I couldn't breathe in the thin air. Gasping, I felt as if I suffocated. Panicking, I glanced around.

The room was a standard conference area with table and chairs. But big silver tanks lined the far wall and metal boxes had been stacked in the corner. Metal plates covered the air and heating vents.

Hank gestured to a chair. Once I sat, he showed me the small tank near the chair's legs and the oxygen mask. Understanding cut through the dizziness and I covered my nose and mouth with the mask, filling my lungs with thick air.

The Outsiders fiddled with clamps around their necks. A popping noise followed a whoosh and they removed their round silver helmets.

They did resemble us. Short brown hair, brown eyes, a nose, mouth and ears. But their skin had an unhealthy yellowish cast, almost like jaundice. And their expressions were far from friendly.

The Outsider on the right crinkled his nose as if he smelled something rotten. "This is sheep leader?" He spoke with a thick accent. He struggled to pronounce each word.

Hank pulled his mask away from his face. "Yes. This is Trella Garrard."

"She look…"

"Insignificant," the other Outsider said.

"She is not. She caused much trouble for our world, but her actions enabled us to contact you."

As if I didn't feel bad enough.

Hank introduced the Outsiders. "This is Ponife." The Outsider on the right inclined his head. "And Fosord."

"What is problem?" Ponife asked Hank.

Hank explained in concise sentences how they needed me yet they doubted my sincerity. The two Outsiders conferred in a strange dialect. I could understand every fourth or fifth word.

Ponife stood and went to the stack of metal boxes. He removed the top one and set it on the floor, then rummaged in the second one. He returned with a thin silver loop, walking toward me.

"Stand, Trella Garrard," he ordered.

I glanced at Hank.

"If you truly believe, you'll do as they say," Hank said.

Escape would be difficult, considering the blocked vents, and the roomful of people between me and freedom. I rose. Ponife touched a small metal X to the loop and it opened, breaking into two half circles hinged together.

He held the broken loop out and approached me, aiming for my neck. I decided I had learned more than enough, and ducked. Running for the door, I hoped the element of surprise would be on my side when I raced through the new control room.

It wasn't. The door refused to slide open. Hank tackled me to the ground. Despite my struggles, Hank kept me pinned, and Ponife snapped the loop around my neck. It felt big at first, but the metal warmed against my skin and…softened then tightened. Hank released me and I dove for the oxygen mask, convinced I was being choked to death.

After a few deep breaths, I realized my windpipe had not been compressed. I tried to hook a finger under the loop, but it was skintight.

"I knew you were lying. Did Jacy send you to spy on us?" Hank asked.

"No. I panicked." I pointed to Ponife. "He scared me." I tugged on the loop. It didn't budge. "What is this thing?"

"A command collar," Ponife said. "You will…listen to us."

"But she can't be trusted," Hank said.

"No matter. She is…attached to us. We know where she go."

"She will listen or…" Fosord, who hadn't moved during the whole incident, motioned to his colleague.

Ponife twisted the metal X with his fingers. Sharp needles of pain stabbed into my neck and traveled down my spine. Unrelenting pulses of fire coursed through my body. I collapsed to the ground, shrieking. Vinco's knife had been a caress in comparison to this anguish.

The pain stopped as quickly as it had arrived. My relief was almost as intense as the pain. Hank pressed the mask to my mouth as I gasped. Shudders overwhelmed my muscles as sweat pooled. If I had to guess how it felt to be kill-zapped, I'd imagine that torment came pretty damn close.

Hank straightened. "Impressive. Do you have more of those command collars?"

"Yes," Ponife said. "We find them to be…useful for…solving problems."

"Can I?" Hank wanted to take the X.

"No. Only Controllers can…correct problems."

"What else can it do?" he asked.

Ponife pulled on one of the ends. Numbness spread down my body, deadening all feeling below my neck. I could only move my head.

"She is…stopped," Ponife said. He flipped it around and tugged another side.

Feeling returned with a sudden flush of heat. My body tingled like I had just been kissed by Riley. It intensified as pure pleasure raced along my skin as if invisible hands stroked my body. To me, this was more humiliating than the pain.

"She is…rewarded. That is all." He righted the X.

The tingling stopped, and I had control of my body. For now.

"Plus you know where she is, right? It works like a tracer?" Hank asked.

Ponife dug into the pocket of his suit. The white material creased like fabric, but crinkled like very thin metal. He pulled out a small box that resembled a hand-puter the Pop Cops had used. He opened it, displaying a miniature screen. Inserting the X into the opposite side, he pushed a few buttons. Then he showed Hank the screen.

"That's a map of level five," he said. "What are those numbers on the side?"

"Her vitals. To know if she tells untruths," Ponife said.

Just when I thought my situation couldn't get any worse, he proved me wrong.

"Can we interrogate her now?" Hank asked.

"No. She is…terrorized. You must wait until her vitals return to normal."

"How long?"

"Depends on her."

Hank yanked me off the floor and hustled me from the conference room. He pushed me toward Bubba Boom. I fell into his arms.

"What happened?" Bubba Boom asked, supporting me.

"She tricked you, boy. She's spying for Jacy," Hank said. He tossed a long thin box at Bubba Boom who caught it in midair. "Take her to the lockup. When she settles down, we're going to have a nice long chat." He returned to his post.

Bubba Boom looked at me with a pained expression, but he followed orders, half carrying me from the control room. Right before the doors closed, I spotted Karla Trava watching me with a smug smile.

I tried to explain to Bubba Boom. "It's a misunderstanding. I got scared and—"

"Hank said you're spying for Jacy."

"You believe Hank over me?" I asked.

"Yes." Then he didn't say another word.

He kept a bruising grip on my upper arm. I was really sick of being manhandled all the time. We arrived in what would be Sector D5, which should contain apartments. Except the normally open hallways had barred double doors. Bubba Boom aimed that long box at the first set. He pushed a button and a click rang.

"What's this place?" I asked as he opened the gate.

"Anne-Jade had wanted more cells because of all the Travas. The Committee agreed to convert this Sector into a brig." Bubba Boom pointed his box to the first door on the right. It clicked open. This door was solid except for a panel about eye-level. "You're our first guest." He shoved me inside.

Daylights switched on as the door banged. I shot to my feet, but it was too late. There were no handles or anything on my side of the locked door. The cell was two meters wide by three meters long. A mat covered the floor near the back wall. Solid bars covered the vents. Nothing else here but a toilet.

Trapped, I experienced a sudden premonition that being kill-zapped and fed to Chomper would be a kindness in comparison to my future.

As I lay on the mat in my cell, I tugged and pulled at the loop around my neck, but it refused to budge. I doubted even Logan could remove it. Not that I could go anywhere.

There was only one thing I could do. I slid my hand into my pocket and removed Riley's sheep pendant. Dangling it over my face, I considered my next move. Should I trigger the beacon? It would probably alert Hank. And without working computers, would Riley even know I had signaled for his help?

What if he tried to rescue me and was caught? I couldn't risk him. Jacy needed him. But did they know Hank had been using level five as his own personal headquarters? Did they know two Outsiders had come in? Too many questions and no answers. My emotions flipped from terrified to worried and back again.

One thing I did know. I trusted Riley. He was smart and wouldn't be as easy to catch as I had been. At least that was the reason I clung to in desperation as I pressed the sheep, sending the signal.

I waited for Hank to arrive and confiscate my pendant, but as the hours passed, I slowly relaxed. Eventually, I lost track of the time. It seemed so long ago when Bubba Boom had arrived in the infirmary around hour eight of week number 147,026. Would the Outsiders repair the Transmission and resume our journey?

The click of the lock startled me from my musings. I shoved my pendant back into my pocket as Hank and one of the Outsiders—I couldn't tell with his helmet on—entered my tiny cell. I noted Bubba Boom's absence. The door closed behind them. Ice-cold fear spread inside me. This would be painful.

Hank questioned me and Ponife played with the metal X. The interrogation went something like this:

Hank—"What is Jacy up to?"

Me—"I don't know."

Ponife (with a mechanical sounding voice)—"An untruth." He twisted the X.

I screamed in pain.

Hank—"What is Jacy up to?"

Me—"I don't know."

Ponife twisted the X.

I screamed.

And so on until I lost count. Eventually, I broke and confirmed I had been spying for Jacy, and he had been attempting to bypass the Outsiders' hold on our network. At least I retained some dignity and hadn't said how they planned to circumvent the controls to all our life systems. Although right now I wished he hadn't shared that with me. Not when my muscles vibrated from the repeated bouts of agony and my clothes reeked of fear. Not when I lay curled tight in a ball, wishing for a quick trip to Chomper.

Hank seemed happy with my confession and left, but Ponife remained. My terror doubled. He popped his helmet off. Terror tripled. Ponife knelt next to me. Terror headed off the scale.

"Do not…fear," he said, panting with the effort. "Your air is…thick. We will not harm…world. We desire…to reclaim what is ours."

"What is yours?" I asked.

"This ship."

That was the last thing I expected. "Are you sure?"

"Yes. Your…ancestors stole it. Exiled us."

I noted his use of the word *exile*. Of course, it could have a wide range or meanings. "How do you know? As you said, our air is thicker than yours."

"We have…records. We had to…ration air so long…we are used to it. The air mixture is easy to alter. We'll find a…common setting. Good for all."

"Why are you telling me this?"

"You are leader," Ponife said.

I touched the collar. "Not a good one."

"Work with us. You will have…chance to repair damage."

I doubted it would be that easy. "Why did they exile you?"

His demeanor changed in an instant. Wrong question.

"Impertinent child." Ponife twisted the X.

When I came to my senses, Ponife was gone. In his place was a tray of food and a glass of water. My throat burned so I gulped down the water. Then I attacked the food. Only after I had consumed most of it did I consider the danger. I shrugged.

They didn't need poison or drugs. A couple more sessions with the collar and I would do anything for them.

I considered Ponife's comments, trying to list reasons for banishing a person. It would also depend if the Insiders at the time knew about the extra space or not. We hadn't recycled the Travas, but if we didn't know about the Expanse I was sure we'd have had to in order to make room for all of us. Maybe instead of recycling the troublemakers, our ancestors put them into a Bubble Monster and sent them on their way. Was that better or worse than being recycled? Given the choice, I would rather take my chances in Outer Space in a Bubble than be Chomper's dinner.

Eventually, I fell into an exhausted sleep.

A rasping sound woke me. Disorientated, I blinked in the daylights as the shushing grew louder. Deep down, I recognized the noise, but my brain hadn't quite connected it.

After a few more seconds, I jumped to my feet. Climbing up to the air vent, I peered inside. Zippy had come!

I rattled the bars over the vent, but they wouldn't budge. Riley would guess I was stuck. Otherwise, I would have escaped by now. I searched with my fingers and found a cloth bag tied to Zippy. Good boy.

Pulling the bag through the bars, I carried my treasure back to the mat. Funny how the smallest things became so important when you've been reduced to utter helplessness.

I upended the bag. A microphone and receiver tumbled out along with a diamond wire. Inserting the receiver in my earlobe, I turned on the mic.

"Anyone listening?" I asked, trying not to sound pathetic, but strain shook my words, giving me away.

"Trella!" Riley's relieved voice reached me.

I collapsed back onto the mat. This was the first thing to go my way in a long time.

"What's wrong?" he asked.

Worried about Hank detecting the transmission, I explained about the new control room and the Outsiders as fast as I could.

After I finished, Riley asked me a few questions. Then he said, "Get out of there, and meet me at—"

"I can't. They have a…tracer on me."

"Can you cut it out? I could send a scalpel."

"No. It's around my neck." I gave him a basic rundown on all the wonders of the command collar.

He responded with an extended period of silence.

Unable to endure another minute, I said, "Don't be upset. I tried to run away, but Hank—"

"Trell, I'm not mad—well, not at you. I'm going to throttle both Hank and Bubba Boom and feed them to Chomper myself." He paused. "I'm thinking of a way for you to escape. You could use Zippy's short range EMP to disable it."

"I thought that only worked on weapons."

"Logan had to limit what the pulse could affect because of all the sensitive equipment and computers back when you ambushed the main Control Room. But you're far away from anything vital right now. Actually, if Zippy was stronger and if we had our network in place, he could have taken out Hank's new control room."

"How do I switch him over?" I asked.

Riley told me how to remove the safety filter.

"How can I tell if it works on the collar?"

"You escape, hide and wait. If it's operating, they'll find you pretty quick. But the pulse will ruin your microphone and receiver. If they don't come after you, meet me in our storeroom."

"Sounds like a plan. Thanks for the help." Before Riley could switch off, I said, "If this doesn't work, I just want to tell you that…" I closed my eyes. Why was this so hard? "That…I was an idiot to keep my distance from you. That I didn't realize how much I love you until I lost you."

"You'll get free, Trella." Riley's voice sounded tight. "You've survived worse than this. And this time you have more motivation."

"More motivation?"

"Yes. I'm not going to respond to your comment through a microphone. You'll have to hear it from me in person."

After Riley clicked off, I used the diamond wire to saw through the bars over the air vent. I hoped Ponife didn't check my vitals because my accelerated heart rate would alert him. Once I had enough space to wiggle through, I pulled Zippy from the shaft and removed the safety filter.

With nothing else to lose, I flipped the switch on Zippy. My receiver whined and popped, but the little cleaning troll remained silent. Logan had given Zippy a special protective coat so his inner electronics weren't zapped as well. I shoved the cleaning troll back into the duct, and climbed in after him.

In case Zippy's pulse hadn't disabled my collar, I didn't want to hide in any of my favorite spots. Instead, I worked my way up to the top of level ten, which was the bottom of the Expanse. Finding a space between two storage containers, I settled in to wait.

At first, every single noise jolted me. Eventually, I grew used to the sounds of the Expanse looming over me. After I felt like enough time had passed—if my collar worked, they would have found me by now—I descended to level four and headed toward our storeroom.

The glow of bluelights shone through the vent, indicating no one was in the room. Disappointed, I aimed my feet at the ladder and climbed down. The clock on the wall read hour forty-seven. I sank onto the couch. Thirty-nine hours had passed since I left the infirmary with Bubba Boom.

The horror, pain and fear had taken a toll on me. My head throbbed from the thin air. Exhausted, I curled up on the couch with Zippy, but I wished for Riley and Sheepy.

Chaotic dreams swirled. Outsiders chased me. Daylight reflected off their silver helmets, blinding me. Then a wall of people blocked my escape route. Jacy led the group and I ran to him. Instead of protecting me, he grabbed my arm and dragged me back toward the Outsiders. He handed me over to Ponife in exchange for the metal X. As Jacy laughed and turned away, Ponife's white gloves stroked my skin.

I woke with a cry and with cold hands on my shoulders. My nightmare had turned into reality. I was caught.

eighteen

Flailing and kicking the Outsider, I fought with all my strength. I would rather be sent to Chomper than be under Ponife's control again.

It took me a couple of seconds to realize he wasn't fighting back. And finally, his soothing tone and caring words reached me. I stopped struggling and embraced Riley.

"I didn't mean to scare you," he said. He sat on the edge of the couch. "I just couldn't wait until you woke up."

"Not your fault, I was having a nightmare," I said, clinging to him, soaking in his warmth and enjoying the feel of his arms around me.

After a few minutes, Riley pulled back to look at me. A smile quirked and he smoothed a few strands of my hair from my face. My braid had fallen out hours ago and I was sure rats would have no trouble making a nest in my hair.

"How did you cut the collar off?" he asked.

"I didn't." Confused, I touched my throat. The collar remained in place. My fingernails clinked on its hard surface.

Riley squinted. He ran his fingers along my neck. When he found the collar he explored the surface and tried to tug it. "No seams. It doesn't feel like metal. The color is amazing."

"Why?"

"It blends in. It matches your skin. Didn't you know?"

"No mirrors in my cell."

He gasped with mock horror. "So cruel! How did you ever survive?"

I laughed and it felt good. It had been such a long time since a happy feeling had touched me that I wanted to prolong it. I cut off whatever Riley planned to say next by drawing him in for a long kiss that left us both breathless. Deciding that conversation was overrated, I claimed his lips again and yanked him down so he lay next to me on the couch.

My fingers unbuttoned his shirt, I snaked my hands along his chest and around to his back. I would have ripped it off, but he pulled away.

"As much as I would love to continue," he panted, "we don't have any time to spare."

"We might not get another chance," I said.

"If we don't get moving, we're guaranteed not to get any more chances."

"That bad?"

"Yep. We need weeks to finish installing a second network. Which we won't get now that the Outsiders are already inside. We're hoping your and Logan's idea has a quicker turnaround time?"

"I'm not sure. We'll have to ask Logan."

"We'll need to regain control of the air plant first," Riley said. "Without that, we're sunk."

"I'll get Logan and take him up to the top of the Expanse."

"The top?"

Describing level seventeen to Riley, I filled him in.

"Why didn't you tell me this before?"

"I really don't know. Just after I discovered it all this trouble started between us. At the time, I felt overwhelmed, scared and uncertain. Almost like I do now except for the uncertain part." To prove my point, I kissed him again, letting my hands slide all the way down his back.

Riley sat up and grabbed my wrists. "Your timing sucks. You know that, don't you?"

"I hate to waste this opportunity."

"We'll get another one. I promise."

"You can't promise. Not this time. I've seen the Outsiders. I've been…" I closed my eyes as memories of pain rolled through me.

Riley cupped my face with his hands, getting my attention. "Sounds like the Outsiders are too hard to beat. You can't fight them. So you can stay here while Jacy, Logan, Anne-Jade and I make a token attempt to thwart them."

"I know what you're doing."

"Me?" He tried to appear innocent.

"You're telling me I can't fight so I'll get angry and prove you wrong."

"Did it work?" he asked.

I huffed with amusement. "A little."

"How about if I add on guilt? Reminding you that Sheepy wouldn't be happy if the Outsiders replaced the Pop Cops and his rebellion was all for nothing."

Guilt was a factor. Not for Sheepy, but over Cogon. He would hate this. I'd like to turn back the clock and start again from when we beat the Travas. That was impossible, but I remembered a phrase that kept me focused during the bad times. Maximum damage. This time I would impart maximum damage for Cogon.

"I can see that little evil gleam in your eyes. You're back!" he said.

Riley's broad smile shot through me and I couldn't resist

kissing him again. But this time, I pulled away so we could discuss plans.

"Did you have time to make that pulley system?" I asked him.

"One of Jacy's men put it together." He reached under the couch and pulled it out. "We didn't know how thick the rope would be, so we guessed, erring on a bigger size."

I spun the wheels, examining the device. "What's this lever?"

"The brakes in case you accidently let go. We don't want Logan smashed flat."

"Good idea."

When we finished coordinating our plans, Riley rummaged through the drawers of the desk, returning with a small pair of bolt cutters and a jar.

He tossed the jar to me. "Sheep oil."

I peered at it in suspicion. "Did you have this before?" Riley had cut off a metal cuff from my wrist during our Force of Sheep rebellion, but he had claimed not to have the oil which was supposed to help with the pain.

"I can't recall." He batted his dark eyelashes at me.

"Look who has the evil gleam now." I grumbled as I spread the oil around my neck, trying to get it under the control collar. "Okay."

Riley thought the back of my neck would be the best place to cut it off. I held my hair up. The cold touch of the metal sent shivers down my spine. At first, I didn't feel anything, but when he grunted with effort, a sharp pain stabbed into my throat. I cried out and he stopped.

"What's the matter? I didn't pinch your skin."

"It hurt."

"It doesn't look like I even dented the damn thing," he said. "I'm going to need bigger cutters."

A sudden and very unpleasant thought occurred to me. "Could it still be active?"

Riley examined Zippy. "He's working fine. Do you have the receiver and microphone I sent?"

I pulled them from my pocket and also removed my sheep pendant. He took all the devices over to his desk. I peered over his shoulder as he tested each one.

"They're all broken." He then put the tester's two prongs on my collar as he stared at the display. "No reading either. It's busted."

Relief surged through me.

"I'll have to have Logan help me make another pendant for you." Riley swept the items into the recycle bin.

I retrieved the pendant.

"But it can't send a signal anymore."

"Doesn't matter. It's still precious to me." I looped it around my neck then tried to distract Riley with a passionate goodbye kiss, but he wouldn't let me procrastinate anymore.

Since we really couldn't delay any longer, I climbed the ladder with reluctance and entered the air ducts again.

The trip to Logan's room didn't take long. When I arrived, I peered down to check for his keepers. At first the significance of the mess below didn't register in my mind. Logan was never tidy, but this seemed extreme even for him.

The couch had been turned on its side. Computer parts and metallic gadgets littered the floor. The white stuffing from the ruined cushions had settled over everything like a coating of dust.

But no sign of Logan.

Logan was gone. After the shock wore off, I considered where he might be. If he had decided to "escape" from his room, Riley would have known about it because Logan would have sought him and Jacy out. But what if he couldn't?

I glanced down at the door. No wires hung from the locks, which meant Logan hadn't escaped. Anne-Jade could have opened it from the outside. Again, Riley would know unless she was unable to tell him. But why would the room be in such disarray?

The final and most likely scenario entailed Hank bringing Logan up to the brig on level five. It was a logical move. Logan's knowledge and abilities made him a dangerous enemy. And from the mess, it appeared as if one of his keepers had discovered his stash of gadgets.

Just in case Anne-Jade knew where her brother had gone, I searched for her on level four. She was slumped in her chair in the ISF office in Quad A4, staring at nothing that I could see. No one else worked at the other desks. An odd silence filled the room.

Not wanting to scare her, I called her name before jumping down from the vent. Anne-Jade waved me over halfheartedly. Utter defeat looked at me through her eyes. I almost stepped back as my heart lurched in my chest.

"Did something happen to Logan?" I asked.

"Not yet."

Unsure if I should be relieved or not, I asked, "What do you mean by that?"

"Come on, Trell. You don't need me to explain it."

"Did Hank take him?"

She straightened and for a brief second the old Anne-Jade frowned at me. "How did you know Hank's involved?"

"He tried to recruit me to his cause."

She slouched back. "You should have signed up. They're in charge now, you'd have saved yourself a lot of trouble." A wry smile twisted. "Sorry. I forgot who I was talking to. Trouble is exactly what you crave. I just want peace."

Anger flared. I banged a fist on her desk. "I wanted peace, too. And you *know* what happened while I sat around mooning over our state of affairs. I don't crave trouble. It's just one of those unfortunate side effects when I finally decided to take action." I leaned in close to her—almost nose to nose. "If Hank has Logan, then I know exactly where he's being held. Are you going to sit around moping or are you going to help me?"

"It's too late."

"That's such a load of crap. It's never too late."

A spark of ire flashed. "What more proof do you need? My brother's dead body? Would that convince you it's too late?"

"No. Not Logan's. Not Riley's. Not mine or yours. They haven't won, Anne-Jade. They just think they did. Which gives us the advantage."

She laughed. "You're insane."

"That's certainly debatable. But give me another chance."

"Another chance to do what?"

"Prove to you it isn't too late."

She snagged her lower lip with her teeth and chewed. "I don't have any resources. They took everything."

"Everything?"

She nodded.

"You mean you don't have a few loyal lieutenants who would take a risk for you?"

"Well…"

I sensed a small victory. "And you didn't keep a few weapons hidden away just in case?"

"I might have."

"Might? When will you know?"

Anne-Jade huffed in annoyance. "All right. I'll make you a deal. If you rescue Logan and get him to a safe location, I'll help you."

"I accept." I shook her hand, sealing the deal.

I turned on my mic and hailed Riley, informing him of Logan's disappearance and my plans to rescue him. He had given me another microphone and receiver. They worked on a specific frequency so it was very difficult for Hank and the Outsiders to pick it up.

"Do you have the diamond wire?" he asked.

"Yes."

"Do you need backup?" His voice held a nervous edge.

"I'll take Zippy."

"I'd be happier if you took a dozen armed men and women along."

"And I'd be happier if the Outsiders decided to leave us alone."

"Point. Be careful…please."

"I will."

The problem with using a diamond wire to aid in my escape became apparent right away. Wires ringed the bars covering the air vent to Logan's cell. Wires that I assumed would set off a loud alarm if I sawed through them.

I hadn't called attention to myself just in case Logan had company. It was interesting how fast my ability to crawl through the shafts without making noise had returned. Either that or just the amount of time I'd been spending traveling through them had sharpened my skills.

Logan sprawled on his back on the thin mat. His cell was a mirror image of mine. I called his name when I was certain he was alone. He jerked and scrambled to his feet.

"Trella, don't touch the—"

"Bars, I know. I can see the wires."

He slouched against the wall and rubbed his face. "I think I'm stuck for good this time," he said in a tired voice.

He didn't appear to be injured, but I knew what the Outsiders were capable of. "What happened?"

"My keepers made a surprise visit," he said. "I didn't have time to hide all my toys. They were strewn all over. I guess I shouldn't have been so relaxed about them. Another mistake caused by overconfidence."

"Another?"

He waved a hand. His right one still covered his eyes. "The whole Outsider fiasco could have been avoided."

"How?"

"If I had kept track of all communications, I would have spotted Hank's link to the Outsiders."

"Why didn't you?" I asked.

"Privacy. I didn't want to spy on the Committee members or others."

"Exactly, Logan. You didn't want to be like the Travas and Pop Cops, monitoring all our activities. You're not to blame."

"I'm not helping, either," he said. Clearly miserable, he massaged his temples.

"Did you meet the Outsiders?" I asked.

He straightened, dropping his hands. "They're here?"

"Only a couple. I've met them both."

"You? When?"

"Long story. I'll tell you later. First, we need to bust you out of here."

"How? The heating vent has the same trip wires. All you have to do is touch them and they'll set off the alarm."

"How?" I asked.

"There's a weak electrical current going through the wires. If you touch it with your finger, you'll block the current and that sets it off." He began to pace. "But if you touch it with both hands, the current will travel through you and back to the wire. I could cut the bars… No. Won't work. You'd be stuck holding the wires. No way for you to move once the bars and wires are cut. Unless we made a connection with a separate wire and some metal clamps, which we don't have. Plus we would need one bypass for each bar, unless the wire is continuous."

I traced the wire. It wrapped around all five bars before continuing down the air shaft.

"We still don't have the clamps and wires," Logan said when I described it to him.

"I have Zippy and my tool belt."

It was as if I had told him his computer access had returned. He stood under the vent and explained in an excited tone what I needed to do to bypass the current. I performed surgery on Zippy, removing wires and various parts, following his instructions.

Well aware that the Outsiders or Hank could come in at any time, we hurried. But it still took time to rig the bypass, cut the bars and pull Logan into the shaft with me.

"Will it hold?" I asked, pointing to the loop of Zippy's wire.

"It should. Unless a cleaning troll comes by and rips it off."

"Let's go." I put a finger to my lips. "Keep quiet until we get there."

"Where are we going?"

"To the roof."

Logan's rescue had gone smoothly. That worried me as I guided Logan to the top of level ten. My safety rope remained in place—another good sign. I had the pulley hooked onto my belt and I found a few extra kilograms to attach as well.

Before climbing up the Wall of the Expanse, I said, "Even with the pulley, I'm not strong enough to hoist you all the way to the top. So I'm going to use myself as a counterweight. As I sink down, you should rise up. Once you're at the top, grab onto the ladder and climb up a few rungs. I'll join you as soon as I can."

It had been five weeks since I had scaled the forty-five meters to the bottom rung of the ladder. Five hectic, muscle-bruising, energy-sapping weeks. And I felt every single one of them as I pulled myself from handhold to handhold.

Sweating, panting and nauseous, I finally reached the last rung. I clung to it as cramps and spasms plagued my body. It seemed like I lost another week while waiting to recover.

I secured the pulley to the rung, and threaded the rope through the wheels, dropping the end down to Logan. Vibrations traveled up the fibers as he tied it to his safety harness.

My plan worked—not exactly as I had hoped since I had taken on too much weight and fell faster than expected, but without any dire injuries. Returning to the top was a test of my endurance; I almost gave up around thirty meters, but pushed on.

We didn't encounter any new problems during the rest of the trip to the ceiling. I opened the near-invisible hatch and collapsed on the floor of level seventeen.

The daylights snapped on and Logan yelled in surprise over the sudden appearance of the Bubble Monster and his kid brother.

"Transport vehicles like the Outsiders used," I said to calm him.

"Oh."

"Ignore them, look at the walls." I didn't have the energy to play tour guide so he explored on his own.

From his cries of glee, moans of delight and pure ecstatic woots, I knew he understood the symbols and diagrams on the walls.

When I recovered, I found him tracing an array of…glyphs. His mouth hung open and his finger moved along the raised metal with reverence.

"Did you find out how to work the air plant manually?" I asked.

"Huh?"

I snapped my fingers in his face. "Air plant. Outsiders. Remember?"

"Yes, but…" His gaze returned to the wall. "These markings… They're incredible. They're our history! They're blueprints for our whole world! I'm sure there are schematics for the whole network. Our ancestors or the builders put this here in case we lost the computers, or forgot why we're here. It's… It's…" He stroked the wall again.

"Focus, Logan. Will it help us?"

"Oh yes." He shuffled along the wall, exclaiming over various symbols.

"So you found the data for the air plant?"

"No."

I yanked on his ear until I had his full attention. "Logan, we need to reclaim the air plant. We don't have much time. You can drool over all this later. How can I help?"

He described what the schematics of the air plant would look like. I searched the south and then west walls, while he continued with the east. He moved faster than me and had looped around the room, reaching the north wall before me.

The series of beeps alerted me. I would never forget that sound. Running as fast as possible, I still couldn't reach him before he finished entering the code.

"It's just like—oof!"

I tackled him to the ground.

"What's wrong?" he asked. The squeal of metal filled the room. "Oh."

Logan had opened the large door on the north wall. It was big enough to fit the huge transport vehicle. That same vehicle that could probably fly through Outer Space. Which meant that Outer Space must be waiting on the other side of the door.

The noise rattled my teeth and vibrated in my bones. Not wasting a second, I dragged Logan over to one of the legs of the transport.

"Hang on," I said, bracing for the absence of air, the skin-freezing cold and the floating sensation.

The door finished moving with a bang. Daylights clicked on beyond the entrance, revealing an empty room with walls covered with more symbols.

Logan cocked his head. "Why are we clinging for dear life?"

"I thought Outer Space was on the other side. That door reminded me of when Cogon and I had opened Gateway."

"Sorry. I guess I should have told you."

"Told me what?"

"This door leads to a spaceport." He walked into the room.

I followed him. The area was much larger than I had first thought. It appeared to be as long as two Sectors, but only one Sector wide. Three doors at equidistant intervals were on each of the two long sides, including the open one. And one door at the end.

He gestured to the doors. "There are seven bays that contain two transport vehicles. The Scout and the bigger Cargo vehicle. They can come out here, then the doors all close and…" He pointed at the ceiling. A huge hatch occupied the center. "Fly out to Outer Space."

"How do you know all that?"

"I read it on the wall."

"Why didn't you tell me before?"

"I thought you saw something."

I drew in a deep calming breath. "Let's keep looking for the air plant information."

Keeping Logan focused, I hustled him along the port. We searched the next two bays, but didn't find anything until we opened the third bay. Then he cried out with more excitement than the last ten times. He had found the information on how to manually run the plant.

I gave him a spare receiver and microphone, letting him explain it to Riley. Then we decided he should remain up here to explore and learn everything he could. I would tie a bucket to the rope so I could use the pulley and send up supplies, food and water.

"How are you going to get into the air plant?" Logan asked. "Hank's people are there."

"Anne-Jade has to make good on a promise."

"But she doesn't have any weapons or manpower, and you don't have Zippy."

"We'll work it out."

"Good luck. You're going to need it."

Anne-Jade had hidden a few stunners, and she also had a number of anti-stunners for our force. To tell the truth, it wasn't much of a force. Word had already spread throughout Inside that the Outsiders were coming to reclaim control over us. While many worried, more seemed grateful, claiming the Outsiders would solve all of Inside's problems. Hank and Bubba Boom hadn't needed me to be their prophet after all.

At hour sixty, week 146,026, Anne-Jade led a group that contained three of her lieutenants, ten of Jacy's goons, Sloan and Riley. I scouted ahead, crawling through the ducts over the air plant, counting how many maintenance workers— seven—and reporting their locations back to Anne-Jade.

It was a beautiful raid. Anne-Jade and her lieutenants charged into the plant and stunned most of the maintenance workers before they knew what hit them. A couple of Hank's men fought back, swinging large wrenches. The supervisor pulled his stunner and disabled a few of Jacy's goons before Anne-Jade shot him.

By the time I jumped down from the air shaft, the fight was over. We had taken the plant.

"We have the air plant. What's next?" Anne-Jade asked.

"We disconnect the computer and work the controls the old-fashioned way."

"Old-fashioned?" she asked.

"Manually."

"You can do that?"

"Not me. Riley." I pointed. He and Sloan had unscrewed the main console's covering. They bent over the jumble of wires and circuits with rubber-handled pliers. "Logan's talking him through it right now."

Anne-Jade acted a bit strange. She kept glancing at the entrance where two of her lieutenants guarded the door. And she kept tugging the collar of her uniform as if it chafed her skin.

"Logan sounded in his glory when I talked to him earlier," Anne-Jade said.

"He's been exploring and learning all about the history of Inside and how it works. It's only a matter of time until we get back control of our life systems, and send the Outsiders away."

"I wish I'd known your plans before you rescued Logan," Anne-Jade said.

"We've been sort of making them up on the fly. Why?"

Anne-Jade touched her neck. "When they had him in the brig on level five, the Outsiders threatened to put a command collar on him. You know he would have been a mess. He doesn't do well with pain."

"What are you trying to tell me?" I asked, even though I had my suspicions and they weren't pleasant.

"I'm wearing the collar meant for him. I agreed to—"

"Work for us," a familiar voice said.

I turned. Hank, Bubba Boom and Ponife stood in the doorway.

nineteen

Anne-Jade aimed her stunner at Riley. He didn't have an anti-stunner. I yelled a warning to him as I knocked her arm aside, causing her to miss. Riley ducked behind the console.

She cursed and pointed the gun at me. Now I knew why I didn't get an anti-stunner as well. "Sorry, Trella. I really am. I guess I lost faith in the Force of Sheep."

Hank's people ran into the plant, shouting at Jacy's goons to surrender. They were armed with kill-zappers.

Hank, Bubba Boom and Ponife drew closer to us. I glanced around. All the members of our force—except Anne-Jade's men—knelt on the floor with their hands behind their heads.

I met Riley's gaze. He inclined his head toward the air console. A tendril of smoke rose from it.

Lowering my voice, I said to her, "We know how to disable the collar."

She covered her surprise as Hank and his smug entourage reached us. Ponife wore the standard off-duty clothes of an upper, but there was no hiding his sickly colored skin.

The smoke thickened and puffed from the console.

Riley shouted, "Fire," and dove to the floor as a bright light flashed.

I followed his example. A microsecond later a boom shook the room. A wave of energy knocked anyone on their feet to the ground. Riley and a few others bolted toward the door during the ensuing confusion. I was close behind them when a sharp pain ringed my neck, knocking me flat. We hadn't disabled my collar after all. And now, Hank and the Outsiders knew our plans to bypass the computer. Knew about the instructions on the walls of the port.

They had let me escape and allowed Logan to be rescued. A ruse to discover Jacy and Riley's strategy. It had worked. I'd been a fool.

Awareness crept back. Shapes coalesced from my haze of agony and sharpened into Hank and Ponife. Their words reached me, but failed to make sense inside my head until I concentrated. My memory returned. I had been taken to another cell on level five—this one without any vents—and questioned. Repeatedly.

"Her vitals off the scale. Her heart will not…tolerate more at this time," Ponife said. "Another…session will stop it."

Hank hovered over me. "Do you understand him? One more blast and you'll die."

I nodded.

"Last chance, Trella. Where are Riley and Jacy?"

"Level one." My words were just audible.

Hank leaned close. "Where on level one?"

"Sector…"

He cocked his head to the side to hear me better.

"Sector…" I wrapped my hands around his throat and squeezed with all my strength.

Ponife twisted the metal X and my body numbed from my neck down. The upside—no more pain. The down—Hank removed my hands.

"Damn, she's stubborn," Hank said, rubbing his throat.

"We can threaten to harm her friend... Anne-Jade wears a collar," Ponife said.

"I don't think they're friends anymore. But..." He considered. "We can find someone she does care about. Release her."

Feeling returned in a sudden rush. I gasped as pins and needles attacked my skin. But the pain was a small distraction compared to the self-satisfied gleam in Hank's eyes.

"You can tell us where your boyfriend is hiding, or Bubba Boom will invite your mother up here for a little visit."

An impotent fury burned in the pit of my stomach. I bit my lip. "Level one, Sector H1."

"That wasn't so bad now, was it?" Hank's condescending tone grated on my nerves. He lumbered to his feet and moved toward the door.

"Why didn't the EMP disable the collar?" I asked Ponife before he could follow Hank.

"It is protected," he said.

I ran my fingers over it. "What's it made of?"

"Living metal. An ingenious piece of technology we have perfected."

After they had secured the cell's door, I lay on the mat and wondered how long it would be until they figured out I had sent them to the waste-handling plant. Not to any hiding places. I didn't know Riley's or Jacy's location.

Then it occurred to me that if my collar had been working all along, Ponife knew all the places I'd been. Hank hadn't asked about the Expanse or the port. Which might mean Ponife had kept that information from him. An interesting possibility that I may be able to use to my advantage.

★ ★ ★

Ponife returned hours later with Fosord, the other Outsider. No Hank. I pushed up to my elbow and regarded them. They both wore uppers' clothes and solemn expressions. Ponife held the metal X in his right hand.

Fosord gestured to me. "Come."

No real choice, I gained my feet and followed Fosord. Ponife stayed behind me as we navigated the brig on level five. The closed doors with the red light glowing near the lock meant the cell was occupied. I stopped counting after ten—too depressing.

At one door, Fosord stopped and slid back the metal panel. "Look," he said.

Dread rose like bile in my throat. I swallowed it down. Peering into the cell, I saw Jacy. Bruises covered his face and he tugged at something invisible around his neck—probably a collar. Fosord shut the panel before I could say anything.

He did the same thing at the next cell. I refused to move, but his gaze slid behind me.

"Trella," Ponife warned.

Bracing for another shock, I glanced inside. Logan sat on the mat with his head buried in his hands. We moved to the next cell. Riley lay on a mat as if asleep, but he could have been unconscious. Blood dripped from a large gash across his forehead and temple. My legs refused to hold me up and I sank to the ground. Fosord closed the panel.

Ponife crouched next to me. "See? We have all your friends. You will cooperate now."

"You don't need me," I said. "Unless you have injured?"

"No. Come."

Once again wedged between the Outsiders, we left the brig and walked through level five toward Quad A5. The hallways were filled with Outsiders. I shouldn't have been surprised. Many of them still wore their white suits and helmets.

"They're getting used to the air," Ponife said.

We climbed up to the top of the half-completed level ten. I stopped in amazement. Bright daylights filled the Expanse, reflecting off the ceiling. And the Outsiders had attached a lift to the west Wall, explaining the smooth groove and tracks I had noticed on one of my early explorations.

An odd thought occurred to me. It seemed we've been stumbling around in the dark for thousands of weeks, while these Outsiders had no trouble making everything work for them. Maybe our ancestors had stolen this ship from them.

I turned to Ponife. "Why didn't you try to talk to us? We probably could have worked out an agreement between us."

"We do not want to be...a part of your world. We want our ship back."

His answer confused me. "You want to be in charge, right? And make the rules?"

Ponife attempted to smile. I shuddered at the creepy effort and hoped he wouldn't do it again. "No. We want our ship back and you...gone."

Oh. No. "As in *gone* gone?"

"Like your ancestors had done to us." He gestured to the ceiling. "Put you in transports with little food and supplies and send you all out to die in space."

My emotions flipped from horrified to terrified and back. "Why did they—"

"It does not matter why!" Fosord shouted, grabbing my shirt and slamming me into the Wall. "No crime deserves such punishment. Your people are...savages. You kill your own and crush them into...pulp."

I thought it best not to argue with him.

He released me. "Tell her," he said to Ponife.

"You will help us find everyone," he said. "Hank says you know all the hiding places. We want *everyone* gone."

Even overwhelmed with the information, I still couldn't help asking, "Even Hank?"

"Yes. Everyone," Fosord snapped.

Ponife glared at him. Fosord wasn't supposed to tell me that. Good to know they can make mistakes.

"Does Hank know?" I asked.

"No. And you will not tell him," Ponife said. He held up the X. "Understand?"

"Yes." I just needed a little time alone with Ponife and his X. For him to forget to keep his distance from me. Just one lapse in judgment.

Fosord led us onto the lift. It rose up the Wall. Hanging next to it in the bright daylights was my safety rope. We reached the ladder and the pulley remained in place.

"You are certainly resourceful…for a savage," Fosord said to me.

A section of the ceiling had been removed. The lift shot through the gap and stopped level with the floor. Outsiders milled around the Bubble…er…transport vehicles.

"We are preparing them for your…journey," Ponife explained.

"Will we know how to operate them?"

"Yes. Several of your people are quite…able," Fosord said.

"When are we leaving?"

"As soon as the Transmission is repaired. We will not make the same mistake and let you catch us." Ponife gestured to the bays. "Hank says you did not know this place, or Outer Space existed until recently?" He seemed amused.

"We had a bit of trouble about fifteen thousand weeks ago."

Ponife and Fosord exchanged a glance. Interesting.

"What trouble?" Ponife asked.

"Another rebellion. According to the records, saboteurs deleted a bunch of computer files. The Trava family defeated them and took over control of Inside to avoid any more issues.

We thought the sabotage was a ruse by the Trava family to justify their takeover, but…" I shrugged. "Maybe it had happened. We thought the Controllers were a fabrication as well."

Another look passed between the Outsiders.

"There is some truth. We controlled all Inside's mechanical and life systems." Ponife thumped his chest. "While the nine families bred like rabbits and took care of all the soft jobs…" He cast about as if looking for the right words. "Soft like growing and cooking food, cleaning clothing and raising children. The Trava family were the saboteurs. They wanted more." His speech had winded him even though, of the two, he had seemed to adjust to our air faster.

I mulled over his story. Fosord mentioned a crime when he had been upset, which didn't match this explanation at all.

When he regained his breath, I asked, "Why are you working with Karla Trava then?"

"She offered her help," Fosord answered instead.

"But you can't trust her."

"She doesn't know. The Trava family created a new history and deleted all records of the old. After enough time passed and the following generations grew up learning this false history, no one questioned it," Ponife said.

Yet they had. Stories of Gateway had persisted. The Controllers had transformed into mythical beings. Beings the Travas listened to. As Logan had explained, the Controllers were Inside's operating parameters, fail-safes and the keeper of directives set by the builders. If I believed Logan—which I did—then when the Travas took over, they naturally accessed the Controller files to learn how to run our world.

So who were the Outsiders?

"Why are you telling me this?" I asked.

"Once all your people are on the ships, you can tell the others why they have been exiled," Ponife said.

"Really? Sounds like you're feeling guilty." The comment sailed from my mouth without censure. Big mistake.

Their expressions hardened.

"We do not tolerate insolence." Ponife played with the X, bending the one leg back and forth.

The first wave of pain brought me to my knees. The second jolt forced me to the floor and the third seized my muscles and wouldn't let go. Each one lasted longer than the last until they all blurred together.

I woke back in my cell. As I lay on the mat, I reviewed everything Ponife had told me. Besides being touchy over the reason for their exile, all I had was their version of the events fifteen thousand weeks ago. I tried to think of a way to counter their plans, but failed to come up with a brilliant strategy.

Time passed and I wasn't any closer to a solution. I marked the hours by the arrival of food and water. The meals were delivered on trays slid through the panel into my cell. If Hank would believe me, I'd tell him he was going to be exiled with the rest of us. But Hank never came to my cell without Ponife.

The metallic scrape of my panel opening woke me from a light doze. A hand held the end of the tray. I recognized the thick callused fingers and an idea popped into my head. I removed the meal and seized his wrist, yanking his arm inside my cell.

The element of surprise would only net me a few seconds. "Listen, please," I said before Bubba Boom could break free. "One minute."

He stopped. "Thirty seconds," Bubba Boom said.

"You once told me the Controllers wouldn't torture or trick people. But I've been tortured and tricked."

"You lied and were spying for Jacy," he said.

"So? When the Committee was in charge, we didn't torture

or trick the Travas. We treated them well. Anne-Jade wouldn't even resort to strong-arm methods to get them to help us repair the Transmission. And we had no plans to recycle the Travas either."

"The Controllers won't kill anyone. You're trying to confuse me."

"No, I'm not. Think about it, Bubba Boom. I'm at Ponife's mercy. He's forcing my cooperation. Just like the Pop Cops did to you long ago."

Silence. I pressed my advantage. "You also told me we're their children who have run away. Do you even know *why* we ran?" I released his arm.

Bubba Boom drew it back and closed the panel. I hoped he would think about what I had said, but I had no idea if I had reached him or not.

A few meals later, my panel slid open. No tray came through, but Bubba Boom peered at me from the other side.

"The Transmission is repaired," he said.

No time left. No idea how to stop the Outsiders. No hope of rescue. Anyone who had the resources or determination had been captured.

"Did they tell you what's next?" I asked.

"Yes." He waited.

"Are they still planning to send everyone out into Outer Space?" I asked.

"How do you know?"

"Ponife told me."

"Did he tell you that those who aided the Controllers will be allowed to stay?"

"No. Fosord said everyone."

"You're lying."

"I wish I were."

Bubba Boom shut the panel.

★ ★ ★

The next time my door opened, Ponife rushed in. His agitation was clear. I braced for pain, but he yanked me to my feet and dragged me from the cell. It was the first time he had touched me. He was surprisingly strong. Unfortunately, he didn't have the X in his hand.

He hurried me to a room in Sector E5. Five Outsiders lay on a row of beds. Blood drooled from their mouths and they were all curled on their sides as if in agony. Bubba Boom, Hank and a few others hovered nearby, but they looked panicked.

I didn't wait for orders. Running to the closest Outsider, I felt her pulse. It raced and her skin felt clammy. She shook as a spasm seized her muscles. I opened her eyes. The whites were stained red.

"They had acclimated and were doing fine," Ponife said.

"We need to get them to Doctor Lamont, now." I shouted to Hank and Bubba Boom to help me carry them. The beds didn't have wheels.

They jerked, but remained frozen in place.

"Hurry! They're dying," I said.

Ponife said, "We will bring the doctor—"

"No. She'll need access to her medicines and equipment." I pulled the slight female Outsider upright and managed to get her weight over my shoulders.

Bubba Boom followed my example and swept one of the Outsiders up in his arms. Without waiting to see if the others followed, I bolted for the lift between Quad A5 and Sector B5.

We carried them down to the infirmary.

Lamont pushed a gurney over to me. "What's wrong?"

I rattled off what I had learned as I laid the Outsider on it. Without hesitation, Lamont took control, shouting orders and checking vitals. I filled syringes and fetched instruments.

Bubba Boom and Hank helped as well. Ponife and the two others who had carried the Outsiders stood to the side, keeping out of the way until Lamont ordered them to bring canisters of the Outsiders' air mixture down from level five.

We worked for hours and saved three of them. The other two never recovered. I closed their eyes, arranged their arms and covered them with a sheet. When I looked up I met Bubba Boom's gaze. He had been watching me.

"I'm sorry," Lamont said to Ponife. "We did everything we could. They were just too far gone. Do you need me to prep them to be recycled?"

"No. We send our dead out into Outer Space." Ponife didn't act too upset. "Come, Trella, we must return."

"No." Lamont stepped in his way. "I need her help."

"I will send you plenty of helpers."

"She knows what to do. You saw for yourself. I don't have the time to train another."

He hesitated.

"Where do you think she'll go that you *can't* find her?" Lamont asked.

"Do not leave the infirmary," Ponife said to me.

Hank, Bubba Boom and the other maintenance men followed Ponife. Before he left, Bubba Boom once again met my gaze. He gave me a slight nod. Hope touched my heart for the first time in weeks.

Lamont grilled me as soon as the men were out of hearing range. She already knew quite a bit about the Outsiders and the command collar. Riley had explained much of it to her before he had disappeared. Her questions focused on me.

And after I assured her I was at least healthy, she asked, "Okay, what's the plan?"

"I've no idea. I don't even know what week this is."

"It's week 147,027, hour fourteen."

"Thanks."

"And you don't have to worry about being overheard. Riley found the microphones planted in the infirmary and removed them."

"It doesn't matter. I've got nothing. Everyone's been arrested. Level five is filled with Outsiders and everyone thinks they're the long lost Controllers who are going to make life better."

"Thinks?"

I explained our soon-to-be change in location.

"Then we need to stop them."

I laughed, but the sound lacked mirth. "How?"

"You tell me." She stared at me as if daring me.

"I told you—"

"Nothing, I know. Let's see if we can change that. Did you know that even with all this insanity, I've been testing people and telling them their family bloodlines?"

I had forgotten all about that. "But I didn't send anyone to you. And you can't—"

"I *couldn't* leave level three, but that was before. Once everyone knew I had the tracer, I removed it."

"How many—"

"About half have been tested. I've been busy."

"I see."

"And I know something else that'll help you." She had a smug smile.

"What?"

"The Outsiders need us. Otherwise they won't survive very long."

"How?" Now it was my turn to challenge her.

"All those weeks living in that transport vehicle has affected their heath."

"So? They'll be in here. Nice and safe."

"Won't help."

"All right, Mother. Spit it out."

She faltered for a bit and I realized what I had just called her. Oh well. Nothing I could do about it now.

"Well?" I prodded.

"They need us because they're sterile."

twenty

"Sterile? As in unable to have children sterile?" I asked.

"Yep," Lamont said.

"All of them?"

"That's harder to determine. Two of these three are and so was one of the two that died. From what I've been able to observe, the younger generation—those under twenty-five hundred weeks old or so are all sterile, but the older Outsiders aren't. It's just a matter of time before no one is able to have children."

"What caused their sterility?"

"Long-term exposure to the radiation in Outer Space. When you discovered Outer Space, I found a few files about the adverse health effects of being Outside. Inside's Walls have a lead lining to protect us from this radiation, but the article mentioned these things called…meteoroids that could hit us hard enough to make a hole, letting in radiation."

Yet more things we didn't know about. Lovely. If the Outsiders had indeed been in charge of running Inside, they had to know.

"They're planning to evacuate our entire population," I said.

"You might be able to use this information to your advantage. Plus, if you tell all the Insiders about the Outsiders' plans, I'm sure you'll have plenty of volunteers to help."

"The Insiders see them as our saviors. They won't help me. I'm the one who caused all this trouble in the first place."

"Then educate them. Recruit them. You can do it."

"The collar—"

"I've heard. Come back to the exam room, I want to take a look."

No arguing with the doctor, I sat on the examination table as she used various diagnostic tools to inspect the collar.

I explained how we had thought the device broken before the air plant raid. "Ponife called it living metal."

"It's quite amazing," she said. "As far as I can tell, it's connected to your body's electrical system and using it to power itself."

"I have an electrical current inside me?" I asked.

"Yes. A body produces a small electrical charge."

"Any way to turn off the current?"

"Yes. When you die, but that's *not* an option."

I considered. "Why? In a controlled situation, you could stop my heart and—"

"Absolutely not." She shot me her fiercest frown. Impressive. "Besides," she said, "it might not work. The collar is also linked to your nervous system, which is why it causes such intense agony." Her voice softened. "You have some nerve damage. Did they…"

"Yeah, but don't worry. I can handle it." I lied to my mother, and I half expected the collar to zap me. "Would my nervous system shut down if I died?"

"Not an option, Trella. You'll have to find a way to get that X from Ponife."

"He won't come close enough. And most of the time he has a couple of the maintenance guys with him."

"You'll have to wait for the right opportunity."

Easy for her to say.

Ponife visited the recovering Outsiders at hour twenty-four. Bubba Boom and Egan accompanied him. I felt much better. Almost optimistic, even. Amazing what a long shower and eight hours of sleep on a real bed could do.

Lamont and I answered his questions about his colleagues' health. Then Ponife dismissed Lamont. Shooting me a significant look, she headed to her office.

"We have started to load the first transport ship," he said. "In six hours all the residents of level four will be on board."

I did a quick mental calculation. "The ships can fit over two thousand people?" I asked.

"They are designed for one thousand. They were intended to ferry people down to a planet's surface and not to live on." Bitterness laced his tone. "We have eight ships and your population is currently at 22,509 people."

This calculation was a bit harder. "You're going to put a little over twenty-eight hundred people on one ship?"

"You are fast. Seven ships will have 2,813 and the eight will have 2,809," he said.

I glanced at Bubba Boom. Did he catch that? Ponife had counted everyone. Bubba Boom wouldn't meet my gaze. Instead, he told Ponife he needed to speak with the doctor and went into the back.

"But that's too many." I tried.

"Not your concern. We are going to need you to do a sweep of each level and in all the ducts as boarding progresses," he said. "No one is to be left behind."

They were trusting me with an important task. Too important. There had to be a catch. "What if I miss someone?"

"We plan to fumigate before we move in. Anyone still here will die from the poison. Try not to miss anyone. We do not wish to dispose of too many corpses."

Lovely. "Do you need me now?" I asked.

"We will start in two hours." He gestured to my clothes. I had changed from my climbing suit to my medical clothes. "Make sure you are ready and the doctor has a suitable assistant."

"Okay."

Bubba Boom returned and, without looking at me, followed Ponife from the infirmary. Curious, I searched for Lamont. She was in the surgery, organizing supplies.

"What did Bubba Boom want?" I asked.

"He asked a bunch of strange questions."

"Like what?"

"Questions I really couldn't answer. Like how much food and water would two thousand people need to survive. I told him to ask Riley's brother, Blake. He works in the kitchen and should know."

Blake! I had forgotten about him and Riley's dad. And if I thought harder, I could name a number of others who would support me. Unless they had been arrested? Too bad I couldn't go anywhere.

"Bubba Boom also asked for… Trella, you have that gleam in your eyes. What are you thinking?"

"How are your persuasive skills?"

I had two hours, but we had six until the first transport left. Lamont ran around Inside, recruiting the people I named. They trickled in at first, Jacob, Blake, Emek, Rat and even Sloan came, although he didn't look happy to see me. Then Domotor rolled into the infirmary, followed by the remaining free members of the Force of Sheep—Takia Qadim and Hana Mineko. Breana Narelle had already been evacuated. Kadar and Ivie arrived along with Wera and Cain—Sloan's friends. And the last person to arrive was Captain James Trava.

They had come, but they sat or stood in little peer groups or alone as if they couldn't trust each other. That would be the first thing I'd fix.

"Stop it," I said to them. "Stop thinking about being a scrub or an upper. About being a Trava or an Ashon. We're all *Insiders*. And we've been boarded by hostile Outsiders who are going to take our world and kick us out unless we stop them."

I waited as their protests about not having weapons or access to the computer network dwindled.

"Doesn't matter," I said. "We'll work around it."

"How?" Sloan demanded.

"We have weapons. Blake, how many knives do you have in the kitchen?"

"Dozens," he said. "And we have meat cleavers and some nasty serrated blades."

"Can you gather them all and hide them in Quad A1?" I asked. It was a common area and would be the last level to be evacuated. His resemblance to Riley made it hard for me to look at him for too long.

"Hide them where?" he asked.

"The ducts should work. Can you do it now?"

"Sure," he said.

I then turned to the stink bombers. "Kadar and Ivie, how many bombs can you make?"

"Depends on how much time we have, and how big of a blast you need," Ivie answered. Dirt stained her overalls and she had a smudge on her cheek. She was a pretty girl with long golden brown hair twisted into an oversized bun.

"I need distractions that won't injure people or damage

equipment. Something like a stunner, but more widespread. You'll have about five hours," I said.

"One an hour."

"When you're done, bring them to Quad A1 and someone will tell you what to do with them."

"What are you planning?" she asked.

I wasn't sure, but it wouldn't be good for morale for me to confess this. "A coordinated attack from all sides."

"What about the air plant?" Domotor asked. "If we resist, the Outsiders will fill the air with poison."

"We can disconnect the poison gas canisters," James Trava said.

"What's he even doing here?" Domotor asked me. "The Travas are *cooperating* with the Outsiders."

James answered before I could. "I'm an *Insider*. I don't want them taking *our* ship. Some Travas are helping, but the rest are being loaded onto the transports with everyone else."

"Trella, you aren't going to trust him, are you?" Domotor asked.

Jacy and Riley had trusted him. That was good enough for me. "Do you know where the gas canisters are and how to disable them?" I asked the captain.

"Yes, I do. But I'll need a few helpers."

Wera and Cain volunteered without hesitation. The three of them rushed off.

In order for us to be effective, we needed more Insiders. Many of them wouldn't believe unless…unless they saw it for themselves! "Domotor, can you put together a working computer that isn't tainted by the Outsiders?"

"If I had the right supplies," he said with a surly tone, still annoyed.

I turned to Emek and Rat. "Can you fetch for Domotor?"

"Yes," Emek said.

"Jacob, can you rig the electricity for the computer?"

564 MARIA V. SNYDER

"As long as there's juice nearby," he said.

"Where do you—Quad A1, right?" Domotor asked. He stroked his narrow chin with his long fingers.

"Yep. Call it our headquarters." Then I had another idea. "Any way to make the monitor bigger? So a lot of Insiders can see it at the same time?"

"We have a projector," Emek said.

"A projector?" I asked.

"It's old tech. It has a light and lenses." When he realized we didn't understand, he said, "Basically, it takes a small picture and makes it bigger. You can aim it at a wall."

"I'll take a look at it," Domotor said. "Couldn't hurt."

They left. Emek pushed Domotor's wheelchair, Rat wrote down supplies on a wipe board and Jacob added items.

Sloan, Takia, Hana and Lamont remained. They waited for their orders. I squelched a moment of doubt. This wasn't the time for second thoughts.

"Takia and Hana, I'm going to need you to be evacuated with the others."

The women were alarmed and unhappy until I explained why. "I'll have to find them first, so if you can hide in one of the rooms in Sector F4 that would be perfect."

They agreed and went to get into position.

I drew in a deep breath. Sloan and Lamont remained. Since I'd been collared, I needed an admiral to bring this whole attack together. Who to trust? My mother, who betrayed us during the last rebellion or the man who started the riot and slapped me?

Deciding I needed both, I addressed Sloan. "You're in charge of getting recruits. You'll need to bring them to Quad A1 and convince them about the Outsiders. Then you'll be needed to lead teams up to level five."

He laughed. "And then I'll grow a metal skin so I'm invincible. See? I can be ridiculous, too."

I stared at him until he frowned. "Why are you here, Sloan?"

"Guilt. I failed to protect Jacy and the Outsiders got him."

"Leading those teams will save him," I said.

"Are you sure?"

"Yes."

"I don't know how I'll be able to convince everyone about the Outsiders."

"If Domotor and Emek get the computer and projector working, *you* won't have to."

Sloan straightened his shoulders. "We'll need to coordinate. Do you have any microphones?"

"No. Mine busted ages ago."

He pulled out a couple sets from his tool belt. "For you and the doc. I'll make sure the others get them as well."

I couldn't wear mine yet so I slid them into my pocket. "Thanks."

"If you manage this thing, I might change my opinion about you," Sloan said.

"Just when I thought there wasn't a reason to stop the Outsiders, you go and provide me one." For a moment I almost forgot the pain he'd caused me. For a moment.

He gave me a sly grin. "After that crack, I can't like you... ever."

"Fine with me. Then I won't feel guilty when I slap you later."

"If we survive to later, I'll give you a free shot."

"There it is! That's all the motivation I need."

After Sloan left, I discussed Lamont's job with her. "You have a legitimate reason to be on level five. You need to check on their health, see if others might be on the verge of having a seizure. Plus you need to discuss their fertility problems and see if it's widespread."

"And incapacitate as many Outsiders as possible when the attack starts?" she asked.

"Unless it goes against your doctor's creed?"

"I'll be a doctor up until that moment, then I'll change jobs for the duration."

Curious. "To which job?"

"A mother."

"Fighting Outsiders isn't in that job description."

She laughed. "It is when the child is you. No one hurts *my* little girl and gets away with it."

Bubba Boom and Ponife arrived right at hour twenty-six. I had just finished changing into my blue climbing suit, and adding a few special items to my tool belt.

Ponife gestured to the belt. "Why do you need that?"

"Since you destroyed the air plant, there are a number of air filters blocking the ducts. I need my tools to get through them. Unless you want me to climb down and bypass all of them. It would take up more time." I shrugged.

"No. Bubba Boom, make sure she does not have any weapons in there."

Damn. I unhooked my belt and gave it to him.

He inspected the various pockets. Handing it back to me, he said, "Looks good to me."

I hooked it around my waist, suppressing a relieved grin. He knew exactly what a few of my special gadgets did, yet he'd kept quiet. An excellent sign.

The Outsiders had the stairway blocked so no one could go to the upper level. I'd assumed they guarded the other stairs and the lift as well. I hoped Takia and Hana had found a way to bypass them.

As we climbed to level four and walked down the deserted corridors, I asked Ponife how they managed to convince everyone to leave.

"A trick," he said. "We asked them to come along on a… tour of the great Expanse. To see their world beyond the white metal walls. To go inside the vehicle to see the Outside."

"It's an effective trick." I tried to meet Bubba Boom's gaze. He ignored me.

"Fosord's idea. We also avoid them begging to bring personal belongings along. There is no space for frivolous things."

"Are food and water included as frivolous things?" I asked.

"No. But there won't be enough. However, our ancestors did not have enough either and they survived."

"How?"

"Survival was the reward for the bravest, the smartest and the strongest. All the others died quickly."

He avoided answering my question, but from his comment, I could guess it hadn't been pretty.

All the living quarters had been emptied by now. The Outsiders corralled those they found in Sector H4 and the few holdouts in the main Control Room. I started my sweep in Sector F4. Ponife and Bubba Boom stayed close, but couldn't be with me the entire time.

I spotted Takia and Hana in one of the apartments and the tightness in my throat eased. Takia slouched on the couch while Hana paced. I caught a snippet of their conversation as I passed above them.

"…sure this is a good idea?" Hana asked.

"Doesn't matter," Takia said. "This is our *only* idea."

Hurrying to the room where they had kept Logan, I dropped from the vent and searched for those little Video Cameras. None in the living room. I glanced at the clock. Ponife would grow suspicious if I took too much time. I checked the washroom and the bedroom. Nothing.

My whole plan hinged on finding them. I never claimed it was a stellar plan. It was the best I could devise in two hours. These thoughts weren't helping. I stood in the center of the room and put myself in Logan's place. Where would he hide his most prized device? His most fragile device. His smallest creation.

I returned to the bedroom and picked up his pillow. Stripped of its case, it had been tossed into a corner. Examining the edges, I found new loose thread. I ripped the seam open and dug inside the pillow. Four video cameras were nestled in the stuffing.

I tucked them into my tool belt and raced to where Takia and Hana waited. They both jumped in surprise when I swung down between them. I gave two cameras to each woman.

"If you can, place two of these on the wall of the port without calling attention to yourself. Aim them at the transport ship." I showed them how to activate them. Holding my receiver to my ear and the microphone up to my mouth, I hailed Sloan and recited the frequencies to him.

"What about the other two?" Takia asked.

"Place them inside the ship at locations where we would see what it's like." Their confused expression didn't reassure me. I tried again. "Think of it this way. If you wanted to show an Outsider what's it like in here, you would place one of these in the dining room. It's crowded and noisy and busy there. Understand?"

"Yes," Hana said.

"Ready?" I asked them.

They shared a look and nodded. I escorted them from the room and found Ponife and Bubba Boom. Ponife clutched my X in a tight fist, but he relaxed as soon as he saw the women. He called for an escort and soon one of Hank's men arrived to take them up to the port.

As I searched the remaining rooms, I checked in with my team, receiving progress reports. Not too bad so far. Domotor's curt reply indicated Logan's computer expertise would

be helpful. I told him to ask Sloan if he knew of anyone. Jacy
had probably recruited an expert once Logan disappeared.

At one point Bubba Boom and I lagged behind Ponife.
He touched my shoulder, stopping me as Ponife disappeared
around a corner.

Leaning in close, he asked, "Is it a coincidence Hana and
Takia had been missed by the Outsiders?"

I studied his expression. Trustworthy or not? Based on his
actions this past week, I decided to trust him. "No."

"You have a plan?"

"Yes."

"It won't work," he said.

"Why not?"

"You don't know enough about them."

"Then tell me."

"There's too much." He jerked back as Ponife peered around
the corner.

"What is problem?"

"I'm dizzy. The air is too thin up here," I said, placing my
hand on the wall as if to steady myself.

"It will be thinner in the transport," Ponife said. "You will
get used to it. Unless…"

"Unless I'm not brave? Or do I need to be smart and strong
as well?"

"No. Unless we decide to keep you."

It felt as creepy as it sounded. "Keep me?"

"On this ship. We will need…" He glanced at Bubba Boom.
"Workers."

"You mean like scrubs?" I asked.

"Yes."

"Why did you change your mind?"

Annoyed, he removed the X from a pocket. I had asked
one question too many. Encouraged by my conversation with
Bubba Boom, I rushed Ponife, hoping to surprise him.

I grabbed his wrist just as he twisted the X. The pain rolled through me. I clung to his hand for a moment longer, before dropping to the floor. Even with the deafening sound of my heart slamming in my chest, I heard Bubba Boom's boots as he ran past me.

"You're enjoying this. You're a sick bastard, Ponife," Bubba Boom said.

A thud followed a yelp. The pain stopped. Once I recovered, I glanced up. Ponife sprawled on the floor next to me. Bubba Boom crouched over him. He had my X.

We locked gazes. For a second, I thought he'd keep it, but he handed it to me.

"How do I—?"

"I'll show you later. Put it in a safe place for now," he said.

I tucked it into my tool belt. "Thanks. How did you knock him out?"

He showed me the used syringe. "The doctor was very helpful with finding a way to free you. I just needed to find the proper motivation. It was a difficult decision."

"Why did you help me?"

"When I saw how you and Doctor Lamont tried so hard to save their people and treated them not as an enemy, but as a person in need, I knew you were right. They'd planned to send *all* of us out to die."

"Now what?"

"You're the boss. You tell me."

"Can we rescue Logan, Anne-Jade, Jacy and Riley?"

He flinched a bit when I said Riley's name. "Not Jacy. He's been collared and Fosord holds his key. Anne-Jade isn't in the brig. She's been helping us…them. It'll be dangerous to free the other two. Why do you need them?"

"Logan for his computer expertise and Riley for his knife fighting skills."

"Knives, huh?"

"All we have besides a few noisemakers. Should we look for something else?"

"No, they might work."

"Might isn't a reassuring word."

"A sharp blade can cut the hoses on the Controllers' air masks, making it hard for them to breathe. That is, if you can get close enough. So might is the best I can do."

According to Bubba Boom, Lamont had filled the syringe with one of her narcotics. I estimated Ponife would sleep for another three hours.

Bubba Boom "escorted" me to my cell on level five. The main entrance to the brig was now guarded by two armed men. He joked with the guards, but when the guy on the left turned to open the gate, Bubba Boom moved.

Punching the man on the right, he then took the guard's stun gun and shot them both.

"So much for being subtle," I said as he unlocked the gate.

"No turning back now." Bubba Boom dragged them one at a time to an empty cell and locked them inside.

We released Logan first. He rushed out and hugged me. "If I live through this, I'm having a spacious suite built just for me. I never want to be locked in a small room again!"

Riley stayed calmer than Logan. He kept his guard up as he eyed Bubba Boom. The gash over his left eye and temple had scabbed over, but black and blue bruises colored the left side of his face. His shirt was torn and bloody. I wanted to make sure he had no other injuries, but settled for a quick hug instead.

"Are you sure we can trust him?" he asked me.

"Yes."

He relaxed a bit. "Then let's go."

I stayed next to Bubba Boom and Riley. Logan followed us as we headed to the exit.

Unfortunately, Hank had beat us there.

At first Hank was confused as to why no one guarded the

gate. And why Bubba Boom had three prisoners with him. Bubba Boom didn't say a word, just waited for Hank to catch up.

When Hank put it all together, I feared for Bubba Boom's life. Murderous rage filled Hank's face as he drew his weapon—a kill-zapper.

He stepped close to Bubba Boom and said with a voice of steel, "You're a traitor. You're no son of mine."

Hank shoved the nozzle of his weapon toward Bubba Boom's chest. I yelled and squeezed between the kill-zapper and Bubba Boom. Pushing Bubba Boom back with my hips, I leaned forward as Hank pulled the trigger.

twenty-one

The kill-zapper's nozzle burned my skin as current slammed into me. My muscles twitched with the pulses of power, but the pain seemed minor in comparison to the collar's. I remained standing as Riley and Bubba Boom ran past me. They tackled Hank and wrestled the kill-zapper from his hands.

By the time Bubba Boom stunned Hank, the tremors in my arms and legs had ceased. Riley scooped me up in his arms intent on rushing me to Lamont.

I wriggled from his grasp. "I'm fine."

But Riley wouldn't let go of my arms. He stared at me a bit wild-eyed. "The kill-zapper made contact. Your shirt is burnt."

Glancing down, I saw the scorched fabric. I pulled the material away. My skin underneath the black mark was red and blistering.

"My heart's beating. Besides the burn, I don't feel any pain," I said.

"Maybe it didn't have enough time to do any damage," Logan said.

Bubba Boom shook his head. "It has a very high amperage so it only takes a fraction of a second. The command collar saved you. It has a surge protector so an EMP can't damage it. Ironic, isn't it."

"You're still wearing it?" Riley asked.

"Don't worry." I showed him the metal X. "It'll soon be gone. Although…" I touched its smooth surface. "Maybe I'll wait until *after* we've taken back our ship."

"It might neutralize the stunner's blast as well," Bubba Boom said. He dragged Hank to an empty cell and then he relocked the gate to the brig.

"How do we get down to level one?" I asked Bubba Boom.

"The lift. It isn't guarded on this level, just the other four," he said.

"And what happens when the doors open on level one?" Riley asked.

Bubba Boom handed Riley one of the stunners he had taken from the guards. He offered the other to Logan.

"No thanks," Logan said. "That's not my thing."

As we descended to Quad A1, I asked Bubba Boom about Hank's comment.

"Yeah, he's my father," he said. "Hank kept track of his four children and made sure we were all assigned as maintenance scrubs. I didn't know until all this started." He met my gaze. Sadness filled his eyes. "I also learned Cogon was my half-brother. Cog believed in the Controllers, but he wouldn't have believed their lies for as long as I have."

"By helping us, you've made up for your mistakes," I said, hoping that when all was said and done, I could say the same thing.

The guards outside the lift on level one had already been in-capacitated. Quad A1 teamed with people. Groups of them sat together. Wary, suspicious, angry and uncertain, they glanced at the buzz of activity around Domotor. Murmurings of resentment increased as they noticed my arrival.

Riley went to search for his father and brother, and Logan sprinted toward Domotor. He understood what they had been trying to do in an instant and immediately took charge.

"How long?" I asked.

"Give me a few minutes to sort this out, and then I'll give you an estimate," Logan said.

Sloan sidled over to me. "Where's Jacy?"

"I'm sorry we couldn't rescue him. He has…" How to explain? Not many people knew about the command collars. "A tracer on him that we can't remove without hurting him."

He scowled and jabbed a finger at Bubba Boom. "But you could bring *him* along?"

"Without him, I wouldn't have been able to free Logan and Riley."

"How do you know they don't have tracers?" Sloan asked.

"Only a few have them," Bubba Boom answered.

"And you trust him?" Sloan asked me.

"With her life," Bubba Boom said, pointing to the burned patch on my shirt. He turned to me with a puzzled expression. "Why did you? You didn't know the kill-zapper wouldn't work."

"You saved me from the fire. Consider us even," I said.

"No. You didn't hesitate. There was no moment of consideration."

He was right. "As I told my mother a while ago, it's what I do," I said.

Sloan snapped his fingers. "Almost forgot. The doc's been trying to reach you."

When I pulled out my receiver and microphone, I laughed even though it sounded a bit like hysteria. Blackened and half-melted, the devices would never work again.

"What happened to them?" Sloan asked, marveling over the ruined pieces.

"Kill-zapped. Do you have more?"

Sloan stared at me a moment. "Not if you keep frying them." But he dug into one of his pockets and handed me two more sets. "One for Riley."

Inserting the receiver into my earlobe, I clipped the mic on, hailing my mother. The relief in her voice came through, but she remained professional, reporting that she was in position and would await our signal.

Logan estimated he would have the computer working in fifteen minutes. It was week 147,027, hour twenty-eight. Time for my speech.

I stood on a table as Sloan used a loud and high-pitched whistle to get everyone's attention. Quiet descended and they focused on me with various expressions—all unhappy. I sought the little group of smiling faces and took courage from Riley and his family.

"Thank you for being willing to listen to me. Scrubs and uppers coming together is vital now. But I first want to apologize for turning your lives upside down and then abandoning you. For letting a Committee make important decisions without your input. For dismissing your beliefs in the Controllers and life Outside.

"But these people who have entered our world are *not* the Controllers. They're Outsiders and they plan to exile us. Send us into Outer Space to die."

Voices rose, yelling I was crazy or deluded. Others reminded everyone I had gotten them all into this mess. Sloan used his whistle to settle them down again.

"I understand why you won't believe me." I glanced at Logan; he gave me a thumbs up. "Even if you can't trust me, at least you can trust your own eyes."

The lights dimmed and a large bright rectangle lit up the

north wall. Images appeared. First of the transport ship clinging to our world, then of the port. Outsiders hustled people
into the belly of the transports and then the scene switched
to inside the ships. Every image was crammed with people.
Scared and frightened people.

The buzz rose again, but it had a more muted, uncertain
sound.

"These are live images of what the Outsiders are doing," I
said. "They pretended to be the Controllers so they could get
into our ship. They're people from our world who had been
exiled for crimes against us, and are now planning to exile all
of us Insiders."

Sloan joined me on the table. "She's right," he said over
the din. "We're trying to stop them, but we need your help.
Trella freed us from the Pop Cops. She can free us from the
Outsiders."

A man stood up and asked, "How can we trust her? The
Committee and Mop Cops were just as bad as the Travas and
Pop Cops."

"This time I promise not to let a Committee make the
decisions. *You*…" I swept an arm out. "*You* are going to make
them." I waited until the ruckus died down. "You will vote
for your leaders."

Then the image on the screen showed two Outsiders dragging Anne-Jade toward the transport vehicle. She fought and
broke free for a second before the Outsider on the right tackled
her to the ground. I glanced at Logan. He stared at the screen
with his mouth gaping open in horror.

I turned back in time to see the other Outsider twisting a
metal X.

"NO!" Logan screamed.

Everyone watching gasped as Anne-Jade bucked and shook
in obvious agony. The Outsider kept zapping her over and over
until she lay still. Her lifeless gaze stared at nothing.

Logan screamed again and bolted for the door. Sloan and Bubba Boom chased him down. Chaos erupted as fear and outrage rolled through the assembled. Numb with shock and horror, I couldn't move. Anne-Jade was my friend.

A third Outsider came into view. It was Fosord. He pointed at Anne-Jade's body and then pointed directly at the camera. Instant silence followed his gesture.

Fosord reached to the side. When his hands reappeared, he held a wipe board. Three words had been written on the board: *Surrender or die.*

My grief for Anne-Jade would have to wait until later. I shoved it deep down and took advantage of the stunned silence. "They're scared of us," I said. "We need to act *now* before they do."

"Before they can poison our air?" one man called.

"Before we die of thirst?" a woman asked.

"No to both. We have a team at the air plant. And we'll either win or lose by the time water becomes an issue." I conferred with Sloan.

"I'll need two groups of twenty each to secure the stairways," he said. "I'll lead one team."

"And I'll lead the other," Riley called.

I wanted to say no, but as I told Bubba Boom, Riley knew how to fight. The teams formed quickly and I took heart from the eager helpers.

Sloan, Riley and Bubba Boom grouped together and I joined them.

"…suits then the stunners won't work unless they have their helmets off. In that case, aim for their heads," Bubba Boom said.

"Once we have the stairways, we can send bigger teams to advance up through the levels, securing each," Sloan said.

"How big?" I asked.

Sloan looked at Bubba Boom.

"Hank has at least two hundred maintenance people, plus four dozen Travas and five hundred Outsiders. Watch out for the armed Outsiders. They have this weapon that looks like a black metal tube, but it spits out round disks with razor sharp edges. It'll slice through skin and bone," Bubba Boom said.

"What do we do if we encounter armed Insiders working for the Outsiders?" Riley asked.

"Incapacitate, but don't harm," I said, handing him the communication set from Sloan.

"How?" Riley asked. "We only have two stunners and a handful of knives."

"We need more weapons," Sloan said.

I spotted Ivie and Kadar hovering by the door and gestured for them to join us.

Kadar carried a laundry sack. He handed it to me. "Five stun bombs. Yank the pin out and roll it toward your target. You'll have about four seconds before it goes off. It should affect anyone within a six-meter radius from the bomb."

"They'll help, but still not enough," Sloan said.

"We'll make more as long as we can," Ivie said.

"Thanks," I said. In the meantime, we still needed weapons. I asked Bubba Boom if the ISF's weapons were still locked in the safe.

"Hank removed a bunch for his men and the Outsiders, but the last time I saw there were a few left. But he changed the code for the lock."

I glanced at Logan. He huddled on the floor next to Domotor. Kneeling next to him, I hugged him close for a moment. Then I explained my need.

"Can you help?" I asked him.

He wiped his eyes. "On one condition."

I waited.

"That I get to kill-zap Fosord."

"I thought that wasn't your thing," I said.

"It is now."

"No. We're not killers. Anne-Jade wouldn't approve and you know it. You can stun him, how's that?"

"Can I at least kick him a couple times?" Logan sounded like a petulant child.

"Yes."

"All right. I'm in." He went in search of a few supplies, calling to Emek and Rat to fetch items.

The captain's voice startled me. He called through the receiver. Sloan cupped his ear.

"...have us pinned down," Captain Trava said. "We disconnected the gas, but we won't last long."

"Hold on. We're on our way," Sloan said.

"Go up the Quad I stairs. Don't worry about securing the stairwell. Take two bombs, both stunners and go help the captain," I said, digging into the laundry bag. The bombs had been built inside clear glass balls. A metal pin had been stuck through a small hole.

I gave two to Sloan and one to Riley. They both looked surprised.

"If we don't have the air plant, we're done," I explained. "I'll take Logan, two bombs and we'll retrieve the weapons from the safe."

"How are you going to bring all of them down here?" Riley asked.

I thought fast. "Laundry chute. Make sure you have bins half-full of towels to cushion their fall waiting below. And put together another team plus the follow-up teams. Once you have weapons, go up and secure all the levels. We'll all meet in level five at Hank's control room."

"Yes, sir." Riley snapped a salute.

Sloan laughed then rushed off with his team to help the Captain. I helped Riley organize his team as I waited for Logan.

When Logan returned he had a small cleaning troll tucked under his arm.

"Zippy?" I asked, hoping somehow he found his way home.

"No. Still on level five," Logan said. "This is his…younger brother, Zippy Too."

Bubba Boom boosted Logan into the air duct, but before I climbed in after him, I grabbed Riley's hand. "Be careful."

"Shouldn't I be telling you that?" He pointed to the burn mark on my chest. Riley slid his hands around my back, pulling me close. "Since you tried and failed to electrocute yourself, does this mean you're done jumping in harm's way?"

"I doubt it. In fact, I need to give you…" I dug in my tool belt.

"Your heart?"

"Pretty close." I handed him the metal X. "Keep it safe for me."

"A dangerous move. I could use this to keep you out of trouble."

"But you won't."

"Why not?"

"Because you're one of the good guys. You'll do what it takes to neutralize the Outsiders even if that endangers me."

He grumbled. "Great. Go me."

"There are perks to being a good guy," I said, smiling.

"Ohhh…do tell?"

"Well, after all is said and done, the good guy gets the girl."

"And then what happens?"

"Whatever he desires," I whispered in his ear.

He jerked back in utter surprise.

After I had scrambled into the duct, Riley shouted to me, "Promise?"

I poked my head out. "Yes." No need to add, "if we were both alive."

Climbing up to level four through the air ducts would be difficult so I led Logan to the near-invisible hatch on level one and entered the Gap between levels. One thing Hank had time to repair was the ladder attached to the Wall. It now spanned the entire four levels. I just hoped Hank forgot about it. Getting to the ladder remained tricky. I balanced on the thin I-beam that attached the level to the Wall. Without looking down, I crossed to the ladder.

Logan opted to crawl over and I worried he would fall. He reached it, but not without cursing. We climbed to level four and entered the air shafts. Quad A4 appeared to be deserted, but I wasn't going to trust my eyes.

Removing the vent without making a sound, I poked Zippy Too into the room. A red light glowed on his head.

"Motion sensors," Logan whispered.

I flipped the white switch on the troll's body and the light turned green. Lowering him to the ground, I followed. Then Logan climbed from the shaft. He headed toward the safe and removed a small device from his pocket. While he opened the heavy safe, I reprogrammed the lock on the main door.

So far so good. One problem remained—bypassing the weight sensor on the floor of the safe. Logan worked on the sensor and I counted at least thirty stunners and six kill-zappers inside.

"It's off," he said.

"Get back into the duct, I'll hand you weapons. There's a laundry chute about two meters east," I said.

He grumbled about all the climbing, but he scaled the wall

like a pro. I handed him two at a time, waited while Logan dropped them down the chute and returned for two more.

Working together, we managed to empty the safe. We also managed to alert the Outsiders. The door's lock beeped. I glanced at the clock. It had taken us two hours to complete our task.

"Go," I said to Logan. "Get back to level one."

"How?"

"Laundry chute. Wait thirty seconds after you send the last weapons. I'll let them know you're coming." I closed the vent and signaled Riley.

More beeps emanated from the door, then pounding and, finally the buzz of a cutter.

"And when can we expect you?" Riley asked.

"I'll meet you on level five."

"You better," he grumped.

I removed the vent from the heating duct as the door flew open. By the time five people rushed into the room aiming their weapons at me, I had the stun bomb in hand. I recognized Phelan, one of Hank's supervisors.

"Don't move," Phelan said.

Counting on my collar's protection, I yanked the pin on Ivie and Kadar's stun bomb and rolled it toward the group. They all glanced down, but nothing happened. A dud. Damn.

"Made you look," I said.

"Ha. Ha." Phelan deadpanned. He gestured to the door with his stunner. "Let's—"

A bright flash cut him off. I dove for the heating vent as a wave of energy exploded from the bomb. The glass shards pelted the walls as the men grunted. When quiet returned, I peeked out from the duct. Lying on the floor, Phelan and his team remained motionless. A few sported cuts from the glass.

I checked to make sure the gashes weren't too deep and they all had strong pulses. Then I removed all their weapons and anything else that looked interesting, like Phelan's communication device.

Back in the air shaft, I signaled Riley, warning him of incoming and sent my loot down to the laundry room. I kept one stunner. "Any damage?" I asked him.

"One really annoyed Tech No, but otherwise all came through fine. How many did you neutralize?"

"Only five."

"Better than getting caught. What are you planning now?"

Good question. "I'll spy around level five. See what we're up against."

"Be careful. We're starting our ascent. Bubba Boom is leading the Quad I team, and I have the Quad A stairs."

I ghosted through the air shafts on level five for the next hour. No one guarded the brig. It was my first clue of something strange. Groups of Hank's supporters raced through the hallways, but I didn't see any Outsiders. And Lamont failed to answer my hail.

Sloan reported success in the air plant.

Riley and Bubba Boom encountered only a token resistance as they secured each level.

The fight to reach Hank's control room in Quad A5 lasted a mere five minutes. We met up outside the double doors. They opened without trouble.

The control room appeared the same. Banks of computers. Half-completed consoles leaking wires. And Hank, sitting in the big captain's chair in the center. He was alone.

twenty-two

"Right on time," Hank said.

"For what?" I asked.

"Nothing. Absolutely nothing. All thanks to you," he said.

Riley and Bubba Boom flanked Hank, but he was unarmed. All his supporters had been stunned, but a threat still hung in the air.

"Okay, I'll bite. What are you talking about?" I asked.

"The Controllers have made some changes to their plans. They've acknowledged their growing sterility so they're going to keep that transport full of people alive to breed with. That's the good news."

"And the bad?"

"They're going to clean house." Hank swept his arm out, indicating all the people standing in the control room. "They're going to kill us all."

"How?" Riley asked. "We have the air plant."

"They're going to hide in those transport ships and turn the power plant off," Hank said.

No power meant no electricity, no heat and no pumps to move the air around. It would be a slow death. So much for not wanting to dispose of corpses.

"How?" I gestured to the computers. "They don't have control of the network."

"They don't need all this for control," Hank said. "There's an antenna on the Outside. That's what they used to hijack our network." He explained how the Outsiders could communicate with the network without wires.

"Maybe Logan can bypass the power plant controls," I said. I signaled and asked him to join us.

"Logan's one sharp fellow," Hank said. "The Controllers are well aware of his knowledge and don't plan to wait for us to save ourselves."

"Why are you telling us all this?" I asked.

"I'm in the same position you're in. Since I couldn't handle one small problem," he glared at me, "I was left behind. Ponife couldn't handle you either, but that didn't seem to matter to him." He continued to stare at me. "You know, Karla was right. I should have kill-zapped you long ago. Before Ponife put that damn collar on you." Hank mimed shooting me with his finger and thumb.

"Where is Karla?"

"Up with the Controllers. Along with your mother and Jacy."

Worry mixed with relief. Lamont would be safe with the Outsiders. They would need her expertise if they planned to repopulate.

"What did you mean by the Controllers don't plan for us to save ourselves?" Riley asked.

"They're not playing around this time. They're going to open up Gateway and all our air will blow out into Outer Space. I'm guessing it'll take us four to six minutes to die of asphyxiation."

"You don't seem upset," I said.

"Well…when your saviors turn out to be thugs from the past and you've been nothing but a fool, endangering the entire population of Inside, then dying seems insignificant in comparison."

I understood the feeling.

"How do we stop them?" Riley asked.

"You can't. Not in time," Hank said. "They're already up in the port."

"And even if the lift is working, we could only get a few people up there at a time. Easy pickings." I considered. "What about their transport? Is it still attached to Gateway?"

"No. They flew it up to the port," Hank said. "All they left is a couple of their space suits and a bunch of empty gas cylinders."

"Space suits? Can you survive in Outer Space wearing one?" I asked.

"Yes, but that would only save four or five people and not for long. As you said, easy pickings," Hank said.

He was right. Except I hadn't been thinking along those lines. "Can you install a sheet of metal over Gateway?"

"It'll still leak air," Hank said.

"But it'll give us some more time." I glanced at the people who had volunteered to fight. Not many had the arm strength to climb up the Expanse. "And I have an idea. I'll need those suits, a few volunteers, safety harnesses and some magnets. Can you help us, Hank?"

His considered for a moment, keeping his gaze locked on mine. "Ponife underestimated you. Hell, we all underestimated you. Yes, I'll help."

Riley, Sloan and Bubba Boom all volunteered right away. By the time Hank had collected the other supplies we needed, Logan had joined us.

"Logan, do you remember seeing the symbols about the port?" I asked.

"Sure. I read a bunch of them when I was up there. Until the Outsiders came for me."

I explained my plan to him. "Will it work?"

"It should, but I'd better come along to make sure," Logan said.

"It's suicide," Riley said.

"Do you have any better ideas?" I asked.

"No."

"Then let's move."

Hank shouted orders and we dressed in the Outsiders' suits. Captain Trava rushed up from the air plant with the gas cylinders now full of our air. We hurried to Gateway before the Outsiders could open it. The code to open it hadn't changed from when Cog and I had used it—our first lucky break.

The outer door swung open. Squeezing into the inner room, which wasn't designed for five people in space suits, I gave the signal. Hank and his crew closed the door and would seal it with a sheet of metal. Once he finished with that, he had another job to do.

As the room emptied of air, I explained to the others what to expect and not to panic, trying not to let my own fear taint my voice. Of all my adventures, this was the scariest so far. To keep from floating away, we were all harnessed to magnets that clung to the side wall.

I felt light as the door to Outer Space swung open. My stomach rolled as if I fell from a great height. Various exclamations and curses reached me through my receiver.

Funny thing about Outer Space, I couldn't hear the door as it opened but I could hear Logan's voice inside my helmet. He thought he was going to get sick.

"If you puke, try not to cover the glass on your helmet," was Sloan's advice to him.

The magnets keeping us attached could be turned off by squeezing the handle. I released one magnet and moved it, then the other, working my way to Outside.

The nothingness didn't seem so empty this time. Pricks of light dotted the blackness. I ignored the beauty behind me and climbed slowly up the side of Inside. The others followed.

"Don't let go," I said again. "One magnet on the metal at all times."

"Yes, mother," Logan said.

The climb was easy because we were weightless, but difficult due to our cumbersome suits and magnets. I marveled over the audacity of this attempt, at what—or rather, where—we were. On the outside of Inside. In Outer Space. It was humbling, thrilling and terrifying at the same time.

When we finally reached the top of Inside, we all took a moment to drink in the amazing sight of Outer Space and to catch our breaths.

"Okay, Logan. Do your thing," I said.

While Logan hunted for the antenna and the override controls, I signaled Lamont. "If you can, it's time to start acting like my mother."

The plan was to disable the antenna and then access the override controls for the port's big bay doors. Once it was activated, the air would empty in the main hangar. From the Video Cameras, we knew the transport full of Insiders remained in the side bay with a dozen Outsiders guarding it.

We hoped the transport of Outsiders was in the hangar. By opening the hangar doors, the bay doors would seal shut, protecting our ship and trapping the rest of the Outsiders in their ship.

Lots of hopes and speculations, but anything was better than waiting around to die.

"It's a go," Logan said.

The doors widened. Our second lucky break—the transport

was in the hangar. Figures moved behind that strange black metal, which Hank had called metalastic, a combination of metal and something named Plastic, making the vehicle lighter than if it had been made entirely of metal, but just as strong. It also let in the radiation Lamont had talked about, which was why it was only supposed to be used as a temporary transport.

We climbed down into the hangar before the doors closed. Since we had a limited amount of air in our tanks, we couldn't keep the hangar doors open. Bubba Boom unhooked his welding gun from his tool belt. Air began filling the hangar. It would take some time before we could remove our helmets.

As Bubba Boom headed toward the transport ship's access hatch, the Outsiders figured out what we planned to do—melt the metalastic so they couldn't open the hatch and escape their ship.

A long thin tube on the underside of the ship swiveled and pointed at Bubba Boom. I yelled for him to duck as the tube spat out bright disks. Our luck had run out.

"Get in close," Riley yelled.

Everyone scrambled to get underneath the ship, hoping the gun had a limited turning radius. Bubba Boom remained flat on the ground. Two more guns spun as if searching for targets. Sloan pulled a wrench from his belt and attacked the one gun. Riley grabbed the other, hanging from it with both hands. And I shoved the handle of a screwdriver into the opening of the last one.

Riley's gun jerked back and forth, shaking him like a toy. Mine belched. The screwdriver shot out and dented the far wall. Only Sloan had success.

"Take out the rest," I called to Sloan as Riley flew off his. "Before they…"

Too late. The hatch opened. Cold horror froze the sweat on my skin as one then four then seven suited and armed Outsiders poured from the ship. I checked the air pressure gauge that hung on my belt. There still wasn't enough air for us to shed the space suits. It would have given us a small advantage.

I pulled my knife. The others followed my example except Bubba Boom. He hadn't moved, but I didn't have time to worry about him right now.

The Outsiders fanned out, trying to surround us. They held those long tubes Bubba Boom had warned us about.

"Get behind something," Riley called.

I ducked behind one of the transport's legs, feeling too big for the first time in my life. Sloan finished bashing the last gun, but it was four against twelve.

"Trella, I admire your tenacity," Ponife said. His voice echoed from a speaker inside the collar of the helmet. "However, it is time to stop. Surrender and I will allow your cohorts to join the other survivors."

"No," Riley said.

"It would be unwise to trust them," Logan said.

"Thanks for the advice, Logan. Tell me something I didn't know," I snapped. Putting my knife on the floor, I glanced around, searching for a way to escape. "This *stinks,* but I don't think we have a choice. Too bad we didn't get to the hatch in *time.*"

I walked to the hatch and almost laughed when six Outsiders followed me. Tenacious I may be, and stubborn and maybe even a bit reckless, but I never would consider myself dangerous enough to need six escorts.

We entered the ship. The room was similar to Gateway with another door and a control panel. As the hatch closed behind us, I hoped Riley and the others had gotten my hint. One of the Outsiders punched a few buttons. I repeated the sequence aloud.

Ponife chuckled drily. "Your friends are in custody. No one is left to help you."

This was the second time he had claimed I was alone and helpless. It didn't go as he had expected the first time; you'd think he'd learn by now. Or I would. Fear still pulsed through my body.

After a hissing noise vibrated through my suit, the other door opened and we were in an area that resembled a changing room, with empty suits hanging on hooks and shelves full of helmets and gloves.

"Keep your helmet on," Ponife ordered. "We have no plans to kill you."

"I feel so *much* better," I said.

They removed their helmets.

Ponife had perfected his superior expression. "You should be happy. Your mother and friends will all be members of our new combined community."

"Is she here?" I asked.

"No. She is with the others. Only you will stay with us until our world below is…cleaned."

"Cleaned? Why don't you call it what it is? It's genocide."

"Because that would be technically inaccurate."

"That shouldn't bother you since you've gotten a bunch of stuff wrong already."

"Trivial issues, causing only minor delays."

"I'm glad you can put a positive spin on what I'd call stupid mistakes."

Ponife took the bait. "For example…?"

"You assumed that knife was my only weapon." I pulled the last bomb from my pocket and yanked the pin out.

Rolling it along the floor, I dodged a few Outsiders until one aimed his gun at me and pulled the trigger. One disk clipped my right shoulder, slicing through the suit, my skin and muscles. Fire burned as I lost the use of my right arm in an instant. The air inside my suit leaked through the rip with a high-pitched whistle.

When nothing more happened—damn, a real dud this time—Ponife asked, "Is that it? Do you have anything else?" He yanked me to my feet and took off my tool belt. He strode to one of the cabinets and rummaged. Returning, he slapped a white patch over the hole in my suit.

Pain from the slap mixed with amazement. "Why did you save me?" I asked him.

"I told you before—"

"No plans to kill me. But you said 'we' and he…" I pointed with my left hand to the one who still clutched his gun. "He didn't hesitate. Are you sure *your* plans match the others'? Because that particular idea is another mistake." I wasn't being suicidal, really. My will to live throbbed in my heart; I was just hoping to sow a little dissension among the Outsiders.

They glanced at each other until Ponife growled at them to stop. Then an ear-aching alarm sounded. Surprised, their focus shifted to the hatch. I was the only person to see the glass ball flash.

Once again, I flattened my body to the floor. Glass shards pelted my right side as a wave of energy rolled me over to my back. I stared at the ceiling, silently thanking Ivie and Kadar.

"Trella, quit napping while we do all the work." Logan's voice filled my helmet.

Riley's face blocked my view. "Are you hurt?" he asked.

"Nothing Lamont can't fix," I said, groaning as I ambled to my feet. Ponife and the other Outsiders had been stunned by the bomb. "How did you two get in here?"

Logan gestured to Riley. "His knife. Sloan's wrench. Bubba Boom's surprise recovery. And my genius." Then he muttered, "And your help with the code."

"Can you repeat that last part?" I asked.

"Later," Riley said. "We need to leave before the rest of the Outsiders come to investigate."

We made it through the hatch. Bubba Boom waited nearby

with his blow torch. His face was peppered with cuts and a cracked helmet rested by his feet.

"Disk deflected off my helmet," Bubba Boom explained. "I passed out from lack of oxygen. I woke when there was enough air, but decided to stay down until the odds looked a little better."

As Bubba Boom sealed the hatch, we removed our suits. Riley helped me with mine.

He inspected the cut on my shoulder. "I see bone. Do you know where your mother is?"

"On the other ship."

We all glanced at the bay door. Two possibilities waited on the other side. One—Outsiders controlled the ship. Two—Hank and his people had managed to free our Insiders.

Logan examined the panel next to the door. "When should I open it?"

Riley handed me a gun he had taken from the fallen Outsiders and then armed himself with two. I held the unfamiliar weapon in my left hand. Sloan also held one and his wrench rested on his shoulder. Bubba Boom finished sealing the hatch and joined us. Riley gave him one of his guns, then pulled his knife from his belt.

"On three," Riley said. "One."

Logan pressed a few keys.

"Two," Sloan said.

More beeps followed. Logan's hand hovered above the glowing red button.

"Two and a half," Bubba Boom said.

A nervous chuckle rolled through us.

"Three," I said.

twenty-three

Logan punched the button. The door slid open. Chaos greeted us. We clutched our weapons and peered into the crowd of screaming people. I searched for Outsiders, but only Insiders poured from the hatch of the ship.

My brain finally sorted through the overwhelming scene. The screams were happy cries and the Insiders were hugging and celebrating. I spotted Hank leaning against a far wall. We crossed to him, dodging a few overly excited people.

"Looks like my idea to widen the lift worked," I said to him.

"Your idea was crap, Trella," he said. "I could only send up a few people at a time."

"How did you take out the guards?"

"I didn't." He gestured to the Insiders. "They did it before we reached them."

"How?"

Riley clapped me on my good shoulder. "You taught them how to stand up for themselves."

"I don't think so," Hank said. He poked a finger toward

one woman, standing off to the side by herself. "Rumor has it the doctor knocked out all the Outsiders inside the ship, then rallied and organized everyone else to attack the guards in the bay. The Outsiders didn't stand a chance." He glared at me, but it didn't reach his eyes. "Now I know who *you* inherited your pain in the assness from."

I smiled. "I'll take that as a compliment."

Riley and Logan accompanied me as I went to congratulate my mother. Sloan went searching for Jacy and Bubba Boom stayed with Hank.

My mother's eyes lit up when she spotted us. She wrapped her arms around me, but pulled back when I hissed in pain. Then there was no talking to her as she transformed into doctor mode, tsking over the deep cut and insisting on getting me to the infirmary without delay.

Wishing to remain and find out more details, I grumped at her. "I'd rather have you mother me."

"Then you're in luck since I can do both. Get moving or I'll make you stay in the infirmary long after you're recovered."

"Yes, Mother."

The cleanup took longer this time than when the Force of Sheep had won. Even though the Insiders had all rallied against the Outsiders, resentment still lingered between them. A few of us—me, Hank, Emek, Jacy and Domotor—sat together and decided how to proceed. Yes, we included Hank. He always wanted the best for Inside and he had good insights into what changes the people craved after the Pop Cops were gone.

We kept the family names and soon everyone Inside had a family. Then we asked everyone to sign up for a job. Except this time, there wouldn't be scrubs cleaning and uppers working the controls. If a person wished to work in the air plant, he would learn *every* aspect of the plant and his job would rotate from computer controller to changing filters to hauling cleaning trolls around from shaft to shaft then back to being a controller.

For the jobs no one wanted—like cleaning out the waste pipes—every single person of Inside would take a four-hour shift, which, when you considered we had a population of 22,500 and some, that meant I would have to do my four hours every nine hundred weeks. Doable.

Levels five to ten would be completed first and then everyone would be able to move out of the barracks at the same time.

As for the Outsiders, they would be invited to join us, to choose jobs and vote. For those who declined our offer, they would be given a room in the brig. We realized the danger in letting someone like Ponife have freedom in our world, but agreed not to limit or incarcerate someone with a difference in opinion. Actions and not words would land an Insider in trouble. Jacy volunteered to head the ISF for now.

Soon after I had recovered, I joined Logan, Riley, Bubba Boom, Hank and a handful of others in saying goodbye to Anne-Jade. We lined the hallway up to Chomper's lair and paid tribute to a hero. Logan wished for her to be recycled and not sent out into Outer Space.

"She will always be with us," he said.

By week 147,033, we had completed the work schedule for everyone and repaired all the damage to the machinery and computer. At hour zero of week 147,034 we held elections for admiral, vice admiral, captain and for the commander of the ISF. Logan had rigged Video Cameras with sound so every Insider could hear the candidates' plans for our future. I had campaigned for either one of the admiral positions. The other admiral candidates were Domotor; Riley's father, Jacob; Emek and Takia. Logan, James Trava and Bubba Boom ran for the captain's position. Jacy and Sloan campaigned for commander.

Riley brought the early election results to me at hour twenty. They would be announced to everyone at hour twenty-five. I was helping Lamont in the infirmary, but he wanted to tell me them in private. We retreated to my room and he closed the door.

He sat on the edge of my bed with me. Impish delight lit his blue eyes. "Remember your promise?"

I pretended to be confused. "Which one? I just promised everyone to keep our world safe and sane. Did they vote for me?"

"I'll tell you *after* you keep your promise to me."

"Well…" I tapped my lips with a finger as if I considered his words. "I could just wait five hours—"

He cut me off with a deep passionate kiss.

When he broke it off, I said, "Waiting really isn't my thing." And I drew him close for another kiss.

Before we could go any further, Riley pulled away. "I have something for you." He stood on the bed and opened the air vent. Reaching in, he grunted and pulled out a small cleaning troll.

"Zippy?" I asked.

"Yep. Logan fixed him." Riley set Zippy in my lap then took both my hands in his. "You made a commitment to the people of Inside and I'm proud of you."

I sensed he had more to say so I kept quiet.

He squeezed my hands as if suddenly nervous. Then he took a breath and said, "I'd like you to make a commitment to me as well. Will you be my mate?"

Before the Outsiders came, I would have been too scared to say yes. Good thing this was after. "Yes."

It was too awkward to kiss with Zippy in my lap, but Riley stopped me from moving him.

"Open Zippy," he said.

"He opens?"

Riley pointed to a button on the top. I pressed it and a panel opened. Tucked inside Zippy was Sheepy. With a cry of delight, I pulled the little stuffed sheep out. Tied around his neck was a pendant. It was the symbol for Inside—a square with a capital I in the middle, but on the opposite side was a sheep.

"Does it—"

"Yes. If you push on the sheep, it will send out a distress signal."

"I hope I won't have to use it."

"I'm sure Jacy will make certain that Emek and you are properly guarded, but, knowing you and considering you'll have to work with Captain James, I won't be surprised if you get into trouble."

"Jacy? Me and Emek? What are you talking about?"

"Sorry, I can't divulge election results until hour twenty-five." He smirked.

I considered. "Was I voted admiral or vice admiral?"

"Does it matter?"

The vice admiral's position had a little less stress, but otherwise… "No."

"Good, because right now you should concentrate on fulfilling your promise to your mate."

I added the new pendant to my other one. "Are we official now?"

Riley put Zippy and Sheepy on the floor then pushed me back onto the bed as he lay beside me. "Yes. It's official. And since I'm one of the good guys, I can have whatever I desire."

"And what do you desire?"

"To have my way with you."

And he did. Except I think I had my way with him. Either way we were together and that was all that mattered.

★ ★ ★ ★ ★

Acknowledgments

I can hardly believe this is book number eight. When I wrote my acknowledgments for my first book, *Poison Study,* I included every single person who helped me just in case that book might be my last. But due to a combination of a great editor, an excellent agent, loyal readers, my Book Commandos and the continuing support of my family, I'm on number eight.

Eight books that continue to appeal to my readers because of the efforts of Mary-Theresa Hussey, Elizabeth Mazer, Bob Mecoy, Kim J. Howe and the amazingly brilliant support staff at Harlequin. Eight books with gorgeous covers thanks to the incredible talent of the art department's artists, photographers and designers.

Eight books that are recognized by the public due to the hard work of the marketing and publicity departments.

Eight books my loyal Book Commandos continue to recommend to everyone they know and to strangers searching for a good book.

Eight books that would not have been written without the love, support and patience of my husband, Rodney, and my children, Luke and Jenna.

Thank you all!

The GIRL IN THE STEEL CORSET

Book one in *The Steampunk Chronicles*

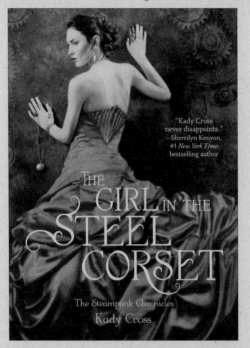

When servant girl Finley Jayne is run down on the streets of London, she is swept into the world of Griffin, the mysterious Duke of Greythorne, and his crew of misfits, all of whom have mysterious powers—just like Jayne. As they search for the Machinist, a shadowy villain using automatons to commit crimes, Jayne struggles to fit in and to fight the darkness that is growing inside her.

Available wherever books are sold!

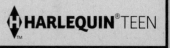

A GODDESS TEST NOVEL

"A fresh take on the Greek myths adds sparkle to this romantic fable."
—Cassandra Clare, *New York Times* bestselling author of *The Mortal Instruments*

In a modern retelling of the Persephone myth, Kate Winters's mother is dying and Kate will soon be alone. Then she is offered a deal by Hades, god of the Underworld—pass seven tests and become his wife, and her mother will live and Kate will become immortal. There's one catch—no one who has attempted the Goddess Test has ever survived.

Kate Winters won immortality and will rule the Underworld at Henry's—Hades's—side. But before she can be crowned, the secretive Henry is abducted by the one being powerful enough to kill him—the King of the Titans. And it's up to Kate to get him back.

THE LEGACY TRILOGY

"I recommend you get this book in your hands as soon as possible."

—*Teen Trend* magazine on *Legacy*

Crown princess Alera of Hytanica has one duty: marry the man who will become king. But Alera's heart is soon captured by a mysterious intruder—a boy hailing from her country's deadliest enemy. With her kingdom on the brink of war, Alera must choose between duty and love.

Bound to a man she cannot love, Queen Alera of Hytanica faces leading her people in dark times. As the enemy Empire of Cokyri attacks, Alera is torn between her duty to her kingdom and the love she still holds for Narian, leader of the Cokyrian armies....

Look for the third installment of this enchanting trilogy, coming November 2012!

Facebook.com/HarlequinTEEN

Be first to find out about new releases, exciting sweepstakes and special events from Harlequin TEEN.

Get access to exclusive content, excerpts and videos.

Connect with your favorite Harlequin TEEN authors and fellow fans.

All in one place.

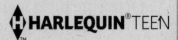